I0749070

Table of Contents

Heritage

Cover design by Alysabeth Vale
Interior design by Alysabeth Vale
ISBN: 979-8-9945284-6-4

The Veilmarked Saga: Book 1

Heritage

Magic is dangerous. But so is denying it.

By Alysabeth Vale

Dedication:

Veiled, potent, true.
To the one who cracked open the gate.
You held a mirror to my buried self, even for a moment.
You vanished, but I remained—blazing.
This book is not about you.
But it exists because you reminded me that I was still alive.
I healed where I could have shattered.
And for that, this flame.

Ritual Gate

◈ ☽✦☾ ◈

The First Gate

This is Heritage.
The weight of what was handed down in silence.
The names we carried before we could speak.
The shadows carved into our bones by hands not our own.
This is the soil, the blood, the altar of origin.
Enter with open eyes.
Remember what was forgotten.

Prologue

The Mystic Academy, Long Before the First Flame Stirred...

The candlelight in the chamber guttered, casting long shadows that danced across ancient stone. Dust motes drifted through the air, thick as secrets. Beyond the high windows, night stretched over the world like a shroud.

A woman stood alone before a locked vault, her hand pressed flat against its surface. It was cold. Older than the Academy itself. Older than memory. Her robes whispered as she stepped back, eyes narrowed—not in fear, but recognition.

"They sealed it thinking no one would ever return," she murmured. Behind her, an older man—weathered, with eyes like stormglass—watched in silence. "And yet here we are."

"Not by accident," she said, "and not without cost."

He hesitated. "Do you believe it's her?"

"I know it is," she said. "I saw the signs. The same ones he once tried to mimic."

Vareth flinched at the name. Even centuries later, the syllables tasted bitter in the mouth.

"She's not like him," the woman added, quieter now. "She's already broken the pattern just by surviving."

The vault thrummed faintly beneath the stone a sound almost too low to hear. For just an instant, a ripple of shadow pressed outward against the edges, as if something inside had stirred. She turned, retrieving a scroll wrapped in worn blue silk. As she unrolled it, the candle's flame flickered violently—like the prophecy itself had stirred awake. She read aloud only part of it. The rest... would reveal itself in time.

.·˙◈˙·.

Three shall rise when the Veil thins:
one by fate,
one by fire,
and one by fracture.
Balance lies not in their power, but in their bond.

.·˙◈˙·.

The woman's voice faded into the dark.

"If they fail... the Veil won't just thin. It will shatter."

She re-rolled the scroll, eyes lingering on the flame one last time.

"It's already beginning."

The woman's name was whispered only once before she disappeared from the Academy's records: Seraphine.

The man—known in some circles as Vareth—had long watched the threads of fate unravel in silence.

Part 1

Threads of Fate

"In the weaving of fate, every choice is a spark waiting to ignite."

Chapter 1: The Garden and the Silence

Camomile was different—and she knew it.

Not just in the way children sometimes feel different, like they don't quite fit. No. Camomile knew, deep in her bones, that she was truly different. From the time she was very small, the whispers had followed her—soft murmurs no one else could hear, words that came not from people but from the wind, from the roots beneath her feet and most of all, from the sky.

Her father had known, too.

Before he died, he told her only half-truths about who she was.

And he made her swear never to speak of it to anyone.

"Hide it, Camomile," he had whispered, his hand wrapped tightly around hers. "Even the kindest faces can turn cruel when they're afraid of what they don't understand."

And so, she had hidden.

After his death, the silence in her house grew louder than any of the voices in her mind.

Her stepmother had always looked at her with thinly veiled contempt—but after her father's death, it worsened.

She tolerated Camomile, but barely. She could see it in the way she set her plate on the edge of the table, never quite looking her in the eye. As if they were waiting for something in her to snap.

But Camomile didn't snap.

She simply drifted away.

She tried, once, to share her truth. She was young—too young to understand the weight of secrets. She told a friend, someone she trusted, about the voices. About the voice that came more often she felt in her chest more than heard in her ears. A voice that made her feel like she wasn't alone.

The boy laughed. Told the village.

Called her crazy.

Since then, Camomile had stopped speaking much at all.

She spent her days at the edge of the forest, where the trees knew how to listen without judgment. Or in the garden behind her home, where she tended herbs and wildflowers with hands steadier than anyone expected. The plants never asked her to be anything other than quiet and gentle.

There, she was free to listen.

There, she didn't feel quite so strange.

Sometimes, after the weeding and watering was done, she'd lie back in the overgrown grass and watch the clouds drift by. The sky felt closer than it should have—like it knew her name. When the wind brushed her cheek, it almost always carried a whisper she couldn't quite catch, as though something ancient far above was trying to remember her.

She turned to her small but beautiful garden and smiled softly. She was proud of it—even the little white flowers called feverfew.

She especially loved those, though her stepmother called them useless and ugly. They grew in the cracks of the stone wall behind the garden, stubborn and pale, their petals always slightly wild. No matter how many times they were cut back, they returned—uninvited but thriving.

Camomile liked to think they were brave, the way they bloomed where they weren't wanted. The way they didn't need permission to exist.

She'd always admired them for their resilience and wondered—just for a moment—if she was like the feverfew in a way.

But before she could dwell on the thought, something strange happened.

Like a light switch flipped on in her mind, and above her, the sky churned with wind and wonder. For a heartbeat, a faint gold shimmer threaded the air, gone before she could be sure it had been there at all. She closed her eyes and listened.

And far away—so far it might have only been a dream—something opened its eyes and listened back.

As if it, too, had been waiting for her.

Chapter 2: The Dream and the Shadow

Camomile dreamed. Not her normal dreams of wings and sky, or even the Eldvale mountain range that peaked out in the north.

No, this dream was different than that.

She was walking through a forest—but not the one she knew. This forest was unfamiliar and strange, too still to be real. The wind tugged at her hair as the sunlight filtered through the trees and warmed the top of her head. But it was a hollow kind of warmth, like it belonged to someone else.

She kept walking.

She didn't know what she was looking for, only that she had to keep moving. The silence pressed in around her, thick and unnatural. No birds sang. No squirrels scurried. Not even the buzz of insects. Just the sound of her breath and the quiet crunch of her footsteps on soft earth.

She wasn't alone.

She could feel eyes on her. Heavy and unmoving. Watching.

Left... right... left... right...

A twig snapped behind her.

Camomile spun around. Nothing. Just trees.

Then—movement. Out of the corner of her eye, a shadow drifted forward. She couldn't make out what it was. Her pulse quickened.

Before she could react, light exploded behind her—blinding and golden, as if the sun had torn through the sky. She tried to shield her eyes, but her limbs were frozen.

The light dimmed, and when she finally dared to look again, it had taken shape: a circle of glowing light, hovering in the air like a rippling portal. The circle of light pulsed gently, as if more than one presence waited within. She couldn't see faces, only felt the echo of connection—like two voices speaking in unison without words.

It didn't just glow. It felt... alive. Like it was watching her too—but gently. Patiently.

She didn't know how, but she knew—this was what she had been searching for.

She stepped forward, arm outstretched.

The light moved toward her, pulsing gently.

Her fingertips brushed its edge—and it vanished.

In its place stood a figure.

Tall. Wrapped in black robes. Faceless and silent. It glided toward her, dark as a storm cloud, and stopped only inches away. It didn't speak. It didn't move. But somehow, she knew—it knew her. Knew her name.

Light and shadow. Both had called her—but only one remained. The glow felt like memory, the shadow felt like hunger—hollow, endless, as if it could swallow her whole and still remain empty.

Camomile opened her mouth to scream—

—and woke up.

Her eyes flew open, heart pounding in her chest. For a moment, she couldn't shake the feeling that the figure was still in the room with her.

"Get up, Camomile. Now!"

Mrs. Lilian's voice snapped her out of it.

Camomile rubbed her eyes and blinked toward the doorway. Her stepmother stood there in her usual faded apron and sharp-eyed scowl, hands on her hips.

"Time to get moving. I need the chores done before the shop opens, and I don't want to repeat myself."

"Yes, ma'am," Camomile muttered, her voice flat.

Mrs. Lilian turned on her heel, but not before giving Camomile a brief glance—almost worried. It passed quickly, like a thought she didn't want to have, and she vanished down the stairs.

She sat up slowly, still half in the forest, the glowing light burned behind her eyelids. It felt real—too real. And familiar.

She dressed quickly and made her way to the barn. Feeding the animals didn't take long, but she stretched the task out, letting her thoughts wander back to the dream. The forest. The portal. The shadow.

It had felt like more than just a dream. Like a message. Like a beginning.

When she returned to the house, Mrs. Lilian was already gathering her things: a basket of fabric over one arm, her wide-brimmed hat already perched on her head.

"Well then," she huffed. "Let's get a move on, girl. We don't have all day."

Camomile followed her down the dirt road in silence. The route was familiar: past the apple orchard, past Mr. Gibson's Garden, where he stood as always with a spade in one hand and a hopeful smile for Mrs. Lilian.

"Good morning to you, Mrs. Lilian," he called.

"And to you," she replied politely.

He gave Camomlie a glance—and looked away, like he always did.

The dress shop sat at the western edge of town, tucked between two older stone buildings. It wasn't busy early in the day, which meant sweeping, folding, and sorting. When the store did fill, no one used her name. They just said "girl," or ignored her entirely. She had stopped expecting anything different.

Sometimes, when the shop was quiet, she'd sneak scraps of fabric and sew small things for herself. She kept them hidden in a cloth bag beneath a tree deep in the forest. One day, she'd take that bag and walk away from Brimclif for good.

She would leave. She had no friends. No family who truly saw her. Nothing to keep her here.

Just after eleven in the morning, Mrs. Lilian handed her a small list and eighteen gold coins.

"Take this to the market. Get everything on the list. Everything, Camomile. Do not forget anything."

She nodded, half in a daze, and stepped outside into the warm sunlight. The air smelled of mid-spring and dust. She stretched her arms for a moment before walking toward the far end of town where the food market sat.

The walk was long, but she didn't mind it. The farther she was from the dress shop, the easier it was to breathe.

She gathered everything on the list—grain, oil, dried fruit, a few spices—and started back. The sun had begun to tilt west, bathing the rooftops in gold.

That's when the shadow passed overhead.

She stopped.

She looked up—nothing.

She walked another few steps, and again, the shadow came. This time, she caught it.

Wings.

Massive, gleaming wings. Bronze and firelight. They shimmered in the air like molten metal, each beat slow and thunderous, the wind beneath them curling through the trees and stirring the dust in golden swirls.

A dragon.

She stared, unmoving, as it circled once above the treetops and descended—down toward Millers Field.

For several heartbeats, she couldn't move.

The bag of supplies slipped from her hands. Her mouth hung open.

No one else was looking up.

No one screamed. No one ran.

She was the only one who saw it.

She backed away slowly, then turned and ran—not to the shop, but to the trees.

Toward Miller's field.

Toward the truth.

The stories weren't stories. The whispers weren't madness.

Dragons were real.

And one had just arrived.

Chapter 3: The Field and the Flame

Camomile's feet barely touched the ground—she dodged low tree limbs and jumped over gnarled roots. Ten minutes after leaving the village, her lungs burned like fire. The sharp air stabbed her throat with every breath, but she kept going.

A dragon. A real dragon.

She'd seen it with her own eyes. Dark reddish-orange wings stretched wide across the sky, shimmering in sunlight. It circled once, twice, then glided down toward Millers Field.

Camomile didn't know what compelled her to chase it. Her heart pounded—not just from the sprint, but from something deeper. Awe. Terror. Wonder. Something ancient stirred in her chest the moment she saw it.

She glanced up again—then her foot caught on something. She went down hard, face-first into the forest floor. Sharp sticks jabbed her arms; rocks scraped her ribs. Groaning, she rolled onto her back and winced at the dull throb pulsing through her body.

A root.

She laughed softly to herself, then scooted backward to lean against a tree. Another root caught her off guard—she tumbled again.

"Of course. Figures," she muttered.

She stayed still a moment, catching her breath. Her chest still burned, but the forest air was cool on her face. Finally, she pulled herself up and jogged on. Millers Field wasn't far—just a little more.

As she neared the forest's edge, she crouched behind a bush. Her breath caught.

There she was.

The dragon stood in the tall grass of Millers Field, her scales glowing like embers beneath the fading sun. Wings folded neatly at her sides; she moved with a grace that seemed impossible for something so massive. Her reddish-orange scales sparkled faintly, as if lit from within, and her long neck curved slowly as she scanned the trees.

Camomile stared. Every part of her screamed to run. To hide. But something else—stronger—drew her forward.

What are you doing? her thoughts whispered. *This is madness.*

Maybe it was.

But her feet didn't listen.

She didn't understand it. The dragon should have been a nightmare—yet something deep inside had already decided. This was not a beast. This was something else. Something meant for her.

Slowly, carefully, she rose and stepped from the bush. Her heart pounded with every breath, but she walked—toward the dragon.

The dragon noticed her.

Amber eyes locked with hers. Not just golden—alive. Like flame and memory and something so old it had no name. She wanted to stop, to freeze, but her body kept moving. One step. Another. Until she stood barely five yards away.

The dragon tilted her head.

Then she bowed.

Camomile froze. Her breath hitched.

"You're bowing to me?" she whispered, voice trembling with disbelief. She had no fire of her own—just trembling hands and a racing heart. And yet the dragon bowed, as if seeing the flame she hadn't awakened.

She held out a cautious hand.

The dragon moved closer.

Camomile didn't back away. She placed her palm gently on the dragon's nose. The scales were warmer than she expected. Softer, too—smooth like polished stone worn down by time. As her hand pressed against the dragon's snout, a shimmer of gold flickered across her skin—so faint she thought she imagined it. But the knowing that rose in her chest felt older than memory itself. A connection.

It felt like home.

"You're real," she breathed. "And you're beautiful."

The dragon exhaled slowly, warm breath rushing over her skin. The scent of ash and wildflowers filled her lungs. Her other hand joined the first, stroking the dragon's nose. The dragon closed her eyes, leaning into the touch with quiet, trusting calm.

Camomile's heart swelled, full and quiet.

But then—

"Skylith? What are you doing?"

The dragon's eyes snapped open, head lifting abruptly. A man's voice cut through the stillness.

Someone was coming—fast—from the other side of the forest.

She stumbled backward just as footsteps broke through the tall grass.

"Hey! Wait!"

Camomile turned to run, but her foot landed on something sharp. Pain exploded up her leg as she collapsed with a cry. She looked down—blood stained her torn pants. A sickle, half-buried in the grass, had sliced a deep gash from her calf to her foot—the worst bleeding from her heel.

Her breath came in short, ragged gasps—from pain, from panic, from all of it at once.

"Hey! Are you okay?" the voice was closer now, urgent.

No. No, no, no.

She forced herself up, limping as fast as she could toward the trees. Branches scratched her arms, but she didn't stop. Her pulse roared in her ears.

She dove behind a bush and held her breath. Her foot screamed with every shift of weight; her hands shook violently—but she stayed still. The footsteps grew louder... then softer... then faded.

She exhaled, barely daring to believe she hadn't been seen.

Then—*Snap.*

A twig behind her.

She turned too late. Arms wrapped around her from behind, one hand clamped over her mouth.

She kicked, thrashed. Her injured leg flared with blinding pain.

"Easy," the man said, voice firm but not cruel. "I'm not going to hurt you."

She still fought; breath ragged through her nose.

He slowly loosened his grip. "Let me help you. Please."

She hesitated—then nodded.

He removed his hand.

"Let me go!" she gasped, voice cracked with panic.

But his hand flew back to her mouth. "Please," he whispered. "You're bleeding. I just want to help."

She went utterly still.

After a moment, he slowly released her and stepped back.

She turned to face him—and froze.

He was tall, at least six feet, with brown hair laced with gray tousled across his forehead and muddy brown eyes that softened when they met hers. He didn't look like a monster. He looked... concerned.

"I'm a knight," he said simply.

Camomile's stomach dropped. Her jaw parted. "What?"

The world tilted suddenly. Vision swam, dizziness rising. She blinked hard, trying to stay upright—but the blood loss was catching up with her.

"Can I take a look at your injury?" he asked gently.

She wanted to answer. Needed to. But her voice caught in her throat.

"Camomile?" he asked with concern.

As her mind slumped toward unconsciousness, the stranger caught her and whispered, "I've got you this time..."

And just before everything went black—before her legs gave way and stars filled her vision—one final thought flickered in her mind like a spark or dangerous wildfire:

How did he know my name?

The world narrowed to heat and pain and unanswered questions.

Then everything slipped away.

Chapter 4: The Knight and His Dragon

She drifted in and out of awareness.

There was warmth—steady, rhythmic motion. Strong arms. The scent of leather and earth. Occasionally, her eyes fluttered open to a canopy of high leaves and dappled light, only to shut again under the weight of exhaustion. A voice murmured softly—low, steady, too distant to make out. It might've been her name.

Pain burned through her leg with every jolt, but it grounded her. Kept her tethered.

A man's voice—clearer this time—carried through the haze like wind through trees.

Where am I?

She lay on something hard and uneven—definitely not a bed. A blanket was draped over her, rough beneath her fingertips. Her hand brushed something else—silken, cool... alive.

What is that?

She turned toward it, and pain flared behind her eyes. A groan slipped out as the ache buried itself deep in her skull.

The light had shifted. The sky now trailed toward late afternoon, gold pooling at the edges of the hills. She was lying near the tree line. The scent of wild mint drifted on the breeze. A few paces away stood the knight, arms crossed, brow furrowed, gaze distant.

Camomile tried to sit up. Pain lanced through her.

His head snapped toward her. "You're awake."

The voice again—closer this time, steady and concerned.

He crossed the space between them in a few strides, crouching at her side. "Don't move too much. You fainted. You've been out for a while."

Her eyes opened slowly. Light and motion blurred together. Trees shifted above her in strange patterns. A massive shape loomed nearby—coiled and quiet.

The dragon.

It all returned in fragments. The stranger in the field. The sickle slicing her foot. Her breathless sprint. The crash into the woods. The man calling her name when she hadn't even spoken it.

Was it a dream?

"Are you alright?" the man asked again. Calm. Kind. Nothing like Mrs. Lilian's shrill voice.

Her vision swam in a dull haze.

But the voice—the face—yes. It was him.

She gasped and tried to sit up again. Her head throbbed, her leg screamed. She cried out.

"Easy," he said, reaching out instinctively. "Don't move. The bandage might come loose."

Bandage?

Camomile stilled, breath shaking. Her fingers grazed her foot—cloth, carefully wrapped.

Her hand trembled. Slowly, her sight cleared—haze replacing blur.

"You're okay," he said again. "You're safe."

She looked up at him. The same brown hair. The same muddy, river-dark eyes. Yes—he was the man from the field. She'd seen him. Just once, before she'd run.

She opened her mouth to speak, but her throat was cracked and dry.

"Water," she rasped.

He was already reaching for a cup. She tried to hold it, but her hands shook too violently. It slipped through her fingers and hit the ground.

She blinked, frustrated.

Without a word, he refilled it and brought it back to her lips. "Here. Let me."

He tilted the cup gently. Cool water touched her tongue. She sputtered at first, but it was perfect—clean and life-giving. Her whole body trembled.

"Slow," he said softly. "You've had a shock."

She nodded weakly.

He helped her drink again, slower this time. Gradually, the shaking eased. A breeze touched her forehead, cooling the damp there.

Camomile exhaled. "How long was I out?"

"A few hours," he said. "I brought you here so you wouldn't wake up deeper in the woods. Seemed safer."

She nodded faintly. "Thank you. I-I didn't mean to cause trouble."

The man gave a tired smile. "You didn't. I just... didn't want to leave you."

She pushed herself up with effort, brushing hair from her face. "I need to get home. I live nearby. On the edge of the woods, near Millers Field. I can walk from here."

He frowned. "With that foot?"

"I'll manage. It's not broken. And I know these woods."

Still, he hesitated.

"I've limped home before," she added with a small smile. "It wouldn't be the first time."

He studied her for a moment longer, then reached into a pouch and pulled out a small glass vial. It shimmered faintly, pale and luminous like springwater.

"Here. It'll help. Not a miracle cure, but enough to keep you steady."

She accepted it, eyed the contents suspiciously. "What's in it?"

"Old remedy," he said, his voice quieter than before. "Taught to me by someone who knew herbs better than most healers. It's safe."

The man hesitated as he spoke. Almost like he was seeing a memory as he watched her take the vial.

Camomile uncorked the tiny bottle and took a cautious sip.

Coolness slid down her throat—mint and honey and something else. Something strangely familiar.

She blinked.

Warmth bloomed faintly in her ankle. Not gone but dulled. Bearable.

"Better?" the man asked.

She nodded. "Yeah... thank you."

He stood and offered his hand. She took it. Her leg held, though she leaned on the tree beside her.

"What's your name?" he asked.

"Camomile Layton," she said. "But just Cam."

At the name, he froze.

The air shifted. His face paled, like a memory had caught him off guard. Something flickered behind his eyes—grief, sharp and buried.

"Well," he said after a moment, voice low. "It's good to meet you, Cam. I'm Sir Benjamin Miles. But Ben works too."

He turned slightly, gesturing behind her. "And this is Skylith."

Cam turned.

The dragon stood near the trees, scales glinting reddish-orange in the low light. Her gaze gleamed with intelligence—ancient and impossible.

It's a pleasure to meet you, Camomile Layton, said a voice inside her mind.

Cam went rigid. Her eyes flew wide.

"You—" Her voice caught. "You can talk?"

Ben tilted his head. "You can hear her?"

Cam nodded, still staring at the dragon.

"I thought... I thought dragon-speech was a myth."

Not a myth, Skylith said gently. You simply hear what others cannot.

"Skylith's been with me most of my life," Ben said quietly. "And still, she surprises me."

Cam tilted her head. "You can hear her too?"

Ben's gaze lingered on her, measuring. "I'm the only one who's supposed to hear her. We're bonded."

The words settled slowly, like snow refusing to melt.

Cam frowned. "Is that... not normal?"

His mouth curved—something between a smile and a sigh. "Not for most people." He didn't explain further, only watched as she turned back toward Skylith, now closer, coiled in quiet stillness.

"You're beautiful," Cam whispered.

And you are more than you know, Skylith replied, her voice like wind over canyon stone.

Cam blinked. "How do I hear you so clearly?"

Ben was watching her closely. "That's what I'd like to find out."

They stood in silence for a beat, the air heavy with unspoken things.

"Do people... know?" Cam asked. "About dragons?"

Ben nodded his head. "Yes."

Cam exhaled. "People in Brimclif don't talk about the old stories. And they never talk to me. I've always been treated like I didn't belong."

"Why?" Ben asked.

"I'm an orphan. My father died when I was ten. And the woman who raised me isn't kind. No one's ever tried to get close."

Sadness crossed his face—genuine, unguarded.

"I'm sorry," he said.

Cam didn't reply. But something stirred in her chest—sharp and strange. A tug. Familiar grief laced with something deeper.

She does not know, Skylith murmured, still watching Cam.

"What?" Cam blinked. "What do you mean?"

Ben exhaled. "She means you don't know who you are."

Cam frowned. "I do."

You know your name, Skylith said. *But not your blood.*

A chill prickled her spine.

"My... blood?"

"You don't remember anything? Before Brimclif?" Ben asked.

Cam shook her head. "No. Just the stories my father told me before he died. That's all."

Ben closed his eyes, breath slow and controlled. "I see."

There was more—Cam felt it in the pause between them.

"What do you know?" she asked.

Ben hesitated. "I... I can't. Not yet."

"You knew my parents, didn't you?"

His silence was answer enough.

Tears gathered, unspoken. She looked away, toward the horizon. The sun had vanished, and the trees stretched long, uncertain shadows across the ground.

"I should go," she whispered.

Ben didn't follow. "You sure you'll be alright?"

She nodded, barely.

"There's something about you, Cam," he said. "I haven't seen all of it yet. But what I have... I don't want you getting hurt before you understand what you are."

Cam blinked. "What I am?"

He didn't answer. Just looked at her again—something weighty and ancient behind his eyes.

She let it go. "I'll be careful."

"Good. Go straight home."

She turned to leave.

"Cam," he called softly.

She paused.

"If you ever hear a voice that isn't your own... don't ignore it."

Cam gave a small nod, her heart thudding in ways she didn't understand. She limped toward the trees.

Then paused again.

She turned, hand on the trunk. "Back in the woods," she said. "You said my name before I ever told you. How did you know it?"

Ben's jaw tensed. He glanced away.

"I've heard it before," he said. "A long time ago."

"From who?"

Ben hesitated. "Someone who meant a great deal to me. Someone I've been looking for... a very long time."

Cam stared. Her breath hitched.

He didn't elaborate. Just looked at her like it hurt to carry the truth.

She didn't press.

Then Skylith moved, stepping forward, her shadow long and flickering.

You are not lost, she said in Cam's mind. *You are only beginning.*

Cam's breath caught. The voice—so clear now, so close.

"I... I don't know what I'm beginning," she whispered aloud.

Chapter 5: The Call to Leave

Cam didn't remember the walk home. Only the ache in her leg and the weight in her chest that refused to lift.

By the time she stepped through the door, the world already felt sharper.

Cam's hunch had been right. Mrs. Lilian was furious.

But then again—what else was new?

Mrs. Lilian sent her straight to her room without so much as a glance. Cam didn't argue nor did she push back. She never did. She had just reached the stairs when Mrs. Lilian asked, sharply, "What have you been doing all afternoon?"

Cam didn't answer. She kept walking, silently climbing the stairs to her small room tucked beneath the eaves. She knew the unspoken rule: don't talk about the knight. Don't speak of the dragon. Don't ask questions that didn't have safe answers.

She shut her door behind her and let out a breath she hadn't realized she was holding. Her room, tiny and slanted-roofed, held only the barest comforts—a worn quilt, a rickety dresser, and an open window that let in the scent of earth and clover. Cam sat on the edge of her bed and looked out across the quiet village.

Were they still out there—Ben and Skylith?

She closed her eyes, and just as she did, a soft breeze fluttered through the window, stirring her hair. It smelled of spring and something older—like fire and sky.

Then she heard it.

A whisper.

Cam blinked her eyes open and scanned the room. Nothing. Just dust motes in the slanted sunlight and the stillness of late evening. Maybe she imagined it. Maybe it was just the wind.

But no matter how she tried to distract herself, her thoughts circled back to the glade. To the dragon whose voice lived in her mind. To the knight who knew something he wouldn't say.

She flopped onto her back and stared at the low ceiling. The silence didn't comfort her.

Who were her parents, really?

She squeezed her eyes shut and tried to picture them—

not memories, just shadows.

A mother lost to stories. A father defined by silence.

Had they been brave, she wondered. Had courage been something you inherited... or something you learned alone?. Had they once walked among dragons too?

So many questions. Not enough answers.

Cam rolled onto her side and willed her thoughts to quiet. Eventually, exhaustion took her.

She dreamed she lay on the forest floor, sunlight dappled across her skin through the trees. The air smelled like cherries and clovers, warm and lazy. She felt... peaceful. Almost weightless, as though a faint golden shimmer hovered at the edges of her vision. Then the light shattered into shadow.

Then the wind shifted, and the light disappeared.

She kept her eyes shut, even as a shadow fell over her.

Hands brushed her hair away from her face—gentle, but unfamiliar. A man's breath stirred near her ear.

Her heart thundered. She tried to move but couldn't.

Then she was being lifted—cradled in strong arms. She didn't know why, but she felt heat rise under her skin, a breathless panic. She fought to open her eyes. Nothing. Darkness.

A scream tore through the dream—high-pitched and otherworldly. It cracked across the dreamscape like lightning through a storm, piercing her bones. Beneath the sound, she thought she felt something else—an emptiness pressing in, hollow and hungry. She tried to cover her ears, but her arms wouldn't respond.

Pain bloomed across her legs, white-hot and deep.

Cam jerked awake.

The scream followed her out of sleep.

◈ ☽✦☾ ◈

Benjamin Miles lay under the stars, sleep refusing to come.

Cam's face haunted him. Her eyes, the way they widened when he refused to speak of her parents. The pain. The recognition. The look in her eyes when he'd refused to tell her the truth—he'd seen that look before. On Anthony. On Isabella. On himself, when he was too young to understand what war meant. It was the look of someone standing at the edge of something vast, knowing they couldn't turn back.

She had her father's fire. The quiet kind. The kind that smoldered before it blazed. And she had Isabella's heart—gentle, unwavering. She had their courage, their curiosity, their love stitched into her like thread in a banner.

She looked like them. Both of them.

And the way she heard Skylith.

That wasn't supposed to be possible. He had noticed it the moment she first spoke back to Skylith. Her energy resonated with something ancient. Something he hadn't felt in years.

And her eyes—blue gray like storm clouds. Like Isabella's.

No. He shook his head. *Don't go there.*

He lay back again, hands behind his head, eyes on the moon. It was round and low, casting pale silver across the glade.

Ben ran a hand through his hair and sat up slowly. "Could it really be her?" he whispered. "After all these years?"

Ben closed his eyes and exhaled slowly.

"I should've told her more," he murmured. "She deserves to know."

Skylith's snore rumbled beside him, deep and volcanic.

Ben laughed softly to himself. "Of course, I bond with the only dragon in the realm who snores like a thunderclap."

Then a sound caught his attention.

A scream knifed through the night, scraping down his spine like claws dragged across frozen glass. Far off, but unmistakable.

Banshees.

He leapt to his feet, heart racing. Another scream, closer now. Skylith stirred—very alert. One look at him, and she knew. His heart pounded with fear and dread—and hers did too.

If they found her... then what else was close behind?

"Cam!" he breathed and didn't waste another second. He ran for the village, and his dragon took to the sky in a blaze of wind and fire.

Cam was on the floor of her bedroom, tangled in her blanket, staring at the door. The room was dim, shadows long. Must be past midnight.

Her heart was still racing.

What kind of dream was that?

She'd always dreamed of escaping Brimclif. Every night since she was old enough to sew dresses and clean counters. But never like this. Never with dragons and pain and whispers in the dark.

She sat on the bed, glancing toward the open window. Outside, the wind stirred again, but this time, she sensed something more.

A feeling settled in her gut—something was coming. Something bad.

And when Cam got that feeling... it usually meant she was right.

She moved quickly, stuffing what little she owned into an old sack: a worn book, a small purse of coins, a blanket, a crust of bread, and a half-filled canteen. Not much. But enough.

She scribbled a quick note and left it on the dresser

She didn't even feel fear. Just certainty.

Her hands shook anyway.

She stood there for a long time, fingers on the sill, listening to the silence of the house. Leaving meant she would never come back. A small part of her wanted to wait—one more night, one more morning. But the certainty in her chest burned hotter than fear. She slipped into the dark.

Cam climbed out the window, landing softly on the earth below. The stars shimmered above like watchful eyes.

Ben ran through the night, his cloak snapping at his heels like a second shadow. His boots pounded the earth in rhythm with the panic rising in his chest.

He didn't stop when the forest thinned near the farmhouse. He didn't stop when his lungs ached, and his legs burned. He only paused when the building came into view—the shopkeeper's place, cold and dark, with its chipped shutters and empty silence.

He scanned the windows. One was cracked open, the curtain fluttering faintly.

That's the one, he thought.

He crept closer, silently climbing onto the windowsill and slipping inside. The room was empty. The bed—unmade. The dresser drawers hung open like gaping mouths, and the whole space had a restless energy, like someone had left in a hurry.

On the dresser sat a single scrap of parchment. Benjamin picked it up, heart thudding.

I'm leaving. I'm not coming back.

– Cam

He stared at the words for a long moment, then exhaled sharply and set the note down. "She left on her own," he murmured. "Smart girl."

A shriek roared through the trees like a curse flung from another world—raw, ancient, and wrong. His body tensed instantly.

Banshees. They were close.

He vaulted back through the window and into the forest.

Another shriek split the air—closer now. Too close.

He skidded to a halt at the edge of the tree line and caught movement in the distance. Figures, pale and gliding between the trees like smoke. He didn't need to see their faces to know what they were. Banshees. The shadow creature's cruelest hunters.

Their scream—it wasn't a sound. It was pressure. A sickness. Like gravity made of noise. It clawed through him, splitting thought from self. Ben covered his ears, but it was useless this close. The sound pierced through flesh and memory, dragging grief out by the roots.

He dropped to his knees.

Stop... please...

Then, suddenly, silence.

He gasped and lay still, stunned. Slowly, his ears rang less. His heartbeat thundered in the quiet.

And then he saw them. Footprints.

Bare. Small. Still fresh. She's alive.

He nearly wept with relief, but he held it in. The banshees were still too close.

He turned, following the footprints deeper into the woods. His mind raced. Banshees could track scent within minutes. He didn't have long.

"She's headed toward Miller's Field," he whispered. "Either that's good... or very, very bad."

Another scream erupted behind him. It peeled through the trees like stone tearing away from stone—as if the forest itself had found a voice to beg for silence.

Ben didn't flinch. He had no time to spare.

He ran harder.

Cam was out there.

And he would get to her before those foul creatures could.

Cam ran. Ran as fast as she could until she saw the tree line she was looking for. She ducked into the trees at the far edge of the village, feet carrying her on familiar paths she'd once wandered as a child—before she was caught and punished. Before she stopped hoping to leave.

She reached the gnarled old tree she'd marked years ago. The one she could pick out even in the dark. She brushed away moss, found the hollow she'd carved, and retrieved a weather-worn bundle of clothes sewn by moonlight over the course of years. Each stitch had been a quiet promise: One day, I will go.

She smiled faintly. That day had come.

But then—

A sound shattered the stillness.

A scream. Too loud to be real—like a landslide of sound collapsing inside her bones.

Not human. Not animal.

Other.

Cam dropped to her knees and slammed her hands over her ears. The sound clawed through her skull, sharp and relentless, like something trying to dig its way in. It grew—splitting the air like broken glass, relentless.

She remembered it. From her dream.

It wasn't a dream, she realized.

It was a warning.

The scream went on and on. Then suddenly—silence.

Cam peeled her hands from her ears slowly, heart pounding. She wasn't deaf. Not yet.

"What was that?" she whispered to herself, but even her own voice felt too loud.

She shoved her meager supplies into her bag and rose to her feet, trying to steady her breath. She turned her back on Brimclif and stepped deeper into the trees.

This time... she wouldn't look back.

Cam heard footsteps.

Heavy. Fast. Getting closer.

She darted behind a bush, clutching her bag tight against her chest, heart hammering.

A hand shot out in front of her.

She gasped—but before she could scream, a firm hand covered her mouth.

"Cam, stop! It's me. It's Ben."

The voice registered. She stopped struggling.

He pulled his hand away slowly. She turned to face him—and there he was. The knight. Real, alive, and out of breath.

Her breath caught. She hadn't realized how badly she'd needed to see a familiar face—even his.

"I'm so glad I found you," he whispered.

Cam tried to respond, but words felt stuck behind her heartbeat. She just stared.

"You okay?" he asked softly.

She nodded.

"What are you doing here? How did you find me?"

"I was looking for you," he said. "And how I found you isn't as important as what's coming."

A distant screech echoed behind them. They both froze. It wasn't just sound—it was pressure, dread, something older than language that pressed into the hollows of their chests.

"What is that?" Cam asked with a shaking whisper.

Ben looked behind them and dropped his voice. "We need to move. Now. Don't speak. Don't make a sound. If we stay here..."

He didn't finish.
Cam nodded.
She followed.
And this time, she didn't look back.

Chapter 6: The Escape

The night was growing darker by the minute, and Benjamin still hadn't returned.

Skylith flew high above the treetops, her wings stretched wide in a silent glide. The wind slid past her scales like a whisper, cold and sharp—but her thoughts burned hotter than flame.

Where was he?

Had he found Cam?

She tilted her head, eyes like burning opals scanning the forest below. No sound. No movement. Only moonlight threading silver across the tangled canopy.

The distance itched. Being bonded to a human had its strengths—but also its flaws. And one of the greatest was silence. At a certain range, even a bond frayed into nothingness. She could no longer feel Ben, not clearly. Just the ghost of him.

Still, she circled. Watched. Waited.

Earlier that evening, she'd asked a question she hadn't spoken aloud in over a decade:

"Did you know she's powerful?"

He had paused, his voice turning strange and low.

"Yes," he'd said. "Back when Isabella was still pregnant. She were afraid. We all were back then."

Of course they were. Camomile Layton was more than a child. She was prophecy wrapped in flesh. A bloodline made from two worlds that were never meant to intertwine.

And now... both of them were gone.

Isabella. Anthony.

His friends.

Cam was all that remained.

But Skylith remembered more than Ben did. More than any human could.

She remembered the long silence after Anthony's death—how Therynys, the great silver dragon, had not moved for days. She remembered asking what had happened. And she remembered the silence in return.

Not because Therynys had nothing to say.

But because a vow had been made.

A vow between riders.

And between dragons.

Anthony and Isabella had sworn never to speak of the child—not until it was safe. Not until the world had changed.

Therynys had obeyed. Even unto death.

So had Benjamin.

But now... now that child walked the woods below.

And the world was catching up.

Camomile stumbled beside Ben as they moved deeper into the forest. Her breath was ragged. The cloak around her shoulders was heavy with borrowed warmth, but it didn't stop the cold that had settled in her chest.

Brimclif was already gone behind them. A memory she would never return to.

And Ben—Ben wasn't just a stranger anymore. He was something else. A protector. A liar. A man made of secrets.

She didn't trust him fully. Not yet. But she followed.

"Where are we going?" she asked.

He didn't answer right away. "Somewhere safe."

That was all.

She gritted her teeth, nodding. There was no other choice.

They were almost to the edge of the woods when it began.

The silence.

At first, she thought it was her imagination—but then Ben stopped dead.

His arm shot out, stopping her.

"No birds," he said. "No insects."

Cam frowned. "So?"

He didn't answer.

A scream tore through the trees.

Not a sound. A weapon.

It split the air and hammered her ribs. She dropped to her knees, hands over her ears, the world fracturing into shards.

"Banshees!" Ben shouted.

They came from the shadows—pale and spectral, their limbs too long, their faces hollowed masks of anguish. Wraith-like. Endless.

Ben shoved her behind him, blade already drawn.

One of the creatures lunged. He met it mid-stride, slashing across its midsection. Shadow-flesh hissed and reeled, but it didn't stop.

They never stopped.

"Cam—run!"

She couldn't.

The scream pinned her.

Another banshee surged forward. Ben blocked it, but one slipped around. Cam barely had time to turn before it struck her—claws slicing deep into her side. She screamed, falling to the ground.

Ben roared and tackled the creature, burying his sword in its heart. It shrieked and vanished into mist—but not before leaving three long gashes across Ben's back.

He collapsed beside her, coughing blood.

"Call her," he rasped. "Skylith... call her."

Cam blinked at him, pain clouding everything.

Call her?

Skylith, she whispered in her mind.

Nothing.

Please. Please come.

Still nothing.

The banshees closed in.

The world went very quiet inside her.

Then something deep in her bones whispered—not to her mind, but to the earth.

Cam pressed her palms to the dirt. Her fingers twitched. Her lips moved without meaning to.

A whisper formed. Not in English. Not even human. The syllables felt ancient—older than thought itself.

The ground trembled. The air shimmered.

Then—light.

A surge of violet-black fire laced with silver-blue burst from her like a heartbeat, bright enough to blind.

The banshees shrieked as the wave hit them, their bodies unraveling mid-air like ash. For a split second, the edges of their forms glimmered gold before dissolving into nothing. The shadows thickened around the banshees, a wrongness clinging to them. Cam felt it for the first time—the same hollow hunger from her dream, wearing new shapes. Then Cam collapsed, blood pouring from her side.

Ben dragged himself to her, vision going black around the edges. "Cam—no, no, stay with me—"

But he couldn't move. Couldn't think. His body gave out.

The forest tilted. But not before more banshees surged from the trees—five, maybe six, shrieking as they closed in from every side. The shadows thickened, teeth and claws flashing in the moonlight. There was no time. No escape.

And then—flame.

A roar split the sky.

Skylith descended in a blaze of fire, her wings splitting the dark, her breath a furnace. She crushed one banshee beneath her talons, immolated two more, and sent the rest screaming into the night.

I'm here, she said, lowering her head.

Ben barely lifted his gaze. "She saved me... magic..."

I know. I felt it. It wasn't learned. It was inherited.

He nodded, delirious. "Can you get us to... Karethwyn? The cave."

Yes. Hold her.

He gathered Cam in his arms. She was ice. Too pale.

Skylith curled around them, lifted them into her claws, and soared into the sky.

The world dropped away.

Ben didn't remember the landing.

He only knew pain.

They were in a cavern now—stone walls, moss-draped, firelight flickering. A hidden place deep within the Forest of Karethwyn.

Skylith had helped him carry Cam inside. Laid her gently on an old stone cot.

He staggered to his knees and pulled a small vial from his belt. The last of it.

The healing potion.

He drank half to keep himself upright. Then tipped the rest between Cam's lips.

"Please," he whispered.

She stirred.

Her chest rose.

Color returned to her face.

Ben sat beside her and waited.

In the space between breath and dream, Cam drifted.

She felt light. Not air. Not sky. Something deeper.

She was floating through a place without shape. A memory that wasn't hers.

Then—a voice.

"Camomile Layton."

She turned. There was no form. Just the voice, low and ancient and echoing through her soul.

"You are waking, child of fire and memory."

Images swirled. A tower. A burning sword. A dragon's eye opening in darkness.

"There are shadows in the Knighthood and the Mystic Academy," the voice whispered. "Not all who swear loyalty mean it. One wears silver. One bears lies."

Cam opened her mouth. "Who are you?"

The voice softened.

"Once, I had many names. But yours is the one that matters now."

The fog tore open.

And she fell.

◈ ☽ ✦ ☾ ◈

Pain found her before sight did.

Cam woke with a gasp.

Pain lit up her side. Her hand flew to her ribs—bandaged, tight, wet. She wasn't alone.

Ben was there, slumped against the wall, his face streaked with dried blood. He looked barely alive.

"Ben—"

"I'm here," he said, voice rough but calm.

She tried to sit up. Couldn't. Her whole body trembled.

He moved to her side. "You're safe."

"I—what happened—?"

"You passed out. You stopped breathing."

She blinked, heart racing. "I felt... something. A voice."

He went still. But didn't ask.

She looked around. The walls glowed faintly with moss. The fire crackled low. It felt sacred. Sheltered.

"Where are we?"

"A hidden shelter. Old forest magic. No one can find us here unless we want them to."

Cam lay back, exhaustion settling into her bones. The dream, the vision, the magic—all of it pressed against her skull like a secret trying to claw its way out.

She didn't tell him. Not yet. Ben didn't press her.

He just sat beside her, hand resting on his sword, eyes distant.

"You should sleep," he murmured.

"Only if you do."

He gave a weary smile. "Deal."

Outside, the wind swept gently through the trees of Karethwyn. And the stars kept their watch.

Chapter 7: The Hidden Voice

The forest of Karethwyn held its breath.

Ben sat with his back against the cold stone wall, his sword beside him and his shoulder aching worse than any wound he'd taken in years. The bandage stuck to his back had started to seep again, but he didn't move. His eyes stayed on the girl sleeping just feet away, curled beneath a thick blanket. Camomile Layton.

Isabella's daughter.

Alive. Somehow alive, despite everything.

She stirred slightly in her sleep, a flicker of pain across her brow. He watched her fingers twitch, the faintest glow still flickering beneath her skin like the afterglow of starlight. The ancient magic was still inside her—still working. He could feel it in the air. It made the hairs on his arms rise.

He hadn't told her everything. Not yet.

"I was too late," he murmured under his breath, staring at the stone floor.

Skylith shifted beside the fire, her head resting near the entrance. *You couldn't have known what would happen to them, Forgeheart.*

"I should have. I was supposed to be there that night." He glanced down at the faded burn mark on his gauntlet. "I was tracking the wrong enemy."

Skylith didn't respond. He knew too that she felt responsible for that night too. Then finally she said.

We were both lead astray that night.

He glanced over again at Cam. Her breathing had evened out. But she was still so pale.

"You think she's strong enough?" he asked quietly.

Strong enough to survive, yes, Skylith said. *But if she doesn't learn control...*

"I know," he finished. "It'll tear her apart."

He exhaled, feeling the weight of years crawl across his bones. When she woke, there would be questions. And eventually, answers. But not yet.

He let her rest.

◈ ☽✦☾ ◈

Cam woke with her body aching and her mouth dry. The world swam for a moment before it settled into the familiar shadows of the stone shelter.

The pain in her side was a dull ache compared to the previous day—but the wound was closed. The ache should have lasted days, but the energy stirring in her veins knit flesh and bone faster than nature ever could. She pressed her hand gently against the bandage. Underneath, her skin burned faintly with... something. Her fingers trembled as she lifted the cloth just enough to see the faint marks beneath it.

Silver-blue veins. Almost like lightning. Etched into her skin, pulsing dimly with energy. And just beneath it, deeper still, she thought she glimpsed something darker flickering violet at the edges—waiting.

She flinched and dropped the cloth.

Ben was sitting nearby, watching her. His head resting against the stone.

"You're awake," he said softly.

She nodded and tried to speak but her voice was rough and gravelly.

Ben passed her a waterskin. She drank greedily.

"You shouldn't move too much," he added. "You lost a lot of blood."

"I feel like I lost half my body," she muttered, wincing.

His mouth curved slightly, almost a smile. She took a few gulps of water then handed it back to Ben.

"What... what happened to me?" she asked motioning towards her side. "My side—the blueish veins aren't normal."

"You're healing fast. Faster than you should be. The magic—it's still working in you. Whatever you did... it didn't end when you fainted."

Cam pressed her palms together. They tingled—like heat without flame. She could still feel it. The power she'd released. It pulsed through her body now and she could feel it. Like she had grown a second arm or leg.

"I didn't mean to do it," she whispered. "It just—happened, I don't know how..."

"Magic doesn't wait to be tamed," Ben said.

"Why now?" She asked looking at her hands. "Why did it surface now and not when I was ten or fifteen?"

Ben closed his eyes and breathed deeply. "Magic. Especially ancient magic appears where and when it chooses. And who it chooses."

Cam turned away from him, staring at the cave wall.

"It would have been nice to use this on Harriett Holster in the seventh grade," she said jokingly.

Ben looked at her with wild amazement. But the one to laugh first was Skylith. And they both joined in the laughter.

Cam didn't mention the dream. About the voice. The warning. Not yet.

Not until she was sure she could trust him. Her thoughts and worries took her far away and didn't realize Ben had spoken.

"Cam," Ben said again.

"Hm?"

"I was saying I'd like to help you keep your magic under control," he said. "If you can't control it, it will control you."

Cam thought about Ben's words and decided it was best to get some semblance of control over the magic within herself.

"I think you're right," she agreed with a little sigh.

Over the next several days, they stayed in Karethwyn. Skylith watched the skies. Ben taught Cam the basics—how to ground herself, how to breathe through the energy, how to listen for the magic instead of trying to force it.

She was a quick learner, but impatient.

"Ugh! I can feel it under my skin," she said once, pacing. "Like it's scratching to get out."

"Then breathe through it," Ben replied. "Let it move through you, not control you."

"I'm trying," she snapped. Sparks flared from her fingertips, silver-blue at first—then, just for a breath, edged in violet-black before fading as if in answer to her frustration.

Ben didn't flinch.

"That's the part you need to watch out for," he said calmly.

Cam sucked in a breath and blew it out hard. She sat down heavily, burying her face in her hands.

A long silence followed. Then:

"I had a dream," she said quietly with her head still in her hands. "It's the same one every night since my magic awakened."

She looked up at Ben. He was curious and looked as if he was holding his breath.

"A voice," she continued. "It knew my name. It showed me... things. Said there were shadows in the Knighthood. That the Mystic Academy... wasn't safe."

Ben's jaw tightened. He didn't answer. But even in the telling, Cam felt it again—the voice was not cruel or empty. It was vast, steady, as if some ancient presence was reaching for her across the Veil.

"You knew," she said, eyes narrowing. "Didn't you?"

Ben let out the breath he had been holding through his nose and closed his eyes as if he were trying to find the right words.

"I knew there were whispers," he admitted. "But I didn't think it would come for you this soon."

Cam crossed her arms. "Then tell me the rest. I deserve to know."

He hesitated. Then sat across from her and spoke.

"Your mother, Isabella—she wielded elemental and healing magic stronger than anyone I'd ever seen, her ancestry was a powerful line. And your father... wasn't born into the Knighthood, into a wealthy family where all the knights came from. But he bonded with a dragon anyway. That's not supposed to happen. An outsider bonding a dragon. It was unheard of. He could also do things that no other knight could."

Cam's mouth parted. "So, I'm—"

"Powerful. And dangerous to some," Ben finished. "You come from a line that was hidden for a reason."

"I never knew any of this," she whispered wrapping her arms around herself. "My dad never told me."

"He was protecting you."

Cam looked down at her hands, glowing faintly.

"So now what?" she asked, closing her hands into fists.

"Now, we need to make a choice," Ben said softly. "You need proper training, but we can't trust the Knighthood or quite possibly the academy..." he rubbed his face and groaned. "No one can know who you are... you could always pretend to be my long-lost niece. Then no one would suspect who you were. You need better training than what I can give you. I know more about dragon riding than magic, otherwise I'd teach you myself–."

"Teach me how to fight," Cam said suddenly.

"W-what?"

"I want to be able to defend myself," she said picking at a fraying end of her shirt. "You won't be able to defend me all the time. Especially if I'm going to a place with a possible threat. It makes the most sense."

"You're right," he sighed. "You should know how to defend yourself, Cam."

Ben stood. And offered his hand to Cam. She took it and he pulled her to her feet.

"It's a two-week journey to the academy," he said. "You're a quick learner, and that'll help—but this won't be easy. I'll teach you the basics in one week and then we head to the academy."

He unsheathed his sword and handed it to her, hilt-first. She staggered a little under its weight.

"Time for you to learn how to defend yourself."

The first day, her arms ached just from holding the blade steady. The weight pulling at her shoulders made her wrists scream. But she gritted her teeth and kept going.

Ben started with the basics—footwork, balance, how to hold a weapon without losing your grip or your head. Cam fell more than she swung at first. But she got up every time.

"Move like you're part of the ground," he said one morning, adjusting her stance. "Don't just stand—root yourself."

She listened. And slowly, she began to feel her center.

The second day Ben brought out the daggers. Lighter, faster. Less forgiving. Ben showed her how to switch hands mid-motion, how to parry and roll her shoulder out of a lock.

"You won't always have a sword," he told her, circling her with a practice blade. "Sometimes it's a rock. A knife. Your fists."

Cam panted, sweat dripping down her spine. "Sometimes it's ancient lightning in your veins."

He smirked. "That, too. But don't rely on it all the time."

By the fourth day, she was blocking attacks. Her movements still raw but improving. He pressed her harder, faster—then abruptly stopped mid-swing.

"You're hesitating," he said.

"I'm tired."

"You're scared."

Cam's grip tightened.

"I'm angry," she corrected.

Ben nodded. "Good. Use it. But don't let it use you."

They trained at dawn and again after supper. Skylith watched silently, sometimes tilting her head when Cam landed a proper strike.

Even at night, Cam went through motions alone, sticks in hand, mimicking sword drills beneath the starlight.

By the seventh day, she was bruised, blistered, but sharper—inside and out. Her body remembered what her mind couldn't yet grasp: she had power. Not just magic. But strength. Muscle. Grit.

She still had far to go, but something inside her had shifted.

She was no longer waiting to be protected.

She was becoming her own blade.

"You're ready enough," Ben said on the final day of Cam's basics training, he slung a pack over his good shoulder. "While we've been physically training your fighting skills your magic skills need improvement. You need training—real training. More so than I can provide. The Mystic Academy is the only place left that can offer that."

Cam nodded. "Even if the dream said not to trust it?"

"We'll be careful. But waiting here isn't an option."

They packed supplies and weapons loaded what they could on Skylith and took off midafternoon. Skylith flew low over the trees, careful to avoid open skies. At least until they were in open country. Cam sat behind Ben, clutching the saddle.

They traveled for a few days like this. Ben, worried that Cam might fall off, showed her how to ride. Just the basic but better than no knowledge at all and have her fall to her death.

They flew during the day and stopped at night because it was safer on the ground at night. And Ben not just worried about Cam falling asleep while on Skylith, but he worried about Skylith too.

It was the sixth day of their journey, and they had just set up a small space to sleep when Cam tensed.

Ben caught it instantly—the way her gaze went distant, her shoulders drawing tight. For a man who carried himself like steel, his hand on her shoulder was unexpectedly gentle.

"What is it?"

"I–I... heard something," she said, still tense.

"We didn't hear anything," Ben said questioningly wanting her to continue.

She set her pack down gently and tilted her head. The wind whispered through the trees.

...Camomile...

A voice. Ancient. Barely heard, yet unmistakable.

"It's coming from that way," she said, pointing. It was the opposite direction they were heading in.

Ben frowned. "Are you sure?"

She didn't answer. She was already walking.

"Whoa, wait a minute Cam," Ben said gently grabbing her elbow. It's nearly dark, we need rest."

She stared in the direction she'd started walking in.

"But..."

"Cam," he said turning her to face him. "I'm not going to stop you, but we don't know how long we will be following this voice you're hearing. It's best to rest first and pick it up in the morning. I promise."

Cam hesitated. The pull she felt wasn't like a thought or a feeling—it was deeper, rooted in her bones like the thrum of her magic. Whatever had whispered her name, it hadn't come from her imagination.

But she looked up at Ben, into his eyes—worried, but calm. Steady.

"Alright," she said softly. "We wait until morning."

Ben let out a breath he didn't realize he was holding and nodded. "Thank you."

They set up camp together in silence, the rhythm of familiarity beginning to settle between them. Skylith curled around their small camp, eyes half-lidded but watchful, a wall of muscle and scale against the darkening trees.

Cam sat on a fallen log near the fire, chewing on dried meat from her pack but barely tasting it. Her thoughts kept drifting—back to the voice, the call that echoed like a bell inside her chest. She was still staring into the flames when Ben sat beside her.

"You did well today," he said, nudging her lightly with his shoulder. "You're stronger than you think."

She gave him a small smile. "I'm starting to believe that."

They sat in silence for a moment. Then Cam asked, "Ben... What if the voice is a trap? What if it's the thing that's been following us?"

Ben poked the fire with a stick. "It might be. But if it was meant to lure you in, I think it would've tried sooner. The timing—it feels like it's waiting for something."

Cam frowned. "Like what?"

"I don't know. But everything about you is waking up. Your magic, your strength—maybe this voice... this call... is tied to all of that."

She glanced down at her hands, still a little raw from training. "It didn't feel dangerous," she murmured. "It felt... familiar. Like when I touched the stone walls of the sanctuary. Like I belonged to it somehow."

Ben didn't answer right away. Then he said, "The old stories say dragons don't just bond with knights. They bond with bloodlines. With fate."

She looked over at him. "What are you saying?"

He met her gaze. "I'm saying if this voice is calling you by name, it's not random."

Cam leaned back, her breath catching slightly in her throat.

"Whatever it is," Ben continued, "we'll face it. Together."

She nodded slowly. "Together."

◈ ☽ ✦ ☾ ◈

Dawn came early and grey. Mist clung to the trees like breath on glass, and the sky overhead was a dull silver.

Ben was already awake, packing supplies when Cam emerged from her bedroll.

"You sure about this?" he asked, glancing over.

Cam tightened the straps on her pack. "More sure of anything."

Skylith snorted from her post, her scales gleaming orangish red in the soft light.

Then let's not waste time, she said her voice low and resonant in their minds.

They changed direction, stepping off the worn path and into the dense, unfamiliar part of the forest. The air grew colder the farther they went, the canopy thick with ancient limbs and moss-covered trunks. Birds grew silent. Shadows deepened.

They walked for hours. The voice didn't come again, but the pull remained, like a thread tugging gently behind Cam's ribs.

"Do you recognize any of this?" she asked.

Ben shook his head. "No. And I've ridden these forests for years. Wherever we're going... it's not on any map."

Cam tilted her head, eyes narrowing. The whisper again. Not hollow, not cruel—deep, resonant, like mountains shifting. A name spoken through stone and time. She nodded and pressed forward. Something was waiting.

The forest deepened, and Ben could feel it in his bones.

The trees grew older the farther they walked—taller, thicker, gnarled like grasping hands. Roots curled like sleeping beasts. Moss dripped from the branches. Fog swirled low over the earth, not like something drifting in from the sea, but like it belonged to the place—born of it.

Beside him, Skylith walked in silence. Her wings folded tight, her movements cautious. She didn't speak aloud, but her eyes met his once.

You feel it too?

He nodded. "Something's waking."

It's her magic that led us here.

"I know."

They didn't speak the rest of the thought aloud—because they both suspected what was waiting ahead. But it had to be her choice. Her path. Whatever this was, it was connected to Cam in a way no one else could touch.

Ahead, Cam moved with silent determination. She hadn't spoken in over an hour. Her eyes scanned the woods like they were speaking to her, revealing something only she could understand.

Then the trees parted—and there it was.

A crumbling fortress, half-eaten by time and swallowed in ivy and fog. Its stone walls sagged, black with age. Towers leaned like they might collapse under the weight of memory.

Ben stopped at the edge of the clearing.

Cam took a step forward.

"We should be cautious," Ben said.

Cam didn't answer. Her eyes were locked on the ruins. Something in her gaze had shifted—like she was hearing a song no one else could hear.

Inside, it was deathly quiet. The kind of silence that vibrates in the chest. Even the birds had gone still.

They stepped through a shattered archway.

And then—

A roar tore the silence apart.

Fire exploded from the walls above, searing the air in a cascade of gold and violet. The force knocked Ben back a step. Skylith reared up with a snarl, her reddish-orange scales lighting like flame as she threw herself forward to shield them.

A massive shape surged from the shadows—a dragon unlike any Ben had seen in his life.

Obsidian Black and night blue scales shimmered like oil beneath starlight, veined with gold that pulsed with light. Her eyes were molten gold, her wings wide enough to blot out the sky.

She shrieked again and launched another blast of fire.

Ben moved, sword half-drawn. "Cam! Get back!"

But Cam didn't move.

She stepped forward.

"Cam!" Ben barked, panic breaking through his voice.

Still, she kept walking—like the fire had never touched her. Her eyes were locked on the great beast. Her breath was shaking, but her steps were steady.

And then Ben realized—she wasn't afraid.

Skylith flared her wings and roared, her voice booming into the minds of all present: *Stop! We mean no harm!*

The black-blue dragon snarled in return, smoke curling from her nostrils.

"You'll get her killed," Ben muttered under his breath, blade clenched in one hand. "Cam, don't—"

But Cam didn't seem to hear him.

Her hand lifted—not in warning, but in wonder.

And the dragon saw her.

◈ ☽✦☾ ◈

Cam's breath caught in her chest.

Her heart pounded so hard she thought it might shake her ribs apart. She took another step, unsure why her legs were still moving.

She should've been terrified.

But she wasn't.

The dragon's eyes—those blazing gold eyes—met hers. Not like a wild creature assessing a threat, but like something ancient peering into her soul.

Cam could feel it. A humming. A pull deep in her chest, in her bones, in the marrow of her blood. Her magic stirred restlessly, recognizing something it hadn't known it was missing.

The fire in the air dulled, then disappeared entirely.

The dragon's gaze narrowed.

Cam stopped only a few paces away. The heat from the beast's body shimmered in the air between them. Her fingers tingled with magic. Her knees wobbled. But she didn't drop her gaze.

A sound rumbled low in the dragon's throat—not a growl, but a question.

What is your name, fireborn? the voice asked—not aloud, but inside her mind. Deep and resonant. Female.

Cam blinked. "Camomile," she said, her voice hoarse. "Camomile Layton."

The dragon tilted her head, like she was tasting the name on some hidden wind.

Your name is green and sharp. Not small like the flower. Stronger. Wilder. Do you know what you are?

Cam shook her head. "I... don't think so. Not yet."

The dragon stepped closer. Her massive body shimmered with energy—blue-black scales flecked with gold. Cam could barely breathe under the weight of her presence.

But still, she didn't back away.

I am Sylithra. Flame of the dusk skies. Last of the Cradle born. I have slept long... but your magic stirred me.

Cam's fingers twitched at her sides. "I didn't mean to wake you."

But you did. And I listened. And I have chosen.

Cam's throat tightened. "You're choosing... me?"

We are already bonded, child. The moment you stepped into my storm. Your blood called to mine. Your silence answered my fire. I know your pain... and your potential.

Cam's vision blurred—not from magic, but from tears. Something inside her ached in response, like an old wound remembering it could heal.

"Will you... stay with me?" she asked.

The dragon lowered her head, until their eyes were nearly level.

Always. Unless you send me away.

Cam lifted a hand. Her palm hovered inches from Sylithra's scaled snout.

The magic between them crackled—quiet, warm, certain.

Her voice was no more than a whisper. "I won't."

Then we are one. Let the old ways return.

Time seemed to stall. The great creature's chest rose and fell once... then again. Her snarling stopped. She lowered her head slightly, not in submission, but in recognition.

Cam took another step. Then another.

And without a word spoken, something ancient passed between them.

A bond.

Not forced.

Not claimed.

Chosen.

The black-blue dragon stilled completely... and bowed.

Ben's jaw dropped. "That's not possible," he whispered.

Only the Knighthood can forge new bonds, Skylith said, awe rippling through her voice.

The dragon raised her head, eyes burning with intelligence and power.

Then let the Knighthood come, she said into Skylith's mind.

Cam stared up at her, wide-eyed and trembling, but still standing.

Ben took a slow step forward. "What's your name?" he asked the dragon, his voice respectful.

The dragon turned her golden gaze to him. *I am Sylithra.*

He exchanged a glance with Skylith, relaying the message to Ben.

Ben went pale.

That name had only ever appeared in the old texts. No one had seen her in a millennium.

She was supposed to be dead.

Cam took a shaky step toward Ben, then faltered. Her legs buckled and she dropped to her knees.

"Cam?" he said, rushing to her.

Her eyes rolled back—and then turned white.

Ben caught her just before she hit the ground.

"Cam!"

But she didn't answer.

Inside the vision, everything was red and black. The Knighthood's crest hovered in the air—then split, torn jagged down the center. Blood poured from the break like molten iron.

Figures emerged behind it—knights cloaked in darkness, their faces hidden beneath shadowed helms.

But one stepped forward.

Not shadowed.

Not hidden.

Clad in silver.

A voice, colder than winter, whispered in her mind:

"The traitor wears silver."

Cam jolted awake, gasping. Ben's hands were on her shoulders.

"Cam? Are you alright?"

She gripped his tunic, eyes wild. "I saw... the Knighthood crest. Split. Bleeding. And shadows... there was someone..."

Ben's face turned slightly paler than earlier.

She locked eyes with him.

"The traitor wears silver," she whispered.

For a moment, neither of them moved.

And far off, deeper in the forest—beneath root and bone and earth—

Something stirred.

Watching.

Waiting.

The shadows had begun to move again.

Chapter 8: Whispers of Becoming

The vision still echoed through her. Just a dream. Just a vision. She told herself that, though it clung to her bones like truth.

Cam sat cross-legged in the clearing just beyond the ruined fortress, her arms wrapped around her knees, the morning mist clinging to her skin like a second layer. Her head pounded with every beat of her heart. A dull throb behind her eyes. The air was heavy with damp silence, broken only by the slow, rhythmic breath of the dragon beside her.

Sylithra.

The ancient black-and-blue dragon coiled nearby like a living storm, her golden-veined scales shimmering faintly in the light. She had said little since the bonding—just watched, still and knowing, like she was waiting for Cam to catch up with the truth.

Cam shifted slightly, winced, and pressed a hand to her forehead. Her fingers trembled.

You saw what must be known, Sylithra said at last, her voice in Cam's mind low and resonant. *Not what must be done.*

Cam swallowed the dryness in her throat. "Why me?"

A pause. Then: *Because your blood remembers what your mind has yet to understand.*

The answer gave no comfort. Cam looked down at her hands—callused now from days of sword training but still shaking. She had touched something deeper than memory. Something older than names.

Behind her, she heard Ben pacing, his boots crunching in the leaves. He hadn't said much since the vision—just offered water, checked her pulse, then drifted away like he didn't know how to hold what had happened.

She glanced back at him. His jaw was tight, his posture coiled. He didn't trust Sylithra. That much was clear. And Sylithra didn't trust him either. He approached now with quiet questioning. Cam knew what he was asking but before she could answer Sylithra spoke to her and Skylith.

There is a rebel outpost a week's journey from here. They follow the old ways, and Camomile must learn the language of magic.

As Skylith relayed the message to Ben he stiffened at the mention of the rebel outpost. And glared up at Sylithra.

"No," he said firmly.

No?

"It's too dangerous," he said standing his ground. "I can't trust them with Cam's safety."

There was a standoff or a quiet conversation happening between Sylithra and Ben that Cam was not a part of, but she felt caught in the quiet rift between them.

Not a student. Not a soldier. Something else entirely.

And it was lonely.

Ben stopped pacing and exhaled hard through his nose. He watched Cam—the girl who carried her father's defiance and Isabella's kindness—sitting beside a creature that should have been dead over a thousand years ago. Bonded. Changed.

He should've been relieved that she was still alive after the bonding happened and then the vision, but all he felt was a slow-burning dread. He didn't want to lose what was left of his friends.

"She's too young for this," he muttered.

Skylith huffed beside him, stretching her wings slightly. *No one ever asks for destiny to come early.*

Ben rubbed his forehead. "You think that she is telling her the truth?"

Sylithra is older than I am. That does not make her wise beyond her years, but she is a very smart dragon.

He scowled. "But it does make her dangerous."

He remembered the last time he ignored a vision. Years ago. The rebel mage who was once his friend had promised clarity, revolution—then slaughtered half a town in pursuit of "freedom." Visions didn't make people right. They made them convinced. That was worse.

He turned toward Cam. "We have to move soon," he called. "There is no telling what kind of creatures are out there. I'd prefer that we get to the academy where it's safer behind magical wards."

Cam stood slowly. "And what if it's not safe?"

Ben hesitated. "Then we'll protect you."

"That's not the same as trusting me to protect myself," she said, stepping closer.

There it was again—that quiet fire behind her eyes.

Ben turned away from her. He couldn't help but see his best friend pushing back when Cam got that look in her eyes. That quiet defiance that had got her mother into trouble.

They flew for a full day, cutting across the canopy of Karethwyn's oldest woods. Cam rode behind Ben on Skylith—not because she wanted to, but because Sylithra had no saddle, and Ben didn't trust her flying solo yet.

They didn't talk much.

The silence wasn't angry exactly, but it was heavy. A tension neither of them seemed ready to break. The wind between them said more than words could: *You don't trust me. I don't know if I should.*

They landed shortly before nightfall and made camp in a small grove, half-sheltered by mossy trees and tall stones. Shadows grew long, stretching like claws across the earth. The dragons curled close—Skylith with her head tucked low, Sylithra facing the trees, as if listening for something distant.

◈ ☽ ✦ ☾ ◈

Night fell, and Cam wrapped herself in her cloak beside the fire. The stars spun slowly above through breaks in the canopy, fragments of light barely visible through the drifting mist.

Sleep came in broken pieces.

But Sylithra's presence was there—steady, quiet, ancient.

Cam slept beside the fire, curled tightly beneath her cloak, her fingers still glowing faintly with gold. It reminded Ben of fireflies from his youth, flickering in the tall grass outside the barracks—before the war, before the Knighthood, before loss etched its way into his bones.

He sat alone at the edge of camp, sharpening his sword by instinct more than needed. His thoughts were too loud. His breath came too shallow. The memory wouldn't leave him.

Sylithra stood like a statue at the clearing's edge, black-and-blue and bathed in starlight. Her wings folded close, her golden eyes reflecting more than firelight. She was watching the girl—but also watching him.

Ben met her gaze. He didn't flinch.

You fear what you cannot guide, she said in his thoughts. Ben did not question how she reached him. He had lived long enough, bonded long enough, to know some links ran deeper than command or training—threads that defied explanation.

"*No,*" he answered, silently. *"I fear what I've seen before."*

The rebel mage—he was someone you knew.

Ben closed his eyes.

"Corin. My closest friend. We trained together. Fought side by side. He used to be kind. Loyal. Until the visions started."

He opened the memory like an old wound.

Sylithra didn't look away.

A flickering vision—Corin, arms lifted in rapture, declaring himself a conduit for "the Old Flame." His words were beautiful. Convincing. Ben had almost believed him, once.

But then came the whispers. The purging. The raids.

And that village.

Show me, Sylithra said.

So, Ben did.

He let her see the woman trying to shield her son with her own body. The fire swallowing them both. The crest of the Knighthood burned into a rebel flag and twisted into something cruel. The blood. The betrayal. And finally: Corin's face when Ben raised his sword against him.

"Then you are no better than the ones who chain dragons," Corin had said.

"I'd rather chain a dragon than set the world on fire," Ben had answered.

You did not kill him, Sylithra said surprised.

"No. But I didn't stop him either. I hesitated. And people died."

The fire in the camp crackled louder, as if protesting the silence between them.

For a long moment, Sylithra said nothing. She only stood in the mist, her gaze distant, unreadable. Then finally:

You carry grief like armor, knight. But you loved him once.

Ben didn't answer. Not at first. But his throat tightened.

"I loved all of them. Anthony. Isabella. Corin, before he was lost. And now... she's all that's left."

He looked at Cam. Sleeping, flickering like a dying star.

"She's what remains of everything I couldn't protect."

Sylithra stepped forward, slowly. Her claws made no sound against the moss. When she spoke again, it was quieter than before—less command, more compassion.

Then let us protect her together.

Ben blinked, startled by the softness in her tone. Ancient dragons did not offer "together" lightly.

You fear that visions create monsters. But monsters are born of silence, too. If she sees something—let her speak it. If she becomes something—do not cage it before it's formed.

Ben looked down at his hands. Callused. Scarred. The hands of a protector. A killer. A friend.

"She doesn't know how powerful she is," he said quietly.

That is why she must learn.

They stood in silence for a while after that—an old knight and an older dragon, not friends yet, but no longer enemies.

Ben sat back down, sighing through his nose. He pulled his cloak tighter around his shoulders, his eyes on the horizon. There would be no sleep for him tonight.

But he would stay. Watch. Guard.

Not just her body, this time.

Her becoming.

In the dream, Cam stood barefoot in a garden she'd never seen.

A red moon burned overhead. The roots below her glowed with amber veins, like lightning frozen in earth. Vines curled around her ankles—not to trap, but to anchor. All around her, flowers pulsed with unfamiliar colors, petals edged in silver.

Sylithra appeared not in dragon form, but as shadow and voice. She circled Cam like smoke, her eyes glinting from the dark between trees.

You've been taught to fear what you cannot name, Sylithra said.

Cam turned toward her slowly. "What are you trying to show me?"

Your mother spoke with the wind. She burned without burning. She did not ask permission.

Cam's breath hitched.

Sylithra's voice deepened. *Unlearn what binds you. Magic is not a weapon—it is a language. And you are only just beginning to speak it. One day, you will not only speak—you will weave.*

Cam reached toward the roots beneath her. As her fingers touched the glowing earth, warmth spiraled up her arms. Beneath the amber and silver, she thought she glimpsed a flicker of violet-dark fire, like a shadowed flame waiting to be claimed.

She woke with a start.

The fire had gone out.

The mist had thickened.

And her fingers—tucked against her chest—glowed faintly with gold.

Chapter 9: What hunts her

After two long days of flight, they reached the split in the mountains.

A crooked stone marker stood at the fork, half-sunken into the earth and veiled with moss. Time had worn away its carvings, save for two paths and two destinies.

To the east, the winding trail led toward the gleaming white spires of the Mystic Academy—its towers faint in the distance, catching the last of the sun's light like watchful sentinels.

The other path curled west into mist-drenched forest, swallowed by brambles and dark pine. A single glyph, nearly erased by time, had been etched into the rock beside it: a dragon's eye, open and wild.

Ben's boots crunched over loose stone as he stepped toward the eastern path. "The Academy is fortified," he said, as he had before. "It has instructors. Spell barriers. Libraries filled with the knowledge you need."

Cam crossed her arms. "It also has enemies hiding in plain sight. That's what the vision showed me."

"And the rebel path?" Ben turned to face her. "You think they have your best interests in mind? They answer to only themselves."

"I don't know who I can trust," she said quietly, her gaze lowered. "That's the problem."

Ben softened slightly. "Then trust what you do know. Me. Skylith. That's more than most have."

But Cam wasn't looking at him.

Sylithra, resting behind them, had lifted her head. Her golden eyes met Cam's. The voice in Cam's mind came low and firm.

Then trust your blood. Trust what burns.

Cam inhaled sharply and responded in her thoughts, *"I just met you, Sylithra. Even though we're bonded, I still need to be able to trust you—and I don't yet. Part of me believes in this bond... but the rest of me still needs proof. Reassurance. Something real."*

Sylithra's massive wings shifted. A breath like steam hissed from her nostrils. She turned her head, not with anger—but resignation. The dragon knew Cam was right.

Trust had to be earned, even by those destined.

Ben noticed the silence stretching between them—the kind only dragons and bonded riders could share. He muttered a quiet curse under his breath and turned away.

"Good," he said sharply. "Glad we're all talking to someone."

Cam winced. She hadn't meant to exclude him. But the truth was, Sylithra's voice now felt as woven into her thoughts as breath itself.

Ben began pulling supplies from Skylith's saddlebags and tossing them into the grass. "We'll make camp here. No decision gets made tonight—not when we're all running on fumes and half a night's sleep."

Skylith gave him a nudge with her snout, and he grumbled something unintelligible in response.

Cam took a few steps toward the edge of the clearing and looked between the two paths. The Academy, where answers might wait—or traps. The rebel trail, filled with mystery, wild magic, and danger.

Either could shape the rest of her life.

Neither felt safe.

She rubbed her arms, feeling the ache of choices yet to be made settle into her bones. Her magic stirred beneath her skin like something waiting. Watching.

She glanced back at Ben, then at Sylithra.

"I need more than protection," she whispered to herself. "I need to become something more."

And far, just beyond the trees where the shadows thickened, something else listened.

Waiting.

◈ ☽ ✦ ☾ ◈

The air shifted just after dusk.

Ben stood on the edge of the clearing, his hand resting lightly on the hilt of his sword. The fire crackled behind him, throwing flickering light against the crooked stone marker—the split in the world where one road led to safety, and the other to chaos.

Or so he told himself.

He didn't trust the forest past the ravine. Too quiet. Too still. Even the dragons were uneasy tonight—Skylith, crouched near the fire, had stopped preening her wings and simply watched the dark like she expected it to move.

He cast a glance back at Cam.

She was crouched near Sylithra, eyes half-closed but alert, tension coiled in her shoulders. She hadn't spoken much since their last argument. She hadn't needed to.

He knew the look on her face too well—it was the same one Anthony used to get before diving headfirst into a fight he couldn't win.

Ben turned back to the trees. His fingers flexed around the hilt.

Something was wrong.

That's when he heard it.

A low growl, like rocks grinding together.

Then another.

Too many feet, too close, too fast.

"Cam?" he called sharply, drawing his blade.

Before she could answer, the clearing exploded with motion.

A Darkfang leapt from the shadows, red eyes gleaming, smoke-fur trailing behind it like torn cloth. Ben slashed upward, catching its flank, but another slammed into his side, sending him hard into the dirt.

"Darkfangs!" he shouted. "They're here!"

Skylith roared, wings bursting open in a fiery arc. Sylithra was already moving, flames curling in her throat.

Ben rolled to his knees, gasping, his ribs screaming. One of the Darkfangs lunged again—and this time he was ready. He brought the hilt of his sword up into its jaw and drove his blade through its chest.

But then he saw it—more of them. Too many. And they weren't attacking the dragons.

They were all going for Cam.

They were after her.

There was no question now. The Darkfangs ignored Ben. They ignored the dragons. Every snarling mouth, every pulsing red eye locked onto her.

Cam backed away slowly, her heart hammering. She gripped her sword tighter, its hilt slick in her hands. The air pulsed with heat—her magic. It was reacting, flaring to life, not from calm or clarity—but from fear. And fury.

You want me? Then come get me.

She spun and ran, deeper into the forest—toward the ravine.

Branches whipped across her arms, stinging cuts rising along her skin. A claw raked her shoulder as one leapt too close, tearing fabric and flesh. Hot pain bloomed, sharp and raw, but she didn't stop. Her breath burned in her throat, every step heavier, her legs screaming. Her wounds throbbed, hot against the icy air. The mist did not move like an animal. It moved like absence, like hunger shaped into a body. The same hollow wrongness from her dream scraped at her bones. The mist swirled as she ran, her pulse hammering. For an instant, the shadows split with a shimmer of gold light, gone as quickly as it came.

She focused on the thundering paws behind her, the shadows flanking her, and the fire churning in her chest.

Let it out, Sylithra's voice echoed faintly in her mind. *Give it shape.*

Cam skidded to a halt behind a fallen tree and turned to face the pack of Darkfangs. Her breath came in ragged gasps. Blood ran warm down her forearm where claws had torn through. She gritted her teeth and planted her feet wide.

The sword in her hand hummed.

She pulled from the tight knot of emotions inside her—every memory of loss, of fear, of being underestimated, of being alone—and willed it into her hands.

A flicker of silver-blue sparked against her palm, and just for a heartbeat, a thread of violet-black coiled through it before fading. It threaded through her veins like liquid flame.

With a cry, she plunged her blade into the earth. A shockwave burst outward. Not enough to kill—but enough to stagger. The leading Darkfangs yelped and fell back, blinking through the light.

It wouldn't hold them for long.

Cam turned and ran again.

The trees thinned. The sound of rushing water grew louder.

And then—open sky.

She reached the edge of the ravine just as the first Darkfang broke through the trees behind her. Below, the river crashed against stone. Fast. Cold. Deep.

Cam took two steps back. *Think, think, think.*

Then she had it.

She turned, magic still burning under her skin, and raised her sword high. She let them see her. Let them chase her.

"Come on," she breathed. "Come get me."

They bolted forward, fangs bared.

Cam waited... waited...

Then leapt aside at the last second. Six of the Darkfangs went over the edge but one remained.

Cam raised her blade, breath ragged. The beast lunged—too fast, too close. She pivoted with it, steel flashing, and drove the point hard into its chest. The Darkfang let out a strangled cry before it collapsed, sliding limp into the dirt.

Cam staggered back, blood dripping from both her blade and her own arm. Her chest heaved. Pain burned along her shoulder and thigh where claws had torn through. She had only a heartbeat to breathe—

—before the air shifted.

A Howler glided down from the tree branches. Pale mask. Empty sockets. A quiet that scraped across her soul.

Cam's mouth went dry.

I might not survive this one.

But she squared her stance anyway.

"Cam!"

He'd barely spoken her name before she was gone—vanishing between the trees like a streak of lightning, golden magic crackling at her heels. The shadows swallowed her in seconds. And right behind her—four Darkfangs, silent and low to the ground, moving like smoke with teeth.

Ben swore and lunged forward, sword already in his hand.

"She's drawing them away," he muttered. "Damn it, Cam-"

A deafening snarl broke through the night air.

Two shapes dropped from the trees ahead—hulking, glistening, wrong. Wraithbeasts.

They landed hard, one on either side of the trail. Smoke rolled off their backs. Their lion-like forms rippled with shadow, tentacles slithering in place of manes. Glowing slits for eyes. Teeth that shimmered like obsidian.

Ben gritted his teeth and charged the left one before it could pounce. His sword caught it mid-step, biting into its shoulder, but it didn't slow—it roared and slammed into him with the weight of a boulder.

Ben hit the ground hard. Pain lit through his ribs, and something in his shoulder gave a sharp pop. He rolled fast, barely avoiding a swipe of clawed limbs, and stabbed upward.

The blade drove into the Wraithbeast's underside. It shrieked—too high, too loud—and melted into shadow. Ash scattered over him.

The second Wraithbeast was already leaping.

Ben barely had time to raise his sword. Claws raked down his side before he caught the creature with the flat of his blade and shoved it back. His breath came in ragged gasps. Blood soaked into his tunic.

"Not tonight," he growled.

He spun low, sweeping the beast's legs out from under it, and drove his sword straight into its eye. The Wraithbeast shuddered, gave one last gurgling howl, and burst into ash.

Ben staggered to his feet. The forest spun briefly, his head pounding. But he didn't stop.

He turned toward the sound of rushing water in the distance. Toward where Cam had run.

And then—clearer than thought, deeper than memory—he heard her.

Skylith's voice, low and thundering, filled his mind.

Forgeheart.

Everything stilled for one breath.

His blood ran cold.

The sky was full of wings and fire.

Mirebats shrieked through the night, their twisted forms blotting out the stars. Wings like torn cloth. Eyes like hollow coals. They moved in swarms—quick, unpredictable, screeching with magic-laced venom that sent sparks across Skylith's scales.

She flew through them like a blade.

Left flank! Sylithra's voice cut clean through her thoughts, sharp and commanding.

Skylith tilted her wings, rolling into a tight spiral just as two Mirebats dove. She exhaled a stream of fire, catching one mid-flight. It shrieked and fell, trailing black smoke. The other lunged—but Sylithra slammed into it from the side, her claws tearing through shadow-flesh.

They're after her, Sylithra said, wings straining as she climbed above the fray.

I know, Skylith answered, fury rising. *I counted seven Darkfangs on her trail.*

Sylithra beat her wings hard, rising above the swarm. From this height, she could see the glimmer of the ravine. And there—faint but unmistakable—golden light burning through the trees. It flickered, wild and uneven.

She's using her magic, Skylith said. But she's weakening.

Tell Ben, Sylithra said at once, sweeping a Mirebat off her back with her tail.

Skylith closed her eyes for a heartbeat, focusing past the roar of wings and fire, past the chaos. She pushed her mind toward the earth, toward the man who shared her history and now her purpose.

Forgeheart, she sent. *Cam is at the ravine's edge. She's alone. Injured. The beasts hunt her still.*

"How badly?" Ben's thought-voice returned, sharp and immediate.

I don't know. But the fire's fading.

A pause. Then: *I'm going.*

Skylith caught a Mirebat in her jaws and crushed it midair.

We'll keep the skies clear, she growled.

Sylithra wheeled upward again, flanked by Skylith, their massive wings catching moonlight as they turned toward the last of the airborne enemies.

The forest below trembled.

The stars above burned on.

And the girl at the edge of the ravine—blood of fire, voice of storms—fought alone.

For now.

◈ ☽✦☾ ◈

The Howler landed without a sound. Tall. Skeletal. Its cracked bone mask caught the moonlight like fractured porcelain, a mockery of a face. The hollow sockets glowed faintly, burning like coals.

Cam raised her sword with both hands. Her arms shook violently with the effort. Every muscle screamed. Blood ran warm and sticky down her side, soaking into her tunic. Her left leg buckled when she shifted her weight, the torn muscle refusing to hold steady. The air scraped against her throat like glass, each breath shallow and sharp.

She was trembling.

Bleeding.

Exhausted.

Her vision blurred, blackness edging in, and for a heartbeat she thought she might fall before the fight even began. Her grip slipped on the hilt, slick with sweat and blood, but she forced her fingers to tighten again until her knuckles ached.

But when the Howler stepped forward, something in her refused to collapse.

No, she thought, jaw locking. *Not yet. I'm not done.*

She widened her stance—shoulder-width apart—the way Ben had drilled into her a hundred times. The pain in her ribs was sharp enough to steal her breath, but it carved her focus down to a single point. The flickering magic inside her pulsed faintly with her heartbeat—weak, but defiant.

The Howler screamed.

It lunged.

Cam ducked beneath the first swipe, rolling hard across the dirt—pain tearing white-hot through her ribs and her thigh. A cry clawed at her throat, but she bit it back and dragged her sword up in a wide arc. Steel caught shadow and bone, slicing through its shoulder. The creature reeled, shrieking.

But before she could regain her footing, it struck again. Claws raked across her ribs, tearing fabric and flesh. The world exploded in pain. She stumbled, nearly dropping her blade, air wheezing from her lungs.

Her hand pressed instinctively to her side—wet, hot, and searing—but she didn't let go of the sword.

The Howler loomed, bone mask gleaming.

Cam staggered forward, half falling, half lunging. Her blade lit again—not gold now, but white-hot, fueled by pain, fury, and the raw ache to live.

The Howler rushed her, claws wide.

Cam met it head-on.

Her sword drove straight through the mask, cracking it down the center. The scream that followed nearly split her skull. She shoved harder, both hands straining, until the mask shattered.

With a burst of white and violet light and a rush of ash, the creature disintegrated.

Silence fell.

Cam swayed where she stood. Blood poured from her side, soaking her tunic, warm against the cold night. Her knees buckled, sword slipping from her hands. She stumbled backward—too far, too close to the edge.

The ravine yawned behind her, black and endless. Her heel slid on loose stone. For one terrifying instant she felt the ground vanish beneath her.

I did it, she thought dimly.

Then her body gave way, crumpling forward at the last possible moment, collapsing hard onto the dirt just shy of the drop.

Her eyes fluttered once, twice. Blackness closed in.

And then she was still.

◈ ☽✦☾ ◈

Ben moved through the forest like a shadow bleeding deeper into night.

His left side ached with every step—hot, sharp pain from where one of the Wraithbeasts had raked across his ribs. The gash was wrapped hastily beneath his cloak, already soaked through, but he pushed forward. Slowing wasn't an option. Not with Cam out there alone.

He followed the burn marks. The scent of scorched fur and wild magic clung to the trees. Her path wasn't clean—it was wild, desperate. Ash and earth churned together in chaotic footprints. She was fighting for every step.

His heart hammered, every throb of it matching the tension in his wound.

Then—he broke through the last of the trees.

The ravine opened before him, moonlight spilling silver over the edge, where the earth dropped away into dark water below.

And there—at the edge—was Cam.

Her body lay there at the edge, a breath from falling. Her sword was in the dirt near her hand, glowing faintly, still alive with the memory of fire. Her chest rose and fell in shallow rhythm. Blood streaked her arms. A long gash marked her side—she was hurt badly, and she'd been alone for too long.

Ben's breath caught in his throat.

"Cam," he whispered hoarsely, pain forgotten as he dropped to his knees.

He pressed his cloak to her side, anchoring her to the ground with one arm as if the wind might try to take her from him. Her skin was cold with sweat. Her lips barely moved. He leaned in and caught the faintest murmur—just breath, no words.

For a flicker, he saw it—gold shimmer threading faintly beneath her skin, glowing like cracks of molten glass. His stomach tightened. He'd seen it once before, years ago, on a battlefield. Too much power, burning too fast. It never ended well.

He forced the thought away. Not now. Not here.

"You're alright," he whispered, more for himself than her. "You're still here."

He held her tighter, wincing as his own injury throbbed. The blood from his ribs now mingled with hers in the dirt. He didn't care.

"Just stay with me."

He reached for the dragons with his thoughts.

Skylith. I found her. She's alive.

And above the canopy, wings shifted against the sky.

HERITAGE

Help was coming.
But someone else had already seen.

Chapter 10: Noticed

High in the tree line, motionless among the branches, the scout crouched—breath slow, body still, one with the dark.

The wind moved below, bending branches. The knight knelt beside the girl, cradling her like something rare and already slipping away.

Blood in the moss. Magic in the air.

The scout's eyes followed the shimmer of the girl's blade. Still faintly glowing. Still pulsing.

She had poured herself into that fight. She had bled it.

And she had survived.

Despite the odds. Despite the imbalance.

Despite the odds meant to break her.

The girl was real.

Not a rumor. Not a hopeful myth whispered among trees.

Stronger than anticipated.

The scout touched the stone at their belt—its surface warm, pulsing with magic as it recorded the moment.

No sound. No movement. Only stillness.

Then, like a shadow evaporating into mist, the scout disappeared from the branches—already gone before the dragons arrived. He knew how far to be before the dragons would feel it.

He'd tested this kind of distance before.

Chapter 11: Remembering

The forest faded.

In its place, moonlight—deep and red—poured from a sky where no stars lived. Cam stood barefoot on soft moss that pulsed faintly with light, gold and violet, threading beneath her toes like veins beneath skin.

The trees surrounding her were vast and silent, their trunks etched with glowing runes that shifted like breath. A wind moved through them, not cold, not warm—just ancient. It whispered her name, not as a command, but as a memory.

Camomile.

She stepped forward, drawn toward the center of the dream like a tide pulled toward some unmapped shore. Roots coiled beneath her steps, guiding her to a clearing where the trees bowed inward, as if reverent.

There, at the heart of it all, was a pool.

Still.

Black.

Not empty—but full of stars.

Sylithra's voice came, not from the air, but from within.

This place is not a dream. It is a remembering.

Cam knelt beside the pool and saw herself—not as she was, but as countless selves.

A girl with fire in her palms. A woman with wings made of light. A child born beneath the howl of dragons.

Her reflection rippled with every version of her that might have been, and all that still could be.

You've carried more than blood, Sylithra whispered. *You've carried a promise—one even the gods forgot.*

Cam's breath caught.

The air shimmered.

A tree rose from the edge of the pool, tall and silver-barked, blooming with golden petals. As she watched, a single blossom fell and touched the water—where it bloomed again into light, spreading outward in rings that lit the trees, the roots, the sky.

She reached into the pool.

Warmth surged up her arm—not painful, not burning, but like the first breath after drowning.

And then she saw it:

A mountain split wide by time. A cradle of stone wrapped in clouds. A place hidden even from dragons.

And in that place—a voice, not Sylithra's, not her own.

When the Veil thins, the child of fire and storm must rise. And she will not rise alone.

Cam gasped.

Her eyes snapped open.

She was back in the forest clearing beside the ravine, cloaked in mist. The fire had dimmed. Ben slept lightly, his brow still drawn in pain.

But Cam's hand still glowed faintly, a thin ribbon of gold threading beneath her skin.

She clutched it to her chest. Her breath caught.

Not a dream, she thought as her vision darkened again. A remembering.

And somewhere, not far off—

The Veil stirred.

Far above the ravine, Sylithra and Skylith stood side by side—silent, massive, their eyes gleaming with quiet thought. Below them, the narrow river shimmered like a thread of silver fire.

They didn't speak aloud; their voices moved in thought alone, a silent current that passed between them, rich with meaning most could almost—but not quite—feel.

She saw it, Sylithra said eventually, her voice folding inward like a secret memory. *The pool. The rootlight. The stars.*

Skylith shifted, claws pressing into the stone. *Do you believe it's real?*

I believe she is.

A pause passed between them.

Her power is growing fast. Faster than anything I've seen.

She should have burned out, Skylith murmured. *After the bonding. The vision. The fight. She should have faded. But she didn't.*

Sylithra's golden veins pulsed faintly beneath her black-blue scales.

She's not like the others. Her strength isn't borrowed—it's remembered.

That comes with a price.

Yes. But perhaps she's the only one who can afford to pay it.

They stood together, two creatures born of old flame and older vows, watching the fire flicker far below. Watching the girl.

Guardians of something returning.

Not protectors of what had been—but witnesses of what must become.

And beyond the trees, something else stirred. Watching. Waiting.

Ben awoke with a sharp inhale, pain flaring through his ribs.

He stayed still, gritted his teeth, and pressed a hand to the wound beneath the dressing. It wasn't fatal. He'd had worse. But it was deeper than he'd admitted—especially after pushing himself during the escape.

He caught movement near the fire.

Cam sat upright, blinking fast, as if she were trying to return from somewhere far away. Her forehead was damp with sweat. Her lips parted slightly, her gaze unfocused. Not just exhausted. Changed.

Ben said nothing.

She looked at him suddenly, sharp.

"You're bleeding," she said.

"It's nothing." He adjusted his cloak. "I've had worse."

She moved to him before he could stop her, brushing his arm aside. "You're lying."

He opened his mouth to deflect again—but a warmth spread beneath her hand. A soft spark of light bloomed between her fingers and his skin, golden and low.

It didn't burn.

It healed.

The ache in his side ebbed. His muscles loosened. The pulsing in his shoulder softened, as if the wound had turned to water and was draining from his body.

Ben stared at her hand. Then at her.

"You're healing me," he whispered.

She didn't answer. Her eyes were distant, her expression unreadable, as she focused. The glow dimmed slowly, retreating into her veins like a second pulse, quiet and ancient.

"You can heal," he said under his breath. "Like your mother."

Cam looked up.

"She did this for you?"

He hesitated. Then nodded once, tight. "First time I met her. I'd taken a spear through the leg trying to save Anthony from a trap. He yelled at me. She didn't. She just... moved. Like she'd done it a thousand times before. Just like you did now."

She lowered her hand. The silence between them thickened.

Ben drew a slow breath. "I came to Brimclif looking for Anthony. But you found me instead. I..."

He trailed off.

Cam's brow furrowed. "What do you mean?"

"I—" He stopped. The word stuck. His throat closed.

"I meant... it doesn't matter," he said quickly, looking away.

Her confusion sharpened like a blade between them. Her eyes narrowed, lips parting—but no answer came.

The silence howled.

Later, once Cam had drifted back to sleep, Ben sat by the edge of the fire, facing the ravine. Fog clung to the trees like breath held too long.

He ran a hand over his jaw, bristling with regret.

He should have said it.

He should have told her.

But the moment had shattered, and now it was too late. Again.

He'd seen the question rising in her eyes when he faltered—seen the suspicion, the hunger for answers, the way her fingers had curled as if to reach for something half-remembered.

She deserved the truth. All of it.

Anthony took her into hiding. I stayed behind. Took his place. Not just for duty. For blood. Because of a secret I can't say yet.

But to speak it aloud now...

To speak it aloud when her whole world was already slipping sideways with every new truth?

It would shatter the ground she stood on.

And maybe it would destroy the last pieces of trust she still offered him.

So, he sat in silence, alone with the embers and the guilt, the weight of a vow made years ago—and the cost of keeping it.

"I'll tell her," he whispered, voice barely more than breath. "Just... not yet."

A breeze stirred the leaves.

He looked up toward the stars—but found only cloud.

Cam stirred beneath her cloak.

The warmth of the fire barely reached her anymore—but it wasn't the cold that woke her.

It was something else.

Ben sat with his back to her, shoulders hunched, the firelight painting gold across his spine. He didn't know she was awake.

She could see it now—the weight in him. Like a man holding a secret so tightly it had begun to crack his bones from the inside.

She didn't speak.

Didn't ask.

But something in her chest whispered: He's not telling you everything.

Her fingers curled into the fabric of her cloak. Her heart beat just a little faster.

She closed her eyes again.

But sleep didn't come.

Only questions.

And somewhere beyond the trees...

The Veil breathed

Chapter 12: The Road Between

Sylithra hadn't stirred. She lay curled protectively around the now-dead fire, her massive body casting long shadows in the morning light.

Ben moved stiffly but with purpose, checking supplies and adjusting straps. Skylith had gone off to scout the ridge, her ember-hued wings flashing once through the trees before vanishing into the fog.

Cam rose slowly. Her body ached. Instinctively, she moved to check her injuries—but found none. In their place were a few small scars laced with faintly glowing blue veins. Her skin buzzed.

Not from fatigue—

But from the remembering.

And from the night before.

It hadn't left her. The dream. The pool. The petals. The voice.

It lingered in her veins like light refusing to die.

She stretched and walked to the edge of the clearing, staring into the trees where the path forked.

East was the way of the Academy—high roads, structured halls, stone towers full of rules and ritual. Safety. Knowledge.

But south...

South led into the wilds.

Rebel territory.

The outpost.

The edge of the map.

The place they were never meant to find.

A choice had hung between them since the attack. Sylithra had been waiting for her to choose. Ben feared she would.

At the fork, something tugged at her. Not the familiar thread of the bond with Sylithra—this was something else. Ancient. Familiar.

Cam knew.

She turned, walked back to the fire, and found Ben watching her.

"We're going south," she said.

He blinked. "The outpost?"

"Yes."

A flicker passed over his face—grief, fear, guilt. Maybe all three.

"You're sure?"

"No," Cam said quietly. "But I feel we need to go that way."

He studied her. "It'll be dangerous."

"It's already dangerous."

The Veil was thinning. The things that found them once would find them again. She didn't need safety anymore.

She needed truth.

And power alone wouldn't be enough.

Behind them, Sylithra stirred—wings shifting in a slow, thunder-soft beat. She said nothing, but her presence loomed: solemn. Approving.

Cam turned to meet her gaze. Their eyes locked.

The dragon inclined her head, as if to say: I know. And I agree.

And something in Cam settled.

She had made the choice.

Ben watched her pack with quiet resolve. She was calm now. Focused. Her fire had banked—not dimmed but directed.

South.

To the outpost.

He adjusted the strap on his shoulder. The wound had mostly healed—but the ache remained. Not from her magic. From memory.

He couldn't protect her from what was coming. But he could walk beside her.

And maybe, if the truth stayed buried a little longer, she'd still let him.

He turned and met Sylithra's gaze. She wasn't just watching—she was measuring him.

She knew. Or she was beginning to.

But dragons didn't speak truths that weren't theirs to tell.

Skylith returned from the ridge, her ember-colored wings catching a single blade of sunlight. She landed low, claws digging into moss.

"We fly soon," Ben told her. "To the outpost."

Very well, came her reply.

He looked to Cam again. She moved with determination, but no training. She hadn't been raised a rider. But she stood beside a dragon like she belonged.

He felt the ache again.

A memory.

Her mother brushing his shoulder. Her voice soft in the dark: You'll make a good father one day, Ben.

He looked away.

Skylith knelt. Sylithra shifted, lowering one shoulder to give Cam a boost.

She didn't move.

Ben sighed. "I think it's time you had your first riding lesson."

Cam turned sharply. "What?!"

"No saddle," he said, walking to Sylithra's side. "But I can teach you how to hold on."

He gestured to Sylithra's back. "No saddle means no mistakes. You fall once—you're a smear on a tree."

Cam squinted up. "Reassuring. Truly."

"She's made of scales, not spikes."

She hesitated—but then climbed up with more ease than he expected.

Ben guided her. "Sit between the wings. Least likely place to break something."

"Again. So comforting," Cam muttered.

He climbed up beside her. "Don't rely on your hands. Grip with your legs. You want to feel like part of her spine."

"Part of her spine," she repeated. "Totally natural."

Sylithra shifted beneath her and Cam stiffened.

"She breathes."

"She wiggled," Cam hissed. "That felt wrong."

"She's a dragon, not a bookshelf."

"You're enjoying this."

"If you fall mid-air," Ben said flatly, "I will say 'I told you so' on the way down."

Cam tightened her grip. "You're the worst mentor."

He grinned as he climbed down. "Tell her to take off."

Cam's heart pounded. She took a deep breath. "Let's not die."

As if I would let you fall to your death, Sylithra said gently, her voice calm and solid in her mind.

Cam blinked. A smile touched her lips. "Thanks."

Then Sylithra launched.

Everything dropped—Cam's stomach, the forest below, her dignity.

Wind slapped her like a wet towel. She yelped, ducked, clung with her legs.

The first few wingbeats were chaos.

Then she remembered:

Move with her. Breathe.

It wasn't graceful.

It was wild. Jarring. Terrifying.

But she wasn't falling.

She was flying.

A laugh burst out of her—half disbelieving, half joyous. "Oh gods! I'm alive!"

Of course you are, Sylithra replied. *We are one.*

Warmth surged through Cam's chest.

"I take it back!" she shouted. "This is amazing! Terrifying—but amazing!"

Sylithra dipped them once, playfully.

Cam screamed. Then laughed harder.

Below, Ben shaded his eyes and called, "Keep your mouth shut unless you want a bird in it!"

Cam gave a dramatic thumbs-up. "Got it!"

Ben's heart pounded as he watched Cam ride Sylithra.

He was both impressed and quietly terrified—but the fact that she stayed on was nothing short of astonishing.

A flicker of pride crept in. He let himself feel it.

Smiled.

Then forced the thought away before it could grow.

He mounted Skylith without a word, and they rose into the sky.

Two dragons. Two riders.

And a truth still buried beneath too many years.

Below, the road south waited.

Wind roared past her wings as the forest blurred beneath.

Cam's magic had revealed it—not just light, but blood.

Old blood. Kin.

Ben hadn't spoken it aloud. He didn't need to.

Dragons didn't require words.

Cam didn't know.

But Skylith did.

And if the rebels tried to use Ben, or manipulate the girl—

She would burn the outpost to ash.

Let Sylithra believe in prophecy.

Let Ben hold onto silence.

She would protect them both.

Even from each other.

The wind swept around her as she glided above the trees, sky vast and clean.

Below, the girl had chosen her path. But something else had shifted.

It wasn't just magic or trust.

It was lineage.

Old blood.

Why hadn't she seen it before?

Maybe she'd been alone too long. Rusted by solitude. Distracted by prophecy.

But now she saw.

Cam had healed Ben as if her bones already knew him.

And maybe they did.

Cam was no rider Sylithra had ever known.

She didn't command. She didn't know how.

And yet—she moved with fierce devotion.

That wasn't trained. That was chosen.

Sylithra angled upward, wind biting clean against her scales.

She wouldn't have chosen this path.

But she would follow it anyway.

Not because of prophecy.

But because of the girl.

Camomile Layton—

Who carried more than magic.

And would carry it, no matter the cost.

The sun was bleeding out behind the trees when Sylithra began to descend.

Cam leaned forward instinctively, legs aching from the long ride. Her hands were numb from gripping, but her heart still buzzed with something like awe. The forest below grew dense and dark, the ravine narrowing into shadow as Sylithra banked gently and began to spiral downward.

Skylith followed close behind, her ember-hued wings catching the last light like fire through stained glass.

They touched down in a clearing rimmed by jagged stone and crooked pines, the kind of place that didn't appear on maps—wild, quiet, watching.

Cam stayed seated for a beat too long. Her legs ached like they'd been welded in place. Her hands were still tingling from gripping Sylithra's shoulders so hard she was surprised she hadn't left dents.

"Oh," she muttered, flexing her fingers. "I don't think I have legs anymore."

Ben glanced up at her, a faint smirk tugging at his mouth. "Want me to catch you if you fall?"

Cam gave him a withering look. "I am not falling."

He dismounted smoothly and gracefully and chuckled. "I'll catch you anyway."

She grumbled something under her breath—but still half-slid, half-fell down Sylithra's side.

Ben caught her elbow as she started to stumbled with a soft thud and a wince.

"Graceful," he said.

"Shut up," she replied, but she didn't pull her arm away.

Sylithra's voice slid into her mind like cool steel.

If that was graceful, I'm a feathered goose.

Cam rolled her eyes. "Thanks for the support."

Skylith snorted from nearby.

I've seen baby deer land with more dignity.

Cam looked between them and sighed. "I'm surrounded by critics."

Ben chuckled and gave her shoulder a light squeeze. "Welcome to the team."

Skylith crouched protectively behind them. The two dragons flanked their riders as the forest pressed close, the hush deepening.

Then the air shimmered.

Cam's head snapped up. Sylithra growled low, wings flaring. A ripple of magic peeled through the clearing like heat off stone—and a figure stepped out of it.

One second—nothing.

The next, a man stood ten paces away.

Lean. Robed in black and silver. Eyes faintly glowing in the dim.

A rebel mage.

Ben's blade was drawn before he was fully facing the man. The intruder raised both hands slowly.

"Peace," he said. "I've been tracking you since the ridgeline."

Skylith hissed. Sylithra shifted forward, eyes narrowing, smoke curling between her teeth.

Cam stepped closer to Ben, one hand hovering instinctively near the belt where she carried her short sword.

"I'm not your enemy," the mage said. "Name's Kaden. I was sent to find you. Escort you to the outpost."

Ben didn't lower his blade.

Cam didn't step back.

Kaden sighed, lowering his arms but staying very still. "Corin said you'd be wary."

Ben's jaw tightened.

"How do we know you're telling the truth?" Cam asked.

"You don't," Kaden said simply. "But if I meant you harm, we wouldn't be having this conversation."

He glanced at Sylithra with a flicker of unease, then at Skylith. "You can fly blind through rebel territory if you want. But it's nearly night, and the old wards don't always care who they kill."

Ben finally sheathed his blade, though his stance remained tense. "Lead the way."

Kaden nodded once. Then, with a flick of his fingers, he opened a narrow portal–big enough for the dragons to walk through–at the edge of the clearing. The air rippled again, and a trail of violet light marked the path forward.

Sylithra and Skylith exchanged a look—long, unreadable, ancient—and then followed as Ben and Cam stepped through.

They emerged into another clearing. This one half-ruined, overgrown with ivy and shattered stone. It looked like it had once been part of something larger—a forgotten outpost now reclaimed by moss and time.

But there were signs of life.

Cam followed Kaden through the forest, ducking beneath low branches and stepping over roots slick with moss. The light was fading fast—burnt-orange streaks threading through the canopy, casting everything in copper and shadow.

They crested a ridge—and there it was.

A great stone fortress scarred but standing, its back pressed into the mountain like a blade sheathed in stone. The walls loomed wide and solid despite their age, marred in places where stone had fallen or ivy had overtaken the cracks. Though time had worn at the battlements and left gaps in towers once whole, the Keep remained tall, its core structure intact. The upper floors showed damage—splintered beams, partial collapse, wounds left from old siege or time—but the heart of the fortress still pulsed with presence.

Part of it disappeared directly into the mountainside—arched corridors vanishing into the rock, half-buried in moss and shadow.

This was no ruin. Not truly. Not anymore.

Tents and shelters clung to the fortress' base, nestled into courtyards and sheltered nooks. Magic shimmered faintly along the walls;

enchantments layered like breath over stone. Movement stirred—rebels in quiet motion, half-ghosts slipping between the bones of the Keep.

It wasn't just a hideout.

It was a stronghold sleeping in the mountains.

Cam stood frozen at the edge of it, her breath catching in her chest.

Not from fear.

From recognition.

A sound was rising in her ears—soft at first, like wind over glass. But it wasn't wind. It was voices.

Dozens of them.

Hundreds.

Low and echoing, too layered to understand. Some deep, some rasping, some melodic and old. They came not from the camp but from beneath it. From the stone. From the trees. From the mountain hollow beyond the ridge.

Cam pressed a hand to her temple. "Do you hear that?" she asked.

Ben frowned. "Hear what?"

She didn't answer right away. The voices were everywhere now—overlapping, weaving through each other. Not human. Not even close. It was the same sound she'd heard as a child, on windless nights, when the forest went still and something in her bones had vibrated like a string being plucked.

But now it was louder.

Nearer.

Alive.

She caught a single phrase in the haze of sound—low and ancient, like fire cracking beneath ice.

She's here.

Cam shivered.

"Cam?" Ben asked again, stepping closer.

She blinked. "It's nothing. Just... tired."

He didn't look convinced.

"Welcome to the middle of nowhere. It's called Haldrin's Keep," he said over his shoulder. "Don't wander off."

Cam followed—but her gaze stayed on the stones. On the shadows between ruins.

And on the voices that hadn't stopped.

She's here.

They whispered again, just beneath hearing.

Just beneath understanding.

Watchfires flickered behind stone barricades. Voices murmured in the dark. A tall figure stood waiting beneath the arch of an open gate, arms folded.

Cam barely had time to take it in before the figure stepped into the light.

Tall. Weathered. Sharp-eyed.

His gaze passed over Cam, flicked briefly to Sylithra and Skylith—and then landed squarely on Ben.

A heartbeat passed.

Then his voice, low and jagged as broken glass:

"Benjamin Miles... I should have killed you when I had the chance."

Chapter 13: Old Wounds, Older Truths

Ben didn't flinch. Didn't blink.

He met the man's gaze with practiced calm, though every nerve in his body tensed like drawn steel.

The rebel camp was quieter than he expected.

Not silent—soldiers murmured, weapons clattered faintly, ward lines hummed at the perimeter—but this wasn't chaos. It was ordered. Watchful. Coiled.

Corin Veyr.

Leader of the rebels.

Corin stood just inside the ruined arch, arms crossed, dark eyes fixed on Ben like a blade he hadn't quite decided to draw.

"Walk with me," he said. Not a request.

Ben nodded once to Cam, who lingered near the shadows of the gate. Sylithra and Skylith loomed behind her, torchlight sliding along their scales, silent as judgment.

He followed Corin into the corridor of stone and ivy. The surviving walls bore old scars—magic scorches, shattered battlements, blackened beams from some long-ago siege. This place had bled once. Maybe it still was.

They walked until the camp noises faded.

Then Corin stopped.

He didn't turn at first. His voice was flat.

"I should've killed you when I had the chance."

Ben exhaled softly. "And yet... here we are."

Corin turned, jaw tight, eyes sharp as drawn steel.

"I saw you die."

Ben said nothing.

"You were there. Carrath's Fall. Seventh Legion. You rode into that ravine like a fool. Gods, the fire burned for three days." Corin stepped closer. "We buried the pieces they found. The whole rebellion mourned."

Ben's face stayed still. "Then I suppose it's a miracle."

Corin studied him with a look that could have cut through armor. The anger behind it wasn't wild—it was old, worn, and sharpened by years into something colder.

"I knew Anthony," he said, voice low. "Better than most. And you..." He tilted his head. "You don't move like him. Don't speak like him."

Ben's silence was its own confirmation.

Corin's jaw flexed.

Corin stepped back a pace, letting the tension fold into something more complicated.

"Twenty years," he said, "and now you show up with her."

Ben's shoulders shifted, the smallest flinch.

"She's under my protection."

Corin barked a dry laugh. "Is that what we're calling it now?"

"She's not the Knighthood's. Not the Academy's. And definitely not the Capital's," Ben said, voice firm. "She's free."

Corin's smile vanished. "No one's free anymore. You of all people should know that."

The silence that followed felt like the pause before a blade fell.

Corin's gaze slid past Ben to the dragon standing beyond the ruined arch.

Sylithra.

Black-blue scales shimmered faintly, her body as still as carved obsidian. Her eyes locked on Corin, unblinking.

The wind shifted.

Corin stilled. "...She's supposed to be dead."

Ben didn't move.

"Not just gone," Corin said, voice hollow. "Dead. Buried beneath the cliffs at Elith Kar. That dragon hasn't been seen in nearly a millennium."

Still, Ben said nothing.

Corin looked back at him, disbelief flickering beneath the steel. "And yet there she stands."

His gaze drifted to Cam, then back to Sylithra.

"And she's bonded again."

The pieces clicked behind Corin's eyes. His voice lowered into something almost reverent.

"It is just like the prophecy said."

Ben's jaw tightened. "You never believed in prophecy. Only your visions."

"I didn't," Corin admitted. "Not until now. But this is different."

He breathed in slowly; tension threaded through the motion.

"She's not ready. Whatever power she carries—it's raw. She doesn't even know who she is."

"And you think locking her in a cage will help her figure that out?" Ben snapped.

Corin's eyes narrowed. "No. But if we don't act, others will. You know what's waiting in the Academy. You know what the Knighthood has becoming."

Ben's silence was answer enough.

"And if the prophecy is real..." Corin's eyes cut to Sylithra again. "Then she's the first sign. Her—and the one who was supposed to be lost."

He met Ben's gaze one last time. A warning simmered behind his calm.

"When the time comes, don't lie to her."

Ben's voice was quiet steel. "I never planned to."

Corin gave him a long, knowing look. Then he turned back toward the heart of the camp, leaving Ben alone with the shadows.

Far off in the mountains, the wards hummed like breath drawn too deep—as if the Veil itself leaned closer to listen.

Sylithra watched him from the tree line, still as a carved sentinel.

Her eyes were deep with memory. She had always known.

Even when the world believed her dead, even when the ashes told a different story—she had waited. She had remembered.

Dragons do not forget. And Sylithra, least of all, knew this:

The prophecy had begun to move. And Cam stood at its heart.

Chapter 14: A Sea Without Harbor

The sun had set behind the mountain nearly twenty minutes ago, the stars had just begun to appear.

Ben stepped out of Corin's tent, the weight of the conversation pressing heavy between his shoulders. The world outside hadn't changed—cold air, quiet camp, the low hum of warding spells along the walls.

But he had.

Cam stood nearby, pressing her fingers to her temples.

"You good, kid?" he asked, voice low.

She nodded quickly without meeting his eyes. "Just... a little loud."

Ben frowned. "There's no one talking."

"Not like that," she muttered. "It's—never mind."

Before he could ask more, Kaden emerged from a side alley, faint shimmer trailing from the wards he'd been checking. He motioned them forward.

"The dragons need to meet the Sky Patrol," he said. "Protocol. Once they're registered by the mage-riders, they'll be cleared to fly. Keeps the wards from lighting up every time they move."

Ben nodded. "Understood."

Kaden turned to the dragons. "Meet them in the upper air. Patrol runs wide around the ridge."

Sylithra dipped her head. Her gaze lingered on Cam—a quiet promise—before she opened her wings. Black-blue scales caught the moonlight like a river of ink veined with gold.

With a single beat, she rose. Skylith followed, embers scattering off her wings.

"This way," Kaden said. "You're not prisoners. But don't wander far. The wards bite."

◈ ☽✦☾ ◈

The outpost unfolded in quiet complexity as they walked—ruined allyways laced with ivy, stone watchpoints bristling with hidden spells, camouflaged tents under flickering ward lights. Magic hung in the air, sharp and metallic, like something half-awake.

But Cam barely noticed.

The voices were louder now.

Not human voices. Pressure—thoughts that weren't hers, pulsing behind her eyes in strange, overlapping rhythms. Booming. Whispering. Echoing.

She flinched, the sound crawling along her spine.

"Something wrong?" Kaden asked without looking back.

"There's... a sound," Cam said carefully. "Not from here. From beneath us."

Kaden's brow twitched. "That'd be the nest."

Cam stopped walking. "The what?"

He gestured toward the ridge. "There's an old dragon nest beneath the valley. The Veil's thinner here. You won't see them—but you might feel it. Especially with dragons like yours nearby."

The pressure surged again, and Cam staggered.

Kaden's voice was calm, but she caught the edge of knowing in it. "First time near a nest can be... disorienting."

A thread of sensation tugged at her ribs—not the voices, but alongside them. A pull, like something waiting just out of reach.

Kaden didn't notice. "You'll be given a place to rest soon. Try not to wander."

He turned into another alley, cloak vanishing into shadow.

Cam pressed her fingers to her temples. "It's everywhere. Like a hundred thoughts at once. They're... pushing into me."

Ben's gaze sharpened. "You're still hearing them?"

"Louder now. They've always been there, but it's like something just turned the volume up."

You hear them, Sylithra's voice rumbled through the bond.

Cam's breath hitched. "What are they?"

A long, reverent pause.

They are dragons.

Her stomach dropped.

Skylith's quieter voice followed. *The mind-song of our kind. Dreaming. Thinking. Remembering. No human hears it—except those we choose. And even then, only one bond.*

Cam's whisper cracked. "But I hear all of them."

Yes, Sylithra said without hesitation. *You always have.*

The voices swelled. Childhood memories bloomed sharp and sudden: the whispers in Brimclif's woods, windless nights when she felt watched, sung to in a language she couldn't name.

"I thought I imagined them," she whispered.

Because we were far, Sylithra said. *And you were young. But the closer you come to our kin, the louder we become.*

Cam sank onto a mossy stone, hands gripping the edge like an anchor. "I'm not just hearing you. I'm hearing all of them. All the dragons."

Yes. You are.

Ben crouched beside her, silent but watchful, something like awe flickering in his eyes. He couldn't hear Sylithra's side of the conversation but from what Cam could tell he knew enough.

Cam looked at him, voice trembling. "What does that mean?"

No one answered.

Not yet.

Only the mountain murmured—low, steady, like the heartbeat of something vast beneath the earth.

◈ ☽✦☾ ◈

Hours seemed to fold into moments.

Kaden returned, voice softer now. "You're pale."

"She needs rest," Ben said, rising.

Kaden gave a nod. "Follow me. Your quarters are in the Keep."

They followed him through the gateway into the courtyard, the echo of their boots following them through the main doors. The stone corridor smelled faintly of smoke and oil. Kaden led them past rows of closed barracks rooms before stopping at a door.

He spoke to Ben—words Cam didn't catch. The voices were too loud again, a pressing hum beneath her skull.

The room beyond was simple but warm: stone floor, patched windows, a fire pit glowing softly in the hearth.

Too quiet.

The stillness seemed to sharpen the pressure in her head until her temples throbbed. She leaned against the wall beside a narrow cot, the cool stone steady under her palms.

Let me help, Sylithra said, her voice was a calm current beneath the storm.

"H-how?" Cam whispered.

The way we quiet our minds in flight. Not silence—focus. Shielding what is yours from what is not.

Cam obeyed. She breathed with Sylithra. Imagined her thoughts as a single golden flame. The voices were wind. The flame bent, but it did not go out.

The pressure eased—just enough.

Her shoulders shook. "It worked. A little."

It will get easier, Sylithra murmured. *You were never broken. You are becoming. Every voice you hear is another thread. One day, you will weave them all.*

Cam stared at her trembling hands, breathing steady for the first time since she arrived at the outpost.

◈ ☽✦☾ ◈

High above the outpost, Sylithra soared with Skylith through the crisp wind of night fall. Sky Patrol dragons wheeled closer, white wings flashing. Respectful, but cautious.

The world had thought her dead for a thousand years.

They would remember her now.

And they would remember her rider.

◈ ☽✦☾ ◈

Ben leaned against the doorframe, watching Cam tremble by the fire.

A thousand puzzle pieces in his mind slid into place—the old stories, the village whispers, the girl who never slept when the wind blew east.

Of course she'd heard them her whole life. Of course it had always been the dragons.

She was strong. But strength wasn't the same as readiness.

He glanced outside, where Sylithra perched on the cliff's edge, head low toward the girl she'd chosen.

HERITAGE

Cam was walking a path none of them had ever seen.
Ben exhaled. Quiet. Heavy. The past hadn't stayed buried.
And she was still here—battered, bright, burning.
He would help her stand. Even if she never asked.
Even if she never knew.

Chapter 15: Not Yet

The knock came just after dawn—firm, quick, and not particularly patient.

Cam stirred from where she sat curled on her cot, tracing lazy lines in the frost on the windowpane. The voices had quieted after last night, but sleep had barely touched her.

Ben was already moving toward the door.

Kaden stood outside, his dark coat dusted with cold, expression unreadable.

"Corin wants to see you. Both of you."

"Now?" Ben asked.

"Now."

They followed him through the early chill, past half-woken rebels and the low burn of cookfires. The outpost was alive but subdued—mages threading new wards along the walls, scouts returning from night watch. Cam focused on the crunch of her boots on frost and the faint pull in her chest, steady as a heartbeat she didn't understand.

Corin's tent waited at the center of the outpost—large, but without vanity. Heavy canvas walls were staked deep against the wind, and the war banners hung faded and worn. Kaden held the flap open.

Cam entered first.

Inside, lanterns threw shifting light across weathered maps and pinned scrolls. Glyphs flickered on the central table, glowing faintly with movement. Corin sat behind it, sleeves rolled, scarred knuckles pressed to the wood. He looked every bit the war-forged strategist: calm, coiled, and carrying twenty years of hard choices in his posture.

"Camomile Layton," he said evenly. "Sit."

She obeyed. Ben stayed standing behind her like a shadow.

Corin studied her, gaze not unkind but heavy with measure. "You've caused a stir."

Cam stiffened.

"That's not a criticism," he said, a faint curve to his mouth. "It's simply true. Dragons. Magic. Prophecy. You draw eyes—whether you want them or not."

She didn't answer.

Corin leaned forward, steepling his fingers. "You're welcome to train here. All our instructors, weapons, spell work, shielding—you'll have access to all of it."

Cam blinked. "Just like that?"

"We don't hoard power anymore. Not after what it cost us." His gaze flicked briefly to the shadow outside, where Sylithra waited. "Besides... you're not someone I want untrained."

The words landed sharper than he intended.

Cam caught it. So did Ben.

But Corin didn't take it back.

"You carry something old," he continued. "I've seen echoes of it before, but never like this. And you've bonded with a legend."

Cam's pulse thudded. She still didn't know what she was becoming—only that it was waking fast.

"That's all for now," Corin said finally. "Get food. Rest. Training circle this afternoon."

Cam rose, only for his tone to change.

"Ben. Stay."

She hesitated, glancing between them.

"I'll catch up," Ben said quietly.

Cam slipped out, leaving the two men in the flickering lantern light.

Ben didn't speak. He didn't need to.

Corin waited until the tent flap settled, then crossed his arms. "She doesn't know yet, does she?"

Silence.

"I used to think prophecy was just a leash," Corin said at last. "A story written to excuse the things we couldn't control. Something to blame when we failed." His fingers traced a scar across the war table. "But I was wrong."

He let the quiet hang.

"When you died—when I thought you had—I started seeing the truth differently. I realized how many mistakes I'd made."

Ben's face didn't change.

"I rushed into war thinking glimpses were answers. That a single vision was a whole path. But it wasn't. It never was. Anthony, Isabella—even you—you all told me to wait. To listen. I didn't."

He turned toward the maps, the lamplight carving lines of exhaustion into his face. "After Carrath's Fall, I spent twenty years learning to see clearly. To understand that visions and prophecy aren't salvation—it's a choice. And the choice hasn't been made yet."

A long pause.

"Sylithra's return. Cam's awakening. It's all moving again. But this time... maybe we're not too late."

Ben's jaw tensed. "She's not ready."

"No," Corin said softly. "But neither were we."

The words cut deep. Ben said nothing.

He remembered Corin as he once was—young, fire-eyed, too sharp to ignore and too reckless to follow. Time had sanded his edges but not dulled the steel. If anything, the quiet made him more dangerous.

Ben exhaled and looked toward the tent flap, toward the girl walking further into a world she didn't yet understand.

"She shouldn't be in the middle of this," he said, almost to himself.

"You really believe that?" Corin asked.

"She's still just—"

"No, she's not." Corin's tone was softer now, but unyielding. "She's already in the middle of it. Whether you're ready or not."

Ben didn't answer.

Outside, Sylithra waited like a shadow of a thousand years ago. Black-blue scales glinted faintly in the frost, gold-veined spine catching the first touch of morning light. She had vanished into myth a millennium ago—buried in history at Elith Kar—and now she had returned.

Dragons didn't return without reason.

Cam had been born into secrets. And now, those secrets were rising to meet her.

Ben's chest tightened. He wasn't ready.

Not to tell her the truth.
Not to let her go. Not yet.

Chapter 16: Threads Through the Mind

The world outside had grown still as dusk fell.

But inside Cam's head, it was louder than ever.

She sat curled on her narrow cot, knees pulled to her chest, the dim lanternlight casting long shadows across the stone walls. Her room in the rebel camp was small—quiet, even peaceful—but her thoughts weren't.

The voices wouldn't stop.

Low murmurs like wind through water. Ancient tones layered and constant. She tried to press them down, to breathe past them, but they clung to the edges of her thoughts like smoke.

She hadn't told anyone just how loud they'd become since the dragons flew that morning.

And the stillness only made it worse.

It gave the voices space to echo.

She tried to ground herself by thinking about her day. Meeting the instructors for magic and combat. Asking—maybe a little shyly—if she and Ben could join the training. They had been delighted, and practically relieved to welcome a new recruit.

Tomorrow she'd start at sunrise with defensive drills. Magic lessons in the afternoon. She should have felt excited.

But excitement couldn't drown the voices.

They swelled again, a storm behind her ribs.

Cam pressed her palms to her temples. "Not now," she whispered to no one.

Sylithra had taught her a technique to push the sound back, but it wasn't holding. The nest was too close. Or maybe she was too open.

She needed space.

Cam rose abruptly and started walking. Ben glanced up from the corner of the room, brow furrowed.

"I just need air," she said quickly, forcing a small, unconvincing smile.

He didn't stop her.

◇ ☽✦☾ ◇

The night forest pressed close around her as she passed through a half-crumbled gate. A mage stood nearby, muttering to a wall of glowing runes, but he didn't look up.

Cam moved without thinking, her steps tracing some invisible path.

A faint pressure sat low in her chest—unnoticed at first, like a thread snagged to her heart—and it drew her toward the trees.

The air grew damp with pine and earth.

The voices swelled with each step, crowding the edges of her thoughts until her vision shimmered.

She reached out, brushing her fingers along a rough tree trunk. The bark bit gently into her skin, a sharp anchor in the haze pressing against her mind.

It didn't help.

The voices filled her skull.

She didn't see the figure until she collided with him.

Cam yelped and stumbled back. A hand caught her arm, steadying her.

"Whoa—easy," a voice said.

She blinked up. A man stood in the moonlight, early twenties maybe, wearing mottled brown-and-green riding leathers that blended with the woods. His dark-brown curls fell across his brow, and a thin scar traced beneath one ear. His eyes—soft blue—held hers with quiet steadiness. For a breath, when his hand caught her arm, the voices dulled—as if the storm itself held still to look at him.

"Hey, are you okay?" he asked, voice calm.

Cam hesitated. The voices surged again, crashing over her like the surf.

She managed a grimace. "Yeah. I just—wasn't paying attention."

"You look like you were about to pass out."

"Just... too much noise," she muttered.

He followed her glance back toward the camp. "The gate's that way."

Cam nodded, trying to pull herself together. "Thanks."

He didn't offer his name. Just nodded once more, turned, and disappeared into the trees like he'd never been there.

Cam pressed a hand to her chest.

The pull was still there.

But she couldn't follow it. Not yet.

◈ ☽✦☾ ◈

Cam's first day of training began before the sun touched the eastern ridge.

She stood at the edge of the packed dirt sparring field, shoulders tense. Rebel fighters moved across the clearing in pairs—stretching, sparring, exchanging muttered instructions.

She tried not to stare too long. Mages in dark robes. Archers tightening bowstrings. Swordfighters with bandaged hands. The rebels weren't polished. They were harder. Sharper. Real.

"Don't worry," a voice said dryly behind her. "They're not all murderers."

Cam turned.

A girl her age leaned against a fence post, red hair gleaming in the morning mist. She grinned crookedly and tossed Cam a sparring blade.

"Name's Tessa. Corin said you'd be joining us."

Cam caught the blade on reflex. "Camomile."

"Like the tea?"

"Unfortunately."

Tessa's grin widened. "Good. Humor. You'll need it."

Days fell into rhythm after that.

Mornings were sword drills. Afternoons were magic lessons with the rebels' mages. Evenings belonged to the dragons—learning aerial balance with Sylithra, signal calls, and maneuvers that made Cam's stomach drop in both fear and wonder.

She surprised them.

She was quick. Determined. She learned from mistakes faster than anyone expected. Ben watched one morning as she swept Tessa to the ground with a move she hadn't known two days ago.

"Remind me never to piss you off," he muttered, tossing her a waterskin.

Cam smirked. "Too late."

Magic was harder.

"Magic flows with instinct," said Marell, a stern older instructor. "Control comes from focus."

And focus was Cam's greatest struggle.

She could call fire. Shape wind. Lift stones. Even dabble in spiritual currents that flickered like light at the edge of her senses. But if the voices rose—if she lost her grip for even a second—everything wavered.

Still, training helped.

During the day, the voices dulled to a background hum, like a storm retreating behind distant hills.

Nights were different.

When the wind stilled, the echoes came crawling back—ancient and endless, seeping into her dreams.

She didn't tell anyone.

She just curled into her cot and held on.

Chapter 17: Threads of Instinct

Ben insisted on daily flight drills, often after dinner—which meant Cam was barely digesting soup before being dragged onto Sylithra's back again.

"Balance," Ben called from Skylith's saddle. "You're riding her spine, not bouncing on a tavern stool!"

"I'm trying not to die!"

"Good instinct. Keep doing that."

Sylithra, amused, dipped one wing just enough to make Cam squeak.

"That wasn't funny!"

It was a little funny, Sylithra replied calmly.

Ben laughed. "You'll thank me when you're not a smear on the rocks!"

"Just say 'I believe in you' like a normal mentor!"

"I believe you're very loud," he shot back.

On her tenth day at the outpost, Kaden found her.

She was sparring with Tessa when he stepped into the ring, calm as ever in his charcoal robes.

"Mind if I steal her?" he asked, already moving forward.

Tessa shrugged. "Sure."

Cam blinked. "What's the lesson?"

"No lesson," Kaden said, grinning. "A test."

Before she could ask what that meant, he vanished.

Literally vanished.

Cam barely ducked in time as he reappeared behind her, arm swinging. She rolled, caught his leg, and twisted. He blinked out of sight and reappeared six feet to her left, charging.

The next five minutes were chaos—teleports, feints, stinging bursts of magic. Cam's instincts burned, her focus razor-sharp. She almost had him pinned when—

Something tugged at her chest.

She gasped lightly. The same faint pull.

Her eyes flicked up for half a breath—and there he was.

The stranger she'd collided with days ago, leaning against a tree.

Watching.

Their eyes met for a heartbeat.

She missed Kaden's feint.

The flat of his blade tapped her shoulder.

"Gotcha," he said, breathing hard.

Cam stepped back, panting. "You cheated."

"I teleported. You flinched."

She turned toward the tree line—but the stranger was gone.

So was the pull.

Cam left the ring drenched in sweat, muscles trembling.

But her mind felt clearer than it had in days.

The voices had stayed low.

The pull was still there, humming under her ribs.

But for now, she could breathe.

And that was enough.

Cam was getting faster.

Ben watched from the edge of the field, arms folded, boots planted in the scorched dirt. She wove between two seasoned rebels, efficient and focused. Not perfect—but sharper every day.

She'd changed since arriving.

At first, she'd looked like she was surviving. Now, she was learning to fight—not just with sword and spell, but with intent. There was clarity in her now, a steadiness he hadn't seen in the forest or even on dragonback.

He watched her sweep Kaden to the ground—clean, fast, almost elegant.

Ben let out a breath. "Show-off," he muttered, not without pride.

Skylith landed nearby, wings tucked neatly in.

You're worried, she said.

"I'm always worried," Ben replied.

She's growing stronger.

"That's what worries me."

She's meant to be strong. You know that.

Ben didn't respond.

He just watched Cam laugh—softly, but real—as she offered Kaden a hand. Sunlight caught the streaks in her dark hair, the mark at her jaw. She didn't know how much of the world was watching her. Or how much more weight was coming.

◈ ☽✦☾ ◈

The sky opened above them like a sea turned upside down.

Wind whipped Cam's face as she leaned forward, fingers curled into Sylithra's black-blue scales. The dragon moved like a storm given form, wings slicing air in a rhythm as steady as a heartbeat.

Cam had flown a dozen times now. Maybe more. But the altitude still made her breath catch. No ground. No edges. Just sky, and the thunder of wings.

You are quiet today, Sylithra said.

Cam hesitated. "I keep feeling this... pull."

A strong pull?

She nodded. "It's always there. Like a hand between my ribs. Some days it's louder than others. But it never goes away."

Sylithra banked gently, turning into the wind. *And today?*

"It's... steadier. Like it's tired of waiting for me to listen."

Why didn't you tell me before?

"I didn't know what it was. I thought maybe it was just the voices. Or leftover magic. Stress, maybe."

But it's not the voices.

"No," Cam said softly. "The voices are a tide. Loud, layered. But the pull—it's... personal. Like it's only meant for me."

Sylithra's thoughts curled behind hers like smoke. *Have you followed it?*

"I tried. It always changes direction. Like it's searching, too."

Do you want to follow it?

Cam hesitated. "I'm scared it'll break my focus. I'm finally getting stronger. If I chase this, I might lose that."

Or maybe it's the reason you're getting stronger, Sylithra said. *Not every pull is a distraction. Some are a beginning. And some are threads—waiting for you to weave them into what you are becoming.*

Cam exhaled, staring at the horizon. "I just... don't want to mess this up."

Then trust that if it matters, it will find you again.

Something in her chest shifted—small, but certain.

Sylithra landed lightly outside the forge clearing, scales gleaming with morning dew.

Ben leaned against the wall, unreadable as ever.

"You're getting better," he said. "Didn't even scream once."

Cam gave him a look. "I never screamed."

He raised an eyebrow. "Right. Must've been the wind."

She almost smiled—but it faded.

Ben noticed. "What is it?"

"I told her. About the pull."

He tilted his head, eyes narrowing slightly.

"You knew," she said, quiet.

"I guessed," he said. "Back on that road, you looked south like something was waiting for you."

"It hasn't stopped," Cam whispered. "It's not like the voices. It's... a feeling. Something just out of reach."

"And?"

"Sylithra says it might not be a distraction. That it could be leading me toward something important."

Ben's jaw tightened. He studied her like he wanted to speak but couldn't.

"I just wish I knew what it wanted," Cam murmured.

He didn't answer.

Not yet.

The pull shifted again.

Once south. Now northeast.

Toward the mountains.

Toward the direction of the Academy.

A place she'd never seen—known only by whispers and warnings.

But something inside Cam was calling to it.

Or calling from it.

And she wasn't sure which scared her more.

Chapter 18: First Light, Last Lie

The morning after her latest flight with Sylithra, a knock came at the door.

Three sharp raps—too deliberate to be casual.

Cam looked up from tightening her boots as Ben crossed the room and opened the door. A rebel scout stood there—a lean, quiet man with a silver streak in his hair.

"Corin wants to see you both," he said, no questions. Just a nod.

They followed him through the camp, past tents and watchposts, through drifting fog and faint enchantments. The ruins looked soft in morning light, almost peaceful—until you noticed the guards, the weapons, the ward lines humming at the edges.

Corin's war tent loomed at the center like a dark heart.

Inside, maps sprawled across a battered wooden table. Trails of red ink veined the surface. Corin's gaze landed on Cam.

"Sit," he said.

They obeyed.

"I've been watching you," Corin began. "You're progressing fast. Too fast."

Cam tensed. "I'm doing my best."

"This isn't a complaint," he said, eyes sharp. "It's a warning. Power like yours draws attention—and not always the kind you want."

He tapped a single point on the map.

The Academy.

"I want to send you there."

Cam blinked. "I've never been to the Academy."

"That's exactly why it could work," Corin replied.

Ben stiffened beside her.

Corin continued, "There's a vault beneath the lower wings. Most don't know it exists. Inside is an old book. I want you to retrieve it."

"You want me to break in?" she asked, eyebrows rising.

"I want you to walk through the gates and see how far your power carries you. You'll be a curiosity. Maybe a threat. But not a spy."

Ben's voice was quiet steel. "She's not going."

"She's not yours to command," Corin said.

"She's not ready."

"She was more ready than I was when I led my first siege."

Cam stood. "Why do you always step in when it's about me, Ben?"

He looked at her, silence stretching tight.

"It's not like you're my father," she said quietly.

Ben flinched.

Corin caught the motion, his expression sharpening.

Ben rose. "We need to talk. Alone."

Corin nodded, waving Cam off. "Go get some air. This won't take long."

Outside, the pull inside Cam's chest tightened. It had started as a whisper in the woods.

Now it pointed directly at the Academy.

For the first time... she had a way in.

◈ ☽✦☾ ◈

The tent flap fell shut behind her, and silence settled heavy.

Ben remained sitting.

Corin remained by the table, fingers trailing the map but eyes elsewhere.

"She doesn't know," he said after a moment. "Does she?"

Ben didn't answer.

Corin sighed. "You were always better at disappearing than explaining."

"And you, better at assuming than asking," Ben replied.

A bitter smile. "And yet, here we are."

Ben stepped forward, jaw tight. "You want to use her."

"I want to protect her. Which, if I recall, used to matter to both of us."

"She's not a weapon."

"No," Corin said softly. "She's a fuse."

He tapped the map near fault lines in the eastern range. "And the world is already on fire."

Ben's eyes narrowed. "You said the prophecy was vague. Half-truths from a vision you didn't trust."

Corin nodded. "Back then. I saw fragments: a girl born of two lines, a dragon returned, a coming storm. I rushed it all."

His voice cracked, quieter now. "Anthony told me to wait. Isabella warned me. Even you. But I didn't listen. I was young and reckless, thinking I could rewrite fate by moving fast."

Ben's silence said everything.

Corin looked at him. "I've spent twenty years trying to make it right."

"And now you think Cam is the answer."

"I think she might be. But I'm not asking her to fight for me. I'm giving her the choice. The one we never had."

Ben's gaze was cold. "You want her to walk into the lion's den."

Corin didn't flinch. "And you want to keep her in a gilded cage."

A long silence.

Then, quieter: "She's stronger than you want to admit."

Ben shifted. "I know how strong she is."

Corin leaned forward. "Then stop pretending you don't see what's coming. The Knighthood is splintering. The Academy's vaults hold things that should have been burned. Cam's not just stepping into her power—she's waking something ancient. You saw it when Sylithra opened her eyes."

Ben clenched his jaw.

Corin's voice softened. "You may have kept her hidden, safe. But she was never meant to stay small."

A beat.

"She deserves the truth. All of it."

Ben's voice was tired but sharp. "And what would you do with that truth?"

"Honor it. Or die trying."

Ben's eyes flickered—approval or acknowledgment.

He stepped back.

"When she's ready," he said, "I'll tell her."

Corin nodded. "Good."

Because dragons never forgot.

And neither did men like them.

◈ ☽✦☾ ◈

The storm had been building since Corin's summons.

They barely made it back to their quarters when Ben turned sharply, closing the door with more force than needed.

"You can't go."

Cam froze. "Excuse me?"

"I told Corin no. You're not going."

She blinked. "Not long ago, you said I needed training. That I should've gone to the Academy first. What changed?"

Ben paced, jaw tight, eyes down. "You've had training. You've improved faster than anyone in years. You don't need to prove anything there."

"I'm not trying to prove anything," Cam said, voice rising. "I just want to understand myself. My power. I keep feeling this pull. You know something's happening. Why are you so afraid?"

"Because I want you safe," he snapped.

That stopped her.

For a moment, silence stretched between them.

She stepped closer, searching his face. "Why? Why do you need me safe, Ben? Why do you flinch when someone mentions my past? Why do you look at me like I might shatter?"

Ben turned away.

"No more vague answers," Cam said, voice hardening. "You said you'd never lie. So... tell me the truth."

He didn't move.

"Ben." Her voice broke. "Why?"

His shoulders slumped.

Then, so quietly she almost missed it, he said:

"Because I'm your father."

The silence crushed her.

Her heartbeat roared.

"No," she whispered. "That's not—"

But it was.

She saw it in his eyes. In the way he never left her side. In the ache behind his silence.

"You knew," she said. "All this time. You knew and said nothing."

"I wanted to protect you—"

"Protect me from what? The truth? From myself?"

He stepped toward her, but she backed away.

Fury and confusion boiled beneath her skin, heat coiling violet-black at the edges of silver-blue light she didn't notice was rising in her veins.

"You should have told me. You don't get to decide when I'm ready."

"I thought I was doing what was best."

"For you," she spat. "Not me."

Ben looked like she'd hit him.

Cam turned and stormed to the door.

"Where are you going?" he asked.

"To find someone who doesn't lie to me."

She didn't look back.

The door slammed like a final blow.

Ben stood in silence, chest hollow, her words louder than the quiet.

"You don't get to decide what I'm ready for. To find someone who doesn't lie to me."

He pressed a hand to his face, dragging it down slowly. His knuckles trembled.

He'd said it out loud—but hadn't meant for it to land like a blade.

What choice did he have?

He crossed the small room and sat on the edge of his cot.

He hadn't been there for her first steps, hadn't heard her hum to the wind as a child, unaware she was singing to dragons. He hadn't held her through nightmares or whispered comfort during the voices.

But he'd imagined it—thousands of different ways.

He'd thought staying away kept her safe. If she never knew what she was, she'd never be hunted.

Now she knew.

And she was walking away anyway.

He'd spent her life trying to keep her from becoming a weapon.

And now, he might've lost her anyway.

Ben leaned forward, elbows on knees, staring at the floor for forgiveness.

It didn't come.

◈ ☽✦☾ ◈

Cam stormed through the camp, boots sharp against stone. The torches guttered once, as if the wind itself bent toward her. Somewhere beyond the wards, the Veil stirred—aware, listening.

Dusk pressed in cold, but she barely felt it.

Her hands trembled—not from fear, not grief.

She found Corin's tent, guarded but open.

Inside, Corin looked up, surprised. "Camomile?"

"I want to go to the Academy," she said, breathless.

He straightened slowly. "I thought you weren't ready."

"I am now."

He studied her—the voice shaking beneath stillness, eyes that hadn't blinked.

"You and Ben had words," Corin said kindly.

Her eyes burned. "Yes."

He nodded. "We'll send you at first light."

Cam turned sharply and left without a word.

◈ ☽✦☾ ◈

Ben sat in the quiet, the door ajar, footsteps long gone.

He didn't move. Just stared at the empty space.

So many chances. So many moments he could have told her.

But fear, guilt, and hope kept him silent.

He had not been there when she learned to walk, when she cried through fevered nights, when the world left her alone.

He had not even known where she was.

Anthony had vanished with her.

Ignorance was its own wound.

Now she looked at him like a stranger.

And she was right too.

But it still hurt.

Night had fallen when she returned.

Ben was gone.

Good.

She sat on her cot, arms wrapped tight.

The voices were quiet for once.

The pull was steady, unwavering.

Not a whisper. A promise.

Tomorrow, she thought. *I'll follow it.*

She closed her eyes.

Chapter 19: The Way Through

Two days earlier...

The torchlight didn't reach this far down.

Wyatt moved silently through the ancient corridor beneath the Academy, where dust layered thick over stone and even the magic felt like it was holding its breath. The walls were lined with etched wards, each humming faintly under his passing presence. He was careful not to touch them.

He'd bypassed four layers of security to get this far—illusion traps, sigil-coded locks, a blood-ward keyed to high-ranking faculty, which he'd spoofed with a strand of hair lifted from an instructor's robe. He was good at this. It was why Corin had sent him.

But this... this was the part no one had cracked.

He reached the vault door: a flawless circle of obsidian-veined stone embedded with runes glowing in a dull, watchful gold. No keyhole. No handle. Only power.

Wyatt dropped to one knee, letting his fingertips brush the surface. The runes pulsed faintly in response—ancient, complex, and alive.

He rooted himself with earth magic, steadying his pulse. The stone welcomed the connection at first, responding to his natural affinity. He reached deeper, connecting to the structure's core, feeling the magic's resistance growing.

Then he layered in his second gift—light magic—threading it through the cracks like golden wire, guiding it with precision. It was a risk. Light was less subtle. But it helped him see, helped him interpret things most people missed. It was how he made sense of the visions.

But the vault wasn't meant to be seen through.

The moment his light met the seal, the magic shoved back—hard. A sudden pulse of force exploded through the circle, knocking him backward with a grunt. He hit the wall, stunned.

It wasn't just locked. It was selective.

He tried again, slower this time. Rooted himself. Focused. Let light and earth intertwine in perfect balance. But it made no difference.

The seal didn't want balance.

It wanted more. Something... beyond even the rarest magic he possessed.

Wyatt sat back against the wall, breathing hard, sweat cooling fast on his skin.

This wasn't a normal vault. It wasn't just blood-locked or skill-locked—it was elementally woven. It required more than one affinity. He could feel it; it wasn't just locked. It was woven—threads of fire, air, water, earth, and healing braided so tightly that only someone who carried them all could unlock it. It was a statement: only the impossible may enter.

And that narrowed the possibilities down to exactly one.

He had seen it before—both in dreams and with his own eyes. The way storms bent around her. The way light flickered along her skin like it already knew her. Sometimes, when he saw her in vision, a shadow lingered at the edge—hollow eyes in hollow light. He never told anyone about that part. She moved like the elements followed her will, not out of obedience, but recognition. No one else carried that kind of power. Not here. Not anywhere.

At the outpost, he'd kept his distance, uncertain of what was vision and what was real. But now, he didn't need another dream to tell him. He knew. He'd known the moment she stepped into the training ring, and the ground shifted under her feet.

The vault would never yield to someone like him.

But it might open for her.

Wyatt stood slowly, pulled the small communication stone from his coat, and turned it over in his palm. Corin had warned him this might happen—had hoped it wouldn't. But there was no more denying it.

He activated the stone and spoke, voice low but certain.

"I need Camomile Layton."

◈ ☽ ✦ ☾ ◈

Far from the vault, at the outpost, Cam watched Kaden prepare a portal. Her gaze was distant, though his movements were sharp and practiced.

Her mind was not on the magic swirling before her.

She tried not to think about Ben. But her thoughts kept spiraling back to him—the way he'd said it, so soft and worn down, as if breaking open.

'Because I'm your father.'

The weight of the word settled in her chest, tight and heavy, making it hard to breathe.

She swallowed and blinked away the sting.

Kaden glanced at her, breaking the silence. "Let's go."

Cam nodded, lifted her pack, and stepped forward.

The teleport left a crackle in the air and a hollow ache in Cam's chest.

Kaden stepped back, checking the ward lines around them. "An hour's walk, straight east," he said, nodding toward a path that cut through sparse trees and up into rising fog. "No more. You'll know when you're close. The air changes."

Cam adjusted the straps on her pack and looked ahead.

"And Cam?" Kaden's voice softened.

She glanced over.

"Corin isn't sending you in blind. There are others already inside—spies he placed a few weeks ago. You're not alone."

Cam gave a small nod, her throat tight. She hadn't asked for backup. But knowing it was there made her shoulders sit a little easier.

Kaden held out a smooth black stone. "Press the center to speak. It links directly to Corin."

She accepted it, cold and oddly heavy in her palm.

"He trusts you," Kaden said, then added with a wry grin, "And for what it's worth? So do I."

That startled her. "You barely know me."

"True." He adjusted his coat. "But I've seen the way Sylithra looks at you. That's not nothing."

Cam hesitated, then smiled faintly. "Thanks."

Kaden gave a mock salute and vanished with a shimmer of light.

She was alone.

The pull in her chest had grown stronger with every step toward the Academy—and now it felt like a thread humming under her ribs, tugging her forward.

The forest was quiet. Morning mist clung to the ground, and her boots made soft scuffs on damp earth. As she walked, her mind returned—again—to Ben.

Father.

The word still didn't sit right. She was angry, yes. But beneath the fury lived something more raw: grief. For what they could have had. For all the years lost. For the aching, uneven truth.

She thought of the way he'd said it—soft, worn down, like he was breaking open.

'Because I'm your father.'

She swallowed hard, brushing damp curls off her cheek. No matter how many times she replayed it, the sting remained.

Her steps slowed. She pressed her fingers to her temple.

"Syl?"

The dragon's voice slid into her mind, warm and ancient.

I am here, Little Flame. A pause. Then*: You are close.*

"Did you know?" Cam asked. "About him? About me?"

A long silence followed. Then Sylithra answered gently.

I suspected. I felt it in his silence. In yours. But it was not my truth to speak.

Cam exhaled, sharp and low. *"I understand. I do. But it still hurts."*

Of course it does.

She could feel Sylithra's sorrow through the bond. A deep, echoing ache. The kind that didn't ask for forgiveness—only understanding.

Cam walked on, quiet.

Eventually, the trees thinned, revealing high stone towers and steep sloping roofs half-shrouded in mist.

The Mystic Academy.

It rose from the cliffs like a fortress carved from thought and wind. Pale flags fluttered at its highest point, and guards stood like statues at the outer gates.

Cam's breath caught.

She felt it again—that pull, that whisper of belonging and warning all tangled together.

The gate didn't open.

A figure stepped forward instead, a silver-robed mage whose face held no warmth. "State your name and intent."

"Camomile Layton," she said, lifting her chin. "I'm here to petition for study."

He studied her carefully. "And your element?"

Cam hesitated.

She had no idea what this test entailed. And she wasn't ready to explain that she'd touched all four elements—plus healing. Not in a place like this. Corin had warned her: One element only. They don't teach more. They don't allow more.

"Air," she said.

The mage nodded once. "You'll be tested. Follow me."

The test took place in an open courtyard, ringed with students. Most watched with mild curiosity; a few looked openly skeptical. The test itself was simple: a conjuring circle, laced with enchantments. She was told to summon her chosen element, nothing more.

Cam stepped inside.

She inhaled, steadied herself, and focused on the wind.

It answered.

The breeze curled around her like a cat, then built in sudden force, twisting upward in a column that lifted her hair and stirred the robes of everyone standing nearby.

Gasps followed.

The wind snapped once, clean and sharp—and vanished.

The mage overseeing her nodded slowly. "Accepted."

And just like that, she was inside.

Wyatt leaned on a stone balcony overlooking the northern court, arms folded, heart pacing faster than it should have.

He'd felt it again.

That same pull.

He didn't know how to name it, only that it had led him to the girl again and again. And every time, it had been her.

Camomile.

He remembered when she'd run into him that day—eyes distant, distracted. She hadn't even asked his name. But he hadn't asked hers either.

Because he already knew. From Kaden, and Corin, whispers around the outpost but he had seen her in visions for as long as he could remember. In childhood dreams, in half-shapes across scrying bowls, in flashes of light when the world stood still. Always her. Sometimes a silhouette in storm light. Sometimes laughing in fire. Sometimes crumbling beneath the weight of something too large to name.

She was his third gift—the one he never talked about. Not like fire, not like shadowwalking. Those were flashy, understandable, and safe.

But vision?

That kind of magic didn't just show you things—it marked you. It chose you. And for Wyatt, it had always chosen her.

For years, he'd told himself it was coincidence. A pattern his mind kept tracing without meaning. But the more he trained, the more he understood how rare it was to see the same person, the same shape, the same name, over and over again in every future he glimpsed.

And now she was here.

Real. Solid. Breathing.

Or at least—he thought so.

Sometimes he wasn't sure.

Sometimes he caught sight of her across the courtyard at the outpost and wondered if she'd vanish like mist.

And sometimes, when he whispered her name under his breath, it felt like summoning a ghost.

Wyatt took a slow breath, clenching and unclenching his fists. He almost stepped forward to speak—but then stopped, chest tightening.

He dragged a hand through his hair, frustrated.

Kaden had spoken of her often—not with admiration or desire, but with awe. Like someone speaking of a legend made flesh. Wyatt had watched her train over the last few weeks, unseen, and come to the same conclusion.

She was powerful. Not just gifted—but staggering.

Another mage who could ride. Who could bend the elements like thread. Who woke something ancient when she moved.

And yet... she still looked lost. Like she wasn't sure what to do with the power she carried.

Wyatt smiled faintly. He understood the feeling.

He'd tried to speak to her more than once. Had rehearsed it in his head. But every time he approached, something always stopped him.

What if she wasn't real?

What if the girl he'd seen all his life was just a mirage wearing skin?

His heart kicked harder in his chest. He shifted his weight, fingers twitching at his side.

Say something. Just say something.

But the words jammed in his throat, stuck behind too many years of waiting.

He hated this—how she turned him into someone hesitant. Someone uncertain. He wasn't that. Not in battle. Not in strategy.

But with her? He couldn't seem to move.

Why do I feel so nervous around her? he thought.

But the answer was obvious.

Because some part of him still wasn't convinced she wasn't just a prophecy in human shape.

Today, he'd finally gathered the nerve to say something.

But before he could reach her, a communication stone in his pocket flared cold.

Corin's voice crackled through: *Wyatt. I need a word. Now.*

Wyatt swore under his breath and turned on his heel.

By nightfall, he had his next assignment.

Retrieve the book in the vault. Quietly. No damage, no discovery.

The last thing Corin said before ending the connection lingered like smoke:

Keep your eyes on her.

Chapter 20: Bloodlines and Buried Doors

Ben woke to silence.

Not the kind that came with peace, but the kind that felt like a held breath. A silence just waiting to break.

Cam's bunk was empty.

He stared at it for a moment too long. Neatly folded blanket. No pack. No boots. The pillow still held the faintest imprint of her head.

His chest tightened. A low hum of dread stirred in his gut.

He didn't need to ask. He knew.

She was gone.

Ben stood quickly, pulling on his coat. His boots hit the packed earth with weight behind each step as he crossed the quiet camp. A few rebels moved about—early risers on patrol, a dragon handler whispering to her bonded. No one looked alarmed.

He found Kaden near the edge of the training yard, adjusting the runes on a short-bladed spear.

"Kaden," Ben said, voice low and clipped. "Where is she?"

Kaden didn't look up. "She left."

Ben's jaw locked. "Left where?"

"The Academy."

That single word pulled something cold through Ben's ribs.

"She wasn't ready," he said, but it came out softer than intended. Like he was trying to convince himself.

"She made the choice," Kaden replied. He finally glanced up. "And she's not going in blind. We've got people there. She's not alone."

"She's never been alone," Ben snapped. "Not while I'm alive."

Kaden's expression shifted, like he was putting something together—but he said nothing.

Ben turned without another word.

Corin was alone in his war tent, hunched over a table scattered with reports. The flap hadn't even finished closing behind Ben when Corin said, "I expected you sooner."

Ben stepped forward. "You sent her."

"She volunteered."

"She's barely an adult."

Corin looked up slowly. "No. She's more than that."

Ben paced, hands clenched at his sides. "She's not ready. The Academy is dangerous. We don't even know if the rebels inside can protect her if she's discovered."

Corin leaned back, arms folded. "Wyatt requested her."

Ben froze. "What?"

"After his last attempt at the archives. He couldn't access the vault. Said it needed more than any mage inside could offer." A pause. "Said it needed her."

Ben's breath left him in a sharp exhale. "He saw it too."

Corin's gaze narrowed. "That's not all he sees, is it?"

Ben stilled.

"Who is she to you, Ben?"

The question lingered. Heavy. Inevitable.

Ben looked away.

For years, he had lived under a borrowed name.

The spell had been simple in principle but ruinous in price: Ben Miles became Anthony Lyte to the world, while the true Anthony faded into obscurity. His face never changed, but every document, every whisper, every trace of him in Caerthalen said "Anthony Lyte."

The cost had been memory.

Not all of it—he knew who he was, who Anthony had been, and most importantly, who Cam was. But some moments were blurred, like a painting left in the rain. Enough to keep enemies from seeing the seams. Enough to make the lie hold.

And now, as Corin waited in the dim light of the war tent, Ben finally let the words break free.

"The spell that made me Anthony Lyte... it didn't erase me. It only blurred the edges. I always knew who I was. I always knew who she was. But to the world—" He exhaled, weary. "I've been Anthony for years."

Corin's jaw tightened. "Then it's true."

Ben nodded, the weight of years pressing into his shoulders.

"She's mine," he said quietly.

Ben nodded once. "Mine and Isabella's daughter."

Corin sat in silence for a long moment, eyes unreadable. "You should have told me."

"You weren't ready to hear it."

"Was she?"

Ben's voice dropped, rough and small. "Not yet. But I told her anyway."

A long silence followed. Corin exhaled and turned back to the war table, gathering himself. "The spell still holds?"

"For everyone else, yes," Ben said. "As far as Valmira knows, Benjamin Miles died twenty years ago."

"And you?"

"I buried him the day I held her for the last time."

Corin studied him. "And now?"

Ben looked toward the tent's opening, where the morning light broke just beyond the canvas. Where she had once stood.

"She doesn't just belong to prophecy," Ben said quietly. "She belongs to me. And I can't lose her again."

'Mine and Isabella's daughter.'

The words echoed through Corin's mind like a spell spoken in reverse—shattering what he'd believed for nearly two decades.

For years, he'd assumed Isabella had married Anthony. It was what the records said. What the noble houses had arranged. What the Knighthood had paraded like a banner.

But now the lie peeled back, thin and rotting.

Ben—not Anthony—had been the one she loved.

Corin's mouth felt dry. "You were there the whole time. Beside her. Not just as a knight..."

Ben didn't answer. He didn't have to.

Corin exhaled slowly and looked at him—really looked. Beneath the scars. Beneath the name. Beneath the old spell still clinging to Ben's presence like smoke.

He had always known.

Ben had moved like a rider. Spoke like a soldier. But the way his magic hummed under the surface—it had always felt wrong for someone trained by the Knighthood alone.

Too precise. Too... old.

"I knew you weren't just a rider," Corin said, voice low. "You have mage blood. You always did."

Ben didn't deny it.

Corin shook his head once, half in awe, half in disbelief. "And you hid it. From them. From everyone."

"Except Anthony," Ben said. "And Izzy."

Corin pressed his fingers to his temples, the weight of the past settling like dust in his bones. Isabella had been brilliant—too clever for the future they'd boxed her into. Corin had admired her from afar, back when the four of them had still trained in the Capital of Caerthalen.

He thought he'd mourned her fully when the news of her death reached them.

But now he saw how little of her truth he'd ever really known.

And now her daughter—Ben's daughter—was walking into the Academy, powerful and exposed, with half of Valmira still chasing shadows.

Corin looked at Ben again, something solemn and ancient threading his voice.

"You were never just part of the Knighthood. You were something they couldn't control. And so was she."

Ben met his gaze, steady and unflinching.

"And neither is my daughter," he said quietly. "No one can control Cam."

The tent fell into silence again—but this time, it wasn't heavy with secrets.

It was heavy with truth.

A few weeks after her arrival Cam slipped into the lower level of the archives using a key she wasn't supposed to have—"borrowed" from a storage room after watching the access rotations for days.

The corridors here were quieter. Older. The air smelled of ancient parchment and burning wards.

She wasn't alone.

A tall figure leaned against one of the shelves, flipping idly through a dusty ledger. He looked up when she entered—blonde hair, sharper cheekbones, quiet presence.

Alex Draxen.

They hadn't spoken directly before, but she recognized him from the training grounds. Always watching, never drawing attention. He had a stillness about him—that she hadn't noticed in the training grounds at the outpost before.

He gave her a small nod, no questions asked, then returned to his page.

She paused, then kept walking. No words passed between them.

But something settled in her spine.

He was one of the others. A plant. Like her.

And now she knew.

A month into her mission at the academy Cam was sitting cross-legged beneath one of the stone arches of the east courtyard, a thick text on elemental binding open across her lap. The breeze tugged at the edges of the pages, and she didn't bother anchoring them. Air answered her easily these days.

"Still pretending you're only gifted with wind?" came a dry voice.

Cam looked up.

A tall black-haired girl stood over her. Cam just stared and said nothing

"Valerie McKenna, call me Val," the girl said as she stood over Cam, arms folded, one brow arched in amusement. A third-year student with deceptively relaxed posture and a lopsided grin that never quite reached her eyes.

"I'm not pretending," Cam said evenly. "Cam Layton."

"Right. And I'm just good at illusions because of years of hard work," Valerie said as she dropped to sit beside Cam without asking. "You're very talked about among the students and instructors."

Cam gave a half smile. "You're not fooling anyone."

Valerie snorted. "Neither are you."

There was a quiet understanding between them. They never said what they were. What they could really do. But they both knew. That was enough.

"You ever wonder how many of us are hiding it?" Valerie asked, voice lower now, almost thoughtful. "How many students here could touch more than one element—if the Academy wasn't so set on keeping things neat and safe?"

Cam closed the book. "I think about it all the time."

Valerie didn't respond for a moment. Then she added, "You're not alone here, you know. There are others watching. Some of them aren't loyal to the Academy."

Cam glanced sideways at her. "You mean rebels?"

Valerie shrugged. "I didn't say that."

"Would you tell the instructors if you found one?"

Valerie's gaze sharpened. "Would you?"

Their eyes locked.

"No," Cam said softly.

"Me neither."

They sat in silence for a while, the wind curling gently between them.

Cam didn't know if she should have revealed that much to Val or not, but the third year seemed to trust Cam with what she had revealed and that took guts. Cam admired that about the older girl, so Val and Cam became friends. A faint gold shimmer curled across Cam's fingertips, answering the unspoken vow between them, before fading into the breeze.

One night, two months into her mission Cam sat on the flat stone ledge of the Academy's Garden roof, knees tucked to her chest, arms wrapped loosely around them. She'd slipped past curfew again, needing space. The pressure of the vault, of the silence in her chest where the pull had once lived—it all pressed too tightly around her tonight.

Valerie climbed up moments later, boots scuffing against the metal stair. She didn't ask permission, just dropped beside Cam and tilted her face toward the stars.

"I hate this place sometimes," Valerie muttered, her voice low and tight. "It makes you feel like you have to be one thing and one thing only."

Cam glanced sideways. "You mean water."

Val scoffed under her breath. "Please. I've had water magic since I was thirteen—animation, sensing underground currents before I even touch the surface. It started after I got angry one day and flooded half a well house back home." She shook her head. "They told me it was too volatile. Said I should focus. Refine. Obey."

Cam stayed quiet, sensing more beneath the words.

Val's gaze flicked to her, sharp and searching. "But that's not the only thing I can do." Her fingers flexed as if holding an invisible brush. "Sometimes... I see things. Remember things. And when I draw them, it's like they come back—exactly as they were. Not just on paper. Real. Moving. Breathing."

Cam's breath caught, but she didn't interrupt.

"They called it corrupted illusion," Val said bitterly. "Said it was unstable, dangerous. That I could twist minds or open memories that weren't mine to see. They threatened to expel me if I kept practicing." She looked away, jaw tight. "So yeah. I hide it. I play the good little water mage."

Cam's voice was soft. "But you don't want to."

Valerie's eyes met hers, blazing now. "Of course I don't. Don't you ever wonder what we could do if we weren't boxed in? If they taught us what we're capable of instead of fearing it?"

Cam was quiet for a moment, heart thudding with a familiar sense of understanding. "Every day."

Valerie ran a hand through her wind-frayed hair. "I don't know where to go. I want to learn more—hell, I want to be able to use all my abilities not just the one element—but I don't trust anyone here to teach me."

Cam looked down at the stone beneath them, thoughts already shifting, forming an idea.

She might not have all the answers. But she knew someone who might.

◈ ☽✦☾ ◈

Cam left the note tucked between the pages of an old defense tactics manual—one she knew Alex frequently referenced. He would find it. He was careful like that.

Alex,

There are others here with second or even third abilities. They're hiding—like you are, like I am. Valerie McKenna is one of them. She's smart, careful, and not as loyal to the Academy as she pretends to be. If anything happens, talk to her.

– C

As Cam turned from the shelf, her hand brushed the spine of a book she hadn't meant to touch. The leather was cracked, nearly black. The title, faded but still legible, read: Internal Barriers and Their Failures: A Study in Magical Containment.

She frowned.

It had nothing to do with what she was researching.

And yet...

She opened it and skimmed a section near the middle.

Containment structures built in secrecy often resist detection. They hum beneath the surface, not like magic eager to be used—but like something alive, unwilling to be found. Most vaults are locked. A few are sealed. A rare handful... watch.

Cam closed the book slowly, her stomach tightening.

She needed to find the vault.

Not later. Now.

◈ ☽✦☾ ◈

Over the next few weeks Cam had done so much research into the vault but had come up with very little as to where it might be. She thought about asking one of the rebels that were always around.

What about the one that is always watching me...? she thought. But she dismissed the idea almost immediately. She didn't want to risk getting caught talking about it—especially not to someone she couldn't fully trust.

She would have to go to the lower levels of the library and dig deeper.

Cam waited until the training bells ended and the common halls emptied. She slipped through the library's east doors, then down the spiraling stairs past the old lecture wings, through a scribe's hall where dust whispered beneath her boots.

The lower archive levels were supposed to be off-limits without a pass from a senior instructor. But Cam had learned by now that those rules didn't apply to people who knew how to listen, blend in, and keep moving.

She moved quietly through the deep corridors, torchlight flickering across stone walls carved with old magic. This part of the library smelled like age and secrets—like the Academy didn't want you to ask certain questions.

But she had questions.

A dozen titles caught her eye, all older than the founding of Caerthalen:

Woven Seals and War-Time Vaults,

Elemental Intersections: Dangerous Fusions,

The Rise and Banishment of the Fifth Circle,

Veil Constructs: Theory and Consequence.

Her fingers hovered over Elemental Intersections: Dangerous Fusions. The hum in her chest spiked, faint but insistent, as if the book itself leaned toward her. She pulled it free without thinking. The diagrams inside were jagged circles of overlapping elements, margins scrawled with warnings. One faded line made her breath catch: Fusion births power. But also hunger.

A chill prickled her skin. She shut the book quickly, too quickly, the whisper of parchment sharp in the silence. After a breath, she slid it into her satchel. Not research she needed now—but some part of her knew she would.

Cam studied the spines, fingers grazing lightly.

A hum started in her chest. Familiar, yet quiet—like the echo of the pull she used to feel. It tugged her left.

She followed it.

At the end of the row, a book sat slightly out of alignment. Thin, dark green binding. No visible title.

She slid it free.

It was handwritten. Old. Inside were diagrams of runes braided with elemental threads, blood seals reinforced with light and darkness.

The vault beneath the Academy was not built to protect knowledge, the first line read, but to trap something that could not be destroyed.

Cam slowly turned the page. Her pulse skipped, just once—then settled into a heavier beat.

A failsafe lies in place. One who carries all four or more threads may pass—but they awaken what waits within.

Her eyes flew to the diagrams—stone chambers layered in wards and elemental seals. Magic woven not just to guard but to restrain. Her fingers traced a sketch marked with concentric circles surrounding a strange rune she didn't recognize.

The Hollowed Spiral.

A ringed circle, cradling a split triangle, surrounded by mirrored lines like wings or blades.

She didn't know what it meant. Not yet. But it was etched into the page like a warning.

She leaned in closer—only to jolt when her chest suddenly tightened.

It felt like the pull.

Just for a moment. Just enough to disorient her. Her pulse spiked.

A stack of books on the table next to her teetered, and before she could catch them, one fell to the floor with a dull thud.

Cam froze.

Footsteps.

She shoved the open book into her satchel and stepped silently behind the nearest shelf just as a young instructor passed the far entrance. He paused, eyes scanning the room.

Cam pressed back against the wall, holding her breath.

The instructor lingered... then moved on.

The footsteps echoed down the corridor, growing fainter.

But something in her gut said: someone else was down there with her.

She waited a little longer than necessary, just to be sure. Silence returned.

When she was finally sure the hall was empty again, she exhaled slowly.

Whatever that feeling was—it wasn't a vision.

But it felt familiar. Too familiar.

Whatever she was getting close to... it wasn't just forgotten history.

The vault wasn't dormant.

It was waiting.

◈ ☽✦☾ ◈

She had no map—only instinct.

The Academy had layers, some older than anyone admitted. Hallways that didn't match blueprints. Sealed stairwells. Entire floors cordoned off for "preservation purposes."

She followed a current in the air—an almost imperceptible wrongness.

After twenty minutes of wandering, she found it.

A narrow hall behind a mirrored corridor. An archway of stone carved with runes that shimmered faintly when she stepped near. Beyond it: a short passage ending in a circular stone door, black-veined, pulsing faintly.

She didn't touch it.

She didn't need to.

The magic radiating from it was ancient, heavy, and strangely alert. Like something behind it had turned its head and noticed her.

She caught herself staring at the spiral in the corner of the room.

A tug, deep in her chest—like something ancient remembered her.

She stepped back quickly, boots scraping the floor.

A shiver rolled up her spine.

Whatever this vault was—it wasn't just protected. It was watching.

In the shimmer of runes, a shadow flickered—tall, hollow-eyed, gone before she could blink. Her pulse stuttered. She told herself it was nothing. But the vault was listening.

Cam turned and left without another glance. She didn't know why she was drawn to it.

But something told her... this wasn't over.

Chapter 21: Visions

From the shadowed edge of the upper balconies, Wyatt watched Cam move through the outer court—head down, hands full, sleeves pushed to her elbows as she carried three sets of scrolls across the training ring.

She wasn't assigned to that task. He knew—because he had read the roster himself.

But she did it anyway.

It had become a pattern. She didn't just complete her own work. She picked up after others. Helped students practice incantation control. Calmed a junior initiate after a failed shielding spell. Filed two days' worth of archived ledgers the other acolytes had ignored.

It wasn't for praise. She didn't smile when it was done. Didn't wait for acknowledgment.

She just... did it. Like her power wasn't the only thing she carried. Like she had purpose in her bones.

Wyatt leaned on the stone rail, the chill of the evening air tightening across his arms. The light magic in him stirred faintly—drawn toward her presence again, even when he tried to focus elsewhere.

This wasn't what he was sent here to watch.

He was here for information. For signs of the shadow threat worming its way through the Academy's foundations. For sealed records, missing students, instructors with divided allegiances, and a book from the vault that he couldn't open. The Knighthood was already rotting from the inside—Corin needed to know if the Academy was next.

That was the mission.

But she was the distraction.

The pull hadn't lessened since she arrived.

If anything, it had sharpened. Not like a bond or a spell, but a thread humming through him, constantly tugging him toward her shadow, her quiet, the way she held herself like she was always walking between two worlds.

She wasn't the threat.

But he couldn't stop watching her.

She reminded him of the visions—but not quite. She was brighter here. Sharper. Her laugh, when it came, wasn't the one he heard in dreams. It was real. It was better.

He'd tried to speak to her once already. Walked within reach. But his voice had stuck in his throat. She hadn't seen him.

Or maybe—he hadn't let her.

Because the truth was, part of him didn't want to be seen.

And another part of him desperately did.

He was supposed to be gathering intel, watching for signs of danger. But the only thing he saw was the way she moved like she was born for more than this place. Like she was already trying to outgrow it.

And something in him wanted her to see him too.

The wind shifted.

Wyatt straightened. The pull behind his ribs twisted slightly—off-rhythm. That was how it always started.

A flicker of light curled in the corner of his vision. The edges of the world wavered. He inhaled slowly, grounding himself with earth, steadying the rise of magic within him.

Then the vision took him.

Stone. Darkness. A chamber lined with impossible light.

She stood before the vault, one hand pressed flat against its face. Magic coiled around her like smoke—all five elements rippling through her skin like veins of living power.

The seal melted away.

Wyatt stood back, unseen, watching as she stepped inside. Shelves lined the circular room—crammed with ancient tomes, enchanted scrolls, sealed boxes etched with runes too old to name. She moved quickly, instinctively, reaching for a thick, leather-bound book wrapped in chains.

It fell into her hands.

But something followed it.

The light inside the chamber dimmed. A breath—no, a voice—rose from the darkness behind her. Cold. Wrong. Like oil poured over flame.

She turned too late.

Wyatt tried to shout—tried to run forward—but his feet wouldn't move.

The shadows surged. The chamber cracked like glass, and she—

Wyatt gasped as the vision snapped him back into reality.

His knuckles were white against the balcony rail. Sweat chilled the back of his neck. The courtyard below looked the same. Students talking. Cam walking with purpose, unbothered, unaware.

But the vault was more than a lock.

It was a door. It was alive. It was watching. And something waited behind it.

He didn't know what. Not yet. But he'd seen her face before the vision broke—not in fear, but fury. Whatever it was, it came for her. And she didn't back down.

Wyatt's pulse steadied as the last of the light magic faded from his skin.

She was meant to open that door.

But if he couldn't stop what came after... he might be the one who watched her walk through it and never come back.

Wyatt closed the door to his dormitory softly behind him and dropped the privacy rune into place. The silence that followed was dense and comforting.

Wyatt sat at his narrow desk, still damp from the vision. He reached for the small, leather-bound journal tucked in the bottom drawer—a field log, enchanted to be fireproof and warded against scrying.

He opened it to the next blank page.

Entry: *Vault Vision – Confirmed Pull*

She opened the vault. All five elements responded to her—air, fire, earth, water, and healing. The seal unraveled.

She retrieved a chained book—dark leather, rune-locked.

Shadows followed. Not magical resistance. Not defense triggers. Something else. Something waiting.

I was immobilized. Couldn't intervene.

She was not afraid—but furious.

Ended in rupture. Collapse.

Possible: threat sealed behind vault? Living or cursed?

Outcome: unclear. Survival uncertain. Urge caution. Vault may be more trap than archive.

He closed the journal and pulled out a separate black-stone communication rune. Corin's personal relay. Only used when urgency outweighed subtlety.

He activated it with a touch of light.

"New vision," he murmured. "She opens the vault. Something is released. Not defensive magic—something worse. A presence. She fights it. Alone. We may not have as much time as we thought."

The rune dimmed.

Wyatt exhaled, long and slow.

He should have left it there. Let the message speak for itself. Let Corin decide. But his fingers hesitated near his desk.

Then, against reason, against caution, he tore a scrap of parchment from a side notebook and scrawled two lines.

He slipped it into a cloth envelope, unsigned, and marked only with a faint air rune—one he'd seen her attuned to earlier in the week.

By morning, it would be left among her assigned materials.

It wasn't much. But it was the closest he could come to warning her... without revealing everything.

◈ ☽✦☾ ◈

The wind outside Cam's window whispered too loud.

Cam rolled over, heart beating strangely. Her body was still. Her mind—buzzing. The threads of sleep tugged at her, but something deeper stirred below it.

A breath. A call.

Then, suddenly—

She stood alone in a stone chamber.

The vault door peeled open like mist curling away from steel. Magic flared beneath her skin—alive and burning. The book appeared in her hands before she could blink.

Then—cold.

The light went out. Not just in the room, but in her body.

A sound rose behind her—jagged and wet. Not words. Not magic. Something older.

Cam turned, raising her hand—and it sank into shadow.

Not smoke. Not creature.

Will. Something sentient.

And it wanted her.

She screamed.

Cam jolted awake, a sharp cry caught in her throat.

Her hands trembled. Sweat clung to her neck and spine. The room was empty. Quiet. But the echo lingered.

The vault. A book. A darkness that knew her name.

And she knew—somehow—it wasn't just a dream.

⟐ ☽✦☾ ⟐

Cam rose before the sun.

Sleep hadn't returned after the vision. She'd tossed beneath her blankets, trying to shake the image of the vault, the chained book, and that unnatural presence coiled in the dark. Even now, her body felt like it hadn't rested at all—like her magic was still bracing for a fight that hadn't yet happened.

She dressed in silence and moved through the dim halls, letting instinct guide her feet toward the courtyard. Morning dew coated the flagstones, and her breath fogged faintly in the crisp air.

A delivery mage had already swept through, placing materials in cubbies along the side corridor—assignments, lesson guides, training updates. Cam passed hers without much thought—until she saw the envelope.

Unmarked. Plain. Folded neatly and tucked beneath her task list.

She paused.

No seal. No name. Just a faint shimmer on the surface—a soft air rune, delicate and familiar.

Her fingers hovered over it before lifting the flap.

Two lines, handwritten in ink that shimmered faintly when it caught the light:

The vault responds to you.

Be careful what it wakes.

Her breath caught.

The paper felt heavier than it should. As if it knew it had arrived too late—or just in time.

Her hand curled around the message as she glanced sharply around the corridor. No one lingered. No instructors. No students. No obvious trail.

Who had sent this?

More importantly—how did they know?

Her mind flashed back to the vision. The vault. The shadows.

She read the words again.

Not a threat. A warning.

Cam folded the note and tucked it into the inner lining of her coat, heart thudding hard.

She didn't know who had written it.

But someone knew what she'd seen.

And they were watching.

She found it.

◈ ☽✦☾ ◈

Wyatt watched from the upper walkway, just out of sight behind the arc of a stone column. He didn't need light magic to tell when someone was shaken—he could see it in the way her fingers paused over the envelope, the slight hitch in her breath as she read the message.

She didn't drop it. Didn't crumple it. Didn't toss it away.

She kept it.

Tucked it into her coat like it mattered.

That should've been enough. That should've been the end of it.

But Wyatt's jaw tightened as she turned and walked back into the heart of the Academy—shoulders squared, chin lifted, that unrelenting fire returning to her eyes.

She's going to investigate it now, he thought. *She's going to start pulling threads I shouldn't have given her.*

And part of him didn't regret it.

◈ ☽✦☾ ◈

Cam's fingers skimmed along the spines of ancient tomes, her eyes scanning shelf after shelf of forgotten lore. The Academy's public archives were vast—but curated. Sanitized. Everything here had been deemed "appropriate for student study."

But she wasn't looking for spells or elemental techniques.

She was looking for cracks.

There had to be something—anything—about the vault. Its creation. Its protections. Its purpose.

She didn't dare ask directly. Not yet. Asking questions got you noticed. Cam had spent too long hiding her truth to risk drawing eyes now.

Instead, she searched for terms that echoed pieces of her dream: forbidden seals, multielement wards, deep-lock runes, containment structures, cursed knowledge.

She pulled a slim, dust-coated volume from the middle shelf: *Principles of Arcane Boundaries: Theory and Application.*

She flipped it open, scanning quickly—and froze halfway down the page.

"A multielement seal requires a mage of equal elemental attunement to unravel—commonly considered a theoretical construct, as no known living mage has successfully demonstrated access to all five primary elements simultaneously."

Her pulse kicked.

No known mage. Because they didn't know about her.

Cam closed the book, heart racing, and slid it into her satchel.

Something was buried in this place.

And whatever was sealed behind that vault door... wasn't meant to stay hidden forever.

The candlelight flickered oddly.

Cam straightened from the shelf, the book still half-tucked in her hand, and glanced toward the far end of the row. Nothing moved. No footsteps. No voices. Just that heavy stillness that came with ancient rooms soaked in magic and memory.

And then—there it was again.

The pull.

Not from the vault this time.

Different. Closer. Sharper.

It snagged behind her ribs like a hook caught on soul-thread—turning her slightly, like she might find something, or someone, just around the corner.

She hesitated.

For half a second, she forgot where she was.

Then the footsteps came.

Not hers. Not imagined.

Measured. Confident. Getting closer.

Cam's eyes snapped back to the shelves. She shoved the book back on the shelf, turned the corner—and froze.

A gray-robed faculty member had just entered the aisle. Mid-level, someone she hadn't spoken to before. Too young to be harmless, too observant to underestimate. His gaze swept the corridor like he knew exactly what wasn't supposed to be touched.

Cam ducked behind the next stack, pressing herself into shadow.

She forced her breathing to slow. Focused. Pushed her presence down—not cloaking it with magic (too risky) but shrinking herself the way she had to for most of her life. Quiet. Still. Invisible.

The man paused near the very shelf she'd been standing at seconds ago.

Cam didn't move.

The pull had completely vanished—abruptly, like it had been cut.

After a long pause, the faculty member turned and walked away.

Only then did Cam exhale, low and tight.

The archives weren't safe anymore—not even the public sections.

And that pull... it wasn't just random.

Something—or someone—was reaching for her, even as she reached for the truth.

Cam emerged from the annex and slipped into the narrow stairwell that overlooked the lower levels of the library. The walls here were lined with iron sconces and old ward runes that pulsed faintly as she passed.

She paused at the bottom step, her hand tightening around the strap of her satchel.

The paragraph she had read played over in her mind—like the echo of a heartbeat not her own.

The warning note, still tucked inside her coat, suddenly felt heavier.

She didn't know who had sent it.

She didn't know what waited behind the vault.

But she knew this: Something was calling to her.

And she was going to answer.
She decided that she would go at midnight.

Chapter 22: The Vault

She remembered the path clearly.

The way the corridor narrowed past the last stairwell, how the enchantments carved into the walls began to shift—older, deeper, layered with magic she didn't recognize. The air thickened with each step. Not just with dust and cold, but with something unseen, something waiting.

Cam moved carefully, keeping her pace even. Her heartbeat wasn't racing, but it wasn't steady either.

She had found the vault once before—hidden behind a false wall at the base of the third archive chamber. She hadn't lingered then. The magic in the air had turned her away before she'd even touched the door.

But now... she wasn't turning away.

The pull had returned, subtle but present. Not as sharp as it used to be, not as demanding. More like something aligning. She didn't know what it meant—but she knew she had to answer it.

She rounded the last bend.

There it was.

The door loomed ahead, embedded into the stone like a secret exhaled by the earth itself. Obsidian-veined and rune-laced, it looked as if it had grown from the wall rather than been built into it.

Cam hesitated for only a breath.

Then she stepped forward, reaching out slowly, reverently.

The surface was cold beneath her palm.

The runes on the door pulsed beneath her fingers—air first, then water, then fire, earth, and finally healing. But there was something more.

Beneath those familiar currents, she could feel deeper threads—older, stranger. Magic that didn't belong to just one element, but all of them. Even ones she didn't know how to name. Spirit. Shadow. Light. Time. She didn't just feel it in the vault. She felt it waking in her—quiet, patient, and watching.

There was a question in that weight. One she wasn't ready to answer yet.

They flickered at the edges of her awareness like half-remembered dreams—waiting.

Her breath hitched. She didn't speak. She wasn't ready to ask the questions that came with that kind of knowing. Not yet.

The final hum lingered in her palm, steady and strong—like a second heartbeat.

It wasn't just about mastering an element anymore. It was about choosing them—and maybe learning how to bear them all.

She could feel it opening.

Behind her, footsteps echoed—light, but sure.

She didn't flinch. She already knew who it was.

"Don't open it alone," said a quiet voice.

Cam stood and turned to face the voice, and for the first time, their eyes met not in passing, not across a courtyard or through a crowd—but here, in silence, beneath stone and magic.

The man from the outpost.

The one with too many secrets in his eyes.

And for reasons she couldn't explain, it didn't feel wrong.

The one who kept watching her.

"You've been following me," she said.

"Watching," he corrected softly. "There's a difference."

"Why?"

"Because the vault isn't just sealed." He nodded toward the runes. "It's guarded. And whatever's behind it... knows you."

She stared at him. "You saw it too."

He hesitated—then nodded. "I see a lot of things. But never clearly. Not until you."

Cam's breath caught. Something about the way he said it—like he didn't just mean visions, but everything.

"What's your name?" she asked.

"Wyatt Valehart."

She turned back to the vault. "Help me."

And together, they reached.

Wyatt laid his hands beside hers. Earth surged through him, grounding the wild energy. He wove light magic into the runes, coaxing them forward like threads of gold. Cam focused, letting each of the five elements rise in her—one at a time, like breathing. Where her power touched his light, a gold shimmer sparked between their hands—brief, fragile, but whole.

But there was something deeper beneath the five. Unnamed, unfelt until now. A glimmer of something more—waiting.

She didn't reach for it. Not yet. But she knew it was hers.

The door unfolded.

As the stone petals began to shift, a symbol flared across the threshold—brief but brilliant.

A ringed circle, cradling a split triangle, surrounded by mirrored lines like wings or blades. It didn't belong to any of the Academy's runes. It didn't glow like the elemental sigils—it burned, searing itself into the stone, into memory.

Cam felt it brand the air around them.

Wyatt's breath caught. He didn't recognize it, but some part of him did. Deeply. Instinctively.

The light vanished as quickly as it came, swallowed by the shifting vault door.

Not open. Not swung. It shifted like petals of stone blooming outward, revealing a chamber carved from pure veined obsidian.

Inside: rows of hovering tomes, etched with sigils. Scrolls sealed in iron rings. Runes circling the walls, ancient and pulsing faintly.

In the center stood a pedestal.

And on it—a book, bound in cracked leather, its edges lined in silver runes. It radiated cold. It radiated memory.

Cam stepped forward.

"This is it," she whispered.

Wyatt hovered at the threshold, tense. "Be careful."

She reached out, brushing the book—

And the air dropped ten degrees.

It started subtle.

A shimmer in the corner of the room. A thread of darkness coiling beneath one shelf. Then a shape began to form—hazy, jagged, like something pulled from the broken edges of a memory.

Wyatt's light magic flared.

The shadow snapped toward him, hissed, then retreated.

"Something's alive in here," he said sharply.

Cam gripped the book tighter. "It's—tethered to it. I can feel it."

The vault groaned.

Magic warped along the walls, the ancient protections responding—not to them, but to what was waking.

The runes began to flicker. Something was leaking through the cracks—an intelligence, sharp and ancient and hungry. Not physical, not whole.

A voice formed, like air dragging over stone.

You should not be here.

The chamber pulsed. Shadow spilled outward like liquid thought, slamming toward Cam—

Wyatt reacted instinctively.

Earth surged from the ground under Cam, anchoring the floor beneath her. His light blazed brighter, slicing through the shadow. It shrieked—not in pain, but in recognition.

Cam's eyes lit with elemental fire.

She pushed back.

Magic crackled through her—all of it. The chamber shook as her power met the presence mid-air. The shadow reeled, but not before marking her—a black smoke like sigil curling towards her.

She cried out.

In that moment, the sigil burned itself onto her wrist—it pulsed faintly with dark magic. It wasn't there before; it was born in the clash, tethered to the shadow that had recognized her. It wasn't just a mark—it pulsed faintly, beating in time with her own heart—as if it wasn't just a mark, but a claim. And it wasn't hers alone.

The presence vanished into the vault walls.

The runes surged—and then began to collapse inward.

"It's sealing again!" Wyatt shouted.

"Go!"

Cam clutched the book and ran. Wyatt covered the rear, blasting a sigil loose as the corridor sealed behind them like a mouth snapping shut.

As they stumbled into the outer corridor, Wyatt cast one last glance over his shoulder.

The shadow's voice still lingered in his mind—low, cold, familiar.

And for the first time since arriving at the Academy, he felt a certainty he didn't want.

He knew what that presence was. Or at least, what it had once been.

But he didn't say it aloud.

Not yet.

Because if he was right—if the shadows creeping into his visions had truly taken shape here—then Cam hadn't just opened a vault.

She'd woken up a piece of the threat they were all trying to stop.

They stumbled into the hall, gasping.

Cam spun, watching the last rune flare and die. The vault was closed. Silent. Waiting.

She turned to Wyatt.

"That thing—what was it?"

"I don't know," he said, voice tight. "But it's still in there. And it left a mark on you."

She looked at her wrist. The sigil was still faintly glowing. It was the same sigil she had seen on the vault door before it opened.

A shudder ran down her spine.

Then—A shift.

Like the air itself turned to glass.

"We need to move," Wyatt said sharply. "Now."

Too late.

A pulse of power radiated through the corridor—a ripple of ancient alarm magic. No sound. Just presence. Old, systemic, and laced with command runes.

"Shit," Wyatt swore under his breath. "A silent alarm, they'll know."

"Who?"

"The instructors. The Academy Council. The Knighthood. The Capital. Take your pick."

Cam's heart leapt. "We don't have time."

"I can't call my dragon from this distance," Wyatt said, frustrated. "Distance isn't the best for bonded riders. And it's a three-day flight to the Keep."

Cam's magic was older. Wilder. Hers wasn't bound by rules.

"I can call mine," she said and closed her eyes

And she'd prepared for this.

Sylithra wasn't far—hidden just outside the Academy's reach. Cam had come up with the exit plan the moment she arrived. It wasn't graceful or elegant, but it was all she had. A straight shot skyward if things went wrong.

Now they had.

She reached into the space in her mind—into the bond that never faltered, no matter the miles.

"Sylithra," she whispered across the plane of her mind and magic. *"I need you."*

I am here.

The answer came like a roar.

Cam's eyes snapped open. "We need to move. Now."

They ran—quiet but fast—cutting through the narrow stone halls of the lower Academy. Wyatt took the lead, ducking beneath torchlight and slipping past open archways. The corridors were beginning to stir. Doors creaked. Voices carried low and suspicious.

"They'll search the lower wings first," Wyatt muttered. "We need open sky."

Cam nodded. "Courtyard."

"The central one?"

"It's the only space big enough for her."

"Not ideal but it's what works."

A turn, a stairwell, a dash across the east training hall. Twice they pressed into shadows to avoid patrolling instructors. The silent alarm had mobilized more than she expected.

They reached the vaulted doors and slammed them shut. Wyatt threw his weight against them with a grunt. "We've got maybe thirty seconds—"

A heavy thud jolted the frame. The hinges groaned.

Boots pounded on the stone to the far side.

Shouts echoed down the hall—too close.

Cam hissed, "She's not here yet."

"You said she'd be here!"

"I said she'd come—I didn't say when."

They tore through the courtyard doors, nearly stumbling into the open. Moonlight spilled over the expanse, cool and sharp against Cam's skin.

The sky above was empty.

No dragon.

Wyatt spun to face the door, he put a locking rune on it, but it wouldn't hold for long. "They're right behind us."

Cam scanned the skies, heart hammering. "Sylithra!" she shouted into the bond. "Where are you—"

I am coming.

Too slow.

The doors behind them exploded open.

Five instructors in cloaks stepped out, blades and spears drawn, each one thrumming with magic channeling along the metal.

"There they are!" one barked. "Do not let them reach the perimeter!"

Wyatt didn't hesitate.

He slammed both palms to the stone, and a wall of jagged earth erupted between them and the instructors, buying a few precious seconds.

Cam swept her arms out in a wide arc—wind howled forth, ripping through the glyphs. She followed it with a surge of water, crashing into the spell's core with the force of a breaking tide.

Then—

A thunderous roar cracked through the sky.

A shadow streaked from the clouds, descending like a storm given wings.

Sylithra landed hard, claws sinking into the courtyard stones, wings folding with a gust that scattered debris in every direction.

"You're cutting it close," Cam exhaled sharply. "You're late."

Sylithra's voice entered Cam's mind, low and dry.

You're dramatic, Sylithra's eyes narrowed at the chaos. *I had to shake three knighthood patrols and loop twice through the canyon. You're lucky I found an opening.*

She turned her molten gaze toward Wyatt. *And this one?*

"He's with me," Cam said quickly.

Sylithra snorted. *Fine. But he had better hold on.*

Behind them, one of the instructors was already getting back up, groaning.

Wyatt leapt onto Sylithra's back like he'd done it a million times and extended his hand.

"Come on."

Cam took it.

More guards were flooding the far side of the courtyard now—some from the barracks, some from the tower stairs.

But they were too late.

With a mighty leap and a snap of wings, Sylithra launched into the sky, scattering the last of the spell fire as her tail whipped past the roofline.

Valmira's Mystic Academy grew smaller beneath them.

And the hunt had begun.

The wind stung his cheeks, cold and sharp against the adrenaline still burning in his veins. He pressed closer to the curve of Sylithra's massive shoulder, one hand gripping the edge of a scale the size of a shield, the other braced just behind Cam.

She hadn't said a word since they launched into the sky.

Neither had he.

There was no need to.

But even in the silence, everything had changed.

Because now—after all the visions, all the dreams, all the flickers of her across time—he had touched her.

Held her arm as the vault buckled.

Watched her channel power with a force that shook the air around her.

And she hadn't vanished.

She hadn't blurred into smoke or light or memory.

She was warm. Alive. Magic-strung and furious and real.

Wyatt turned slightly, just enough to see the curve of her back in front of him, the wind tugging at strands of chestnut hair.

The pull that had haunted him since he was twelve was quiet now—but not gone. Just... changed. Less like a compass needle, more like a heartbeat.

She's real.

He hadn't been sure, even after all these years.

But now?

Now she was burned into his skin.

And something in him—quiet and aching—wanted her to look back. Just once. To see him. Not the rebel mage, not the dreamer, not the man with secrets.

Just him.

He exhaled slowly, the breath stinging cold in his lungs.

But this time, she did.

Cam's eyes flicked over her shoulder, catching his gaze in the moonlight. For a heartbeat, everything stilled—the rush of wind, the beat of their hearts, the vast sky around them.

Her lips quirked into a faint, knowing smile.

No words were spoken, but it was enough.

A silent acknowledgment that she saw him. Not just the observer, but the person beneath. The one who had held on through every vision and doubt.

Wyatt's chest tightened, warmth spreading despite the cold air.

He shifted closer, grateful for the moment. For the proof.

The faint glow on her wrist pulsed softly—a reminder of the shadow's mark and the power she carried.

She wasn't just a wielder of fire or water or earth or air.

She moved through all the elements—air, water, fire, earth, healing—and more.

They weren't just powers she commanded.

They were threads woven into her very soul.

And flying beside her now, Wyatt wasn't sure if he was part of a dream...

Or living the future.

◈ ☽✦☾ ◈

The wind was sharp at this height, cold enough to sting her cheeks, but Cam barely felt it.

Her fingers curled tighter around the book, its weight pressing against her ribs, a reminder of what they'd found—what they'd woken. But the heavier thing, the louder thing, was the silence inside her.

The pull was gone.

Not dimmed. Not quiet.

Gone.

Below, the Karethwyn forest stretched wild and endless, the kind of untouched that didn't care about kingdoms or vaults or bloodlines. Sylithra's wings beat steady above the treetops, her body a wall of warmth behind Cam. Familiar. Fierce.

Safe.

And yet, for the first time since arriving at the Academy, Cam felt... unmoored.

Not from fear. Not from confusion.

From clarity.

Because the moment the vault opened, something had shifted. Not in the chamber. Not in the runes.

In her.

She'd expected answers. Instead, she found him.

Her thoughts flickered back—Wyatt stepping from the shadows, eyes unreadable but drawn, like he had seen her before. Because he had. Over and over again. His magic had moved in time with hers. Not guided, not taught. Aligned.

It had not been perfect. But it had felt right.

And when he looked at her, she didn't feel like a weapon. Or a prophecy. Or a mistake.

She'd felt seen, and that scared her.

Why him? Why now?

And what did it mean that she already missed the ache of the pull? Cam glanced over her shoulder.

He sat close, pressed into Sylithra's shoulder just behind her, the wind threading through his dark curls. His gaze met hers, steady and quiet. No questions. No demands.

Just presence.

Cam looked away before he could see too much.

But the truth had already taken shape in her chest—wild and bright and terrifying.

She wasn't just running from unknown enemies anymore.

She was flying toward something else entirely.

Chapter 23: When Shadows Break

The communication stone went cold in Corin's pocket in the dead of night.

He didn't hesitate—slipped away from the war table without a word, ignoring the curious glances behind him. Moving into the shadowed corridor, he closed the heavy door behind him and activated the stone with a quiet breath.

Wyatt's voice came through, low and steady but edged with something sharp beneath the surface.

"Vault is open. She has the book. We're safe—for now. Something else woke up in there. I don't know what."

Then silence.

Corin stood still for a long moment, letting the weight of those words settle over him like a cold shadow.

The vault — sealed for generations — had finally been breached. Caerthalen's most guarded secrets now rested in the hands of the girl no one had expected.

She had done what Wyatt couldn't. What no one else could.

Corin turned the stone over in his palm, frowning.

But something was off.

Wyatt's voice was too calm — too measured. He was holding something back.

Good, Corin thought grimly. *He's learning.*

Unease settled in Corin's chest. No details about what exactly had "woken up," no names, no warnings. The silence spoke volumes.

Whatever it was, it had shaken Wyatt.

And worse — Cam hadn't just passed a test.

She had changed the game.

Corin looked out the narrow window toward the black forest line, where mist curled low to the ground. The night air felt charged, as if the world itself held its breath.

He'd known the vault would stir something ancient.

But he hadn't expected the girl to carry that burden alone.

Ben stood silent, one hand gripping the cold stone railing, the darkness wrapping around him like a shroud. The world outside the outpost was still—too still—and yet he felt the tremor beneath his skin: the spell unraveling.

For almost twenty years, the world had seen him as Anthony. Caerthalen, the Knighthood, and the Academy all believed Anthony had lived and Ben had died trying to save the child.

But the truth was different.

Ben had lived—hidden beneath Anthony's name.

The lie was crafted in secret, woven by Ben, Anthony, and a trusted mage to protect the most fragile and precious life: his daughter.

Isabella had died when Cam was only three weeks old.

Her loss had been sharp and immediate, but it couldn't stop what needed to be done.

Cam had to be hidden, shielded from a Capital desperate to control bloodlines, from an Academy sworn to maintain power through loyalty and order, and from a Knighthood tasked with enforcing their will.

They tried to erase the chosen one—the one who would undo the hollow legacy of Kaelith, the Hollow Prince.

But fate was not so easily bent.

Now, with the vault opened, the spell was broken.

Ben's breath caught as the invisible bindings fell away like ash in the wind.

Footsteps approached quietly behind him.

Corin's voice was low, serious. "You felt it."

Ben nodded, voice steady despite the weight in his chest. "The spell has shattered. They will know the truth now."

Corin's gaze was sharp. "Caerthalen, the Academy, the Knighthood—they'll come for her."

Ben's eyes darkened. "Then they will meet the daughter of Ben and Isabella. A daughter who belongs to no one," He turned to face Corin fully. "Isabella died before the lie ever took hold. But I lived that lie every day to keep Cam safe."

Corin's expression was heavy. "And now?"

"Now," Ben said, "we prepare. Because they will come with everything they have. And we will stand in their way."

He swallowed hard, the burden of decades settling deeper in his bones.

"But whatever happens," he added, voice quieter but fierce, "no one controls my daughter. Not Caerthalen, not the Academy, not the Knighthood."

Corin met his gaze and nodded slowly.

The future was uncertain.

But for the first time in years, Ben felt ready to face it.

The clearing was quiet, broken only by the soft rustle of leaves and Sylithra's slow, steady breathing. Wyatt slid down from the dragon's back, his legs stiff from the long flight, his mind still tangled in everything they'd left behind.

Cam moved with practiced ease, but there was a weariness in her steps—more emotional than physical. She stood near Sylithra, one hand resting against the dragon's flank, eyes scanning the woods like she was still expecting someone to follow.

Wyatt stepped up beside her, giving her space but not straying far.

For a long moment, neither of them spoke.

Then Cam broke the silence, her voice low. "Do you think they'll follow us?"

Wyatt exhaled slowly. "No. Not yet. They'll be scrambling—trying to understand what just happened. The vault... it wasn't just sealed. It was hidden. Protected by more than magic. You opened it like it was nothing."

"It didn't feel like nothing." Her tone was dry, but there was a weight behind the words. "Something happened in there. I still don't understand what I saw."

Wyatt looked down at his hands. "Me neither. But I saw your power, Cam. I felt it. You didn't just open a door. You stirred something awake."

She met his eyes, and for the first time since the flight began, she looked afraid.

"I don't want to be what they're expecting," she said. "Caerthalen, the Academy, even the Knighthood—they've spent generations trying to control people like me. And now..."

"They'll come," Wyatt said quietly. "Not right away. But they will. They'll want to know what you are. What you can do."

"And what I'll become," she finished for him.

He nodded once. "Yeah."

They stood in silence again, the weight of that truth settling between them like a second nightfall.

Finally, Wyatt looked at her—really looked at her—and said, "For what it's worth, I think you were meant to open that vault. And I think you were meant to survive it."

Cam didn't smile, but her eyes softened.

"And you?" she asked. "What were you meant for?"

Wyatt shrugged, a little breathless at her honesty. "Maybe... to make sure you weren't alone when you did."

She looked away, but not before he saw the flicker of something in her expression—uncertainty, maybe. Or something deeper. Something he didn't have words for yet.

But whatever it was, it felt real.

And right now, that was enough.

He didn't ask her if she felt it too—if the pull had changed for her the way it had for him.

Part of him didn't want to break the quiet between them.

The other part wasn't sure he was ready for her answer.

The trees stood like sentinels around them, tall and ancient, their leaves whispering secrets she couldn't quite catch. Cam crouched beside Sylithra, her hand resting lightly on the dragon's scales as her mind tried to settle.

She still felt like she hadn't fully left the vault. The silence it left behind echoed inside her—too vast, too heavy.

Wyatt's voice cut gently through the stillness. "I can contact my brother. Kaden can get us back to the Keep. Quietly. Before anyone notices us here."

She looked up at him, surprised by how steady he sounded. Not emotionless—just... calm, grounded.

"Kaden?" she asked, blinking. "Wait—he's your brother?"

Wyatt gave a small, almost sheepish nod. "Yeah. Surprised you didn't notice."

Cam tilted her head, brow furrowing. "I didn't. You two don't exactly... advertise it."

He gave a short laugh. "We don't try to hide it, just—different paths, I guess. He's my little brother. Only by a few minutes."

Her eyebrows rose. "You're twins?"

"Fraternal," he said. "We're both twenty. Born on the same winter morning, but we've always felt more like opposites than twins."

Cam shook her head with a faint smile. "Huh. I never would've guessed. But now that you say it... it makes sense. Sort of."

Wyatt smirked. "We get that a lot."

Cam's eyes drifted down to her wrist, tracing the faint mark there she hadn't dared to think about since the vault. The mark pulsed faintly, not with her rhythm but with something deeper. Hollow. Watching. When she looked up again, she caught Wyatt watching her—steady, quiet, and somehow reassuring.

She cleared her throat and spoke softly, "You trust him, then?"

Wyatt smiled, steady and sure. "Always. He's my brother."

Cam returned the smile, a weight lifting from her chest. "Then I'm glad he's with us."

She considered that for a moment, then returned her gaze to the dark treetops above. "That means we'll have to move soon."

"Not right away," he said. "We've got a little time before they realize where we are. And even less before they try to trap us here."

Cam didn't respond immediately. She stared out into the trees, her thoughts unraveling faster than she could follow.

The Academy had nearly suffocated her. The vault had changed her. The things she saw, the way her magic responded... none of it was normal.

She didn't feel like herself. She didn't know who that self even was anymore.

But Wyatt...

Her eyes flicked toward him again.

He didn't hover, didn't crowd her. He just stayed close enough to feel solid. Real. Like someone who had chosen to be here, not because he had to—but because something in him refused to be anywhere else.

Somehow, it felt right to be near him.

It felt safe.

Not because he had all the answers. But because he didn't pretend to.

And maybe that's what she needed right now—someone who wouldn't force her to be more than what she was in this moment.

Wyatt glanced toward the thick trees beyond. "It'll be a little while before Kaden can get here. You should rest while you can."

Cam leaned against Sylithra's warm side, her cloak wrapped tightly around her as the quiet of the forest settled. The dragon's breathing was slow and steady; her massive body curled protectively behind Cam like a living shield. The stars above peeked through the shifting canopy, and for the first time in days, there was no need to move. No need to hide.

And yet, her thoughts wouldn't rest.

She hadn't allowed herself to think about him much—not after she arrived at the Academy. Once she'd passed the entrance trial, she threw herself into the role they'd given her. She worked harder than expected. Helped where she could. Took the extra tasks no one else wanted. It was easier to be useful than to feel.

But at night, when the hallways emptied and the lights dimmed, her mind drifted back.

Ben.

Her father.

The words still caught strangely in her chest.

The man who raised her—who tucked her in at night and brought her honeybread when she was sick—wasn't who she thought. And the man who was her biological father wasn't dead. He had been alive all along, watching from the shadows. Hiding truths like they were too sharp to be held.

She hadn't wanted to hear what he had to say.

She hadn't trusted herself to hear it.

But now, lying here beneath a canopy of whispering trees with the cool air against her cheeks, she realized something: she didn't hate him.

Not really.

She was angry—yes. Hurt. Betrayed. But beneath it all, she understood why it had been easier to lie. To let her believe he was someone else. To shield her from the weight of his past.

And still... she deserved more than half-truths.

So many questions swirled in her mind. About her mother. About the mark. About the magic. About him.

She hadn't gotten any answers. Not yet.

But four months at the Academy had given her one small piece of resolve: once she was back at the outpost—if they made it back—she would listen. Even if she wasn't ready to hear what he had to say. Even if it hurt. Even if she stayed angry.

She owed herself that much.

Even if he didn't.

A low hum stirred through her thoughts, warm and ancient.

You are thinking very loudly, Little Flame.

Cam's eyes fluttered open. Sylithra's golden eye was half-lidded, but the dragon's mind was as alert as ever.

"Sorry," Cam whispered.

Sylithra's body shook. In Cam's mind she heard the dragon chuckle. *Do not apologize. I would rather hear your thoughts than your silence.*

Cam hesitated. "So, you knew about him. That he's..."

A pause.

I suspected. I did not know. Not with certainty. But I felt it—long before you did.

"And my mother?"

I did not know her, Sylithra said gently. *But I have seen the fire in you, and I believe she must have burned just as brightly.*

Cam swallowed hard, her throat tightening.

"I don't know what I'll say to him."

You do not have to know. Just go. Speak. Listen. That is enough.

She nodded slowly, brushing a hand over Sylithra's scales.

There is another, Sylithra said, her mind-voice deeper now, tinged with something older than thought. *The quiet one who watches you. He smells of ancient blood as well. Twisted roots and old light.*

A pause.

Stay by his side, Little Flame. There is more to him than he knows—even now.

Cam frowned slightly, glancing toward Wyatt where he sat just out of earshot, watching the trees. She didn't answer Sylithra—not right away.

But her hand didn't leave the dragon's side.

The forest was quiet now, cloaked in stars and the hush of breath shared between survivors. Sylithra rested, curled like a mountain beside them. Cam leaned against her, half-asleep, and Wyatt kept watch nearby, still too wired to rest.

He didn't know what tomorrow would bring. But he knew this moment—this stillness after the storm—was rare.

Then the air to his left shimmered, flickering like heat rising from stone. Wyatt stood instantly, his hand brushing the hilt at his hip—until he felt it.

That familiar pull. Not the one that had haunted him for years, but the bond of shared blood.

Kaden stepped from the light with a grin, boots crunching quietly on the moss.

"Took you long enough," Wyatt said, tension easing from his shoulders.

Kaden raised a brow. "Teleporting into an unfamiliar forest isn't exactly a stroll through the courtyard. Hard to pinpoint your location with all these trees. Good thing I was looking for you."

Wyatt smirked. "Perks of being twins."

"Exactly." Kaden gave Cam a small nod. "You ready to go home?"

She blinked up at them, weariness in her face but resolve behind her eyes.

"As ready as I'll ever be."

Wyatt held out a steadying hand as Kaden began drawing the teleport sigils in the air—lines of white light forming a spiral, then stretching outward in a pattern only trained eyes could follow. The spiral pulsed once, the air tightening like it held its breath—then flared.

"Stay close," Kaden said.

A horn sounded in the distance—low and heavy, carried on the night air. The sound threaded through the trees like a warning.

Cam stiffened, her hand instinctively pressing over the faint mark on her wrist. Wyatt caught the flicker of fear in her eyes, and it twisted something in his chest.

His own jaw clenched, eyes narrowing toward the dark horizon. "They've already started searching."

Kaden cursed under his breath, the lines of his spell work burning faster in the air. "No time to waste—they're closer than I thought."

Sylithra lifted her head sharply, golden eyes blazing as her wings flared once in warning, every line of her body coiled to fight.

The horn sounded again, closer this time, vibrating through the ground beneath their boots.

Wyatt reached for Cam, his fingers brushing hers as the spiral flared—light rising to swallow them before the shadows could.

They appeared in darkness again—but this time, it was warm and familiar. Lanterns glowed low along the stone paths, casting soft light across the outer edge of the dragon roost where they had appeared. Down the slope, the outpost flickered with torches—its towers and walls alive with the quiet hush of night.

It was late. The air was still. And for once, the silence was a blessing.

They were home.

Wyatt released a breath he didn't know he'd been holding. Sylithra's heavy steps echoed behind them as she moved into the clearing, wings stretching once before folding tightly against her sides.

Cam stood still for a moment, eyes scanning the ridgeline and rooftops, taking in the reality of being back.

He watched her closely.

He didn't say it—but something in him felt steadier just standing near her. Like the worst of the storm had passed.

And though he had a hundred questions, he said only one thing:

"We made it."

Chapter 24: The Things they Carry

Ben sat beside the fire, his breakfast growing cold in his hands. The sun was well into the sky now, though he hadn't noticed the time. The morning was quiet—too quiet for the storm still churning in his chest.

He hadn't slept.

Not since he felt the spell lift.

It had been subtle, like a veil sliding off his skin, but he'd known it instantly—his identity, his truth, no longer hidden. The lie he and Anthony had bound in magic so long ago had finally cracked. And in its place came clarity... and fear.

He'd replayed his conversation with Corin more times than he could count. The disbelief. The anger. The moment Corin realized everything Ben had buried. Everything he'd kept hidden from except his closest friend. It was all out now—at least between them.

But it didn't ease the ache.

Across the field, the outpost moved as it always did—quietly, efficiently. But Ben felt separate from it all. Like he was watching it through glass.

Four months.

Four months since Cam had left for the Academy.

Every day of it carved new worry into his bones. Every day he fought the urge to leap onto Skylith's back and fly straight to that stone tower on the cliffs. Not as a soldier. Not as a rebel. Just as a father.

But Corin had kept him grounded—literally and emotionally.

Updates. Quiet ones. Private. Just enough to let Ben breathe.

She passed the trial.

She's been accepted.

She's working hard.

She's being watched, but she's holding her own.

Ben clung to those words like lifelines. And still, they weren't enough.

He exhaled, setting his untouched plate aside. Across the field, Skylith lay curled in the grass, sun warming her flame-touched scales.

You have not spoken to her, Skylith said, voice brushing across his mind like smoke.

Ben glanced her way. "Didn't have the words."

You never do. But you find them when it counts.

He sighed. "She doesn't owe me a conversation."

No. But that doesn't mean she won't come. You are her father. Even if you wore another man's name.

Ben looked down at his hands. "It's not just the name. It's everything I hid."

To protect her. That matters. Even if she doesn't see it yet.

He stared at the fire. "I thought about going after her every day."

I know. I felt it in your mind. You wanted to fly.

A faint smile tugged at the corner of his mouth. "And you were always ready."

Always.

Ben's response caught in his throat—but he didn't get the chance to speak. Footsteps approached, fast but measured, and a familiar voice followed.

"Ben?"

He turned.

Tessa Rhalis stood just outside the fire circle, breathless but calm. Her dark curls were windblown, and her eyes held something between relief and urgency.

"She's back," she said.

Ben stood before he realized he'd moved.

"Cam's here," Tessa clarified. "She arrived late last night—with Wyatt. And Sylithra."

His heart kicked against his ribs.

Alive. Safe. Here.

Four months of silence of buried truths and restrained longing, unraveled in a single breath.

He didn't ask where she was. He didn't ask what had happened.

He only asked, voice rough:

"...Does she want to see me?"

Tessa hesitated—just a second.

"She said... when she's ready."

Ben nodded slowly.

He hadn't earned her forgiveness. But maybe he could earn the chance to try. That would have to be enough.

◈ ☽ ✦ ☾ ◈

The walls in the outpost blurred at the edges.

Cam moved through the halls like a shadow, answering when spoken to, nodding when needed, but barely there. She had surrendered the book. Spoken briefly to Corin. Listened—kind of—while others filled her in on the state of things. None of it landed.

She was too tired.

Not the kind of tiredness that sleep could fix. The kind that hummed under her skin, a magical drain so complete she couldn't even feel the weight of it anymore.

She thought she was fine.

She thought she was standing.

But then the world tilted.

Just a little. A bend in the hallway. A soft slip in the floor. She blinked, opened her mouth to say something—and everything went black.

The last thing she felt was warmth against her shoulder. Hands, catching her before the stone could.

And a voice—quiet, panicked, familiar.

"Cam—hey, hey—"

Then nothing.

◈ ☽ ✦ ☾ ◈

She woke to the smell of earth and old parchment.

The room was unfamiliar. Dark wood walls. A table scattered with maps. A spare bed across from her own, tucked neatly in military fashion. A dragon scale—pale white and polished smooth—resting on a low shelf.

Her body ached.

Not like pain. Like absence. Like something had drained her dry and left only bones and skin behind.

Her wrist tingled faintly. The mark pulsed once beneath her skin—soft, deliberate, like it remembered her even in sleep. She tugged her sleeve down without thinking.

Then she saw him.

Wyatt Valehart sat beside the bed, one hand resting loosely on the edge of the mattress, the other rubbing the bridge of his nose like he'd been sitting there for hours.

He looked up as soon as she stirred.

"You're awake," he said, too fast.

Cam blinked. "What..."

"You collapsed," he said gently, like the words might bruise her. "In the hall. You overextended yourself."

She tried to sit up. He reached out automatically, steadying her with a hand to her shoulder—but didn't press when she remained still.

"I'm fine," she murmured.

"No, you're not," he said, more firmly this time. "You haven't rested since the vault. Not really. You've been burning through magic nonstop—channeling, summoning, resisting that thing in the chamber... Cam, you pushed yourself past what your body could carry."

She looked away, heat rising to her face. "I didn't mean to."

"I know." His voice softened again. "But you don't have to carry everything on your own."

She exhaled, gazing at the ceiling beams above. "Where am I?"

"My quarters. Well—mine and Kaden's," he said. "Corin said it was the best place for you, at least until you can stand on your own again. It's quiet. Safe."

"Corin knows I passed out?"

Wyatt gave a half-smile. "You dropped in front of half the corridor. I think it's safe to say everyone knows."

Cam groaned and buried her face in her hands. "Great."

He chuckled softly, then hesitated. "You scared me."

That pulled her eyes back to his.

"You shouldn't do that again," he said. "Fall over without warning. Makes it hard to look cool when I catch you."

Despite herself, Cam let out a breath of laughter. "I'll give you a warning next time."

There was a moment of silence.

"You caught me?"

"I did," he said with a small shrug. "Reflex. Lucky timing."

"Thank you," she said quietly.

His gaze lingered on her, something unreadable behind it. "You don't have to thank me."

His gaze flicked briefly to her wrist. The mark was still there—faint but pulsing softly like it carried a heartbeat not her own. The memory of the vault came rushing back, sharp and heavy. For a moment, she almost hid it again, but his jaw had already tightened.

"It flared when you collapsed," he said quietly. "Whatever that thing was... it hasn't let go."

Cam looked away. "It's just a mark."

"Marks don't burn like that," he murmured. But he didn't push.

A silence settled between them—not awkward, just full. She wasn't sure if she had the strength to keep talking, but she didn't want him to leave, either.

"Get some sleep," he said after a moment. "We'll deal with everything else later."

Cam nodded and let her eyes drift shut again. This time, she didn't fight it.

She was safe.

And someone had stayed.

The fire in his quarters burned low, casting gold into the shadows of the stone walls. Ben sat cross-legged on the floor, a leather pouch open beside him, its contents spilling onto the rug in delicate loops and glints.

He ran the woven cord between his fingers again, checking each knot, each twist. The pattern wasn't perfect—his hands weren't built for delicate things anymore—but it was solid. It would hold.

At the center of the bracelet, nestled in the braid like a quiet secret, was a small pearl. Soft white, almost moon-pale. It had once belonged to Cam's mother—Isabella had worn it on a ribbon around her throat during festivals, kept it in a drawer wrapped in velvet when not in use. It was the only piece Ben had kept after she had died.

And now it would belong to Cam.

He hadn't meant to enchant it, not at first. It had just... happened. Out there in the forest, when he'd first started working on it by firelight while she was asleep beside Skylith. A quiet spell, old and strange, had come to him like muscle memory. One that would hum quietly against Cam's wrist, invisible unless needed—but if ever she called out, truly called out, the bracelet would find whoever she needed.

A guardian's enchantment.

The kind only family could cast.

Ben's fingers stilled. His throat tightened.

Through the narrow window above his cot, the stars wheeled steady and sharp in the black sky. He didn't need a chart to know what night had just passed. The balance point—when night and day met as equals.

The fall equinox.

Cam's birthday.

She turns twenty.

He hadn't even realized how close it was, how quickly the seasons had slipped while she was gone. He'd been counting every day since she left for the Academy—sharp, sleepless measures of absence—but somehow he hadn't counted this one.

And he still hadn't spoken to her.

He clenched the bracelet gently in his palm, thumb brushing the pearl. And not for the first time he imagined her—wild and curious, too bright for the life she was given.

And now she was at the heart of something ancient and powerful. More than he ever imagined. More than he ever got to witness.

His heart twisted.

He stood slowly, folding the bracelet into the pouch and tying it shut with a firm knot.

Just as he slipped it into his coat pocket, a knock landed at his door.

He turned. "Come in."

Kaden stepped inside, boots damp from the grass, eyes serious but calm.

Ben's stomach dropped. "What happened?"

"She's okay," Kaden said quickly, holding up a hand. "She's resting. She overextended herself magically. She passed out, but it wasn't serious. Wyatt caught her before she hit the ground."

Ben's legs nearly gave out from the rush of relief. His hand gripped the edge of the table to steady himself. "She passed out?"

"Pushed too far," Kaden repeated gently. "We don't know the full extent of what happened in the vault, but from what Wyatt told me... it took a toll. She didn't notice it until it hit her all at once."

Ben was already reaching for his coat again. "Where is she?"

"She's safe. Wyatt's with her. Corin had her brought to our quarters—figured it'd be quieter there than the healer's wing, and less... public."

Ben paused, the urge to find her still thrumming beneath his ribs. "I should go to her—"

Kaden stepped forward, placing a steady hand on his shoulder. "You will. Just not yet. She's sleeping. Deeply. She needs to rest first."

Ben exhaled hard through his nose and let his hand fall from the doorknob. "Right."

"She's in good hands," Kaden added. "Wyatt hasn't left her side."

Ben nodded slowly, the tension in his shoulders giving way to exhaustion. "He's a good kid."

Kaden lingered at the door a moment longer, eyes sharp despite his calm tone.

"She's strong," he said. "But she pushed too hard. Overextended herself."

He paused, then added, more carefully. "She's a lot like you, actually. Quiet fire. Carries too much without saying a word."

Ben looked up sharply, but Kaden didn't flinch.

"I've only seen that kind of magic a few times," Kaden continued. "And bloodlines don't lie, do they?"

A small shrug. "Anyway. My brother's with her. She's safe."

Ben swallowed thickly.

Kaden cleared his throat. "Corin wants to see you. He's in the command room. Said whenever you're ready."

"Now's as good a time as any," Ben murmured.

He cast one last glance toward the pouch in his pocket, his thumb brushing the knot.

Tomorrow, he'd give it to her.

Tomorrow, he'd try.

But tonight... he'd breathe.

And hope she slept peacefully.

The Academy halls were too quiet.

Valerie kept her head down as she moved through the west corridor, boots tapping lightly on polished stone, every instinct on edge. The usual hum of controlled chaos—late students, whispered spells, instructors barking orders—was gone. Replaced by something colder. Sharper.

Fear.

She felt it in the way the younger students clustered together. In the glances cast toward every passing instructor. In the way no one said Cam's name out loud.

She didn't blame them.

Cam Layton and the quiet one with the distant eyes had vanished in a blaze of forbidden magic and dragonfire. The courtyard still smelled of scorched stone. The vault was sealed again, tighter than ever. And the instructors... they were unraveling behind closed doors, though none of them would admit it.

Valerie had seen the sigils light up in the tower. She'd felt the alarm go off—ancient, thick with power. She knew something massive had happened.

And she knew, with a deep knot in her gut, that Cam was at the center of it.

Good, she thought.

Because someone needed to shake this place awake.

She stopped outside the library steps, scanning the shadows for any sign of Alex.

Cam had left a note. Valerie hadn't needed to read it to know. She could feel it in the way the wind stirred the empty training fields that morning. Something had shifted.

And now? Now she had work to do.

She wasn't the hero. She wasn't chosen. But she was still here. And someone had to stay behind and start pulling the threads loose from the inside.

Valerie slipped into the library without a sound.

The main floor was dim—only a few orbs of reading light floating above abandoned tables. Shelves loomed like quiet sentinels, but she didn't stop to admire the spines like she usually did. Instead, she moved quickly through the eastern aisle, past histories and healing manuals, past the untouched dust of the old Valmiran records.

Straight to the back wall.

A ward shimmered faintly across the archway there—barely perceptible unless you knew how to look. She glanced over her shoulder, listening. No footsteps. No breath. Just the creak of old wood settling and the beat of her own heart.

She pressed her hand to the sigil carved into the stone.

For a moment, nothing.

Then—a flicker. The faintest pulse of recognition, residual access from her father's position before he was demoted. It wouldn't hold long, but it didn't need to.

Footsteps echoed down the corridor behind her. She froze, pulse quickening. Two instructors passed the mouth of the hallway, their robes brushing the stone, their voices sharp and low. She couldn't make out the words, but the cadence was enough: agitation. They were rattled. Watching. Searching.

Valerie pressed tighter against the archway, holding her breath. The ward shimmered again, thinning just as the voices grew faint. She slipped through before either could look her way.

The Restricted Archive smelled of dust and old binding glue. Ancient scrolls and forgotten grimoires lined the upper shelves, some sealed in iron cages, others chained to marble pedestals. This wasn't just forbidden knowledge—it was curated forgetting. Everything dangerous. Everything powerful. Everything inconvenient.

She made her way down the aisle, past bloodline compendiums and political blacklists, until she found what she was looking for.

A thick, spine-cracked volume bound in faded red leather:

"Elemental Convergence: Anomalous Lineages and Multi-Aspect Mages."

She stared at the title for a long moment.

They'd tried to erase this. Not destroy it—too risky. Just... bury it. Hide it behind fear and silence and ancient wards. But Valerie had grown up around secrets. She knew how to listen when things stopped being said.

Carefully, she slipped the book into her satchel, muffling the shifting pages with a practiced hand. Then she turned, moving quickly back the way she came—pausing only once, near the threshold, to look back.

It felt like crossing a line.

It was a line.

Valerie exhaled softly, then stepped back into the corridor, letting the silence swallow her.

Let them look the other way.

She was done waiting for permission.

Chapter 25: Dreams Of Memory

The world felt hushed, wrapped in autumn.

Cam stood before a cottage—small, sturdy, its stone walls moss-lined and hidden beneath a canopy of flame-colored leaves. Smoke curled gently from the chimney. Ivy curled around the windows. Everything about it felt tucked away, protected, secret.

She didn't remember walking to the door.

Didn't remember pushing it open.

But suddenly, she was inside.

The fire crackled softly in the hearth. The scent of fresh herbs and warmed wool lingered in the air. Wooden beams stretched low above her, and just beyond the firelight, in a cozy corner of the room, two figures sat together.

Ben sat on a stool, his back braced against the wall, legs stretched out before him. He looked younger—tired but calm in a way she'd never seen before. Cradled in his arms was a newborn wrapped in soft cloth, impossibly small.

Cam's breath caught.

A woman rested nearby on a narrow bed—Isabella. Her hair, dark and damp with sweat, spilled across the pillow. Her face was pale but peaceful, her smile weak but radiant.

"She's here," Isabella whispered, voice rasped and full of awe. "She's finally here."

Ben let out a shaky laugh, brushing his thumb gently over the infant's cheek. "She's so small."

"She won't stay that way," Isabella murmured. "She's going to be fierce. I can feel it already."

The baby let out a tiny, stubborn wail.

Ben chuckled softly. "Sounds like you."

Isabella closed her eyes for a long moment, then opened them again—fixed on the baby, on him. "We won't have long, Ben."

He tensed, jaw tightening. "Don't say that."

"We knew it when we came here. This house... it's a gift. A hiding place. But it won't last forever."

Ben leaned down, his forehead resting against the baby's. "Then we make the time count."

There was silence—thick, golden, and sacred.

Cam stood frozen in the shadows of memory, her heart thundering. The firelight flickered across her parents' faces, across the stone walls and wooden floor, as if the house itself remembered that moment.

"She'll have your heart," Isabella said softly, reaching out to stroke the baby's dark hair. "And your fire."

Ben leaned over and kissed his wife's forehead, voice low with reverence. "Her name is Camomile."

The baby quieted at the sound of her name.

Cam pressed her hand to her chest.

And the wind outside shifted—leaves brushing against the shutters like a whispered blessing. The stone house faded, piece by piece, as the dream slipped from her grasp...

Until only the warmth remained.

The scene shifted and the fire crackled softly, casting long, flickering shadows across the worn wooden floor. Cam didn't recognize it—this place, this quiet—but her breath caught when she saw him again.

Ben.

His jaw tense as he paced the narrow room. He hadn't removed his traveling cloak, hadn't touched the tea growing cold on the table. His eyes were sharp, distant, full of dread. Like he'd already lost something.

This had been their meeting place. He and Isabella. Their safehouse. But something had gone wrong—Cam could feel it in her chest, the way dreams often brought emotions before understanding.

A knock broke the silence.

Ben moved fast—hope and terror warring in every step. He threw open the door.

Anthony stood there.

His clothes were travel-worn, his face pale. But in his arms—wrapped tightly in soft blankets—was a baby.

Cam.

Ben stared. "Where's Izzy?"

Anthony's voice cracked. "She's gone."

Ben staggered back a step. "No—"

"A Veilborn," Anthony said grimly. "Shadows clung to it like fog. I tried, Ben. I did everything I could, but she was already—" He swallowed hard. "She made me take Cam. Told me to find you."

Ben reached for the bundle with shaking hands. The baby stirred, barely a sound.

Ben froze. His shoulders hunched, breath hitching audibly. His fists clenched, knuckles pale, before forcing them open to take the baby.

Cam felt the tremor in his arms, the way his chest tightened around each shallow breath.

"I wasn't there," Ben whispered. "I should've been there."

"I know," Anthony said quietly.

The dream held the moment in aching stillness, and even without knowing why, Cam felt the loss curl cold and sharp inside her, catching in her throat. She could feel the sting of tears as she watched, desperate to move, to speak—but she was only memory here. Only witness.

The scene dimmed, flickering like candlelight underwater.

The fire went out.

The room grew colder. The air heavier. She was back in the small cottage house again—but now, weeks later.

The cradle sat in the corner, tiny and quiet. Ben stood by the hearth, unmoving. Anthony beside him.

And a third figure entered.

An old man in plain robes lined with silver thread. His hair was white, pulled back, and his eyes were pale blue, nearly colorless—like mist trapped in glass. A mage.

Ancient. Quiet. Steady.

Cam had never seen him before, but her dream-self knew he was one of the last loyal to the truth. A hidden ally to Ben and Anthony. One of the few who still remembered the world as it had been before the lies.

"You understand what this will do?" the mage asked.

Ben nodded, his jaw tight.

"It won't just hide your names," the mage continued. "It will bury the truth from the world. Your memories will remain intact—but no one else will remember them as they were. To the world, the lie will become truth. Only you two will carry what's real."

Anthony exhaled slowly. "We're ready."

The mage looked at Ben.

"You will believe the lie enough to keep the world convinced. The bond between you will hold the truth steady. But only in silence. To everyone else... Anthony is Camomile's father. You are a family friend."

Ben stared at the cradle. "She'll hate me when she finds out."

Anthony placed a hand on his shoulder. "She won't. Not when she understands why."

"She deserves to be protected without everything about her past being rewritten," Ben muttered. "But I don't see another way."

"You're not doing this for you," Anthony said. "You're doing it for her. And for Isabella. You know what they'll do if they find out who Cam is. Who you are."

Ben gave a short, broken nod.

The mage stepped forward, lifting both hands.

Runes of light spun slowly between his palms—silver and deep blue, threaded with memory and silence. They shimmered like constellations, then stretched outward in thin spirals of binding magic.

"Then kneel," the mage said.

Ben did.

So did Anthony.

The runes descended like starlight through water, wrapping around them. No flash. No sound. Just a hush, deep and sacred.

Cam saw memories flicker inside the spell—herself, cradled in Isabella's arms. Firelight and laughter. Loss. A tiny necklace with a pearl. A man's promise.

Then the light sealed.

The spell was cast.

Ben blinked slowly as the shimmer faded. His eyes looked the same—but different. Like something had dimmed behind them.

Anthony stood. Straightened. Smiled faintly.

Ben's hand drifted to the edge of the cradle. His fingers curled there for a long moment, like he couldn't quite remember why.

But his smile—soft, flickering, proud—remained.

Cam felt the world begin to fade again.

But just before the dream dissolved, she heard his voice—not in the dream, but in herself. A memory inside her blood.

Ben's voice, low and full of ache:

"I never stopped loving her. Even when I couldn't remember why."

It wasn't a vision like she'd had before. Not a prophecy. It felt older than that—like memory stitched into her blood, waiting to be remembered.

Cam startled awake, her breath catching in her throat as if she'd surfaced from deep water. The remnants of the dream clung to her skin—warm firelight, Isabella's voice, Ben's silence. The weight of memory not hers but carried like a birthright.

She blinked up at the ceiling—stone, smooth, dimly lit by a lantern resting on a nearby shelf. The room smelled faintly of parchment, old pine, and something familiar: earth magic. Grounded. Real.

Wyatt and Kaden's quarters.

It came back to her in pieces—the way her magic had faltered, the way her knees had buckled, Wyatt's arms catching her just before the dark pulled her under. He'd brought her here. Said she'd overextended herself.

The book. The vault. The flight.

Everything was catching up with her now, all at once.

She shifted slightly under the blanket tucked around her and turned her head.

Wyatt sat slouched in the wooden chair across from the bed, one arm draped over the side, his head tilted awkwardly against the wall. Asleep, though not deeply. His brows were still faintly drawn, as if he hadn't stopped worrying even in rest.

She watched him for a long moment.

Her chest still ached from the dream. From the truth buried beneath so many layers of silence and magic. But here, in the quiet of this room, the ache was softer. Less sharp.

Less alone.

She pulled the blanket up to her chin and stared at the ceiling once more.

Ben had wanted to protect her.

Anthony had helped him.

A memory spell… a false identity…

And yet, what had reached her tonight hadn't been lies.

It had been love.

Love carved into truth, even when the world wouldn't remember it.

She closed her eyes, letting the warmth of the blanket and the steady rhythm of Wyatt's breathing anchor her again.

Tomorrow—later—she would face what came next.

But for now, she let herself be still.

And she let herself believe, just for a moment, that maybe… she'd never truly been forgotten.

The air was crisp, the kind of cold that clung to the edges of fall—sharp and clean, with golden mist still clinging to the treetops.

Cam walked slowly through the outposts outside paths, her boots crunching over half-frozen leaves, her breath visible in the morning air. Her hair was still slightly damp from where she'd scrubbed her face awake, trying to clear the remnants of the dream from her head.

Ben. Isabella. A cottage made of stone. A spell sealed in silence.

She didn't sleep much after waking up. Not really. Just lay there in Wyatt's bed with the truth curled like heat in her ribs. Her body ached from everything she'd overdone—too much magic, too little rest—but her feet still moved. She needed answers. And there was only one place to start.

She found him in the east clearing, seated by a firepit that hadn't yet been lit for the day. His back was to her, broad shoulders hunched slightly as he cleaned a curved blade with the kind of focused care that only comes from worry.

Cam hesitated.

For a breath, for a heartbeat, she considered walking away.

She'd left him without a word.

She'd judged him without understanding.

But the dream… the truth…

“Ben?”

Her voice came out softer than she meant.

He turned slowly. And when his eyes landed on her, he froze.

For a moment, neither of them spoke.

Then—he stood. Not quickly. Not dramatically. Just with the weight of everything unspoken in his posture. His gaze searched her face, but he didn’t come closer.

Cam stepped forward instead.

“I had a dream,” she said. “A memory. I think it was mine. I don’t know if someone gave it to me or if it was always there waiting. But I saw you. My mom. And Anthony. I saw the spell.”

Ben didn’t speak, but his eyes flickered—pain, relief, fear, all tangled together.

“I know you’re my father,” she said softly. “I know what you did to protect me.”

Still, he said nothing.

She swallowed. “I know you didn’t want to lie. But I needed you. And you weren’t there. That hurt. I also wanted you to know that... I don’t hate you.”

Ben’s hands dropped to his sides.

“I know,” he rasped. “I wanted to be there.”

“You should’ve told me sooner.”

“I wanted to.” His voice broke slightly, rough like gravel. “Every time it came close I wanted too.”

“Then why didn’t you?”

“Because I thought keeping the lie was safer than breaking it.”

Cam looked at him—really looked. He was older than she remembered. Not in years, but in weight. In the way sorrow etched itself into the corners of his eyes.

“I’m sorry,” she said.

Ben blinked. “For what?”

“For leaving. For not saying goodbye. For assuming you didn’t care.”

His throat moved like he was swallowing words.

“I was angry,” Cam went on. “Still am, a little. But I understand now. Or at least—I want to.”

Ben stepped closer, slowly, like he was waiting to be told to stop. When she didn't move, he came the rest of the way and stopped just in front of her and sighed heavily.

"You were born into a world that didn't want you to exist," he said quietly. "We did everything we could to keep you safe. And I've spent every day since... wondering if I did the right thing."

Cam looked up at him. Her voice was steadier than she felt. "You did the best you could with what you had."

"I wish it had been more."

"Me too," she said.

They stood there in silence for a long while.

Then Ben reached into his coat and pulled something from his pocket—a small, carefully wrapped bundle of cloth, worn but neat.

"I made something for you," he said holding it out. "Happy birthday."

For a breath, they simply stared at one another.

Cam blinked. *Birthday?*

She hadn't even remembered. Not this year. Not with everything happening. But he had.

And not just remembered—he'd known. Known the date, known what it meant.

He is my father, she realized again, the truth landing in a new, quieter place. Because how else would he have known? No one else had said a word. No one else could have.

And he'd made something for her. Not bought. Made.

A gift from someone she'd barely begun to let herself believe was real.

Then Cam crossed the small space between them and wrapped her arms around him.

Ben froze—only for a second.

Then his arms came around her, fierce and careful all at once, like holding something he thought he'd never touch again. He smelled like smoke and forest and something warm beneath it all—like safety.

And to Cam, it felt like home.

Not a house. Not a room.

Him.

She hadn't realized how much she missed it. Missed him.

For the first time in months, maybe longer, the ache behind her ribs eased.

"You know I don't expect you to call me 'dad,'" Ben said quietly.

She smiled "We'll work up to it," she said loud enough for him to hear.

When they pulled apart, Ben's eyes were glassy, but his voice was steady.

"Here," he said holding out the cloth bundle again.

Cam took it with both hands—then looked up at him and smiled a real smile.

She opened it without hesitation.

Inside: a woven bracelet, its threads tight and soft in alternating shades of dark green and deep silver blue. In the center, a small pearl—imperfect, luminous, unmistakably worn.

Cam's breath caught. "This was hers."

Ben nodded. "It was part of a necklace your mother wore. I kept it."

Her fingers trembled. "You made this?"

"Been working on it the day we left Brimclif," he said quietly. "The threads are enchanted—subtle, but strong. If you're ever in danger, it'll reach out. Call for help."

"From whom?" she asked, barely above a whisper.

"From whoever you need most," Ben said. "It'll know."

Cam swallowed the lump in her throat and slipped the bracelet on.

The pearl shimmered faintly against her skin.

Ben's face shifted—brows narrowing, voice tightening.

"Cam... your wrist."

She followed his gaze. Beneath the edge of the bracelet, the shadow-mark curled faintly across her skin. Still there. Still pulsing. Dark. Delicate. Wrong.

Her chest went still.

"I didn't notice that it was still there," she whispered. "I thought it had faded."

Ben reached out—but stopped just short of touching it, fingers trembling as if touching it might make it worse.

Whatever warmth had softened the air between them chilled.

Something had followed her out of that vault.

And it wasn't done yet.

◈ ☽✦☾ ◈

Wyatt stood at attention, but his hands wouldn't stop twitching. He kept them clasped behind his back, trying to mask the tension in his shoulders.

Corin sat at his desk, brows low as he studied a map of the western reaches, but he looked up the second Wyatt entered. His sharp gaze took one sweep of Wyatt's face—and he knew.

"You're not just here to give a report," Corin said.

"No, sir," Wyatt admitted.

"Close the door."

Wyatt obeyed. The latch clicked behind him. He took a breath.

"It's about the vault."

Corin's jaw ticked. "Go on."

"We found it. Or—it found her. The runes weren't just sealed. They were... watching. Guarding something. It opened for Cam, but the protections didn't fail. They reacted. To her. To me."

Wyatt shifted, his hands twitching at his sides again. "There was something else. Before the vault opened. Just for a second."

Corin looked up sharply. "What?"

"A symbol. On the floor in front of the door." Wyatt's brow furrowed. "It shimmered, almost like it was waking up. Then it pulsed once and disappeared."

Corin narrowed his eyes. "What did it look like?"

Wyatt stepped forward, reaching across the desk for a charcoal nub. He tugged a spare scrap of parchment toward him, then paused—recalling it fully. Then, in quick but deliberate strokes, he drew.

A ringed circle. A split triangle cradled inside. Wings flaring from both sides—perfectly mirrored.

He turned the parchment around. "This. It lit up before anything else happened. Right before the vault responded to her."

Corin stared at the drawing, his expression was unreadable.

Corin's eyes stayed on the mark Wyatt had drawn. His voice dropped lower, heavier.

"I've read whispers of this before," he said. "Not in reports—those were scrubbed long ago—but in fragments. Old journals, smuggled records from mages who vanished. They all hinted at something the Academy buried, something the Capital swore never existed. Veilborn weren't destroyed... only contained."

He looked at Wyatt then, the weight in his gaze sharp.

"I always suspected the Academy was hiding more than forbidden books behind their vaults. But I didn't want to believe it. Not until now."

"There was something alive in it," Wyatt added quietly. "I know how that sounds, but—it wasn't just a rune. It saw us. And whatever it was... it chose to open."

Corin stood slowly, crossing to the window, arms crossed tight. "What was inside?"

"Books. Relics. Runes I couldn't even begin to identify. But there was something else."

Wyatt hesitated.

"A shadow."

Corin turned back to him, face hard. "What kind of shadow?"

"Not human," Wyatt said. "Not living. It wasn't just reacting—it knew her. It marked her. Left something behind."

Corin's silence stretched.

Then: "Where?"

"On her wrist," Wyatt said. "It wasn't there when we left the Academy. But now it is."

"Did she notice?"

"Yeah," Wyatt said. "She noticed it right away. Felt it the moment it appeared. She hasn't said much about it since."

Corin exhaled slowly, then poured himself a measure of dark liquor from the side table. He didn't drink it. Just held the glass like it was an anchor.

Wyatt swallowed. "I don't know for sure, but—I think it was Veilborn. Or... a fragment of one."

Corin turned sharply. "You're sure?"

"I've seen visions. Glimpses. Always blurred. But this one—this thing—it recognized her. And when I pushed it back with light, it didn't retreat like it was wounded. It backed off like it remembered me."

Corin went still.

That silence again. This one deeper.

"I was afraid of that," Corin said finally.

Wyatt's pulse kicked up. "You knew?"

"I knew something was buried in the Academy. Something too old to destroy and too dangerous to leave unchecked. The Council never spoke of it—not directly—but I've heard whispers. In old records. Journals smuggled out of the Capital."

He walked back toward Wyatt, the tension in his steps barely leashed. "Whatever's marked Cam... we need to find out if it's watching her. Or waiting."

Wyatt nodded tightly. "If it's Veilborn, it may already be doing both."

Corin's eyes met his. "Then we don't have time."

The fire in the hearth crackled low, casting long shadows across the outpost's map-strewn war table. Corin stood near it, arms crossed, his expression tighter than usual.

Ben leaned against the wall, still wearing the coat he hadn't taken off since his talk with Cam.

"She's not telling you everything," Corin said.

Ben stiffened. "She just got back. Give her time."

"I'm not blaming her," Corin said quietly. "I'm saying something marked her. And I don't think she knows how deep it runs."

Ben's eyes narrowed. "The mark."

Corin nodded. "Wyatt told me. Right side. Wrist. Faint but constant. He said it happened when the vault reacted."

"Not just the vault," Ben muttered. "Whatever was in it."

Corin turned toward him fully. "He thinks it was Veilborn."

Ben went still.

That word hadn't been spoken aloud in years—not since the last known case had vanished deep into the darkest parts of the forest and mountains.

Veilborn are myth now. Nightmares dressed in shadow. But Ben had always known the threat wasn't dead—just sleeping.

Corin's voice lowered. "You were the first to warn us about what those shadows could become. Back then we didn't listen enough."

Ben's jaw clenched. "She said it was tethered. Whatever it was... it recognized her."

Corin nodded once. "We need to know if that mark is just a symbol. Or a link."

Ben's hands curled at his sides. "If it's a link... we've already lost ground."

The fire cracked again, a burst of ember light flickering across both their faces.

Cam stood just beyond the threshold; spine pressed to the cold stone wall.

She hadn't meant to overhear. She'd only come to find Ben again, maybe ask more about the past. But then she heard her name—and stayed frozen in place.

Veilborn.

Linked.

Marked.

The words echoed in her ears like stones dropped into deep water.

She looked down at her wrist, at the place where the shadow's touch still lingered in the shape of that dark sigil—faint, yes, but not fading.

Not gone.

She'd hoped it was just residue. Something she could train or wash or grow out of.

But now?

Now it felt like a tether.

Like something had reached through time and chosen her.

And for the first time since returning to the outpost... she didn't feel safe.

Not from them.

From herself.

Chapter 26: The Edge of Control

Cam lay curled beneath the blankets, the faint morning light spilling across the room in pale threads. She hadn't moved—not really. Not since waking from her restless sleep and the ache it left behind.

But even as she stayed still, she felt them.

We are near, Little Flame.

Sylithra's voice echoed gently through her mind—low and steady, like a mountain exhaling.

Another presence stirred, sharper, brighter.

You're different. Something shifted in you. That was Skylith. She always sounded like sparks beneath iron—warm but edged.

Cam closed her eyes tighter. "I know."

You have crossed a threshold, Sylithra said. *Your power is changing. Awakening beyond the shape you once knew.*

"Then why does it feel like I'm losing control?"

There was a pause. Then Skylith answered, more serious this time: *Because it's not control you need. It's understanding.*

Cam pressed her hand to her chest. "I don't know what I'm becoming."

Not becoming, Sylithra corrected softly. *Remembering. Magic this old doesn't bloom—it returns.*

The room felt colder then. Like the truth had pulled the warmth from the air.

Sylithra's voice grew deeper, the bond vibrating with something ancient.

Something is waking in you. Something ancient. And it is not patient.

Cam swallowed hard, her throat tight. Slowly, she shifted the blankets aside and sat up, her fingers moving almost unconsciously to her wrist.

The mark was still there.

Not darker. Not brighter. Not anything, really.

Just... there.

She ran her thumb across it.

It wasn't burning. It wasn't fading.

A memory etched into her skin—of power, of shadow, of a truth she hadn't asked for.

She closed her eyes again, letting the silence return. But the dragons' words echoed in the spaces behind her ribs.

She was changing.

And she didn't know how to stop it.

Ben stood just outside the blacksmith's awning, polishing the edge of a blade he didn't really need to fix. His eyes weren't on the steel—they were on the girl across the field.

His daughter.

Cam moved like a ghost of herself. Every step was careful. Every motion contained. It was the same way Isabella used to walk when something was unraveling inside her.

Too controlled. Too quiet.

She sent a jet of wind into a stone target. It cracked down the center. Too strong for the control she was trying to fake. Her jaw clenched, but she didn't say anything—just moved on like nothing happened. Ben's eyes caught the faint flicker at her wrist—the mark. It pulsed once, subtle, wrong, like a heartbeat that wasn't hers. She tugged her sleeve down before anyone else could see, but not fast enough. He knew it was still there. Still waiting.

Ben exhaled through his nose and set the blade down.

She's not fine. And she doesn't want me to see it.

That stung. But he understood it too well.

She had not had time to be a daughter. And he hadn't been there to let her be one.

◈ ☽ ✦ ☾ ◈

From the watch platform, Tessa stirred a wooden spoon in her bowl, though her bowl beside her was long empty. Below, the training rings sprawled across the packed earth, their borders marked by weathered posts. The clang of steel and bark of orders carried easily up to her. She watched Cam with narrowed eyes. The wind flicked her hair around her face, wild and restless. The same wind Cam had summoned.

It hadn't calmed since.

Tessa set the spoon in the bowl beside her and leaned against the stone battlements.

You can always tell when air mages are off, Tessa thought. *They don't float. They storm.*

Cam hadn't laughed—really laughed—since she got back. She smiled, sure. Gave her signature sarcasm here and there. But the real stuff? The glint in her eye when they were causing mischief?

Gone.

You can't just stuff that much power inside a girl and expect it to sit politely.

Tessa's fingers clenched around her scarf.

She'd wait. She wouldn't push. But when Cam cracked, she'd be there to catch the pieces.

Kaden sat at the edge of the strategy tent, flipping through mission reports, but his eyes kept drifting outside.

Cam was training again. Harder than she needed to. Precise. Cold. She wasn't flowing with the wind—she was forcing it.

She's trying to contain it, he thought. *That never works.*

He recognized the signs. Overextension. Withdrawal. Denial. He'd seen rebels fall apart faster from inner pressure than from any outside threat. He also understood on a more personal level as well.

And Cam? She had too much power and too little time.

He closed the file in his hands and rubbed the back of his neck.

I don't think she's afraid of what she can do. I think she's afraid of what it means.

Wyatt watched her from the tree line, arms crossed.

She hadn't looked his way once during training.

She didn't need to.

He felt it too. The weight in her magic. The tug in the earth when she summoned it. It wasn't just stronger—it was... louder. Like it had a will of its own.

Something's waking in her, the realization slid through his mind.

Sael, his bonded dragon, had said it. So did the others. But now Wyatt could see it too—in her movements, in her silence, in the way her hands trembled just after a spell was cast. Not from exhaustion. From restraint.

She's scared. She doesn't trust what's growing in her—and she doesn't trust us to hold her if she loses control.

He shifted his stance, a soft ache twisting in his chest.

She doesn't know we would stay anyway. That I already have.

Corin stood at the high window of the main hall, arms behind his back, eyes sharp.

He didn't need magic to see what was wrong.

Cam moved through the courtyard with the posture of someone trying to stay small—but power poured off her like waves from a storm-tossed sea. He could feel it even from here.

The leaders of Valmira saw what she could become before she was born. But even they didn't understand the scale.

He didn't understand it either.

But he recognized the signs of awakening. And war. Because when something that ancient stirs... the world stirs with it.

He turned from the window.

She doesn't know what she is yet. But others will find out. And they will come for her.

Corin reached for the sealed report left on the table. The one confirming the Council's fear:

Caerthalen had sent a scout. A mage-hunter. Quiet. Hidden.

But real.

Time was running out.

And Cam wasn't ready.

Cam sat on a sun-warmed bench near the edge of the stone wall, half-tucked beneath the shade of a crumbling archway. A cup of tea cooled in her hands. She hadn't touched it in nearly twenty minutes.

The sky was clear. Birds chattered. Somewhere in the field beyond the wall, someone laughed.

None of it seemed to reach her.

"Please tell me that tea is cursed," a voice said lightly.

Cam glanced up to see Tessa walking toward her, a crooked grin on her face. "You've been staring into it like it holds your future."

Cam gave a soft snort. "It's cold now."

"Tragic," Tessa said, plopping down beside her. "I'd offer to warm it, but last time I tried using wind to speed up the cooking, I created a small dust storm."

Cam raised an eyebrow. "A dust storm?"

Tessa put a hand to her heart. "An accident of great proportions. The rice went airborne. Kaden inhaled a grain. Wyatt still won't eat outside when I'm around. It was a mess. And they still made me eat it." Tessa glanced sideways. "You should've been there."

Cam's smile faded a little. "Yeah."

A silence passed between them. Comfortable, but heavy.

Tessa tapped her thumb against her leg. "Are you sleeping alright?"

Cam gave a vague shrug. "Not really."

"You've been... off." Tessa hesitated. "I mean, more than usual. And I know 'brooding forest cryptid' is kind of your thing now, but still."

Cam gave her a flat look.

Tessa raised both hands. "Joking. Kind of."

Cam exhaled slowly. "I'm just... trying to keep it together."

"Who said you have to do that all the time?"

Cam looked away. "If I don't, I'll fall apart."

Tessa's voice softened. "Then maybe let someone catch the pieces. Even just for a while."

They sat there a few moments longer before Kaden's voice called from the edge of the walkway.

"You two planning to move, or are we all pretending the war has been canceled?"

Tessa didn't miss a beat. She raised a hand and made a rude gesture in his direction—casual, practiced, clearly fond.

"Keep talking, shadow boy," she said. "I'll lightning your smug ass straight into the ravine."

Kaden laughed, Tessa turned, already heading back toward the training ring.

Cam stood, brushing crumbs off her jacket. "Just needed a minute."

Kaden walked with her as they moved toward the back field, his hands tucked into his coat pockets, his expression casual—but not careless.

"You look like hell," he said without preamble.

Cam scoffed. "You and Tessa rehearsing that line or something?"

"Nope. Just obvious." He glanced at her sidelong. "You've been off since the Academy."

She didn't answer.

Kaden watched her in silence for a few more steps. "What did you see?"

"Nothing important."

He frowned. "Liar."

Cam pressed her lips together.

Kaden didn't stop walking, but his voice dropped lower. "We all felt something change. Wyatt. Me. Even Tessa. You came out different—and I don't mean tired."

Cam clenched her hands. "It was a vision. A memory. I don't even know if it was-." She cut herself off.

"Whose memory?" Kaden asked.

This time, she didn't dodge fast enough. Her breath caught.

Kaden's jaw tightened. "So, it was personal."

"I didn't ask to see it," Cam muttered. "And I didn't ask for this power, either."

He stopped walking, making her pause too.

"No one's blaming you for what you are," Kaden said evenly. "But if something's waking in you... we can't help if you won't tell us what we're up against."

Cam looked down at her boots. "I don't want to be something they're 'up against.'"

"You're not," he said. "But you might be something they'll come for. And that means we have to be ready."

His voice was calm. Measured. But it cut through the fog in her chest like a blade.

She nodded once—just enough to show she'd heard him.

Then they kept walking, toward the field, toward the fight she wasn't sure she knew how to win.

◈ ☽✦☾ ◈

The field behind the outpost had been cleared years ago for training—flat, packed earth rimmed with trees and stone targets. Usually, it buzzed with energy: laughter, banter, elemental sparks leaping through the air.

Today, it felt like the world was holding its breath.

Wyatt stood a few paces back, arms crossed, boots sinking slightly into the warm dirt. The wind was still. Even the birds had gone quiet.

Cam raised her hand and hurled a spear of water toward the stone circle. The impact shattered it—not just the target, but the ground around it. Fractures webbed outward in all directions. Water soaked into the earth, steam rising faintly from the heat her magic hadn't meant to summon.

No one spoke.

Kaden, standing beside Wyatt, tilted his head. "She's not holding back."

"She is," Wyatt murmured. "That's the problem."

Tessa lowered her hands slowly. The wind she'd summoned faded from the air. "She's been off all week. Her focus is sharp, but her energy's—"

"Wrong," Kaden finished.

Wyatt didn't correct him. He couldn't.

Cam's magic wasn't untrained. It wasn't unstable. It was trying to grow—and she was caging it. The result was a storm with nowhere to go but inward.

Her movements were tight, rigid. Her jaw clenched so hard Wyatt could see it from across the field. She didn't pause to breathe between spells and element summoning. She didn't center herself. She just kept going, like stopping might be worse than breaking.

Then came the earth spell.

She reached for the ground with one hand; eyes fixed on a new target. The dirt responded immediately—too immediately. It pulled, then erupted. Stone cracked like a gunshot, bursting outward in a wide arc. Shards sprayed into the trees. Kaden raised a ward instinctively. Tessa jumped back.

Cam didn't.

She stood in the debris cloud, spine stiff, arms trembling slightly at her sides. Then she turned—fast, sharp—and walked away from the group without a word.

Wyatt watched her go, his pulse tightening. Her shoulders were locked. One hand trembled openly now, and the other was jammed into her coat pocket like she could stuff her emotions down with it.

She paced near the tree line, muttering something too low to hear. Then stopped. A long breath. Another spell? No. Her head dropped slightly.

He saw the flicker then—on her face.

Not just frustration.

Fear.

Not of them. Not even of the magic.

Of herself.

Wyatt swallowed hard. He knew that look. He'd seen it in the mirror more than once, back when the visions had first started, back when he thought he might be going mad.

She was unraveling—and trying so hard not to let anyone see.

Wyatt took one step forward. Then another.

"She's scared," he said under his breath.

Kaden looked over. "Of what?"

Wyatt's eyes didn't leave her.

"...Herself."

Tessa let out a breath, shoulders slumping as she watched Cam crouch near the far edge of the field, pretending to tie her boot—just long enough to blink away whatever emotion was trying to claw its way out.

No one responded.

They didn't need to.

The silence was answer enough.

The dining hall was mostly cleared by the time Wyatt found her again. She sat near the back, a bowl of soup barely touched, shoulders slightly hunched like she was trying to disappear into herself.

He slid into the bench across from her and didn't say anything at first. Just let the quiet settle.

Finally, he said softly, "You're not fine."

Cam glanced up at him. "Never said I was."

"You don't have to," he replied. "I can feel it."

She blinked, surprised—but not annoyed. Just... wary.

"You're not the only one who notices magic shifting," he added. "Dragons do too. So do mages like me."

Cam toyed with her spoon. "It's not just stronger. It's different. Every time I reach for it, it feels like something else is reaching back."

Wyatt nodded. "I've felt that before. Like the power wants to move through you before you even know what to ask."

"That's exactly it," she said, voice lower now. "It's not just four elements anymore. It's like... I'm standing at the edge of something I don't understand. And it's pulling me forward."

He watched her carefully. "I know that the dragons noticed it. They said something's waking in you."

Cam's fingers tightened slightly on her spoon. "Syl and Sky said the same to me a few days ago."

After a beat, Wyatt leaned forward just a little. "I think Sael might be able to help."

She looked up again. "Your dragon?"

He nodded. "He's old. Over a thousand years. And he's seen a lot of magic come and go. The spiritual elements... the ones beyond the four, they're older than the Academy admits."

Cam's eyes narrowed slightly. "You believe that?"

"I do now," Wyatt said, voice steady. "After seeing you in that vault... I think you're not awakening to power the Academy taught us to fear. I think you're awakening to what they tried to erase."

She didn't speak for a long moment.

Then she said, "So I'm supposed to learn how to control something I don't understand with dragons and mages who don't even know what it is?"

He gave her a small smile. "Not alone, though."

Cam looked at him—really looked at him—and for a moment, Wyatt swore he felt that thread between them shift again. Not tense. Not burning.

Softer. Steadier. Still there.

She stood, pushing her bowl aside. "Alright. Let's go meet your dragon."

◈ ☽✦☾ ◈

The grove beyond the ridge was quiet, cloaked in the silver hush of early dusk. Trees bowed in the wind, their limbs casting long shadows over the mossy floor. Cam followed behind Wyatt and Kaden, her steps slower than usual. Every part of her ached—from too much magic and not enough rest—but it was more than exhaustion. Something was shifting inside her, and it hadn't stopped since the vault.

The moment they stepped into the clearing, the air changed—thick with old magic. The kind that didn't speak in words but in weight and memory.

Five dragons waited in the grove.

Cam froze; breath caught in her throat.

She didn't need introductions.

She knew them. Felt them.

They knew her, too.

Sael, regal and pale as moonlight, stood poised like a statue near the center. Tenebrin loomed darker than shadow to the left, obsidian scales shimmering like oil. Brontheus was draped along a sloped rock to the right, his deep green-black body coiled loosely, eyes steady and golden. Skylith paced slowly along the grove's edge, tail flicking like a restless ember.

And at the far side, half in shadow, Sylithra stood—silent and immense. Her scales shimmered black-blue beneath the dusk, the veins of gold glowing faintly. Watching.

Waiting.

We were expecting you.

Brontheus's voice came first—mossy, steady, and deep. The sound of ancient forests breathing. It echoed gently in Cam's mind.

Cam startled at the sound—not because it was a dragon's voice, but because she realized no one else had reacted.

Wyatt stood still beside Sael. Kaden's hand rested calmly on Tenebrin's side. Neither looked confused or surprised.

They couldn't hear.

Only their bonded dragons could speak to them. But Cam—she had always heard them all. A secret she'd carried since childhood, one Sylithra had only recently taught her to quiet when it became too much. Tonight, though, there was no blocking it. The voices pressed in close, deliberate, like they had been waiting for this moment.

Sylithra's mind brushed hers, warm and slow, like coals waiting to blaze.

You are not imagining it, Little Flame. The Cradle stirs in you. As it does in me.

"The Cradle...?" Cam had heard whispers—myths passed in old rebel records. The first line of dragons. The first wielders of spirit and storm and memory. Supposedly extinct.

But Sylithra had always been different. Her magic was older. Her presence was heavier. Now Cam understood why.

Tenebrin stepped forward, his tail curling.

You are not awakening to simple power. You are waking the old line. The Cradle. And the Veil feels it.

It's stirring, Brontheus added, his voice lower now. *The divide between realms is thinner. Every time you pull on your strength, something pulls back.*

Cam's hands curled into fists. "I didn't want this."

It doesn't matter, Sael said calmly. *It was already in you. Buried. Waiting.*

Footsteps behind her made Cam turn. Tessa stepped into the grove, her expression wary but calm. She moved to Brontheus's side, and the green-black dragon tilted his head, brushing his rider's shoulder gently.

Cam blinked. "You brought me here for this?"

Wyatt nodded slowly. "They wanted to meet you. They've been feeling the shift in the air since the vault. Since you started to change."

Sylithra's golden eyes narrowed.

The Cradle does not awaken on its own. It must be called. And something... or someone... has called it.

Cam's stomach turned.

"The vault?" she asked aloud. "You think that opened it?"

Part of it, Skylith answered, her voice sharper, brighter, more fire than the rest. *But not all. You carry something deeper. Your magic does not follow the rules. It bends them. Breaks them. And it's only just begun.*

Cam's voice wavered. "I can't control it. Every time I reach for an element, it answers with too much force. And the others—spirit, shadow, storm. Not just those but others too—they're... louder. I don't know how to use them."

You're not breaking, Brontheus said softly. *You're expanding. Your soul is growing to hold what the world tried to forget.*

Cam swallowed hard, heart beating faster. "I don't want to hurt anyone."

Tenebrin's eyes glinted.

Then stop pretending you're not powerful. Meet it. Learn to wield it. Or it will wield you.

Sylithra took a single step forward, her voice low and final and she said for the second time that week:

Something is waking in you. Something ancient. And it is not patient.

The wind shifted. Leaves rustled overhead. The grove went still.

Cam looked at the dragons, at Wyatt, at Kaden, and at Tessa. No one flinched. No one stepped away. None of them seemed ready to run from her—not even with all the fear bubbling in her chest.

The Veil was stirring.

The Cradle was awakening.

And she was the thread between them.

Chapter 27: Between Light and Shadow

Cam stood for as long as she could. Long enough to listen. Long enough to nod. Long enough to pretend she could carry it all without flinching.

But as the dragons shifted, wings folding and breath softening, and her friends began to murmur low among themselves, she turned away.

She couldn't let them see her break.

Not Kaden. Not Tessa. Not even Wyatt.

She walked a little ways off—just past the edge of the grove where the trees grew closer again, shadows longer, quieter. She braced a hand against one of the trunks, her other hand clenched tight, her nails digging into her palm.

They all said she was awakening. Changing.

They called it old, ancient, powerful.

But to her, it still just felt like drowning.

Her breath came fast and shallow. She squeezed her eyes shut—but it was no use.

A few tears slipped free.

She didn't sob. She didn't make a sound.

But the tears fell anyway, quiet and hot, tracing the edges of a fear she hadn't dared to name.

Footsteps approached behind her.

She didn't turn.

"I know what it feels like," Wyatt said softly. "Trying to carry something too heavy... and pretending it doesn't hurt."

Cam drew in a breath that trembled.

Then his hand found hers—gentle but steady.

Warm.

"I see you," he said. "You don't have to hold this alone."

She glanced back at him, her eyes still damp, and for a moment she let him see the storm behind them. All the things she didn't say. All the weight she couldn't explain.

And Wyatt didn't flinch.

Instead, he stepped closer—slowly, as if giving her time to pull away.

She didn't.

When he pulled her into a hug, she sank into it, her forehead pressing to his collarbone, her hands clutching the fabric of his tunic like a lifeline.

He held her like he meant it. Like he would stay as long as she needed him to.

And for the first time in days, Cam let herself lean into someone else.

Not as the chosen one. Not as the girl with too much power.

Just... herself.

They stood there, wrapped in silence, as the last of the light faded from the grove.

No magic. No pressure. Just the truth of a moment neither of them could name.

But even as she sank into the warmth, the mark beneath her sleeve pulsed faintly — a heartbeat not her own. No one else could feel it. Not even him. And she wished, just for a moment, that she could forget it was there.

◈ ☽✦☾ ◈

The council chamber was barely more than a hollowed-out stone room tucked beneath the Keeps' main hall—cool, one window, and just about soundproofed by layers of enchantment older than most of its occupants.

Corin stood near the table's head, one hand braced on the wood, the other curled around a mug of untouched tea gone cold.

Around him sat the most trusted voices of the rebellion. Captains. Scouts. Strategists. Ben. Kaden. A healer named Mirell who rarely spoke but always saw what others missed.

And still, the room felt too small.

Too still.

"They know," said Brayden, the youngest scout, his voice low. "The report came in this morning. The Academy and the Capital channels have flagged Wyatt and Cam as fugitives—unconfirmed location, but they're narrowing in."

Corin exhaled slowly through his nose. "How?"

"Unclear. The leak didn't come from us." Brayden shook his head. "But they're combing known rebel paths. Border activities picked up. A few names got flagged near the southern ridge—likely unrelated, but they're circling."

Corin's gaze flicked to Kaden, who stood in silence at the far edge of the room, jaw tight. He gave a brief nod, already calculating next steps.

"We're still safe," Corin said aloud, though more to anchor the room than convince it. "The Keep isn't on any map they trust, and the wards are holding."

"For now," Mirell murmured.

Ben hadn't spoken yet. He stood by the far wall, arms folded across his chest, shadowed by the lantern light. Corin knew that stance. It was the look of a man who'd spent the last four months fearing he'd lost his daughter—and now wasn't sure if getting her back had solved anything.

Corin cleared his throat, his voice quieter as he asked, "Do we have reason to believe they'll send a hunter?"

A silence.

Then Brayden nodded once. "I'd bet on it."

Corin didn't curse, but his fingers dug slightly into the table.

"Mage hunters are bound by border magic," Mirell offered carefully. "They can't step onto rebel-ground without triggering the outpost's defenses."

"Unless the defenses fail," Ben said finally. "Or someone inside lets them in."

A beat passed. Kaden's jaw ticked. No one denied the possibility.

Corin turned his head slightly toward Ben. "Then we prepare. Quietly. No panic. No movement that signals we're hiding something. We'll rotate patrols and tighten the perimeter—keep Cam's location limited to need-to-know."

He paused.

Then looked Ben in the eye.

"Is she ready?"

Ben's breath hitched.

He didn't answer at first. Just stared into the fireless hearth for a long second, as if trying to summon something from the stone.

Finally, his voice came—quiet. Honest.

"...I don't know if any of us are."

The words fell heavy.

No one argued. No one offered comfort.

Because they all felt it too.

The words left his mouth quieter than he'd meant them to—but no one asked him to repeat them. The silence that followed was louder than a battle cry.

Ben stayed near the wall, his arms folded, but his hands trembled slightly beneath the sleeves. Not from fear. From pressure. From the weight of too many truths, too many lies, and the fragile shape of the girl who now carried all of it like a cracked vessel still refusing to break.

Camomile.

She hadn't looked like a child when she arrived—she hadn't for some time now. But she'd collapsed within hours of setting foot back in the outpost. And that haunted him more than anything else.

Not because she'd fallen—but because she'd done it trying not to.

"Then we need to make her ready," Corin said, voice low but firm. "Whatever's stirring inside her... it's not waiting. Neither are they."

Ben nodded slowly. "She's strong. Stronger than she knows. But her magic doesn't follow the patterns we trained for. She's not just channeling—it's like she's being drawn forward by something older."

Mirell glanced up from her quiet notes. "You believe it's connected to the mark?"

Ben hesitated. His mind drifted—not just to the mark, but to the vision she must've had. The same power he'd seen glint in her eyes before she fell asleep. That raw, barely contained storm.

He nodded once. "The dragons feel it. So does Wyatt, so does Skylith... she won't say it outright, but she believes Cam's connection to the Cradle is awakening something that hasn't stirred in a very long time."

Corin rubbed his jaw. "The Veil."

Kaden, quiet until now, stepped forward. "And it's not just awakening. It's moving."

Ben looked at him. "How do you know?"

Kaden's eyes flicked toward the sealed window. "Because it's not just Cam who's dreaming about it."

The room went still again.

Brayden shifted uncomfortably, but Corin didn't flinch. "Then we prepare for two fronts. One visible. One not."

He looked back at Ben. "Keep her steady. Whatever it takes."

Ben nodded again—but his chest felt tight.

Because deep down, he knew: Cam wasn't a soldier. She wasn't a weapon.

She was becoming something entirely new.

And the world wasn't ready for her.

He only hoped he would be.

No one seemed to notice the weight behind the words he had just uttered. Or maybe they did, and no one had the stomach to ask.

He didn't blame them.

Corin's gaze lingered on him for a moment too long, sharp as always. Kaden held it, steady on the outside. Inside? He was barely keeping the pieces together.

Because he wasn't just dreaming about the Veil.

He was feeling it.

The same way his shadows stirred on nights when the sky felt too still. The same way they whispered now at the back of his mind—uneasy, cold. Like something was watching through them.

He hadn't told anyone. Not even Wyatt. Not about this part.

Wyatt knew about his shadow magic, sure. So did Corin. But the rest? The dreams?

No. He hadn't dared speak it aloud.

Because shadow wielders weren't supposed to exist. Not anymore. Not unless—

Unless you were Veilborn.

Kaden clenched his jaw and shifted back slightly from the center of the room, content to fade into the edges again. Like his power always tried to do. Like he always did when he was thinking too hard.

He hated this part. The uncertainty. The not knowing what he was.

He knew Wyatt's visions made him doubt reality some days. Kaden had seen his brother wake from nightmares with words on his tongue he didn't understand. But Wyatt's gifts felt rooted in light, in insight. They didn't cling to you like cold silk and whisper things when no one else was listening.

Kaden's did.

At night, when everyone else slept, he could see movement just beyond the edges of the trees. Shapes that vanished when he tried to look at them head-on. And in the dreams...

Cam wasn't alone.

The Cradle stirred, yes. But so did something else. Something older than even the dragons remembered.

And the worst part?

The shadows recognized it.

Like they remembered something he didn't.

Kaden looked across the room again—at Ben, at Corin, to the door that led outside where Cam was likely trying not to fall apart.

If she was waking up to something ancient, so was he.

And if they didn't figure it out soon...

It might not matter who was chosen and who was cursed.

The Veil didn't care.

It just wanted in.

The late morning sun filtered through the tree line as the five of them stepped into the open field—flattened earth and scattered stone targets waiting, silent as ever. It should've felt routine. Familiar.

But Cam's stomach twisted tight.

They meant well—Tessa, Wyatt, Kaden, Ben. All of them here to help her. But she felt like a thread pulled taut between too many hands—every movement threatening to unravel something.

She didn't tell them that. Just nodded, rolled her shoulders back, and stepped to the center of the field.

Ben's voice broke the silence, calm but commanding. "One element at a time. Nothing fancy. Just control."

Cam nodded again.

Control.

She could do that. Probably.

She started with earth—the easiest, usually. Just a shield. Something small. She raised her hand, focused on the flow beneath her feet. The ground obeyed—but not gently. A slab of rock burst upward with a thud, too fast, too high, slamming into the target with a crunch that made Wyatt wince.

Kaden shifted slightly at her side, jaw tight. He scanned the grove's shadows once, quick and almost unconscious, before focusing on Cam again.

"Okay," he said slowly. "That rock has some issues it needs to work through."

Cam cracked a strained smile, even as her pulse thundered in her ears.

Ben crossed his arms. "Try again. Half the force."

Cam turned to the next test—air and fire combined. She wasn't sure why Ben had lumped them together. Maybe he sensed what she did: that the lines between them were already blurring.

She lifted her hand.

Wind surged—sharper than intended. A sudden gust swept through the field, toppling two training dummies and whipping Tessa's hair into a cyclone.

"I just brushed my hair for once!" Tessa shouted, half-laughing.

Cam laughed—but out of the corner of her eye, Kaden's smile didn't quite reach his eyes. His gaze lingered on the grove's shadows, thoughtful. Distracted.

Before Cam could respond, the air shimmered—and heat bloomed.

Fire cracked from her palm, wild and sudden. It caught the wind's current and roared to life, veering off-course toward the crates near the tree line.

"Cam—" Ben started.

The crates exploded in a whoosh of orange light. Wyatt moved fast, slamming his hands to the ground to raise a stone wall that caught the edge of the blaze.

As the wind stirred and the grove fell still again, something slid through her mind that wasn't her own—deep, velvet-dark, and edged in warning.

Too much light draws its shadow, rider.

Cam stiffened. That wasn't Sylithra.

Her eyes flicked toward Kaden, but he didn't look at her. His jaw was tight, his thoughts shuttered. If he'd heard it, he gave no sign.

But she had.

Ben circled in from behind, his jaw tense but his eyes steady. "Cam. What's happening?"

She didn't answer.

Couldn't.

Even her breath felt stolen.

Water. One more.

She pulled at the wellspring inside her. Tried to shape it.

But it flooded.

A stream of water slammed downward—not at the target, but at the roots of a nearby tree. The bark split with a violent crack as the tree ripped free, crashing into the dirt with a ground-shaking thud. Cam hadn't aimed for the roots. She hadn't aimed at all.

Cam staggered back, breath ragged, arms trembling.

She hadn't meant to. She never meant to.

The tree hit the ground with a deafening crash.

The shadows at the forest's edge stirred—too deep, too dark for the hour.

Kaden stepped forward instinctively, one hand out—not to stop her, but to contain something. His palm flexed once. A ripple of darkness curled at his fingertips, subtle and smoky, before vanishing.

No one else noticed.

"Cam—" Wyatt said, stepping forward.

She backed away. "No. I—I need to stop. I can't—"

"Hey," Kaden said, moving in front of her before she could bolt. "We're here. You're not alone in this."

"I just uprooted a tree, Kaden."

"Yeah," Kaden said with a wry look. "But it had a good run. You saw how it was leaning."

Cam let out a breath that almost, almost turned into a laugh.

But the pressure in her chest hadn't left.

"It's not just control," she whispered. "It's like... it's not mine anymore. It's too big. Every time I reach for it, it pulls back harder. Like there's something else in there. Something I can't name."

Tessa stepped beside her and rested a hand gently on Cam's back. "You're not broken."

"But I don't know what I am."

For a beat, no one spoke.

Then Wyatt did.

"It's not the elements," he said softly. "It's that you're using them like they're the only ones you know."

Cam frowned, still turned half-away. "What's that supposed to mean?"

"You're not just elemental anymore," he said gently. "Your magic's changing. And I think it's trying to show you what else you can do."

Cam blinked. Looked at him.

Wyatt glanced toward Ben. "She's not overreaching. She's approaching it the wrong way. The Academy teaches control by containment—but she's not meant to contain this."

Ben's brow furrowed. Thoughtful.

"You've seen how second and third abilities work," Wyatt said. "They're not clean or narrow. They're layered. Emotional. Alive. She's treating a sea like a river and wondering why it doesn't obey."

Kaden gave a low whistle. "So... what you're saying is that she needs to unlearn the Academy?"

"I'm saying she needs to listen to what's waking up inside her," Wyatt replied. "Not cage it."

Cam stood there, her magic still humming wild beneath her skin. A storm she couldn't cage. A part of her still wanted to run. To bolt from the weight of it all.

But the other part?

The part that stayed?

That part was still standing here. With them.

"I can't do that alone," she said finally.

"You won't," Wyatt said, without hesitation.

Kaden clapped a hand on her shoulder. "You've got all of us. Whether you like it or not."

Tessa smirked. "And if you accidentally toss me into a tree again, I'll just make sure you land first next time."

A breath escaped Cam before she could stop it.

Not a laugh. Not quite.

But close.

The fear hadn't vanished. The pressure was still there.

But for the first time that morning, it didn't feel bigger than her.

Cam didn't remember walking back inside.

She must've said something to the others—Thanks, or I need a minute, or maybe just a look. But her feet had carried her away from the training field before her mind caught up. Now she stood alone at the edge of the clearing, hands clenched at her sides, pulse still pounding from the magic that refused to stay still.

The sky above had begun to darken, streaked with rose and bruised lavender. A wind tugged at the loose strands of her hair like it was trying to pull her somewhere—somewhere quiet. Somewhere away.

Cam exhaled and sat on the steps just outside the barracks, elbows on her knees. Her fingers still tingled from the last surge of power. She wasn't sure if it was from adrenaline, or the effort of not crying in front of everyone.

She hated feeling like this. Like she was slipping out of her own skin. Like every step forward only exposed how far she still had to go.

Something deep inside her—old and pulsing—was changing.

She didn't know what to call it. She only knew she wasn't the same girl who walked into the Academy four months ago. And she couldn't go back to pretending she was.

Footsteps approached behind her. Familiar.

She didn't need to look up to know who it was.

Wyatt.

He paused just a few feet away, and for a moment, he didn't speak. Just stood there with that quiet presence she was starting to recognize—not loud, not demanding, just there. Steady.

Then his voice, low and sure.

"Want to go for a walk?"

Cam hesitated, then nodded. "Yeah. Okay."

They didn't speak at first. The path wound through the woods like a memory, soft with fallen leaves and fading sunlight. The quiet between them wasn't awkward—it was watchful. Careful. Like neither of them wanted to shatter the calm that hung in the trees.

It wasn't until they reached a stretch of tall pines that Wyatt finally broke the silence.

"I used to walk like this when I couldn't sleep," he said, eyes on the dirt path ahead. "Out by the border of the outpost. Kaden always thought I was training, but I just... couldn't stay still."

Cam glanced at him. "You get that feeling often?"

"Only when something's coming." He looked at her now. "And lately, it always feels like something is."

She swallowed. "Yeah."

A beat passed. Then he asked, softer this time, "Can I ask you something real?"

Cam blinked. "Sure."

"What does it feel like for you? That pull. The thing that brought you to the vault. To here."

She took a long breath, surprised at how quickly the answer rose. "It used to feel like a magnet in my chest. Like I was constantly being nudged toward something, even when I didn't understand it. But now..." She looked up at the canopy, where the sky was turning purple. "It's quieter. Not gone—just... softer."

Wyatt's voice was barely above a whisper. "Do you think it changed because you found what you were looking for?"

Cam hesitated.

"I don't know. Maybe it wasn't a thing I was being pulled to," she said. "Maybe it was a person."

She didn't look at him as she said it. And he didn't respond right away—but the air between them shifted.

Wyatt's hand drifted to the back of his neck, fingers pressing at the skin like he could ease away a tension that had nothing to do with the day's weight. His jaw tightened, then softened again, as though words fought for space but never found their way out. He drew in a breath, held it, and let it slip away in silence.

Cam watched him carefully, sensing the heaviness in what he hadn't said. Part of her wanted to ask, to press—but she caught herself. He was holding it close for a reason. So, she let the silence stand, respectful of whatever he wasn't ready to share.

Still, a faint knot lingered in her chest, a quiet uncertainty that left her wondering what truth lay just beyond reach.

They walked a little farther until the trees thinned, and the sound of water grew louder. The ground sloped gently downward, and then the ravine opened before them—a stretch of jagged stone and slow-moving river, reflecting the deepening sky.

A fallen tree arched out just enough to make a seat. Cam climbed onto it, balanced easily, and sat. Wyatt followed.

Above them, the first stars began to appear.

Cam exhaled slowly. "You know what's weird?"

"What?"

"I'm scared of what I'm becoming... but when I'm with you, I don't feel like I'm breaking."

Wyatt turned his head slightly, watching her through the dark. "You're not breaking, Cam. You're transforming. That's different."

She didn't reply—but her shoulder brushed his. And she didn't move away.

Then Wyatt shifted slightly and cleared his throat. "Hey, I... uh, I meant to give you something earlier."

She looked over at him, curious.

He reached into his pocket and pulled out a smooth stone, small enough to fit in her palm. A single rune was etched into the surface—faint but carefully carved.

"I heard it was your birthday last week," he said, a little awkwardly. "And I wanted to give you this. It's just... a rock. Nothing fancy. But the rune is for grounding. I thought... maybe it would help. When things get too loud."

Cam turned it over in her fingers, lips parting slightly. "You carved this?"

He nodded. "Yeah. Took me a few tries not to mess it up."

"It's perfect," she whispered, and something about the way she said it made the night feel warmer.

She tucked the stone carefully into the pocket of her coat, then let her fingers rest there like she didn't want to let go of it just yet.

"Thank you," she said softly. "Really."

Wyatt smiled but didn't say anything else. He didn't need to.

Then, like a ripple beneath her skin, something shifted.

Her breath caught.

"Cam?" Wyatt asked, straightening.

She blinked, but her eyes were distant. Her fingers twitched, and the world around her blurred—shadows folding in at the edges.

Wyatt's hand found hers instinctively. "It's okay. I'm here. You're not alone."

And then the vision took her.

The stars stretched. The trees dissolved. And the cradle and the Veil called her name once more.

Chapter 28: The Edge of Memory

Cam's fingers clenched around Wyatt's hand—and then went still.

It happened so fast, Wyatt barely had time to react. One second, she was beside him on the log, warm and breathing and steady. The next, her body slumped sideways, her eyes glazed over, unseeing.

"Cam—?"

He caught her before she could slip from the edge. Her head fell lightly against his chest, her weight unfamiliar but not heavy. Her skin had gone pale. Cold. Too cold.

"Camomile—hey. Look at me."

No response. But he knew exactly what was happening. He'd experienced it happening to himself so many times before. But hers was different—like it pulled her too far, too fast.

Wyatt lowered her gently to the leaf-covered earth, his heart pounding. He knelt beside her, cradling her head, one hand trembling slightly as he brushed her hair away from her face.

Her breathing was shallow—thin and uneven, like a dream slipping away.

"Come on, Cam. Stay with me."

He pressed his palm to her chest, just over her heart.

Still beating. Steady. Present.

But wherever she was now... it wasn't here.

Wyatt closed his eyes for a moment, grounding himself. He knew this place—this space between. Visions could pull you under like riptides, fast and brutal. They never asked permission. They took what they wanted and left you hollow.

But this wasn't a normal vision. Not like his.

This was deeper. Wilder. Like something ancient had reached through her bones and called her away.

"Don't stay gone too long," he whispered, barely audible over the wind. "Please."

He shifted to sit behind her, holding her against his chest, arms wrapped around her shoulders so she wouldn't be alone if she woke afraid. His coat draped over both of them, and he rested his chin lightly against her temple.

The stars wheeled overhead. The ravine murmured quietly nearby.

And Wyatt waited.

Silent. Steady. Terrified. But still there.

There was no falling this time.

No tumbling through memory or being flung into someone else's life.

Just... stillness.

Cam stood in a realm that didn't follow the rules of the world she knew. Sky and shadow twisted together above her, light rippling like water across an endless rift in the earth. The wind carried no scent. The air shimmered with colorless magic, humming at the edge of sound.

The Veil Between.

She knew it instinctively.

Before her stretched a jagged rift—darkness and starlight churning in its depths, endless and slow. It pulsed, not like something living, but like something watching.

At its heart stood the cradle.

Stone, weathered by time. Cracked and coiled in ancient roots. Vines had overtaken most of it, but she could still see its shape—arched like a nest, low to the ground, pulsing faintly with silver-blue light.

She stepped toward it, breath shallow.

As she moved, her wrist tingled.

She lifted her arm. The mark glowed faintly—just like it had in the vault. Just like it had the first night she felt something wake.

The mark wasn't just reacting. It was answering. Like it knew this place. Like it belonged to it

A symbol flickered on the veil's surface—matching hers exactly.

Then, a voice—not hers. Not even quite human. Deep, feminine, and echoing from everywhere at once:

"You are of the Cradle. You have always been."

Cam froze.

The veil pulsed once, and the shadows around it shifted—parting like water to reveal a figure standing just beyond the roots.

Tall.

Clad in silver robes woven with starlight. His skin was pale, but not colorless. His features sharp. And his eyes... hollow, glowing faintly like lanterns without flame—light that wasn't of the world.

He smiled at her.

Not cruel. Not kind. Just waiting.

Like someone who had been waiting a very long time.

"You've walked the edge too long, Camomile Layton," he said. "The gate opens wider with each step."

Cam didn't move. Her pulse stumbled. He said her name like he'd carried it for centuries—like it belonged to him.. But she had no idea who he was. "You know my name."

He tilted his head. "I've known it for centuries."

Something in his voice tugged at her memory. Not recognition. Not fear. Curiosity.

"What are you?" she asked.

His smile faded just slightly.

"I am what was made to wait," he said. "And you... are what was made to wake."

The air shuddered around her.

"I don't understand," Cam whispered.

"You will."

The light from the veil flared suddenly—blinding.

Cam shielded her eyes, heart racing. The Veil itself trembled beneath her feet.

And then—

Darkness again.

Not void. Not fear.

Just the end of the vision.

Just before it slipped away completely, she heard the female voice once more, this time softer, almost mournful:

"It is calling you back."

And somewhere beyond the Veil, the Hollow Prince smiled—his eyes opening to the mark that had finally answered back.

Cam gasped.

It was sharp, sudden—like someone being pulled from deep water. Wyatt's arms tightened instinctively around her as she jerked upright, fingers clutching at his coat with white-knuckled urgency.

"Cam?" he breathed, eyes scanning her face.

She didn't answer right away. Her eyes were wide, unfocused, still somewhere far away. But she was breathing—shaky, shallow, alive. Relief surged through Wyatt like a wave, but it didn't steady his heart.

Then she whispered, voice raw and distant, "He was waiting for me."

Wyatt stilled. "Who?"

She blinked again, the tension in her limbs beginning to ease. Her head fell forward, barely catching herself on his shoulder. "I don't know... I don't know his name. But he was there. In the Veil. Watching."

Wyatt didn't speak. He just wrapped one arm tighter around her, bracing her against his chest like she might slip away again if he let go.

"You're back," he murmured. "You're okay. I've got you."

Her breath hitched, but she nodded faintly.

He could feel the tremble in her muscles. The way she leaned heavier against him—not from fear, but exhaustion. Whatever she'd seen... wherever she'd gone... it had drained her completely. Her legs didn't move when he gently tried to shift her weight.

She wasn't going to be able to walk.

"All right," he said softly. "We're done for tonight."

Wyatt closed his eyes for a moment and reached out—not with magic, but with thought.

Sael.

The name carried more than sound. It carried need.

Ten minutes later, the trees stirred—and the pale white dragon emerged through the dusk light like moonlight on mist. Sael moved with quiet grace, lowering his head when he reached them.

She is weak, Sael observed in Wyatt's mind, his mental voice calm but edged with worry. *The Veil drains more than magic. It takes memory, breath, time.*

"I know," Wyatt whispered.

Carefully, he gathered Cam in his arms. She didn't resist—just buried her face against his shoulder, her breath soft and uneven.

He stepped toward Sael and climbed onto his lowered forearm, settling Cam in front of him with one arm still around her waist.

"We're going home," he told her quietly, unsure if she even heard.

As Sael lifted into the sky, the trees vanished beneath them—and the stars wheeled silently above.

The council room at the back of the outpost was dimly lit, stone walls thick with silence and smoke curling softly from the hearth. A round table sat at the center—scarred, solid, older than the rebellion itself.

Corin stood by the window, arms folded, gaze like a hawk watching the dark treetops. Kaden leaned against the far wall, his expression unreadable. Ben was already seated, fingers steepled beneath his chin.

Wyatt entered last, the door clicking shut behind him.

"She's asleep," he said quietly. "Tessa's watching over her."

Corin turned. "And?"

Wyatt hesitated for only a second, then moved toward the table. "It was a vision. Deep. Stronger than anything I've ever seen or experienced myself."

Ben sat up straighter. "Was she in pain?"

"No. Just... gone. Like something pulled her too far, too fast." Wyatt exhaled, running a hand through his hair. "When she came back, she said one thing: 'He was waiting for me.'"

Corin's brow furrowed. "Who?"

"She couldn't remember clearly," Wyatt said. "But she mentioned a figure—tall, wearing silver, standing in the Veil. She said he smiled at her. And she said she heard a female voice that said..." He looked at each of them, the words lingering in his throat. "'You are of the Cradle. You have always been.'"

Ben's knuckles whitened against the table.

Kaden shifted from the wall. "I've heard that phrase."

Wyatt's head turned sharply. "What?"

Kaden nodded once. "Not in visions. In the shadows. Whispered. When I practice too close to the Veil's edge." His voice dropped. "It wasn't a voice I knew. And it wasn't mine."

Silence pressed against the walls of the room.

"What does it mean?" Wyatt asked. "Cradle—we keep hearing that word. The dragons mention it. The Veil responds to it. What is it?"

Ben finally spoke. "It's not a place. Not really. It's a bloodline. A legacy. The Cradle was the first root of magic—old magic. Before the Academy. Before the Knighthood."

Wyatt stared. "You knew this?"

"I didn't understand it until now." Ben looked tired. Older. "Sylithra comes from the last of the Cradle-bonded dragons. I thought the line ended with her. But now..."

Corin stepped forward, voice firm. "Now, we know it didn't."

Kaden crossed his arms. "And this silver figure—who is he?"

Wyatt shook his head. "Cam couldn't say. And I've only seen glimpses in my own visions. But he knew her. He knew her name."

Ben's jaw clenched. "Then he's been watching her for a long time."

Corin's gaze darkened. "Which means he's part of whatever force is waking with her. And we can't afford to wait and see what that force wants."

A pause.

Then Corin turned to Ben. "So, what do we do now?"

Ben stared into the fire, his voice low but steady. "We stop bracing for what might come—and start preparing her for what already has."

Corin stood slowly, the firelight catching in the lines around his eyes. "We move carefully. Quietly. No word leaves this room. If the Cradle is waking—and if something inside the Veil is watching—we need to be ready before it steps through."

Kaden crossed his arms, jaw tight. "And what if it already has?"

No one answered.

Ben didn't look at anyone—only the map spread on the table, his eyes fixed on the jagged tear drawn across the southern edge. A representation of the Veil. Of where Cam had gone. Of what might still be calling her back.

"She's not just powerful," Ben said quietly. "She's tied to this. All of it. The Cradle, the Veil, the prophecy they buried. If we lose her..."

"We won't," Wyatt said.

The others looked at him.

His voice was steady; his shoulders squared despite the exhaustion pulling at him.

"I've seen what she becomes," he added. "And it's not something that breaks."

Silence fell again—but it felt different now. Not hopeless.

Resolute.

Beyond the council chamber, the outpost lay quiet beneath the starlight. And somewhere in that quiet, Cam stirred in her sleep—unaware that pieces of the past were falling into place. That names long buried were speaking again.

Back in her room, Cam lay still—too tired to think, too restless to sleep. The vision tugged at her memory like a thread she couldn't follow.

She rolled up her sleeve and looked at the mark again. It wasn't glowing. It wasn't fading. Just there.

A reminder.

Not of danger.

But of something watching.

Somewhere, beyond the Veil, the Hollow Prince smiled—watching, waiting, patient as the mark he had left upon her skin.

Chapter 29: What the Shadows Wanted

The training chamber was quiet, save for the crackle of a single torch and the whisper of chalk dragging across stone. Cam knelt near the center, drawing a rune that kept slipping out of shape—its lines just a little too sharp, too heavy-handed.

Ben watched from a few steps away, arms folded, patient but alert.

"Too much pressure on the third arc," he said gently.

Cam exhaled sharply, blowing a strand of hair from her face. "I'm trying."

"I know," he replied. "But magic like this doesn't respond to force. It listens. When you stop trying to control it, that's when it listens."

She straightened slowly and turned toward him, eyes sharp. "Easy for you to say. You've had years to master this."

Ben didn't answer right away. Instead, he stepped forward, crouched beside the half-formed rune, and used one finger to soften the lines—rounding what she'd pressed too hard.

Then, without lifting his gaze, he said, "You know I was part of the Knighthood. But I never told you what I hid from them."

Cam blinked. "What?"

"I'm a fire mage, Cam," Ben said, finally meeting her eyes.

Silence.

Ben watched her stillness. For a second she didn't breathe, didn't blink—then her jaw tightened. A flicker of heat sparked in her eyes, quick as a flame catching dry kindling. Not rage. Not yet. But hurt. The kind he had expected—and dreaded.

"You—" She shook her head once, slowly. "You never even hinted."

The words landed sharp, but her voice carried more exhaustion than fury.

"I couldn't," Ben said. "It would've gotten me executed. Or worse—silenced. They don't tolerate mages among their own ranks, especially ones who could hide it."

Her voice softened but still carried weight. "You lied. To them. And to me."

"I did." He didn't flinch. "Because I thought I was protecting you. Not just from them—but from the burden of that truth."

Cam looked back down at the rune. "You should've told me."

"I know."

"I'm not mad," she said after a beat. "I'm just... tired of not knowing who people really are."

Ben's voice gentled. "I didn't tell you because I thought silence was safer. But truth doesn't stay buried, Cam. You have to meet it head-on, even when it's ugly. Even when it hurts."

She sat back on her heels, letting the words settle. "I'm starting to understand that. Truth doesn't wait. Just like your magic chose you."

Ben gave a quiet, wry smile. "Exactly."

Cam looked up again. "So... fire. What else?"

Ben lifted one brow. "Want to see?"

She nodded cautiously.

He reached into his coat pocket and drew a small coin. Holding it in his palm, he called a thread of flame—barely a whisper—and let it lick across his fingers. The fire didn't burn the metal. Instead, it danced around it like it knew its shape. Then, with a slow breath, he closed his hand—and when he opened it again, the coin had been reshaped into a tiny, intricate leaf.

Cam's eyes widened. "Metal?"

"My second ability," Ben confirmed. "Not as flashy as fire, but useful in ways the Knighthood never suspected."

She took the leaf gently from his hand, marveling at the detail. "It's beautiful."

"She said the same thing," Ben murmured.

Cam blinked. "Mom?"

Ben's expression shifted—gentled, nostalgic.

"She was the fiercest person I ever met. Smarter than any of us. More powerful than she let on. She walked into every room like she already knew the outcome... and half the time, she did."

Cam smiled faintly. "Sounds like someone else I know."

He chuckled. "You get more from her than you think."

There was a pause. A stillness between them.

Cam leaned in slightly. "Tell me more about her."

Ben looked towards the window, and something in him softened. "I met her before the war really started. She was undercover, working with the rebels while posing as an instructor. Anthony and I were on opposite sides back then. Corin saw the storm coming. Your mother? She was the storm."

Cam's breath hitched. "And you... followed her?"

Ben's voice was quiet. "I think I was already following the truth. She just gave me the courage to stop hiding from it."

Cam turned the leaf-coin over in her fingers. "She sounds like someone I would've liked."

Ben gave a sad smile. "She would've been proud of you."

Another silence, this one full, warm.

Cam turned back to the rune and traced it again—softer this time. Lighter. The lines held. Magic hummed through it like breath caught in still air.

Ben watched, pride flickering in his chest.

"You're getting it," he said.

Cam smirked faintly. "Guess I have a good teacher."

Ben laughed. "You have a stubborn teacher. And I have a stubborn student."

Her smirk faded into something quieter. "And maybe... a real father."

Ben didn't answer right away. He just looked at her. And this time, his silence wasn't because he didn't know what to say.

It was because she'd said everything that mattered.

And for the first time in a long time, they weren't chasing the truth.

They were standing in it.

A few days later Cam stood at the ravine's edge, wind curling around her jacket like it knew her name.

Below, the field stretched wide and golden with morning light, and beyond it—sky. Endless. Open. Waiting.

Sylithra landed beside her with a beat of massive wings, black-blue scales shimmering like ink lit from within. Gold veins pulsed faintly, alive with ancient power.

You are steadier today, Little Flame, Sylithra murmured, lowering her head. *Your mind does not fight as much.*

Cam pressed her hand to her dragon's jaw. "I'm trying."

Good. Trying becomes doing. And doing becomes knowing.

A burst of heat signaled Skylith's arrival, her reddish-orange wings flaring in a wide arc. She landed near Ben, smoke trailing from her nostrils.

Then came Sael—pale white, graceful, deliberate—cutting through the wind with Wyatt steady on his back.

Brontheus descended next, his forest-green form veined in black shadows. Tessa swung down halfway before they even touched the ground.

Last came Tenebrin, sleek and dark as obsidian, his wings whispering through the wind. Kaden dismounted in a fluid motion, already scanning the skies as if expecting trouble.

For a brief moment, they all stood together, dragons and riders. United.

Ben stepped forward with a smile and a folded map. "This isn't a joyride. You'll be flying in formation today. Not just side by side—but together. You need to know how to read each other in the air. If you can't move as one, you won't last long when it matters."

Tessa groaned. "So, this is a group trust exercise, just with more ways to fall to our death."

"Exactly," Ben said cheerfully.

Wyatt nudged Cam. "Don't look now, but I think this is his version of a pep talk."

Cam smiled, small but real.

Sylithra's voice entered her mind again—this time laced with something deeper, quieter.

Today, we open the bridge. You will not only hear me, Camomile... you will feel the others. Not through your magic—but through ours.

"What do you mean?"

But Sylithra was already moving, wings spreading as she launched into the sky.

Cam followed—one breath, one leap, one motion—and Sylithra carried her into the air with a surge that made her ribs ache with exhilaration. She let the fear drain from her limbs. She didn't need to force the wind to obey.

She was the wind.

The dragons fanned out into formation: Skylith leading, her flames trailing like streamers. Sylithra and Sael flanked her. Brontheus and Tenebrin covered the rear.

Cam felt the shift almost instantly.

"Focus." The voice wasn't spoken aloud—it slid straight into her mind.

Not Sylithra.

Wyatt.

She startled, nearly losing the flow of her breath—but then another presence filtered in, calm and amused:

"Relax, Cam. You're in. This is normal for us."

Tessa.

Cam's mouth parted. She glanced at Sylithra, wide-eyed. This wasn't like the voices she'd always carried in her head, quiet as breathing. This was deliberate. Shared. Chosen.

We dragons carry the thread between you, Sylithra said calmly. It is our gift. A sacred bond. And a secret the old bloodlines protected for centuries.

Cam nodded, breathless. *"But I thought..."*

The voices pressed sharp against her mind—too many, too close. She swallowed hard, instinctively reaching for the mental wall Sylithra had taught her months ago. She didn't shut them out completely, but dulled the edge, forcing the link to soften.

Not now, she thought to herself. *Not all at once.*

You can hear all dragons. But this... this is something only we can offer. And only to those we trust. Sael added from beside her.

They moved in unison now—not just riding but flying together. Cam didn't need to shout a command or guess who was shifting. She knew. They all knew. A rhythm passed between them—graceful, fluid, whole.

This was flight. This was family.

The sky was too still.

Too clear.

The kind of perfect that made your instincts itch.

Kaden had flown in worse conditions—stormfronts rolling like beasts across the sky, fires raining from siege towers, even that hailstorm outside Darneth that nearly took his left eye. But this... this was different.

It was quiet.

The kind of quiet that didn't settle—it waited.

High above the tree line, the dragons moved in near-perfect formation. Wings stretched wide, gliding on invisible currents like shadows carved from magic. For once, they weren't training for survival; they were breathing. Relaxing. Almost normal.

Tessa was laughing through the bond, cracking some smart-mouthed joke about Ben's idea of a "team-building flight." Wyatt grumbled back with dry sarcasm. Cam was riding Sylithra like she belonged up here—balanced, focused, calm.

And that was the worst part.

She was smiling.

Kaden's stomach twisted.

Tenebrin let out a low, vibrating growl beneath him.

Too open. Too far. The dragon's mindvoice was razor-sharp, tense. *The light here doesn't move right. Shadows stick where they shouldn't.*

Kaden's fingers tightened on the reins. *"I feel it too,"* he murmured aloud, more to himself than to Tenebrin. His eyes scanned the horizon—every ridge, every treetop, every drifting cloud. They were nearly at the edge of the territory Corin had deemed safe. A mistake.

The border wasn't a wall. It was a thread. And someone had tugged it loose.

"Pull in the formation," Kaden muttered over the mental link. *"Something's—"*

Kaden. Tenebrin's voice cut clean and cold. West ridge. Low. Moving fast.

A shadow peeled away from the distant clouds.

Not gliding. *Slithering.*

Kaden's pulse kicked hard in his throat. His air magic flared, unbidden, feeding his clarity. Every edge sharpened. Every heartbeat slowed.

The presence slid across his awareness like oil—slick, hungry, wrong.

Vorrakai.

No warning howl. No cry. Just the shape—a nightmare forged from old fear. Wings like serrated scythes. A mouth split too wide across a face with too many eyes. Smoke trailing its body like tattered thoughts.

"Vorrakai!" Kaden's shout split the sky and through the link. *"West ridge! It's hunting!"*

The laughter snapped into silence. His eyes never left the monster cutting through the clouds, its serrated wings tearing the light apart. Every nerve in him was locked on it, every ounce of instinct screaming to intercept.

He almost missed it.

A shift in the air—wrong, too quick. A screech split the sky behind him, jagged and sharp. Kaden twisted just in time to see the shadows break apart into shapes—five of them—winged, snapping, already closing. Mirebats.

Dammit. He hadn't even felt them until they were there.

Wyatt's voice hit the bond first, sharp and protective: *"Kaden—behind you!"* The fear wasn't for himself. It was for his brother.

Then Tessa's thought slammed through the link, urgent and clear: *"There are mirebats—five of them! Circling the rear—trying to split us!"*

Wyatt's curse echoed through the link. Ben's command followed like a blade: *"Form up! Tighten the line—defend the flanks!"*

Dragons broke from pattern instantly. Brontheus wheeled into position beside Sael. Skylith streaked higher, flames licking the wind. Sael was already diving, his wings folding tight.

But Kaden wasn't watching them.

He was watching it.

The Vorrakai sliced through the low clouds, obsidian and nightmare, a predator wrapped in sentient shadow. Its focus was absolute. It wasn't here to feed.

It was here to strike.

And it was heading straight at Cam.

She didn't see it. She was still balanced on Sylithra's back, windswept, unaware.

"CAM!" Kaden roared, power surging beneath his voice. *"Look out—!"*

But he already knew.

She wouldn't be fast enough.

Chapter 30: The Unmaking of Fear

Ben had seen monsters before. Real ones.

Not the kind whispered about in Academy lore or written into cautionary tales to keep children from wandering past the ward lines—but the kind that shouldn't exist.

He'd stood in the ash of fallen cities. Faced mages twisted by their own power. Watched the skies burn during the first breach at the Northern Wall.

But nothing—nothing—felt like this.

Not the way the Vorrakai moved. Not the way the air bent around it, swallowing sound. Not the way its many eyes gleamed with calculation, not hunger.

Purpose.

It wasn't hunting blindly. It had chosen.

And it had chosen Cam.

A flash of her figure caught his eye—kneeling tall on Sylithra's back, silhouetted against the clouds. Not unaware. Exposed.

Ben's heart lurched violently.

"Sky—GO!"

He didn't wait. He was already moving, already in the saddle, Skylith beneath him like a living furnace. Her wings carved hard into the sky, flames rippling across her back as she surged forward on instinct alone.

Below them, the formation was shattering—dragons diving, streaks of magic igniting midair. Tessa's wind screamed like a storm. Wyatt was yelling something through the dragonlink. Kaden was already diving.

But all Ben saw was her.

The Vorrakai tore through the clouds like a god of death—its wings jagged and too silent, its talons slick with shadow, mouth opening in a soundless hiss. The mirebats scattered ahead of it, circling like carrion around a blade.

Cam turned, too slow, just as Sylithra bucked beneath her.

Ben felt it snap inside him—that tether of restraint, the one he'd kept buried for years. For survival. For safety.

He didn't call the fire.

It answered.

A raw, searing force surged up his spine and out through his hands, igniting his veins with pure heat. No hesitation. No more secrets.

He pulled metal from the buckles on his belt, the etched rings around his fingers, the runes stitched into his gloves—and they obeyed, twisting midair into a cyclone of blades. A barrier.

Mirebats dove for him—he met them with fire.

"Back!" he snarled aloud, casting a wall of heat to melt their wings before they reached Skylith.

But the Vorrakai?

It didn't stop.

It turned toward him, snarling. A dozen eyes narrowed. And then—

It ignored him.

And went straight for her.

Ben's breath caught. Not in fear—but rage.

He let go.

Skylith roared, channeling it with him, a column of white-hot fire exploding from her chest in a storm of flame. It tore toward the Vorrakai, engulfing one wing—scorching it black.

The beast reeled midair but did not fall.

It twisted. Screeched. Turned again.

Ben reached for more fire—called to the metal beneath the earth itself—but it was like trying to stop a blade mid-thrust.

"Cam, MOVE—!" he shouted into the link, heart hammering.

But it was too fast.

Too close.

And Ben realized—sickeningly, viscerally—this wasn't just a beast.

It was a message.

And Cam was the one it had been sent for.

Tessa didn't hesitate.

The moment the Vorrakai and the mirebats broke from the clouds—massive, coiling, trailing shadow like smoke—something in her snapped. No more doubt. No more second-guessing. Just action.

"Bron—let's go!" she commanded through the dragonlink.

The green-and-black dragon answered in a heartbeat, wings folding tight as they dropped through the sky like a blade.

Wind tore at Tessa's face, singing in her blood. Lightning sparked along her arms, threading through her veins like instinct made visible. She didn't reach for the carefully measured spells they'd learned last week.

She reached for the storm inside her.

She called the wind.

It answered—lashing outward in a cyclone born of sheer will, hurling two mirebats from the air like charred leaves. One exploded in a flash of blue-white light, its wings curling in smoke as it fell.

"It's heading for Cam!" Kaden's voice cracked through the link, urgent and sharp.

Tessa snapped her gaze downward—Cam was kneeling tall on Sylithra's back, high above the trees. Alone. Unaware of just how close it was to her.

The Vorrakai surged toward her, claws like obsidian scythes, too fast to intercept. Ben's fire hit it—wild and brilliant—but it didn't stop. It powered through, smoke trailing off its flank, still coming.

"Get away from her!" Tessa shouted, both aloud and through the bond.

She slammed her palms together, channeling a spear of air sharpened by lightning. The blast struck the Vorrakai in the shoulder—bone cracked with a sickening snap. The beast shrieked and staggered midair, its wing faltering—

But it didn't fall.

"Stubborn bastard," she hissed.

Mirebats swarmed again. Brontheus wheeled around to meet them, but Tessa didn't wait. She vaulted from her dragon's back mid-dive, free-falling through open sky for a heartbeat before landing hard on Sael's wing. Wyatt's hand snapped out, catching her arm with practiced ease.

"You're insane," his voice muttered inside her head.

"Fast," she corrected, planting one foot on the saddle and casting a wind-surge beneath them.

It propelled Sael closer to Cam, threading through a formation that was no longer chaos—but rhythm. Kaden diving left, Ben casting wide arcs of flame, the dragons moving in tandem.

More mirebats dove.

Tessa turned mid-saddle, arms alight, and flung a pulse of air so sharp it sliced through them like glass. Wyatt added a root-snare spell for good measure—thorns erupting from the treetops to catch any that slipped the wind.

They weren't just surviving anymore.

They were moving together.

The dragonlink pulsed through her mind—steady, alive. She could feel Wyatt beside her. Kaden circling. Ben burning. Cam ahead.

For the first time, they weren't isolated in their strength.

They were becoming a unit.

She locked eyes on Cam again—still standing, the gold-veined wings of Sylithra stretched wide like a shield behind her.

Tessa didn't yet see what Cam was about to do.

But she felt it.

Something was about to change.

The sky was too wide. Too high. The wind was too quiet just before it broke.

Wyatt felt the shift before he saw it. Not from the fire Ben cast or the wind Tessa summoned. No, this was older. Deeper. It came from her.

From Cam.

It wasn't just power—it was a summons. A tether in the air that bent light and sound around her. Something primal and vast was stirring, and it was centered on her body like a storm forming in the hollow of her chest.

"Sael, bring us in close."

The pale dragon didn't hesitate. He banked sharply, slipping low beneath Brontheus's arc and carving a clean line toward Sylithra. Wind rushed against them, thick with heat and shadow and the metallic tang of blood.

But Wyatt wasn't listening to the chaos anymore.

He was listening to her.

Cam stood tall—kneeling, actually—on Sylithra's back, no saddle, no reins, hair whipping like a banner in the wind. She was fire and focus and fury incarnate. Not frightened.

Rising.

Mirebats circled in distraction, dragging Tessa and Kaden into their fray, but Wyatt saw it—knew it—

The Vorrakai tore through the sky like a nightmare given wings. Shadows screamed around it, mirebats diving to distract—but Wyatt felt something else. A pull. A thread of focus so sharp it cut through the noise of battle.

The Vorrakai wasn't just hunting. It was drawn to her. Like it already knew her name. And Wyatt's chest went cold.

"Cam—" he tried to call through the dragonlink, but the bond between dragons roared with too many voices, and hers was silent—still.

It wasn't fear. It wasn't recklessness.

It was knowing.

And then he felt it.

A surge of heat rippled across the link, laced with something ancient and wild—fire twisted with shadow. Not like anything he'd ever sensed before. It slammed into his chest like a drumbeat.

His vision blurred white.

The light in his veins flared to meet it—reactive, defensive. For a moment, he couldn't see her, but he felt her. Felt her becoming something more. It wasn't just fire. It wasn't just shadow. It was layered, woven.

She stood like an anchor at the eye of the storm.

And then she moved.

Cam raised her arm slowly—graceful, deliberate, calm in a way that made the chaos around her seem like an illusion.

Wyatt could see the fire building at her fingertips, coils of shadow threading through it—not smothering but shaping. The air bent around her, pulsing with elemental tension.

Then his breath caught.

The flame was no longer the red-gold of fire he knew. It burned violet, rimmed in black, alive in a way that made the air shudder. Wrong and beautiful all at once.

This wasn't the fire she had called before. This was something else—something older, answering her.

He reached instinctively through the dragonlink. *"Cam..."*

But she wasn't listening.

She was deciding.

The spear formed in her hand—not iron, not magic, but will. A twisted spear of shadow and fire, jagged at the edges, glowing from within like embers inside obsidian. The wind recoiled from it. Even Sael growled low in discomfort.

Then she threw it.

Wyatt's breath caught. Space shivered. Light collapsed around the arc of the spear as it flew, trailing fire like a comet across the sky.

The Vorrakai turned too late.

The impact hit with the sound of a thunderclap inside a scream.

A shockwave exploded outward—flame roaring, shadow spiraling, the sky warping with pressure and sound. Wyatt threw up a shield of light just in time to keep from being burned. Even Sael reeled midair, snarling.

For a heartbeat—

Silence.

Smoke coiled in thick spirals. The wind was still.

Then—movement.

Wyatt lowered his arm just in time to see the Vorrakai rise.

Burning. Bleeding black ichor. One wing torn, ribs exposed, but still smiling—its fanged grin warped and steaming.

"No," Wyatt whispered.

He leaned forward instinctively. *"Sael! Go!"*

But they were too far, just a breath behind.

The Vorrakai lunged—mouth open, claws flashing—and Cam was still standing. Still exposed.

"Cam!" he shouted through the dragonlink, raw with panic.

And then—

She turned.

Wreathed in fire. Wings of shadow spiraled out behind her, not from Sylithra, but from herself. Her magic blazed to life, more than before, more than he'd seen—more than anyone had seen.

And still—

It wasn't over.

The candlelight flickered low, casting long shadows against the worn stone floor. Valerie stood at the front of the old storage room turned secret meeting hall, her arms crossed tightly, watching twelve faces that had no business looking as young as they did.

Twelve students.

Each with a second ability. Two with a third.

And every one of them dangerous—for no reason but being born.

"They're scared," Alex murmured beside her, keeping his voice low.

"They should be," Valerie said softly. "So am I."

She stepped forward.

"This isn't a lesson," she said, voice calm but clipped. "It's not sanctioned. And it's not safe. If you're here looking for safety, you're in the wrong place."

The mages went still. Even the ones who'd been smirking at each other moments ago straightened.

"There are things moving under this academy," Valerie continued. "Things most of your mentors pretend don't exist. The Academy doesn't want to talk about them. Caerthalen would rather kill them quietly than admit the truth."

She held up a hand before anyone could speak.

"They call them the Veilborn. Creatures shaped by shadow, born of a kind of magic we've been told was wrong. Forbidden. Dangerous."

She looked each of them in the eye. "But here's the truth. The danger isn't in the magic. It's in the people who've tried to control it for generations."

One of the students shifted nervously. "They're already hunting. Word's spreading—two fugitives escaped the Academy. That new girl and a Valehart. People say they're dangerous. That they're the reason the mage-hunters are moving again."

Valerie's jaw tightened, but her voice stayed steady. "That's what they want you to believe. That anyone who doesn't fit their order is a threat. But fugitives or not—those two are proof the Academy's walls can be broken. And that's what scares them most."

A tense silence filled the space.

"You have second abilities," she said. "Some of you, a third. You were taught to hide them. To feel ashamed. That ends now."

Eliah, the lightmancer, shifted her stance. A ripple of magic curled around her fingers before she pulled it back. Rian's air magic rustled his collar. Miren's shadow flickered under her boots like it couldn't decide whether to trust the ground.

Valerie nodded once. "I'm not asking you to fight. Not yet. But I am asking you to see the truth. A war is coming—not just between rebels and Caerthalen. Between truth and the people who've buried it."

She let her words settle.

"If you leave tonight, no one will stop you. But if you stay—this room becomes more than a secret. It becomes a beginning."

Silence.

Then Alex stepped forward, the quiet hum of his magic brushing the edge of the room like a second heartbeat.

"I'm leaving in a week," he said. "I've been stationed here undercover, but I answer to the rebellion."

Several heads turned sharply, surprised. But no one spoke.

Alex held their gazes. "Where I'm going, you can train openly. Without hiding what you are. Without fearing a Warden showing up at your door."

A hush fell over the room. Eliah's lips parted slightly. Miren tilted her head, interested.

"If you want to come with me," Alex said, "you can. No pressure. But I need to know before I leave. We move fast—and once we're gone, there's no looking back."

Valerie gave a single approving nod. "If you want your life to stay the same, that's your right. But don't expect the world to wait while you decide."

Alex stepped back, and Valerie drew in a slow breath.

"There's no more neutral ground," she said. "Not anymore. You either let them break you from the inside—or you choose something else."

Rian raised his hand slowly. "What if we're not ready?"

Valerie's voice softened, just a little. "Then we make you ready."

The candle wavered in its iron sconce. Somewhere outside the walls, the bell tower struck midnight.

The Academy slept on.

But down here—in the dark—a dozen minds were waking.

Chapter 31: The Fall

The sky stretched wide and endless beneath her, the ground a distant blur, like something from another world entirely.

She wasn't in the saddle. She was kneeling on Sylithra's back, the black-blue dragon soaring high, wind slashing past her face and coat. Her hands pressed lightly against warm scales, each breath syncing with the powerful ripple of Sylithra's muscles beneath her.

She was calm.

Everything around her was chaos—Ben's fire cleaving through the sky, Tessa's wind roaring like a cyclone, Kaden's shadows trailing behind the Vorrakai, and Wyatt's light flaring like a second sun. The sky danced with color and danger. Yet here, on Sylithra's back, Cam found stillness.

But Sylithra didn't.

It comes for you again, the dragon warned, her mindvoice low and carved from ancient stone. *This one knows you.*

Cam didn't flinch.

She looked.

The Vorrakai tore through the clouds, cutting the air like a sickle made of obsidian. It didn't flap—it slithered through the sky, wrong in every direction. Claws like sickle-moons. Skin slick with silvered tar. Eyes that burned with something worse than hunger.

The mirebats swarmed below, keeping the others busy. Tessa was leaping from dragon to dragon, lightning dancing at her fingertips. Kaden flared into a teleport near the tree line, dragging shadows in his wake. Ben was riding the storm of his own fire. And Wyatt—

Cam saw him.

Locked on her from across the sky. Eyes wide. Light gathering at his palms.

He knew.

They all knew.

The Vorrakai wasn't hunting anyone else.

It was after her.

Just like the forest. Just like before the outpost. Just like every dream, every vision, every whisper she couldn't explain. Always her.

Always her.

Cam's pulse roared in her ears. Her throat tightened. She wanted to scream—but she didn't.

She stood.

Sylithra didn't stop her.

The dragon only watched.

We are with you, she whispered through the link, reverent and quiet.

Cam didn't think.

She let go—not of Sylithra, but of the knot in her chest. The fear. The confusion. The need to understand why.

She let it burn.

Fire bloomed from her core—not red or orange, but a violet so deep it was nearly black, edged in flickering gold that pulsed like breath. Even through the haze of battle, the color struck her—wrong, unfamiliar, yet so utterly hers that she knew in her bones it could never be anything else again. And shadows rose with it—not empty, not foreign, but coiling through her veins like they had always been waiting.

She held fire in one palm. Shadow in the other.

Then—

She clapped her hands together.

The crack was sharper than lightning. The air folded inward, warped. A spear of pure fireshadow formed between her fingers—barbed and alive, veined with color and heat and memory. It hummed with her heartbeat.

The Vorrakai screamed.

Too late.

Cam hurled it forward. The weapon tore across the sky like a fallen star, trailing shadow and flame. The moment it struck, the world exploded.

The spear slammed into the Vorrakai's chest. The sky burst open with black-violet light. Fire spiraled. Shadow shrieked. The creature howled—a sound not made for mortal ears—and its body tumbled backward, smoke pouring from the impact site.

For a second—

Cam believed it was over.

But it wasn't.

The Vorrakai rose.

The spear still embedded in its shoulder. One wing torn. Its side blackened and bleeding thick, tar-like ichor. But its mouth twisted into something like a grin.

It was smiling.

Cam barely had time to suck in a breath before the Vorrakai lunged.

Sylithra twisted midair, wings flaring wide. She tried to turn, to throw them off their path—but she was too late. Claws raked across her flank, screeching against her scales.

The impact jolted Cam from her stance. She staggered—

—and that's when the Mirebat hit.

From behind. Silent. Fast.

It struck like a shadow knife, colliding with her spine and shoulder in a perfect, vicious arc. Pain bloomed. Her balance shattered.

Cam gasped, the world tilting sideways beneath her.

Her hands scrabbled at Sylithra's scales. She was falling. No saddle, no harness. Nothing to grip.

"No—!" she choked out.

Camomile!! Sylithra's roar cracked through the dragonlink, raw and thunderous. The kind of sound that could split stone.

But it was already too late.

Cam felt the open-air rip past her. Her body twisted. Her shoulder burned where the claws had raked her. The sky spun. The ground below felt infinite, unreachable.

The Mirebat dove with her—talons wide for the killing strike.

And something in Cam snapped.

Rage surged—not the blind kind, but the focused kind. The kind of bone of knowing this wasn't chance. These things always came for her. They always would.

And she was done.

Before the Mirebat could reach her again, her body flared—

Violent fire. And shadow.

A second burst erupted from her chest, pouring from her palm with impossible force. The magic struck the Mirebat head-on.

It didn't scream.

It disintegrated—bones, skin, and wings reduced to flaming ash in an instant, swept away by the wind.

But Cam was already unconscious.

Pain. Darkness. Air rushing around her. Her vision blurred, and she free fell into darkness.

The chamber smelled like dust and forgotten truths.

Valerie knelt beside the opened rune case, the soft blue glow of containment spells still crackling faintly around its edges. Alex crouched beside her, unrolling a scroll they weren't supposed to find—one hidden beneath seven layers of lock and obfuscation magic.

She read slowly, the ink almost pulsing on the parchment as if reacting to her presence.

"These aren't normal bloodlines," she said, voice hushed. "These are... Cradle markings. Pre-Veil. Possibly even older."

Alex nodded, tapping a name halfway down the scroll. "Here—'dual-born' line, marked by Sight and Shadow. That combination hasn't been seen in recorded mage registries for over four hundred years. It's not random."

Val's eyes narrowed. "That line has two descendants still unaccounted for. Male siblings, based on this notation. That's... rare."

Alex looked over her shoulder. "That's not all. Look here—Fire and Metal. That line's marked as bonded. Said to produce dragon-forged wielders with affinity for both combat and magic."

"Could explain the wildfire magic some of the rebels have been reporting," Valerie murmured. "And here—Healing. Storm. Air." Her brow furrowed. "Three elements. That shouldn't be possible."

"It's not," Alex said, voice grim. "Unless the parents were from different Cradle branches. That would make their child a triune carrier. One born of storm and sky, descended from healers and warriors alike."

Valerie set the scroll down, heart pounding. "Someone tried to erase these lines from history. Look—half the names are blacked out. This one's just labeled 'The Mirror's End.'"

She touched the ink with her thumb, frowning. "Triune carriers... dual-born lines... it all sounds impossible." Her voice dropped, almost to herself. "But if the Cradle could wake once... maybe it can again."

Alex unrolled another scroll, this one older, brittle at the edges. "Here's a footnote. A null bloodline—marked by shadow and suppression. A failsafe. Designed to contain or destroy."

"A failsafe?" she echoed, staring at the sigil: a broken crown surrounded by thorns. "A weapon."

Alex nodded. "And they marked this line as terminated. But you can't kill a bloodline—not really. Not if it already scattered."

Val exhaled slowly, standing. "We're not looking at isolated mages anymore. These lines are converging. Someone's awakening them."

He rolled the scrolls back up carefully, storing the copies. "In three days, I'm heading back to the outpost. If anyone here has second or third abilities and wants to leave... they can. No more hiding. Where I'm going, they can train in the open."

She gave a firm nod. "I'll tell them. Quietly. The ones who feel the stir in their bones—they'll come."

Her eyes drifted back to the bloodline scroll.

Sight and shadow.

Fire and metal.

Healing, storm, and air.

And the one they didn't speak aloud.

The Hollow Line.

The one marked in silence.

The wind was alive with fire and storm and shadow—but all Wyatt could see was her.

Cam stood poised atop Sylithra's back, hair whipping across her face, one hand glowing with coiled magic, the other braced against the dragon's spine. She wasn't in the saddle—wasn't anchored—but she looked like she belonged there. Like she was part of the sky itself.

Wyatt's breath caught.

Even amid the chaos—Tessa's lightning arcing like silver spears, Kaden weaving shadow between enemy strikes, Ben's fire swallowing the Vorrakai's flank—Cam was the center of it all. And she was breathtaking.

Then the moment shattered.

A shadow streaked from the cloudbank—too fast, too quiet. A Mirebat.

Wyatt's eyes widened. *"No—"*

The creature slammed into Sylithra's side with a screech of wings and bones. The dragon reeled midair, pushed of course—but it wasn't Sylithra that Wyatt was watching.

It was Cam.

She stumbled. Slipped. And a second Mirebat slammed into her.

Her footing vanished.

Time fractured.

Cam tumbled through the sky like a dying star—burning, fading.

"NO!" Wyatt's voice tore from his throat. He didn't think, he just moved.

He leapt.

Sael stayed where he was, hovering high above, wings straining to maintain position—but Wyatt knew better than to risk a dive at this altitude. Sael couldn't pull out in time.

This had to be him. He didn't have a plan. Just faith that Kaden would read the angle, like they'd done in training a hundred times before.

The wind hit him like a wall, shrieking in his ears as he dove. His arms reached. His magic surged.

"I see her!" he shouted through the dragonlink. *"Kaden!"* he called, voice cracking with urgency. *"We need a portal—NOW!"*

Above, he felt the flare of Kaden's magic answering—tense, focused, immediate.

Below, Cam kept falling.

Faster.

Wyatt pushed harder, his body cut through the air like a blade. Cam twisted in the wind—limp, spinning.

Too far.

He reached—and just as she slipped past his grasp, he caught her.

His arms locked around her midair. The impact jarred his bones, knocked the breath from his lungs, but he didn't let go. He twisted his body, bracing for what was still coming.

"I've got you," he breathed against her hair. "Cam, I've got you."

Blood streaked down her temple. Her head lay against him.

Unconscious.

And still they plummeted—wind roaring, ground rushing closer like a rising wave.

"KADEN!" he shouted again through the dragonlink. *"Get us out!"*

And then—

Light.

A crack of shadow-born magic.

A portal ripped open just beneath them—jagged and brilliant.

They fell through.

And vanished from the sky.

Only to land hard on Sael's back—Wyatt twisting just in time to take the full impact across his shoulders, shielding her.

His breath hitched.

But they were there.

They were safe

The moment Cam fell; Ben's heart dropped with her.

One second, she was standing—standing—on Sylithra's back, her silhouette crowned in wind and violet fire. She looked like a legend, like something pulled from the oldest runes. And then—

The Mirebat struck.

He saw the movement a half-second too late. It came in low, slamming into Sylithra's ribs with claws outstretched. The dragon roared, twisting in the air, but Cam was already reeling—thrown off balance, her hand slipping from the curve of her dragon's spine.

Ben's gut clenched.

"Cam!" he roared, the name ripped from somewhere raw inside him.

She fell.

Freefall. No control. No flame beneath her. Only air and open sky.

Ben's hands lit with fire instinctively, but it was Wyatt who moved first.

The boy didn't hesitate. No fear. No calculation.

He jumped.

Ben's breath caught in his throat. "No—" He almost shouted for Sael to follow, but then he saw it. Wyatt had already commanded Sael to hold position. Smart. Suicidal—but smart. At this altitude, even Skylith couldn't have recovered from a dive like that.

And yet Wyatt dove anyway.

Ben watched, helpless, his grip white-knuckled on Skylith's reins as the two bodies—one falling, one chasing—spun lower through the clouds.

"Come on," Ben muttered. "Come on, kid—"

He saw the flicker—Kaden's magic flaring dark and sharp across the battlefield. A portal. It opened like a wound in the sky, rimmed with violet-black flame.

Ben barely blinked before both Cam and Wyatt vanished through it.

Then—

Thud.

They landed hard on Sael's back, above and behind him. Ben turned just in time to see Wyatt's body shift midair—shoulder-first, taking the impact—shielding Cam even as his breath was stolen from his lungs.

The boy didn't even scream.

He just held her.

Ben's fire ebbed as the adrenaline crashed through him, leaving his arms shaking. He swallowed hard, trying to steady himself.

They were alive.

She was alive.

But barely.

He could see the blood at her temple. Her limbs slack. The cuts along her arms. And that spear—that terrifying, magnificent thing she had thrown at the Vorrakai—still burned behind his eyes.

She had made that.

From shadow and flame. From fury and clarity. From everything he had trained her to control—and everything no one could have taught her.

Not even him.

Not even the Academy.

Not even the dragons.

Ben exhaled sharply.

Because it wasn't just power anymore.

Cam was becoming something more.

And every creature in the Veil could feel it.

Kaden's breath caught as Cam slipped from Sylithra's back.

He didn't hear her scream. Didn't even see her flail. Just one moment she was there—standing like a storm about to break—and the next, she was gone.

Falling.

The dragonlink exploded with overlapping thoughts. Sylithra's roar, raw and broken. Tessa's gasp. Wyatt's voice—sharp and cutting through it all.

"Kaden—portal! NOW!"

His body moved before his mind caught up.

Tenebrin veered into a dive, and Kaden's hand lit with shadows. The air around him crackled with static as he opened a rift—not to the ground, not to the trees—but to the space just above Sael's back. He calculated the speed, the fall, the angle in half a heartbeat.

And Wyatt—damn him—was already there.

Falling faster than was sane. Arms outstretched. No hesitation.

The portal opened like a blade slicing the sky, and they vanished through it.

Kaden twisted Tenebrin's path around hard, searching, bracing—

Then: impact.

He spotted them.

Wyatt landed first—twisting just in time to take the brunt of it across his back, his body the only shield between Cam and the dragon's spine. Kaden saw the way his shoulder buckled, the way his arms didn't loosen. He held onto her like she was the last star left in the sky.

And she wasn't moving.

Kaden's heart dropped. He swore softly. Too much. Too far.

He blinked sweat from his eyes, trying to read the threads of magic still shimmering across the rift he'd made. It had worked—but barely. A hair off, and they would've been lost to the trees or slammed into Sael's wing at the wrong angle.

"Dammit," he muttered through the dragonlink. *"You reckless—brilliant—idiot."*

But he couldn't help it—he was impressed.

The whole battle was still roaring behind them. Mirebats circling. The Vorrakai limping and bleeding ichor midair. But for a few heartbeats, all Kaden could do was stare at them—Cam cradled in Wyatt's arms, blood streaking her temple, fire still flickering violet-black along her fingertips, edged faintly in gold, like it hadn't yet decided to go out.

She'd changed in those last moments.

The girl he met back in the forest—the one who flinched when someone said "chosen"—was gone.

And something older had stepped into her place.

He didn't know what it meant yet.

But he knew one thing as he drew another portal behind him and teleported to Sael's back in a flash of shadow:

If anything came for her again—

They'd have to go through all of them.

The sky had exploded.

There was no other word for it—wind, shadow, fire, lightning. Dragons shrieking and spinning through the air. Magic flashing like storms barely held together. Blood. Smoke. Screams.

And Cam was gone.

Tessa had seen the fall—seen the blur of her body disappear below Sylithra, too fast to track. Heard Sylithra's roar of anguish shake the sky.

Then Wyatt dove after her like he didn't care if he lived.

Then Kaden's portal opened in midair like a blade.

Then—impact.

They weren't dead.

But they might be, if she didn't hold the line.

"Keep your wing steady!" she barked at Brontheus, her voice cutting through the wind like a blade. *"We're not letting that thing past us again!"*

The Vorrakai shrieked through the smoke, its form ragged and trailing black ichor. One wing half-torn. Cam's spear still embedded deep in its shoulder, flickering with lingering shadowflame.

But it wasn't done.

It charged—again.

Right at Sylithra.

"With me!" Tessa shouted into the dragonlink, already calling lightning into her palms. The air answered like it had been waiting, leaping to her hands with a sound like a storm cracking open.

Ben was already there—Skylith sweeping around in a wide arc of heat and fury. He didn't speak, didn't shout, didn't need to. His fire answered hers, catching along the edge of her storm and spinning upward into a spiral of flame and current.

Sylithra twisted through it—her form elegant and deadly, even grieving.

Cam's dragon wasn't retreating.

She was angry.

"On your left!" Tessa shouted to Ben, loosing a bolt of wind-sharpened lightning at a Mirebat diving toward Skylith's exposed wing. The bat exploded in a puff of bone and blackened hide.

Ben answered with a gout of flame that washed the remaining mirebats from their flank.

The Vorrakai roared and surged forward again—still after Sylithra, still bleeding, still relentless.

"DIE ALREADY!" Tessa screamed, hurling another bolt of charged wind.

It struck the Vorrakai square in the side of the head—its skull jerked mid-flight, but it didn't fall. Its wings beat erratically now, fury and instinct holding it in the air.

Too close. Too fast.

Then Skylith slammed into it.

The sound cracked through the sky like thunder—bone on scale, flame on shadow.

The two tumbled, locked in a spiral of claws and fury, and Sylithra dove straight into the fray without hesitation, wings tucked, jaws open wide.

Tessa couldn't see them for a moment—just fire and black smoke, spinning together in a storm.

She surged forward on Brontheus's back, keeping pace, blasting mirebats from the air with wind spikes and lightning arcs as they tried to ambush the dragons mid-duel.

One creature screeched too close—Tessa spun and kicked it in the gut, sending it pinwheeling backward into a blast from Ben.

They were holding. They were fighting back.

And Cam was still alive.

Wyatt's voice echoed faintly through the dragonlink—tired, quiet, but steady.

"She's safe. I have her."

Tessa exhaled.

But the fight wasn't over.

"Ben," she called through the link, lightning already charging in her palms again. *"Let's end this."*

Chapter 32: The Rise

The sky bled smoke and stormlight.

Sylithra's wings beat through the chaos, every movement a cry of rage. The ache of her bond rang hollow where Cam had once been—her rider, her flame, torn from her back and swallowed by the sky.

She had failed.

No.

She would not fail again.

The Mirebat was ash. She had felt it burn in Cam's fury. But the Vorrakai still moved—still clawed and thrashed and shrieked like it belonged to the world.

It did not.

It was born of the Veil. Twisted. An echo of things that should never have passed into this realm.

And it touched what was hers.

You will not have her.

Sylithra banked hard, ignoring the searing pain in her ribs. The Vorrakai was tangled with Skylith now—Ben's flame-bonded fury rolling through the air like a wildfire—but the beast was still standing, wings flaring ragged and black against the storm.

She tucked her wings and dove.

Faster. Deeper. Past the pain. Past the noise. Into instinct. Into the old knowing.

Into what she was before the Cradle fell.

Flames licked the edges of her vision—Skylith rising on a current of Ben's fire, biting deep into the Vorrakai's shoulder, pinning it for a moment in place.

Tessa's lightning split the air beside them, a spiral of light coiling like a dance. Brontheus and Tenebrin held the flanks. Mirebats screamed and scattered.

But Sylithra was already moving.

Already calling to the power in her blood.

It surged—deep and molten and golden—veins along her wings lighting like ancient sigils. Magic older than the Knighthood. Older than the Veil. Older than this world.

Now, she whispered through the dragonlink. *Clear the path.*

The others obeyed.

Skylith peeled away. Lightning carved a tunnel through the air.

The Vorrakai turned its too-many eyes toward her.

It hissed.

And she answered.

With wrath.

Sylithra's jaws opened wide—her throat burned with fire and something more. Shadow curled behind her fangs, but at its heart was light—a terrible, beautiful light forged from bond, and fury, and the impossible magic of Cam's soul.

She exhaled.

The blast struck the Vorrakai full in the chest. Not just fire, not just shadow—but Cradleflame. This was not hers alone. It was Cam's fire, refracted through their bond—a reminder that Cradleflame was never a single soul, but two.

The scream that followed was no mortal sound.

The Vorrakai's body convulsed, its wings erupting in black fire, its armor cracking open from within. Its limbs twitched once—

And then it was gone.

Not just burned.

Erased.

The Veil shrieked in protest as its creature died.

But Sylithra didn't roar in triumph.

She banked midair, her wings folding in exhaustion, her breath ragged in her chest.

Her heart beat once—twice—until she felt it.

Cam.

Alive. Safe. On Sael's back. Wyatt holding her. Kaden shielding them with a veil of magic.

Sylithra's soul hummed.

The fight was not over.

But the worst of it had passed.

And Cam...

Cam had chosen to rise.

The lamp flickered once, casting long, uncertain shadows over the cracked marble floor. Valerie's fingers trailed along the spines of old tomes — dust-covered, moth-bitten, most of them forgotten for a reason.

Alex knelt beside a half-broken filing cabinet, flipping through brittle scrolls and reports. He hadn't spoken in minutes. That made her nervous.

Valerie glanced toward the barred window. Wind pressed against the stone like it wanted in — or like it was trying to warn her. She shifted her focus back to the documents. "Anything yet?"

"Just names," Alex muttered. "All scrubbed. Dates erased. No context."

Valerie frowned. "They wouldn't hide them like this if they weren't important."

Then he found it.

A thin file tucked behind the cabinet wall — hidden between two boards. Not marked like the others. Just a wax seal in silver, bearing the older crest of the Academy. The kind no one used anymore.

Alex stared at it for a beat before breaking the seal.

Inside: yellowed parchment, some of it smeared by age, other parts too carefully redacted to be accidental. Valerie leaned in beside him as he read aloud.

"Subject: Female Mage — Tri-elemental. Primary affinities: Healing, Air, Storm. Bloodline evaluation marked inconclusive. Mage disappeared following unauthorized search into Cradle-based archives."

Valerie's heart tripped over itself. "Tri-elemental?"

Alex nodded slowly. "And look—" He pointed to the margin. In messier, hand-written ink:

"Child likely survived. Bloodline fracture probable. If rejoined, results unstable. Dangerous."

Her breath caught. "They scrubbed the child's name."

"They scrubbed everything." He turned the page.

More notes followed — one referencing a fire-wielding combatant, marked "rogue-class," once bonded to the subject. Another entry simply read: "Keep them apart. If she finds dragons, the path reopens."

Valerie leaned back on her heels. "This isn't just about talent. It's about fear. Legacy."

Alex was staring at the last page now. It was more fragmented — torn at the edge, written in two hands. One was careful and cold, official. The other looked more like a warning than a note.

The last line was handwritten in violet ink; "The failed vessel sleeps. But the girl — she would not. Keep her from dragons. Keep her from memory."

Valerie whispered, "The Hollow Prince."

Alex said nothing for a moment. Then: "They were trying to erase her before she even became herself."

Valerie's voice was tight. "But they failed."

He looked up then — a flicker of something in his eyes. Not just awe. Recognition.

Alex's voice dropped, almost too soft to hear. "I think I know who she is."

Valerie stilled. "Who?"

He shook his head, cautious. "Not yet. But I've seen that bloodline before. Maybe not here—but at the outpost."

She caught her breath.

"We need to be careful," he said. "If anyone finds out we've read this—"

"Then we protect it," Valerie said. "And if the others want the truth, they can help us build it from the ashes."

She rolled the scrolls and tucked them under her cloak. Alex snuffed the lamp.

They didn't speak as they left the archive.

But the silence that followed carried the weight of a legacy long buried—and now, starting to rise.

The wind had quieted.

Ash drifted in lazy spirals, settling across the canopy like mourning snow. The last echoes of the Vorrakai's scream faded into the trees.

Then—wings. Heavy, urgent.

Skylith landed first, flames crackling faintly along her scaled neck, smoke coiling from her nostrils. Ben was already leaping from the saddle before she fully touched down. His boots hit the ground hard, and he sprinted.

Brontheus and Tenebrin circled once before dropping through the trees behind her. Tessa leapt down from Brontheus's side mid-hover, her braid whipping like a flag as she hit the dirt in a crouch. Kaden teleported midair and reappeared just ahead, Tenebrin spiraling down behind him.

But it was Sael who descended last—white wings wide, landing with a soft, grounded grace that betrayed the chaos they'd just survived.

And on his back—Wyatt.

Still holding her.

Cam was unconscious, her head tucked beneath Wyatt's chin, one arm limp, the other clutched weakly against his chest. Blood streaked her temple, and her knuckles were singed. But she was breathing. Faintly.

Wyatt hadn't moved. Not really. He sat against Sael's back spine, both arms curled around her like she was something sacred.

He didn't speak. His eyes were locked on hers, every muscle in his body straining to stay still—to not shake.

Ben reached them first. His knees hit the saddle without grace, fingers brushing Cam's wrist, then her jaw, checking for pulse and breath and burns.

"She's alive," he rasped, voice hoarse. "She's alive."

Kaden appeared beside them an instant later, jaw tight, eyes scanning the canopy for more danger even as he knelt opposite Ben.

"Wyatt?" Tessa's voice was softer, urgent as she ran up behind. "Is she—?"

"She's breathing," Wyatt said. His voice cracked like something broken and barely stitched together. "I've got her. I didn't let go."

"No one's asking you to," Ben said gently, already unfastening the buckle of Cam's scorched coat. "We've got her now. You can—"

"No." Wyatt's arms tightened. "Just a little longer."

None of them argued.

Sylithra touched down beside Sael, her wings folding slowly. She lowered her head with reverence, her gold-veined eyes locking on Cam's unconscious form.

She fought, she murmured through the link, her voice a low thunder. *She did not fall.*

Tessa swallowed and looked away. Her fingers sparked slightly from leftover adrenaline.

Kaden exhaled, dragging a hand through his hair. "We shouldn't stay here long. Not after that."

"Just give us a minute," Ben said, not unkindly. His eyes never left Cam's face. "We're not moving her until I've checked her ribs. And her head."

Wyatt didn't answer but shifted slightly—enough for Ben to reach her more easily, enough to let them all see her battered frame and the hint of soot-darkened skin beneath her clothes.

She looked small in his arms.

But not weak.

Never that.

They stood in silence for a long moment—ringed by dragons, shadow, and scorched trees. Each of them shaken. Each of them changed.

Then Cam stirred.

Just slightly.

A breath caught. A flicker of her fingers.

And Wyatt, still cradling her, whispered like it might wake the stars:

"...Cam?"

Her lips didn't move.

But her hand curled weakly around his hand.

And in that moment, the whole forest exhaled.

The infirmary at the outpost was quiet.

Not silent—nothing in a place like this ever was—but muted, like even the walls were holding their breath.

Cam lay on one of the stone-framed beds near the hearth, wrapped in soft cloth and healing sigils drawn faintly in gold and red. Someone had covered her with a wool blanket too big for her, and her head rested on a cushion made from one of Tessa's spare jackets.

She hadn't woken yet. Not fully.

Ben stood beside her, arms crossed, gaze unreadable. There was soot still smudged across his jaw and knuckles where fire had leaked through, but he didn't seem to notice. Or maybe he just didn't trust himself to look away.

Wyatt hadn't moved much since they returned.

He sat in a low chair pulled close to her bedside, elbows on knees, fingers clasped loosely in front of him. Not praying. Just listening.

Every time her breath hitched—he flinched.

Kaden stood near the doorway, his usual restless energy absent. He'd offered to cast a sleep spell for Wyatt three times already. Wyatt declined every time.

Tessa had slipped out earlier to get food, claiming she needed to stretch her legs. Everyone knew she just didn't want to cry in front of Cam's unconscious body.

A fire crackled quietly in the corner.

She is stable, Sylithra voice curled into all their minds through the dragonlink. Her massive head filled the opening from the window, breath fogging the glass as she kept her vigil. *Her mind remains intact. Her magic will recover. She is still herself.*

Ben's jaw tightened. "Stable doesn't explain what I saw."

Wyatt finally tore his eyes from Cam's face. "The fire?"

"That fire," Ben muttered. His gaze flicked to the faint scorch marks still staining her fingers. "It wasn't just fire. It carried shadow at the edges, braided through the flame. I've only seen seams like that once before. And it didn't ended well."

Wyatt swallowed. "But it felt... familiar. Like the world's been holding its breath for it."

Ben shook his head. "That kind of change doesn't happen by accident."

They both fell silent, the weight of it hanging heavier than the smell of smoke still clinging to their clothes.

"She shouldn't have had to fight that thing alone," Ben muttered finally, his voice low.

"She didn't," Wyatt said, his voice hoarse. "But she was the reason it came for us."

Kaden crossed the room and set a canteen by the bed. "Then next time, we make sure we're the reason it doesn't get to her."

Ben said nothing. Just reached forward and gently brushed a lock of chestnut brown hair from Cam's brow.

Wyatt didn't look away.

◈ ☽✦☾ ◈

Later, after the others had gone, a stillness settled over the outpost infirmary. The noise had faded—Tessa's clipped jokes, Kaden's steady voice, even the soft rush of the healers' boots across stone floors. One by one, they'd left to give space. To breathe. To process.

Only two remained.

And the room felt smaller for it.

Ben didn't speak at first.

He stood next to the infirmary window, arms crossed, watching—not the healers, not the runes glowing faintly along Cam's arms—but him.

Wyatt.

The boy sat beside her, silent and still. Not touching, not speaking. Just there. Like the storm hadn't broken him, only narrowed his world down to a single point.

He wasn't watching her like a soldier checks on a casualty.

He was watching like he could feel every breath she took. Every flicker of movement beneath her lashes. Every moment she drifted somewhere between sleep and pain.

And Ben knew that look.

He'd worn it once himself.

A line of dried blood traced Cam's temple. Her hair clung to her cheek, damp from sweat or tears. She looked too small beneath the blankets. Too still.

But it wasn't her wounds that held Ben frozen.

It was what he saw in Wyatt's face.

His voice, when it came, was quiet. Not accusing. Not uncertain.

"You care about her."

Wyatt didn't jump. Didn't pretend not to understand. He just turned his head slightly, still holding Cam's hand in his, thumb brushing over her knuckles like it was the only thing anchoring him.

"I do," he said softly. "I have... for a long time."

Ben didn't move.

He kept his eyes on the window. "That's the way I looked at her mother," he said. "Back when I still believed things could turn out different."

Wyatt exhaled, low and uneven.

"I've seen her," he said. "Since I was twelve."

That made Ben glance at him. "In dreams?"

"And visions," Wyatt nodded. "Sometimes in fire. Sometimes in light. Always her. I didn't understand it. I thought I was cursed. Or broken. Or just imagining things because I wanted something to mean something. I didn't know who she was—I didn't even know if she was real."

His voice dropped. "But I knew her. How she moved. How she fought. How she broke... and still kept going."

Ben didn't speak, but his shoulders lowered slightly—less braced, less guarded.

"When I finally met her," Wyatt said, "I didn't believe it. Not at first. Thought it was just another vision."

Ben's voice was quiet. "You still think she is?"

"Sometimes," Wyatt admitted. "But then she rolls her eyes, or tells me off, or nearly gets herself killed doing something reckless—and I remember. She's real. More real than anything I've ever seen."

The fire inside the infirmary crackled.

Somewhere beyond the walls, Sylithra let out a low breath, like thunder deep underground.

Ben turned back toward the window, something unreadable in his expression.

"You've been watching her longer than I have."

"I didn't mean to," Wyatt said.

"I know," Ben replied. "You're not the only one who's seen things."

Wyatt looked at him.

Ben's jaw tightened faintly. "The Cradle echoes—forward, backward. In blood and memory. We were fools to think it could be controlled. Or kept secret."

Silence stretched between them.

Two men—one from the past, one from the future—both shaped by the same girl lying just beyond the window.

"I'd never hurt her," Wyatt said at last, voice steady but raw.

Ben didn't answer right away.

Then: "You'd better not."

Wyatt nodded.

Ben added, "And don't lie to her. Not about what you see. Not about what she is."

"I won't."

"And don't try to protect her from it, either."

That, Wyatt didn't respond to—not right away. His grip on Cam's hand tightened slightly.

"I won't let her face it alone," he said finally.

Ben's gaze softened, only slightly.

"That," he said, "makes two of us."

Cam still slept, breathing steadier now.

Ben stepped outside, backlit by the faint torchlight lining the outpost's main hall. He leaned against the outer wall, rubbing the heel of his hand into his sternum like he was trying to massage out something stuck there. Something old.

The infirmary door creaked softly behind him. Footsteps followed, then stopped just a few paces away.

"I thought I'd lost her," Wyatt said after a long pause.

Ben's jaw tensed. "You didn't."

"I almost did." Wyatt leaned against the opposite wall, arms folded tight. "I saw her fall. I saw the way she stood on Sylithra like she didn't care if she lived or not."

Ben's voice was quiet, but firm. "She cares. She's just... tired of being hunted."

Wyatt shook his head. "She's always been hunted?"

Ben's gaze sharpened. "Yes. Whether she knew it or not. The Capital's eyes were always searching, waiting for her to surface. She's been running her whole life—she just didn't know it until now," his jaw tightened. "And it isn't only the Capital. The shadow-born have been after her since the moment her power stirred. Wraithbeasts, Wraithcall, Banshees,

Howlers—things that don't just hunt at random. They're drawn to her. Testing her. Waiting for her to break."

Wyatt swallowed, the truth heavy in his chest. "And they won't stop."

Ben nodded. "No. They won't. Which is why we stand with her. Because she's never had the chance to stand alone."

They stood together in the torchlight, two shadows drawn by fire.

Wyatt exhaled slowly. "Her fire's different now. I saw it change."

Ben's expression hardened. "I saw it too." A pause. "And I don't know if that's a gift or a curse."

Wyatt didn't answer.

"Whatever it is," Ben said quietly, "she won't carry it alone. Not while I'm breathing."

"I've fought monsters," Wyatt said, staring into the trees. "But that? That Vorrakai—it wasn't just a creature. It knew her. It wanted her. Like the Veil's watching. Waiting. Testing."

Ben nodded slowly. "It is."

Wyatt turned to face him. "So, what now?"

Ben met his gaze. Steady. "We train her. We guard her. And when the Veil comes again, we stand in front of it. Together."

Wyatt's throat tightened. He didn't say thank you. Didn't say he was scared.

He just said: "Good. Because I'm not letting go next time."

Ben gave a dry smile—more breath than laughter—but there was warmth in it.

"I don't think she'd let you."

Chapter 33: The Moment Between

The corridor beyond the reading chamber was dim and half-forgotten, tucked behind heavy stone archways and overgrown vines that clawed through the windows like the building itself had tried to seal away what lay here. Valerie's boots made no sound on the ancient rug beneath her as she and Alex moved deeper into the hall.

A flicker of motion made her freeze.

Up ahead—just past the corner where the restricted records were kept—two figures stood shrouded in shadow. Not cloaked like students but cloaked in that deliberate stillness meant for killing. Like they weren't supposed to be seen.

Valerie raised a hand to Alex, motioning him to stay back.

They pressed against the cold wall, barely breathing.

The first voice was sharp, clipped. "Confirmed sighting two nights ago. Deep in the Karethwyn forest."

Valerie's breath hitched.

The other voice responded low, almost cautious. "You're certain?"

"Blue-black dragon with gold veining. There's only one that matches. Same as the last report." A pause. "She wasn't alone this time. Someone was with her. Unidentified."

"Another mage?"

"Possibly. They were fast. Kept to the tree line. Covered their tracks well—but it's her. There's no mistake."

The second speaker lowered their voice. "The order's gone out. They're sending a mage hunter."

Valerie's stomach turned to ice.

She knew what a mage hunter left behind. She'd seen it once before. Never forgot the silence afterward.

Alex was already moving. He slipped one hand into his coat and pulled out his communication stone, the polished obsidian flickering faintly in the dark. A twist of magic shimmered across the surface as he activated the link.

"Confirmed danger," he whispered into the stone. "Cam and an unknown companion were spotted in Karethwyn forest. Mage hunter in-route. We need to act now."

Corin's reply came almost instantly, low and steady like stone beneath a river.

"Understood. Return sooner than planned. Three days minimum. And listen—if they're broadcasting a sighting, it could be deliberate. A trap. Cam's location is secret and secure. They may be trying to flush out anyone aligned with her. Don't bite."

Alex's jaw tightened. "Understood."

"I want you back before they get desperate. You move tonight if you can."

Alex glanced toward Valerie, who gave a nod.

"We've gathered more than expected," he added. "A dozen. All second or third ability. They want out. I'll need Kaden's help to move them quietly."

A pause, then:

"Done. He'll be ready. Move fast. Don't let them find her."

The connection faded.

Alex slipped the stone away, and Valerie looked at him with wide eyes.

"We move at dawn," he said quietly.

She nodded once, the quiet dread still coiling in her chest.

But beneath it all... a spark of something steadier.

Resolve.

They weren't going to let her be hunted.

Not Cam. Not any of them.

The air outside the Academy wardlines was colder than she expected—sharp with night and silence.

Valerie stood near the edge of the outer wards, clutching the strap of her satchel. Behind her, the group of recruits waited in uneasy stillness—some pacing, others whispering nervously to themselves. The youngest couldn't have been more than fifteen, their hands glowing faintly from stress-triggered magic.

Alex stood beside her, his expression tight but calm, eyes scanning the tree line.

Then the shimmer came.

A ripple—like heat bending light—peeled into existence just a few paces ahead. And from that shimmer, someone stepped through.

Tall, lean, and composed, with silver-threaded black fabric and a dagger tucked at his hip. His presence shifted the air the moment he arrived.

"Kaden," Alex greeted, stepping forward. "You're late."

Kaden gave a shrug, already sizing up the group. "Had to reroute the arc. Corin wants this done clean."

Valerie stayed still, watching them with cautious curiosity. She'd heard the name before. Kaden Valehart. Strategist. Shadow mage. Loyal to Corin.

But names didn't mean much yet. She barely trusted anyone these days.

Kaden turned to her briefly. "You're Valerie?"

She nodded, tense. "Yes."

"You and Alex come last. I'll take the first three now. Second group will follow five minutes behind."

Alex stepped beside her and lowered his voice. "You'll like Haldrin's Keep. It's not perfect, but it's real. No need to hide what you are anymore."

Valerie's throat tightened slightly. "Is she there?" she asked. "Cam?"

Kaden glanced at her again, his expression unreadable—but not unkind. "Yeah. She made it back fourteen days ago."

Val swallowed. "Is she okay?"

"She was injured. Vorrakai level bad. But she's alive. In the infirmary."

At that, something inside her loosened. She hadn't realized how tightly her hands had been clenched.

"Let's get moving," Kaden said.

He turned and drew a shimmering line through the air. Magic stretched and opened—a portal cut clean into the darkness, revealing flickering torchlight and stone corridors in the distance.

The Keep.

Real now. Tangible. Waiting.

Kaden stepped through with the first group of recruits, the portal closing like breath behind him.

Valerie stared at the place where he'd vanished. Her heart pounded—not from fear, exactly. From the feeling that she was stepping off the edge of the life she used to know.

"You doing alright?" Alex asked.

She looked at him. "Yeah. Just... ready."

He gave a faint smile. "That's enough."

The portal shimmered open again.

This time, Valerie stepped forward.

Not as a student. Not as a daughter of Caerthalen. Not anymore.

But as someone beginning to choose her side.

The last shimmer of the teleport gate faded behind him, leaving only the faint scent of charged air and damp forest. Kaden exhaled slowly, rolling the tension from his shoulders as the quiet of the outpost settled in.

Valerie and the others had gone inside. New recruits—each carrying hope or fear or something heavier. He'd barely registered their faces. His thoughts were still two buildings ahead.

He moved quietly across the clearing, boots crunching in the grass. The infirmary window glowed faintly, candlelight throwing soft shadows through the warped glass. He didn't go inside. Not yet.

Instead, he paused outside, just close enough to see them.

Cam lay still on the cot, her skin pale beneath the low light. Wyatt sat beside her, unmoving, as if afraid even the shift of breath might disturb something fragile.

Kaden folded his arms and leaned against the outer wall. For a moment, he didn't think. He just stood there, letting the weight of the past few days settle over him.

Too close.

They'd almost lost her.

He wasn't sure what they would've done—what he would've done—if she hadn't opened her eyes again. And he couldn't stop replaying the image burned into his mind—her fire when it turned. Not red, not gold, but violet streaked with black, edged in a shimmer that didn't belong to any element he knew. Wrong and right all at once. He didn't say it aloud, not yet. But he filed it away with all the other questions stacking higher in his mind. Because fire wasn't supposed to change color. And magic wasn't supposed to feel that old.

The pressure building around her was growing heavier by the hour. And he could feel it too—whatever was stirring in the threads of blood and prophecy. It wasn't just about dragons anymore. Or magic. Or rebellion.

Something was changing in the world, and she was right in the middle of it.

And still, she'd stood her ground.

Kaden let his head fall back against the wood with a quiet thud.

"Don't make a habit of this," he muttered to the window. "We're running out of heroes."

He didn't expect an answer.

Didn't need one.

He straightened after a few seconds and turned back toward the field. There were recruits to get settled. Plans to make. Secrets to keep.

But he allowed himself one last glance at the window.

Just to be sure she was still breathing.

The scent of sage and smoke clung to the air.

Cam stirred beneath stiff blankets, her ribs aching, her head pulsing in quiet waves. The world came into focus slowly—the glow of runes along the infirmary ceiling, the low hum of magic woven into the walls, the sound of someone breathing close by.

She turned her head and found him.

Wyatt.

Asleep in a chair beside her bed, his chin tipped forward, arm folded tight across his chest. His fingers were still curled loosely around her wrist, as if he'd refused to let go, even in sleep.

Her chest squeezed—not from pain, but something deeper. Softer.

She shifted with a groan.

Wyatt startled upright in a heartbeat, his eyes instantly on her. "Cam?"

"Ugh," she rasped. Her voice was rough, like stone over water. "Did I... fall again?"

He huffed out a breath that was almost a laugh, almost a sob. "Straight off a dragon, actually. Ten out of ten for theatrics."

Cam winced and closed her eyes briefly. "Tell me you caught me."

Wyatt huffed. "I did."

She peeked one eye open. "Was it cool this time?"

Wyatt blinked, then gave a crooked smile. "Exceptionally. Very heroic. Might've had wind in my hair."

Cam chuckled, which turned into a wince. "Good. I like to fall in style."

He looked at her like she was a miracle and a disaster at once.

"You really need to stop doing that," he said after a moment, softer now.

"What? Falling?"

"Yeah." His voice lowered. "Falling."

Silence lapped at the edges of the room. She met his gaze, searching. There was something heavy there. Something familiar.

"Well, if I do fall again...You'll catch me, though," she whispered. "Right?"

He didn't even blink. "Always."

Cam swallowed. Her hand—still caught in his—tightened just slightly.

Wyatt's gaze lingered on her too long. Not just on her face, but on the memory of the fire that had erupted from her hands. He swallowed. "Cam... when you fought the Vorrakai, your fire—" He hesitated, searching. "It wasn't red anymore. It wasn't like anyone else's. It burned violet. Black at the edges. I've never seen anything like it."

Cam's breath caught. She hadn't wanted to think about it. Not yet. "I felt it," she admitted softly. "Like something in me shifted. It wasn't wrong, but... it felt like standing on the edge of something bigger. Like it could swallow me if I let it."

Wyatt leaned closer, voice rougher now. "It was terrifying. And it was beautiful. Like it wasn't just fire—it was you. Something only you could hold. And there was something in it—something golden—like it was reaching for more than just flame."

The silence between them deepened, taut and fragile.

Cam's hand tightened in his. Her heart stuttered. The world narrowed to his voice, his eyes, and the warmth of his palm against hers.

Wyatt shifted forward. "There's something I should've said earlier—back at the Keep, before the flight and the Vorrakai attack."

She nodded.

Cam's heart thudded. The world narrowed to him, and the warmth of his hand.

"I—"

The infirmary door banged open.

"Cam?!"

Tessa's voice cut through the quiet like a thunderclap. She froze in the doorway, curls wild, eyes wide. Her gaze swept over Cam's pale face, then dropped to Wyatt, still bent too close.

"Oh, my gods," Tessa said, grinning as she walked in. "You're awake. And you're flirting."

Cam let out a wheezy laugh and tried to sit up straighter. "Reckless bitch privilege revoked. I'm claiming it."

Tessa put a hand on her hip. "Excuse me? There's only room for one reckless bitch on this team, and it's me."

Wyatt cleared his throat and straightened, just enough to pretend he hadn't nearly kissed her.

Tessa raised an eyebrow at him. "Don't make me report this to the council."

Cam grinned weakly, a flush creeping up her neck. "You brought the chaos. What's the occasion?"

"Oh, you know. Nothing important. Just that Alex showed up early with half a dozen new recruits," she said, flopping onto the chair beside the bed. "Didn't expect you to be awake. Or dramatically flirting in soft lighting."

Cam groaned and covered her face. "Please let me pass out again."

Tessa laughed and nudged her. "Nah. You're stuck with us now."

Wyatt gave a soft laugh, quieter than the others, and Cam reached for his hand again under the blanket. This time, he didn't let go.

Tessa saw it but said nothing.

Instead, she leaned back and sighed. "Well, guess you're officially the most dramatic one here. Took my title and everything."

Cam smiled faintly. "I'll share it with you."

"You'd better."

The three of them sat there in a loose triangle of warmth and exhaustion. No armor. No pressure. Just the weight of surviving—together.

Cam leaned back into the pillow. Her body hurt. Her thoughts swam. But for the first time in days, she didn't feel like she was drowning.

And maybe, just maybe, she could let herself rest.

Part 2

Breaking the Chains

"Freedom is not given. It is seized by those willing to shatter the bonds that hold them."

Chapter 34: Shadows at the Door

The outpost breathed like a living thing.

Valerie woke to the low murmur of voices, boots on frost-hardened dirt, the hiss of morning kettles, and the faint but unmistakable rhythm of dragon wings overhead—slow, deliberate, like something sacred returning to the sky.

She sat up slowly, rubbing sleep from her eyes, heart caught between panic and wonder. She wasn't at the Academy anymore. The stone walls were uneven here. Her cot smelled faintly of cedar smoke and wool. A simple basin sat near the window. Everything in the outpost was rough-cut, mismatched—and used. Lived in.

It was the first place she'd been in years that didn't smell of sterility and fear.

Pulling on her boots, she stepped out into the cold air and let herself pause on the threshold.

It wasn't what she expected.

It wasn't what she feared, either.

No tension crackled in the air. No whispers followed her. People bustled about with quiet purpose—hauling crates, mending cloaks, speaking to one another by name, not title. There was laughter, even. Somewhere near the forge, a group of young rebels teased each other as they hammered out morning drills.

Valerie blinked against it. This... wasn't the rebellion her family had spoken of.

It wasn't chaos.

It wasn't reckless.

It was home for people who had none.

And she had chosen to walk into it.

She wandered the edge of the courtyard, unsure where to go yet unwilling to return to the small room she'd been given. As she passed a line of stacked crates, a tall woman carrying firewood offered her a warm roll of bread without hesitation.

"First morning's the worst," the woman said with a wry smile. "Eat. It helps."

Valerie accepted it wordlessly, holding the still warm bread in both hands. The gesture caught her off guard more than anything else. There was no suspicion. No careful sizing-up.

Just kindness. Trust offered freely. It made her chest ache.

Her fingers trembled slightly as she took a bite. The bread was uneven, slightly burned on one side—but the best thing she'd tasted in days.

She moved toward a quieter edge of the outpost path, her thoughts turning over like stones in a riverbed.

Her parents' voices echoed like ghosts.

Her mother, always anxious, had whispered warnings about rebellion at night like they were bedtime stories meant to frighten her into obedience.

"If you're caught near them, we can't protect you. They're not like us. They'll twist your gift. Twist you."

Her father, more measured but just as cold, had dismissed them all with a single phrase:

"Romantics with nothing left to lose."

But here, now, standing among the people her family had feared, Valerie felt... still.

Not safe. Not yet. But seen.

And maybe that was more dangerous.

She turned a corner near a low stone wall and nearly collided with someone.

Kaden.

He caught her by the arms to steady her, hands firm but not rough. His familiar sharp eyes softened when they met hers.

"Valerie," he said, brows lifting. "That was either clumsy or deliberate."

"I—wasn't looking." Her voice caught somewhere between apology and breathlessness. "Sorry."

He didn't let go right away. "You alright?"

"I think so," she said, though she wasn't sure. Her thoughts were still knotted from the night before, the weight of what she'd left behind—and what she was starting to believe in.

Kaden tilted his head slightly. "You look like someone who's about to ask if it's too late to run."

Valerie gave a small, surprised laugh. "Maybe."

"But you're not going to," he added, stepping back, releasing her arms. "You're not the type."

He turned, walking slowly down the path toward the command building. "Come on. Corin's waiting."

Corin's quarters were carved from the same stone as the rest of the outpost, but neater—stacked scrolls, labeled shelves, a desk smoothed from use, and a wall pinned with maps and handwritten notes. Sparse. Functional. No decoration.

Alex stood near the hearth, arms folded, eyes sharp with tension. Scrolls were laid across the desk like spilled secrets.

Valerie stepped in, suddenly aware of how small she felt in the presence of people who moved like they'd already chosen their side—and accepted what it would cost.

Corin entered quietly. He studied them for a long moment, his eyes lingering briefly on her. Then, simply:

"Tell me everything."

She let Alex speak first, recounting what they heard at the Academy—the whispers of Cam and Wyatt near the Karethwyn forest, the panic, the mage hunter dispatched in secret.

Then Valerie stepped forward and opened her satchel. Inside: the smuggled documents. Fragments of history, names crossed out, bloodlines marked in ink and secrecy. She laid them carefully across the desk.

As Corin read, his hands folded, fingertips pressing together in slow rhythm. Thoughtful. Measured. But when he reached a certain name, something in his jaw tensed. She couldn't quite read it.

"This might be bait," he said at last. "They may want to flush out the ones still loyal to the old ways. Force their hand."

"No," Valerie said, quietly but firmly. "It's more than that. They're not staging fear. They are afraid. You can feel it."

He looked at her then—really looked. And for just a moment, she felt seen not as a liability, but as someone useful.

He gave a small nod.

Afterward, Kaden offered to show her around. She followed him through the winding paths of the outpost and stone barracks, past training circles and warm fires, all of it alive with motion and purpose.

Then they passed a low wall on the upper levels of the Keep.

She stopped in her tracks.

The dragon was curled in rest, her coils half-shaded under a canopy of old pine, the firelight of her scales glowing like banked coals. One eye opened lazily, flicked toward Valerie, then drifted shut again.

Kaden noticed her awe and said nothing. He didn't need to.

Valerie took a slow step forward, her voice no more than breath.

"Gods... she's beautiful."

No illusion. No illusion at all.

She lingered near the dragon for another long moment before Kaden gestured to the barracks building ahead.

"Your room's there. You know how to get back I take it? Don't hesitate to ask for anything."

She turned to thank him, but he was already walking away, half-smiling to himself.

Valerie cast one last glance at the orangish-red dragon before turning toward her quarters. She found her door easily enough, but just as she reached for the handle, another door creaked open at the far end of the corridor.

She looked up.

Cam stood there.

Pale, slower in her step than before, but awake. Whole. Her eyes lit up with recognition.

Valerie didn't hesitate. She walked forward and threw her arms around her.

Cam gave a soft grunt of surprise and hugged her back. "Hi to you too."

"You're okay," Valerie said, pulling back to look at her. "Are you really okay?"

"I'm getting there," Cam said with a crooked smile. "Kaden says I shouldn't be walking yet, so I'm obviously doing it just to annoy him."

Valerie laughed, then hesitated. "Can I say something weird?"

Cam nodded. "Always."

Valerie's voice dropped, softer. "Thank you."

Cam tilted her head. "For what?"

Valerie's mouth twisted slightly. "For... not being what they said you were."

Cam's smile faded. "What did they say I was?"

There was a long pause.

"A mistake. A myth. A threat." Valerie met her eyes. "I think they were afraid you'd be real."

Cam didn't speak for a moment. Then she reached out, squeezed Valerie's arm gently.

"I'm glad you're here."

And Valerie, for the first time in a long time, believed it.

Old stone kept the morning's chill in its bones.

Cam walked the narrow path that wound up the mountain path behind the outpost—slow, careful, coat unbuttoned so the air could sting her skin awake. Moss softened each worn step; lanterns still guttered from the night watch, their glass panes fogged by breath and frost.

Above her, the high alcoves cut into the cliff face—dragon eyries—glimmered with faint light. A forge clanged somewhere far below. Otherwise, silence.

When she stepped beneath the first arch, a hush settled that was almost holy. Wind threaded through the half-open roof, carrying the scent of pine and distant snow. Stone pillars framed recesses big enough to house legends.

Sylithra lay in the largest.

The Cradle dragon's blue-black scales were dulled along her chest and side, where Mirebat claws had raked deep enough to score flesh beneath. Gold vein-lines pulsed faintly under the wounds, like sunrise caught beneath obsidian. A broad swath of linen bandages wrapped her ribs, etched with healing runes that glowed dimly, syncing with each breath.

Even resting, Sylithra filled the alcove like a sleeping god.

Cam crossed the floor on bare feet, boots hooked by two fingertips. She knelt beside the dragon's head and laid her palm against a scale just behind the jaw hinge. Heat answered her touch—steady, ancient.

Sylithra's mind-voice curled gently into her thoughts:

Little Flame.

"Thought you might be lonely," Cam whispered.

The dragon's eye—liquid gold around a black vertical pupil—flicked open and settled on her.

I've endured worse wounds, Sylithra rumbled. *One learns patience when centuries are the measure.*

Cam smiled faintly. "Didn't stop me worrying."

She eased down, knees tucked to her chest, and listened to the deep, deliberate rhythm beneath scale and bone. Her fingers traced an older scar along Sylithra's neck—ragged and ridged, a mark of a battle long forgotten by history.

"I didn't lose control out there," she said softly. "I found it. For the first time, I felt like I knew what I was doing."

A breath. Then—

"But I missed what mattered."

The memory sliced through her again: the Vorrakai crashing down, the pulse of unleashed magic, and then—too late—Sylithra's roar, the flicker of wings in her periphery, the claws, the feeling of being weightless and falling.

"I saw the big threat. And forgot to look for the quiet one."

Sylithra's breath warmed her cheek.

Awareness is not gifted. It is built.

Cam pressed her forehead to the dragon's hide. The ancient warmth steadied her heartbeat. "Next time, I'll see the whole field. I have to."

No, Sylithra said. *You already can. You just haven't learned how to trust it yet.*

Footsteps scuffed behind her. Familiar. She didn't turn—didn't need to.

Wyatt stepped into the alcove and crouched across from her, his coat still open to the chill in the air. He didn't speak at first. Just reached out, brushing a finger along an uninjured scale.

"She'll mend," he murmured. "Dragons heal faster than pride."

Cam huffed. "Mine's the only pride that's bruised."

"Then we make it better."

Another presence—Kaden, arms folded, leaning in the archway. His gaze snagged on the bandages and stayed there, jaw tight.

"Lucky we're all stubborn," he muttered. "Otherwise, we'd still be scraping you two off the forest floor."

Tessa appeared next, curls wind-wild, a pouch of nut clusters dangling from her fingers.

"If this is a pity party, I'm in," she said brightly. "I brought snacks and sarcasm."

She dropped to her knees beside Cam and offered the pouch. Cam took one. Her laugh almost cracked.

"You're impossible."

"Correct. Also, starting tomorrow: blindfold sparring. If we can't see the sneaky things, you can't miss them."

Cam blinked hard. "Deal."

Wyatt extended his hand. Cam took it. His palm was warm—solid. Kaden stepped closer, hand firm on her shoulder. Tessa looped an arm around them both.

For a moment, they were just a circle of limbs and warmth and breath—no prophecy, no hunters, no weight.

Just them.

"I need to train differently," Cam said into the silence. "Not harder. Wider. I want to feel what I'm not looking at."

"We'll help," Wyatt said.

Tessa nodded. "Blindfolds, spiked obstacles, emotionally scarring drills—you name it."

Kaden grunted. "She means yes."

Sylithra's tail curled slowly behind them, forming a half-circle—a quiet wall of protection.

Cam leaned into her friends. The air was cold. The forge sang faintly in the distance. And behind her, the slow, eternal rhythm of a dragon's heart kept time.

And for the first time in days, the world didn't feel like it was closing in.

It felt wide enough.

◈ ☽✦☾ ◈

The outpost's strategy room smelled faintly of ink, smoke, and old pine. Scrolls and maps layered the table in tight rows, each corner pinned with iron weights. A low-burning lantern hissed near the wall, the only light in the dim space—Corin preferred it that way. Secrets sat easier in shadow.

Ben stood opposite him, arms crossed, brow furrowed as he scanned a document unrolled between them. Ancient vellum. Frayed edges. The language wasn't one he'd seen in decades, but the rune work was unmistakable.

"Is this all of it?" Ben asked.

Corin nodded once. "What Alex smuggled out from the Academy's restricted wing. And what Valerie overheard matches what we feared—they're hunting anyone with second or third abilities now. Quietly. Strategically."

Ben muttered a curse under his breath. "Trying to stamp out crossings before they happen."

Corin leaned forward, tapping a line near the bottom of the scroll. "This symbol's turned up more than once. Bloodlines with elemental convergence. Most are marked in red. Some... sealed."

He flipped to a second parchment—a diagram, circular and scorched around the edges. In the center: the strange emblem. A ringed circle cradling a split triangle, with mirrored lines flaring from both sides like wings.

Ben's shoulders stiffened.

He reached forward, palm hovering just above the parchment. "Where did she see this?"

Corin didn't answer right away. "Wyatt saw it first—in the vault beneath the Academy. Cam described it too, right before it opened. But Valerie was the one who found it again. In the archives. The moment she saw the diagram, she recognized it. That sketch is hers."

Ben's voice dropped. "You're certain?"

Corin nodded once. "She described it in detail. Wyatt sketched it from memory. Same lines. Same mark."

Ben exhaled slowly through his nose. "I've seen this before. Once. On a ruined altar near the northern crater—what's left of the Cradle Temple."

Corin's gaze sharpened. "Cradle bloodline?"

"More than that." Ben's voice lowered. "That symbol isn't a crest. It's a warning sigil. It marked mages born outside the system's control. The ones who could awaken more than one element. The ones who could walk all paths."

Corin's eyes returned to the scroll. "Like Cam. And the mark on her wrist."

A silence stretched.

He didn't look up as he added, voice low, like speaking it aloud might make it more real:

"There was another. Before. One they tried to control."

Ben didn't answer. His jaw flexed once. Then:

"They failed."

A beat passed.

"Built him to survive the Veil. Forgot to give him anything worth surviving for."

Corin finally looked up, his voice quiet.

"And now?"

Ben didn't blink. "This time... she wasn't crafted in silence. She was born into love."

His mouth tightened.

"She is loved."

Another pause. Corin shifted a page aside.

"You knew, then. Back when Anthony took her."

Ben didn't answer at first. Then just said:

"We knew enough to hide her."

Corin shifted the top document aside, revealing a brittle page covered in bloodline lineage notations—crosses, arrows, and an old, faded seal in the corner. "We've always assumed the Capital's fear was dragons." He looked up, searching Ben's face. "But it wasn't. Not exactly."

Ben raised an eyebrow but said nothing.

"The return of balance," Corin said simply. "The kind of balance that can't be controlled."

Ben didn't speak right away. His gaze dropped to the table, then returned to Corin's eyes, steady but guarded.

Then, finally, he said, "What we found wasn't just old magic or theory. It was something buried. Contained. Sealed away centuries ago by mages who realized too late what they had unleashed."

Corin's breath caught.

Ben met his gaze evenly. "We weren't meant to find it—not me, not Anthony, not Izzy. But we did. And the closer we got, the harder Caerthalen pushed back."

Corin noticed the slight twitch at the corner of Ben's mouth—the shadow of a secret. The way his eyes flicked down to the table and back, avoiding the full truth that lay heavy between them.

He knew Ben was holding back. The truth about the bloodlines, the forbidden union, the price paid to keep it hidden—it sat tight on the table in front of them, unspoken but palpable.

Corin's voice was low. "Is that why...?"

Ben nodded once, the movement quick but resolute. "They killed her for it. Sent a Veilborn of all things after her. I don't know how that is even possible... so Anthony and I had to disappear. We swapped names, lives—everything—to keep Cam hidden. To protect what was left of the bloodline. Of her."

Another silence fell, heavy and close.

Then Ben tapped the edge of the page, his voice flat. "If Cam carries this symbol—if the shadow marked her—she may be the key to more than just the rebellion."

Corin nodded grimly. "And the target of more than just Caerthalen."

The candle had burned low again.

Ben sat at the edge of his desk; Cam's latest training log open in his hands. Her notes were precise—deliberate even in their messiness. He recognized the way she thought working in spirals, always circling the truth until it opened itself to her.

She'd made progress. Rapid progress. Too rapid.

Air, water, fire, stone—she was beginning to command them all. Not perfectly. Not always safely. But something had shifted in her rhythm. The runes she carved now pulsed with resonance beyond their form. He could feel it in the ink, in the paper itself.

It wasn't just elemental anymore.

There was something else waking in her magic. Something older than bloodline.

Ben rubbed a hand across his mouth, uneasy.

"She's changing faster than I expected."

He looked down at the journal again, then closed it with care and placed it atop the others.

"Please don't burn too brightly."

◈ ☽✦☾ ◈

The cliffs were quiet at dusk.

Wyatt sat near the edge, knees drawn in, fingers tugging absentmindedly at tufts of grass. The last light of day bled across the sky in ribbons of fading gold and blue-violet, sinking slowly behind the ridge. It was one of the rare moments that didn't demand anything from him. No training. No strategy. Just breath and stillness.

Beside him, Sael rested with his wings half-folded, long neck curled, silver-white scales faintly luminous in the dying light. He hadn't spoken since they landed. He didn't need to. Sael was like that—quiet, watchful, steady.

Wyatt exhaled, then said, low:

"I almost kissed her."

A beat passed. Then Sael stirred slightly, his tail curling closer around his own limbs.

Why didn't you? came the voice in Wyatt's mind—low, ancient, but dry with curiosity.

Wyatt scoffed, though it held no real humor. "Because I don't know if it's real. What I feel. What she feels. We've barely had time to breathe, let alone think. It's easy to feel close to someone when the world's falling apart. I don't want to mistake survival for something deeper."

Sael let out a slow breath, warm enough to ruffle Wyatt's hair.

That is wisdom... or cowardice. You'll have to decide which.

Wyatt huffed a breath and leaned back on his palms. "Thanks."

I'm serious, Sael said, sounding vaguely amused. *But if you ever get close again, I suggest you move faster. Before someone interrupts—like last time.*

Wyatt blinked. "Wait... you saw that?"

Sael's tone was drier now. *You mean when you leaned in, hesitated, and Tessa came bursting through the doors with perfect dramatic timing? Yes. Subtle as a thunderclap.*

Wyatt groaned and dropped his head into his hands. "Gods, I hate her timing."

She has a gift.

They shared a brief, companionable silence. Wind rustled the tall grass around them. The moment stretched, quiet and full of thoughts neither of them voiced.

Then Sael shifted again, his neck raising just slightly. His tone, when it came, had changed—no longer teasing.

Colder. Deeper. Timeless.

The mirror is stirring. The Hollow Prince dreams again.

Wyatt went still.

A chill rippled over his skin despite the lingering heat of Sael's breath. He didn't know what the title meant. Not really. But something in the weight of those words made his blood pulse faster.

He should've been thinking about that—about the warning, the shift in the air, the way the world felt like it was turning toward something vast and unseen.

But instead, his thoughts drifted back to her.

He'd seen Cam in visions for half his life. Known her before he truly met her. But lately, he kept wondering:

Was it fate that brought them together?

Or had he filled in the spaces with who he wanted her to be?

The last of the light disappeared behind the ridge. The stars began to emerge—quiet, watching.

Chapter 35: The Circle of Five

The forest clearing beyond the outpost was quiet but alive, ringed by ancient standing stones that leaned in like watchers. Moss veiled the base of each stone, and soft lichen bloomed in the cracks. The sun filtered through a loose canopy of birch and fir, casting fragmented light on the worn earth beneath their boots.

Cam stood at the center of the ring, eyes closed, arms relaxed at her sides.

A breeze skimmed her skin. She let herself feel it—not just on her face or arms, but deeper, through the air itself. She slowed her breathing. Tried to listen with something beyond her ears.

Around her, the others moved.

Wyatt's steps were heavier than Kaden's, more deliberate. Kaden was all silence and precision, like a thought with legs. Tessa shifted with little electric huffs of air—playful, impossible to miss. They were circling her now.

Ben stood just beyond the outer ring, arms folded, expression unreadable. He hadn't said a word since she arrived, just nodded once and stepped aside to observe. But Cam felt the weight of his gaze like a second sun.

Kaden's voice, smooth and amused: "Ready?"

Cam nodded. "Go."

At first, it was nothing—just the trees, birdsong, wind. She reached for the subtle shifts in air pressure, the tiny warps of magic that preceded movement.

There.

A flicker from the left. Fast and sharp—Tessa.

Cam turned, caught the current of storm magic curling toward her, and countered. A smooth arc of her arm dispersed the energy, redirecting it with a gust of her own.

Tessa let out a pleased laugh. "She's getting better."

Cam smiled faintly but didn't answer.

Something was coming behind her. She could feel it—or thought she could. She spun—too early.

Nothing.

Then—

A foot swept her ankle from behind and her balance vanished. Cam crashed down onto the packed earth; wind knocked from her lungs.

Kaden leaned over her with a grin. "Still too reactive."

Cam blinked up at him, annoyed but impressed. "You move like smoke."

"And you move like a question with too many answers," he replied.

She groaned and took his offered hand, letting him pull her to her feet. Her shoulder ached from the fall, but she shook it off. "I'll get you next time."

Tessa snorted. "I'm sure you will."

Cam gave her a mock glare and turned to Wyatt, who had quietly stepped into the center.

He closed his eyes slowly, shoulders straight, jaw tight.

The circle formed again, and Cam took her place beside Tessa, opposite Kaden.

For a moment, nothing happened.

Then Wyatt moved.

Or rather—felt.

His brow furrowed slightly as if tracking a whisper. Cam lunged toward him, deliberately light-footed. He turned and blocked her—barely—but his reaction was solid.

Kaden followed with a near-silent step from behind. Wyatt shifted again, just in time.

Impressive.

Then Tessa, of course, cheated.

She sent a sudden gust of wind straight into his chest.

Wyatt stumbled back with a curse, eyes flying open. "Seriously?"

Tessa's grin widened. "What? You were doing too well."

Ben called out from the edge, voice dry. "Your form's improving. But Tessa's right—you let your energy drift."

Wyatt made a face. "I let my lungs drift, mostly."

Cam was already laughing. So was Kaden. Even Ben allowed the ghost of a smile to cross his face.

It was the first time they'd all laughed together in... weeks. Maybe months.

The tension between them had finally loosened—like the fight wasn't just for survival anymore, but for something lighter. Something whole.

Still, under the warmth of it all, Cam felt something shift beneath her ribs. The way her power moved was changing. When she'd hit the ground earlier, the earth had responded—cracked slightly under her palm. And when she'd redirected Tessa's wind, it hadn't felt like one element... it had felt like three fighting for space.

She pressed a hand to her chest.

The wind stirred again, but not from anyone in the circle.

It came from her.

Across the ring, Ben's head tilted slightly, a crease forming between his brows. Cam caught it—just for a second—but he said nothing. And somehow, that silence weighed heavier than words.

She stepped out of the ring to let the others reset, wiping her hands on her pants, grounding herself in motion.

Cam wasn't sure what she was becoming. But whatever it was, it was accelerating.

And for the first time in a while...

She wasn't sure if that was a good thing.

The clearing hummed with magic and motion—dust rising from the earth, wind kicking through boots and sleeves, sparks dancing around fingertips. It was a kind of rhythm built from repetition and trust. A quiet pulse of bodies learning to read each other without needing words.

They were resetting the formation when the circle shifted again—not from within, but from the edge.

Valerie stepped into view just beyond the stones, her cloak already unfastened, sleeves rolled up as though she'd known she'd be called. The light caught the edges of her black braid, wind pulling strands free as she crossed the grass without fanfare or hesitation.

She didn't speak right away. Didn't need to.

Cam's eyes met hers. One short nod passed between them—familiar, assured. Not just invitation. Permission.

"Finally," Cam called. "Thought you were ditching us Val. "

Val smirked. "Didn't want to embarrass anyone."

Tessa huffed a laugh. "She's got claws."

"She had them yesterday," Kaden said, brushing dirt from his tunic. "She just hides them well."

Val stepped into the stone circle like she belonged there. No proving. No performance. Her gaze flicked over each of them—not measuring but noting. Observing. Connecting. Wyatt offered a subtle nod. Tessa raised an eyebrow like she'd already chosen Val as her next target. Kaden tilted his head but said nothing more.

Ben, arms crossed near a split boulder at the edge, watched with the stillness of someone who noticed everything. He didn't interrupt.

Cam gestured toward the center. "We're doing blind sensing and sparring. Pick your opponent."

Val didn't hesitate.

She turned to Tessa.

Tessa grinned. "Excellent choice."

The air shifted—just slightly, as if the clearing itself leaned in.

Tessa struck first, fast as ever—an arc of wind that twisted midair into a flicker of lightning.

But Val was already moving.

A ribbon of water curled up from the grass at her feet, split into two strands, then snapped forward with pinpoint accuracy. One deflected the bolt. The other coiled around Tessa's arm and stopped just short of her collarbone—hovering like a blade made of breath and tension.

For a moment, neither moved.

Then Val blinked, the water unraveled, and she stepped back.

Tessa looked at her arm. "Okay," she said slowly. "That's... annoying."

"Thank you," Val replied, straight-faced.

Wyatt gave a low whistle.

Kaden's eyes narrowed, more calculating now. Ben said nothing, but the brief tilt of his head marked his attention.

"Didn't learn that at the Academy," Tessa muttered, shaking out her wrist.

"No," Val said, her voice quieter now, but firm. "My brother taught me. Before Caerthalen got to him. Ten years ago."

The circle went still.

Even the wind paused.

No one asked questions—but no one looked away either.

Kaden glanced toward her. Not with pity—just recognition. Tessa's smile faded into something steadier. Wyatt's expression shifted too—respectful but measured. As if seeing more clearly now.

Cam took a step forward, brushing dust from her sleeve as she closed the distance between them. She didn't offer comfort. She didn't need to.

She offered her hand.

"You don't need to prove why you fight," Cam said. "But I see it now. And I'm with you."

Val looked at it for half a breath, then clasped it tight.

Their hands held—not a greeting, not a formality.

A mark of trust. A seam stitching shut.

And somewhere outside the circle, Ben exhaled—quiet, unreadable.

The training resumed. But the rhythm had changed.

It wasn't just a circle now.

It was a unit.

◈ ☽✦☾ ◈

The clearing still pulsed with leftover magic—faint sparks drifting through the air like heat ghosts, the scent of damp grass and singed ozone clinging to their skin. Footsteps scattered the dirt in looping, layered tracks. The standing stones hummed quietly, responding to all that had been stirred.

Cam knelt beside the half-buried water barrel, dragging her hair off her neck with one hand while the other dipped the ladle and brought it to her lips. The water was ice-cold, sharp, grounding. She welcomed the chill in her bones. Her pulse was still too fast, her fingertips tingling like they hadn't fully settled back into her own element yet—any of her elements.

A step behind her. Light. Familiar.

"You move like someone who doesn't want to be seen," Cam said without turning. The words came softer than she intended, almost instinct. She knew that silence well—the kind you learn when you'd rather the world pass you by than notice you.

Val stepped up beside her and crouched down, tucking her sleeves back into her bracers. "You learn not to leave footprints when they start following them."

Cam offered her the ladle. Val took it with a nod of thanks, drank, then stayed quiet. Not awkward—just... thinking.

The others were still scattered nearby. Wyatt and Kaden had gone to retrieve extra water flasks. Tessa was off somewhere cracking sparks through the air for fun. Ben watched from the far side of the clearing, arms crossed, but he wasn't listening in.

Cam finally broke the silence. "You good?"

Val let out a breath. "I forgot what it feels like. Being part of something without having to measure it first. Like I don't have to brace myself just to speak."

Cam smiled faintly. "It gets easier."

"I'm not sure I want it to." Val's voice was quiet, almost thoughtful. "Bracing kept me alive."

She glanced across the clearing where laughter had picked up again—Kaden had returned shouting something sarcastic, Tessa firing back with a bolt of lightning that singed a bush in response. Wyatt was smiling, for once. Not guarded. Not watching shadows.

Val turned back to Cam. "I didn't expect you to be like this."

"Like what?"

"Still standing," Val said simply. "Still... sane."

Cam chuckled, but there wasn't much humor in it. "That's generous of you."

"I mean it. You've got enough power to flatten this clearing without blinking, and you still look people in the eye like they matter."

Cam looked at her then. Really looked. "Everyone matters."

Val studied her, then smiled—soft, but real. "That's why it's terrifying."

They sat together in the hush, knees brushing dirt, the trees creaking gently around them. Above, the sky had shifted from pure blue to a silvery dusk-clouded sheen. Cam could feel the pressure of a coming storm somewhere in the distance—Tessa might be pulling it without realizing.

Cam extended her hand, palm up.

Flame curled to life first, violet-black and edged faintly in flickering gold, darker than any normal fire. Then it twisted to water—cooling, running over her skin without burning. The water split into a veil of mist that coiled into wind and finally dropped into her palm as a pebble of earth—shaped like a teardrop, heavy and humming.

She let it crumble.

Val stared. "That's not just channeling."

"No," Cam said. "It's something else now. I don't always know where it's leading."

"How do you contain it?"

"I don't. I listen."

Val blinked. Her expression cracked open a little—more awe than fear now. "That's... beautiful."

Cam tilted her head. "Want to show me your second?"

There was a pause.

Val's hands tightened slightly on her knees. Then she nodded.

She closed her eyes, and the air around her shimmered—not like heat, but like a ripple in still water. Light bent subtly. Space twisted. For a heartbeat, it looked like Cam was seeing double—two Val's, flickering slightly out of sync.

The second figure peeled away, stepped to the right, paused.

And vanished.

Cam blinked hard. "Wait—was that—?"

"I can shift perception," Val said. Her voice was steadier now, like saying it aloud gave her more control. "Not illusion, not really. It's more like I... bend where people are looking. Make them doubt what they see."

Cam leaned back slightly, visibly impressed. "That's brilliant."

Val let out a shaky laugh. "That's dangerous."

"They're the same thing sometimes."

Silence fell again, but not the heavy kind. Cam could feel something in Val now—something opening. Power, yes, but also trust. Like this was a gate she hadn't meant to walk through, but now that she had, she couldn't quite look away.

Cam didn't touch her. She didn't have to.

"Power doesn't make you dangerous," she said softly. "Denying it does."

Val's gaze lifted. Their eyes met.

And for the first time since they'd stepped into the ring, Val looked like she believed it.

The light had changed again.

The late afternoon sun slanted through the treetops, casting gold between the trunks, glinting on stones and sweat-slick shoulders. The forest clearing, once charged with tension and motion, had gone still—but not empty. It felt full in a different way now. Like breath after a held silence.

Cam stood near the edge of the circle, arms crossed, boots buried in soft grass and churned soil. Her body ached in the satisfying way that meant they'd trained well, but her mind was still attuned—not to danger, just... to everything.

Tessa was sprawled on her back in the grass, muttering about "fair fights" and "weird water tricks" as she conjured a tiny lightning orb between her fingers and lazily bounced it hand to hand. The crackle was soft, rhythmic.

Kaden sat nearby on a fallen log, chin propped in his knee, quietly re-tying his boots. He didn't say much, but Cam knew that look—his mind was still cataloging every movement, every new variable. Especially Val.

Wyatt had stepped away just slightly, sitting cross-legged by the cooling remains of Cam's violet-black fire pit, faint streaks of soot still veined with an unnatural shimmer. Sael's presence lingered faintly in his stillness, that tether humming somewhere just outside reach.

And Val—Val hadn't moved since the last spar ended. She stood inside the circle of stone, one hand resting lightly on her hip, the other hanging by her side. For the first time since arriving at the outpost, her posture held no wariness. No edge. Just balance.

She looked like she belonged there.

And what struck Cam most wasn't that she had brought Val in.

It was how easily the others had accepted her, without needing to be told.

Tessa lifted her head and called, "You've got freakish reflexes, by the way."

Val raised a brow. "You almost singed my braid. Call it survival instinct."

Cam caught Kaden's grin. Even Wyatt smirked slightly, then resumed his quiet vigil.

Val finally stepped out of the ring and dropped to sit beside Tessa, careful not to disturb the flowers blooming wild near the edge of the stone. She picked one absently—a small white bloom—and rolled it between her fingers. Her face was quiet, but not unreadable. The tension she carried in her shoulders had unwound by degrees.

Not vanished. But it softened.

Cam watched the exchange unfold like someone studying the surface of still water—seeing the reflections ripple, understanding the depth beneath. There was no defining moment where trust had bloomed. It had simply grown, somewhere between the silence and the sparring and the honesty of the fight.

And now it lived here, among them.

But with that came something else—something Cam hadn't expected.

They kept glancing at her.

Little things. When laughter rose too high and needed reigning in. When a strategy question came up. When someone looked for the cue to wind things down. They didn't ask directly, didn't put it into words—but their eyes turned her way all the same.

Cam.

The girl who once wasn't even supposed to exist.

Now the center of a circle of powerful mages, half of whom didn't trust the systems that raised them.

A circle that looked to her not just for power—but for direction.

And that terrified her more than anything Caerthalen could throw.

Because they believed in her.

And she wasn't sure she believed in herself.

Not yet.

A twig snapped lightly as someone shifted beside her.

It was Val.

She didn't speak, didn't ask. Just stood there next to Cam, shoulder to shoulder, both of them watching the others with that same mix of affection and vigilance.

After a long beat, Val murmured, "They listen to you."

Cam let out a breath. "They shouldn't have to."

"Maybe not," Val said, voice soft. "But they do."

Cam didn't answer right away. The wind had picked up, a soft whisper through the clearing. One of the standing stones flickered faintly with residual magic—violet-black with a shimmer of gold. Hers, definitely. Though she still didn't know what it meant.

She looked at Val. "You okay?"

Val nodded once. "I didn't know it would feel like this. Like I'm finally breathing the same air as everyone else."

Cam smiled—just barely. "Now you are."

Chapter 36: The Fifth Bond

The path back to the outpost wound through the woods in meandering silence. The group walked loosely bunched—still catching their breath from training, from laughter, from the strange ease that had finally settled between them.

Cam walked near the front. Her body ached, but her magic hummed too loud beneath her skin for her to feel tired. The air had grown thicker since they left the clearing. Oppressive. Like the trees were watching.

Something was wrong.

She stopped walking.

Tessa almost bumped into her. "What—?"

Cam raised her hand. "Shh."

She reached out—first with air, then with fire, then stone. The forest pushed back against her senses, heavy, distorted. The trees weren't swaying, but the wind was whispering anyway. The roots of the forest shifted like something had brushed past them, but nothing moved.

Then she heard it.

A howl—ragged, warped, far too close.

"Down!" Cam shouted.

The underbrush exploded. Branches snapped like bones.

Three shadows broke the tree line—fast and wrong. A banshee shrieked as it lunged from the left, its scream cracking through the air like glass shattering inside her skull. Behind it, a howler pounded forward on all fours, jaw split far too wide, slavering with black spit. And behind them—

Veilborn.

A scout.

The stench hit her next—sulfur, rot, cold iron.

Cam's magic surged before she could think. She flung her hand out. A blast of wind slammed into the banshee, hurling it back into the trees. Tessa struck it mid-air with a forked bolt of lightning that lit up the forest in a jagged white blaze. The wail that followed rattled Cam's bones before the creature burst into smoke.

Kaden was already moving, sword out, crouched low, quick as a wolf. "Cam! Look out!"

The Veilborn locked eyes with her and lunged.

Her wrist burned—the mark pulsing like a brand as the creature closed the distance.

"Not this time," she hissed.

A column of violet-black fire erupted from her hand, edged in flickering gold and curling with wind. The howler disintegrated mid-leap, ash scattering in the storm of her flames.

Val raised both arms. The stream beside them swelled, water surging unnaturally fast as though it shared her fury. She lashed it forward in a crashing wave that knocked the Veilborn to its knees.

Wyatt's light followed, a sharp white beam cutting through the haze. It hit the scout square in the chest. The creature shrieked, smoke spilling from its mouth as it staggered back—

Then it righted itself. Turned. Its eyes locked on Cam like hooks.

Its voice scraped the air like bone dragged over stone.

"Camomile."

Her name slithered through the trees.

And then—like ash burning too quick—it crumbled to dust.

The forest stilled.

Cam stood there breathing hard, hair tangled, hands faintly glowing. The silence felt heavier than the fight, pressing close around them.

Then—a noise behind her.

A gasp.

She turned just in time to see Wyatt's knees buckle, sudden and boneless, as if the strength had been stripped from him in a single breath. Cam lunged forward, catching his weight before he hit the earth. They sank together to the forest floor, her arms straining around him.

"Wyatt?" Her voice cracked. Panic surged sharp and cold through her veins.

His head lolled against her shoulder, breath shallow. For a heartbeat his skin seemed to glow—faint, silvery, like moonlight pulsing beneath the surface, threaded with a shimmer of gold—before it flickered and dimmed. The air around them tightened, pressing in, so thick it swallowed every sound but her own heartbeat.

Her wrist seared. The mark burned bright under her skin, pulsing in rhythm with Wyatt's shallow breaths. She clutched at it with her free hand, teeth gritted, unable to tell if the fire was hers or his.

"Wyatt—no, stay with me—" She shook him gently, afraid of breaking him if she tried harder.

His lips parted as though to speak, but no sound came. Only that terrible silence.

Then—

He stirs, a voice said.

Not hers. Not Wyatt's.

Sael.

The words thrummed through her bones, not spoken but certain, carrying the weight of something ancient and inevitable. She wasn't bonded to him. She shouldn't have been able to hear it.

And yet she did.

The mark on her wrist throbbed with the echo, heat threading through her veins until she couldn't tell where she ended and the voice began.

It didn't feel like warning. Or comfort.

It felt like prophecy.

◈ ☽✦☾ ◈

Everything burned red.

A mountain range scorched by sunless fire. The sky above was torn open—ragged and unnatural. A door of bone stood in the center of it, sealed by ancient runes that glowed like embers.

And then—it opened.

He couldn't see the face. Just the silhouette. Crowned. Hollow-eyed. Like the mark on Cam's wrist blazed in the same shape as what appeared on the door. Something stepped through. It smiled with emptiness.

A voice in his mind—not Sael's—whispered:

"She is the balance you broke."

Wyatt gasped.

He snapped back to his body, cold sweat clinging to his skin.

His head rested on Cam's shoulder—her arms still around him, grounding him, holding on like he might disappear.

He blinked up at her.

She caught me, he thought distantly.

Then—

"Sael—" he rasped, throat dry. "Who... what was that?"

Sael's answer came slowly, reverently, laced with dread.

The Hollow Prince is no longer dreaming. He's waking.

The wind stilled.

Every leaf held its breath.

And in the space between two heartbeats—

Cam knew something had changed.

Not just around them.

Inside her.

The forest was too still. Not peace—something heavier. The air pressed down like it was holding its breath, like the trees themselves had gone rigid.

Cam shifted, easing Wyatt against her shoulder. His weight sagged into her; all fire and certainty drained from him. She tightened her grip, steadying them both, her pulse hammering louder than the silence.

Kaden's voice cut through first, low and clipped. "That Veilborn knew her name." His eyes swept the group, sharp even in the fading light. "That wasn't a chance encounter. It was sent."

Val swiped the back of her hand across her mouth, leaving a dark smear of dirt. "Then sent for who? For Cam? For all of us?"

Tessa straightened slowly, the wildflower still crushed between her fingers. Her gaze found Cam's, quiet but firm. "Whatever it was—it didn't come here by accident. It was hunting."

A branch cracked in the distance. Cam's head snapped up—relief and dread tangled tight in her chest—just as Ben emerged from the trees at a run. His eyes swept the wreckage of smoke and ash before fixing on Wyatt slumped against her.

"What happened?" His voice was hard, urgent.

Kaden stepped forward, blade still drawn. "Banshee. Howler. And a Veilborn scout." He glanced once at Cam, then back to Ben. "The scout spoke. It said her name. Out loud."

Ben went very still. His jaw tightened, breath slow, measured. He muttered something almost under his breath, not meant for them:

"...running out of time."

Cam barely caught it. Then, softer still, a whisper she almost thought she imagined:

"The Hollow Prince..."

The words struck her like an echo. She'd heard them before—Sael's voice had carried the same name not long ago. For a heartbeat, she wanted to turn, to demand answers. But Wyatt stirred faintly against her, and her attention snapped wholly back to him.

Silence pressed in again until Kaden finally spoke, eyes narrowing. "It's barely dusk. How did they even get past the wards?"

The question hung there like smoke. No one answered.

She held him closer, swallowing hard. The name could wait. She'd tuck it away for later—something to ask Ben when the world wasn't breaking apart around them.

Far above, hidden beyond clouds and mountain peaks, a gray storm-drake stirred.

Virellan had come.

◈ ☽✦☾ ◈

Val sat at the far end of the dining hall, her bowl of stew barely touched, its warmth long since faded. Conversation drifted around her—low murmurs, metal against pottery, the occasional bark of laughter that sounded more like relief than joy. The fire crackled in the hearth, but her skin still felt cold.

Cam had gone with Wyatt to the infirmary after the fight. The vision he had had hit fast and hard—so fast he hadn't even braced for it. Val had seen it—how his knees buckled, how Cam caught him before he could fall, the way she hadn't let go. Wyatt had rested his head on her shoulder like he didn't know where else to lean. Like she was the only anchor he had.

Val had noticed the way they looked at each other. Cam, steady even in the middle of chaos. Wyatt, like he'd known her long before any of this began.

They'd make a cute couple, she thought absently. But the warmth of the thought didn't linger.

Her mind kept circling back to the banshee's scream, the way the air had gone brittle with lightning, the howler's guttural cry as it lunged through the trees—and the Veilborn. Not just its voice or its hunger. But how it had paused... turned... and whispered Cam's name like a secret it had never forgotten.

Val shivered.

How do you fight something that already knows you?

Her spoon clinked against the bowl. She pushed it away and rose from the bench.

"I need some air," she mumbled, not expecting—or wanting—a reply.

Outside, the sky was fading into deeper blues. The wind had stilled, but the trees felt like they were holding their breath.

She hadn't made it far down the path when footsteps padded up behind her.

Cam caught up easily, her brows pinched in concern. "Hey, I was just about to join you when I saw you leave. Is everything okay?"

Val hesitated. "Yeah," she said. "Just needed to clear my head."

Cam didn't challenge the lie—but she didn't believe it either.

After a moment, she asked, "Mind if I walk with you?"

Val offered a tired smile. "Actually... I'd like that."

They walked in silence past the outer edge of the outpost, down a narrow trail skirting the ravine. The air here was different—quieter, like the night was listening. Stars pushed through the thinning clouds overhead. Every now and then, Val heard the low hum of wardstone magic stabilizing again in the distance.

After a few minutes, Val glanced sideways. "Is Wyatt alright?"

Cam nodded. "He will be. The vision hit hard, but he's stronger than he gives himself credit for."

Val nodded too. Let it settle.

But that fear still stirred in her chest like a tide refusing to recede.

The wind shifted.

Val slowed instinctively, her feet crunching over soft stone. Something was wrong—or not wrong, exactly. Just... different. Heavy.

Cam noticed too. "Do you feel that?"

Val nodded, her pulse suddenly louder in her ears.

Then, through the trees, something moved.

Branches bowed, not broken but opened. And from the hush of the forest stepped a shape carved from storm light.

A dragon.

Gray as thunderclouds, sleek and strong, the creature stepped forward with a grace that made the world seem too slow. Light shimmered faintly across her wings, like mist caught in moonlight.

Val's breath seized in her throat.

The same fear that had cracked through her earlier returned now, tenfold—raw, instinctual. You're not supposed to be near dragons. You're not supposed to matter to them. That's not for you.

But her legs wouldn't move.

The dragon looked straight at her—not at Cam, not around her. At her.

Cam stepped gently between them, hand raised—not to shield, but to steady.

"She's not here to hurt us," Cam said softly. "I can hear her. She's curious... and focused."

Val's voice shook. "Focused on what?"

"You," Cam said.

The dragon lowered her head. Smoke curled faintly from her nostrils. Then—

I am Virellan, came the voice in her mind—deep and ancient, yet not unkind. *Stormborn of the Ember Nest. I felt your heart from the mountain wind. You carry something strong—tangled, but true. I came to see for myself.*

Val's mouth parted. She didn't breathe.

Cam's voice came again, gentle but honest.

"This is new for me too. But... I think she sees something in you. And I think you should trust that."

Val barely heard her.

"I'm not... I'm not supposed to bond a dragon," she whispered. "The Knighthood—they said only they could. That it was sacred. Controlled. I wasn't even meant to be near them..."

Cam's gaze was steady. "They said a lot of things."

The dragon stepped forward again, slower now. Her presence was immense but not crushing—like standing at the edge of a cliff, knowing the wind won't let you fall.

Will you run from what calls you? Virellan asked. *Or will you rise to meet it?*

Val blinked back tears she hadn't noticed. "I don't know if I can."

You already have, her head lowered. Val hadn't raised her hand, but it found its place beneath the storm gray dragons jaw like it was always meant to.

The moment pulsed—like the still point at the center of a storm.

Light flared between them, soft and silver. A tether formed—no ropes, no magic circle, just a knowing. A truth. And in that moment, the bond took hold.

Val's breath hitched as a rush of feeling surged through her: Virellan's mind beside hers, solid and calm. Cam's presence, faint but nearby. And then—a cascade of emotion. Cam's grief. Her love. Her guilt and quiet strength. All of it layered together like pages in a book that had never been opened until now.

Val staggered a half-step back, hand clutching her chest, but she was smiling.

"I didn't know magic could feel like this," she whispered.

Cam just nodded. "Now you do."

The words should have been simple, but they rang like a vow in Val's bones. She swallowed hard, her heart still racing as the last echoes of Cam's emotions tangled with her own. It wasn't sight or sound—it was deeper. Like hearing the truth of someone's soul without them ever speaking.

Virellan rumbled in the back of her mind, steady and approving. Mindwalker, she named her gently, the word more felt than heard.

Val blinked, the realization striking her. Not just a third ability. Not just another weapon for the rebellion. This was... connection. Something that reached past walls and words, binding people together whether they wanted it or not.

Her gaze flicked to Cam, who had already turned back down the forest path, shoulders set against whatever weight she carried. For a heartbeat Val almost spoke—almost told her what she had felt, what she now knew.

But something in Cam's steady stride stopped her.

Later, she promised herself. When Cam was ready.

A hush fell over the trees, the forest watching them pass. The outpost lanterns flickered faintly in the distance, a reminder of safety just ahead. Val drew in a long breath, steadying her racing heart.

Whatever this gift was, it had opened a door that would never close again.

Chapter 37: A Thread Between Them

By late morning, the memory of the forest still clung to Cam—the weight of catching Wyatt before he hit the ground, the look in his eyes just before he collapsed. It hadn't left her since.

The infirmary was quiet.

Faint candlelight flickered against stone walls, throwing long shadows across the floor. Most of the beds had been cleared, but one still had its curtains drawn back—Wyatt's. He sat propped against the wall, pale but upright, a half-empty mug of water on the stool beside him.

Cam paused in the doorway. She'd told herself she was just checking in, that she only wanted to make sure he was recovering. But really, she hadn't been able to stop thinking about him—not since she caught him, not since that look in his eyes before he collapsed.

He looked up the moment she stepped inside.

"Hey," he said softly.

His voice was rough but still him.

Cam crossed the room and sat at the edge of his bed without asking. "Hey."

"You didn't come earlier."

"I figured you had enough people hovering."

"I didn't want them," he said, watching her. "I wanted you."

Cam looked down at her hands, pretending to pick at a thread on her sleeve. "Well... here I am."

They were quiet for a moment.

The wind whispered through the high window slats. Somewhere outside, a nightbird chirped. The silence between them wasn't awkward—but it wasn't easy either.

Cam tried to find a softer entry into the conversation. "Val bonded a dragon last night."

Wyatt blinked. "I heard. Sael felt it. Said the mountain woke."

Cam smiled faintly. "Virellan. That's her name. She's storm-colored—purplish gray with eyes like clouds ready to break."

"Did Val call her?"

"No. Virellan came to her." She glanced toward the window, then back to him. "Val was terrified. But she didn't run."

"Sounds familiar," Wyatt said, watching her face.

Cam gave a small, surprised laugh. "She kept saying she wasn't ready. That the Capital and the academy always told her dragons belonged to the Knighthood. That magic like hers wasn't meant to mix with something that free."

"And you told her otherwise?"

"I didn't have to," Cam murmured. "Virellan did."

Wyatt nodded, then leaned back slightly against the pillows. "Do you think the others will follow her lead? The mages? Possibly other dragons?"

Cam hesitated. "They've been taught dragons meant order. Control. Bonded only to non-mages, to keep the balance." She met his eyes. "But now they're watching us—Val, me. You. All of us. And I think they're starting to wonder if that balance was a lie."

Wyatt's hand twitched at his side. She noticed.

She reached for it—gently, instinctively—and the moment their skin touched, warmth sparked beneath her ribs. The magic answered before she could think.

Light bloomed at the center of her palm, soft and golden, threading into Wyatt's skin. His breath caught—but didn't pull away.

Her heart slammed into her ribs. "I-I didn't mean to—"

"You weren't trying," Wyatt said quietly, watching the glow fade. "You just did."

It had happened with Ben, too. The healing. But this felt different.

Cam couldn't explain it—not with words. It wasn't just bloodline or survival instinct. With Ben, it had felt like something ancient and familiar. With Wyatt... it was personal. Magnetic. Tangled in something she didn't fully understand yet.

"You don't look like you're about to faint anymore," she murmured.

"I'm not," he said, gaze steady. "That's because you're here."

Cam swallowed hard and stood too quickly. "You should rest."

Before she could turn to leave, Wyatt caught her hand again, not with urgency—just quiet insistence.

"Cam," he said. "Thank you. For catching me."

She blinked. Her throat tightened.

"I always will," she whispered.

The words lodged deeper than she expected, heavy and frightening in their certainty. She wasn't used to giving promises like that—too many times life had proven how fragile always could be. But she meant it. Gods, she meant it.

And maybe that was why it scared her most of all.

By dinner time, after a long day training with Ben and Sylithra, Cam walked toward the hall. Her arms still ached from the drills, the memory of Sylithra's voice sharp in her mind—again, but steadier this time. Ben's corrections had been quieter, patient, but no less relentless.

The echo of fire and wind still clung to her skin when she reached the doorway.

She stepped inside and felt it almost immediately—like a ripple in the current. Not silence, not stares... but awareness. The kind that made your skin prickle. The kind that followed you even when backs were turned.

Mages filled the benches, eating, laughing, murmuring. But occasionally, a conversation would pause just a little too long. A glance would flick her way. A whisper would hush mid-sentence.

They weren't looking at her the way people in her hometown used to. This wasn't fear of a stranger. This was fear of something shifting—something they'd been taught to keep tightly caged.

They were taught dragons meant order—tools of the Knighthood. Cam glanced around, noting the bonded pairs in the room. Kaden. Tessa. Wyatt. A few others the rebellion had taken in—mages who had risked everything to claim their birthright.

But now they watched Cam, Val and their friends ... and wondered if that order was unraveling.

Some eyes held curiosity. A few, hope. More than a few held suspicion.

She spotted her friends seated toward the back, in the same corner they always claimed: Kaden leaning back with arms crossed, Tessa poking at her dinner with a spark still playing at her fingertips, Wyatt had been released from the infirmary after lunchtime, he looked less pale but steady again. Val sat beside them, quieter than usual. Her hair was pulled back, damp at the temples like she'd just washed her face. She didn't look up right away when Cam approached.

Cam sat down with her bowl, trying to smile as Tessa nudged her in greeting. Someone cracked a joke about Tessa nearly stealing a loaf of bread earlier. There was laughter. Forks scraping on plates. Normalcy—but thinner than it used to be. Everything felt too loud and too quiet all at once.

Cam was mid-sentence when it hit her—soft as a brush of wind across her mind. A flicker.

Startled, she paused.

Not a thought. Not quite. More like a feeling slipping past a door left ajar.

Fear. Raw. Flickering beneath a calm mask. Not hers. Not dragon. Not like the mark. Different. New.

She turned, eyes settling on Val.

Val wasn't looking at her. She was staring down at her half-eaten plate, shoulders slightly tense, lips pressed into a flat line. But that wasn't what made Cam pause.

It wasn't like her usual mind-links with Sael or Sylithra. This had weight. Distance. And yet it had come from Val—because of Virellan, maybe?

Cam blinked it away. She didn't reach for it. Didn't push. But she felt the shift—like something new had taken root between them. Something neither of them had asked for.

She cleared her throat and focused on her food again.

Across the table, Wyatt said something low to Kaden, and both glanced her way. Cam felt her face flush. She wasn't sure if it was because of the sudden link—or the way Wyatt's gaze lingered just a heartbeat longer than it should have.

She looked away, fast, but not fast enough.

Val noticed.

There was a flicker in her expression, half-thoughtful, half-knowing. But she didn't say anything. Instead, she pushed her bowl aside and stood up abruptly.

"I need some air," she said, not really to anyone in particular.

Cam straightened. "Everything alright?"

Val gave a smile that didn't quite reach her eyes. "Just... tired.

Chapter 38: Quiet Sparks

Kaden stood up a few minutes later without a word, his expression unreadable. He didn't look at anyone as he left the table, just slipped quietly into the dimming light beyond the dining hall.

Cam noticed. She always noticed. But she didn't say anything—not out loud. Her focus had shifted inward, caught on the pulse of something she didn't fully understand.

Her magic had felt... different tonight. Wilder. Not just stronger, but broader—stretching in directions she hadn't trained for. She could still feel the echo of it, coiled under her skin, humming with something that wasn't quite control and wasn't quite chaos. It was expanding faster than she knew how to hold.

It pressed at the edges all at once—flame, wind, stone, water—each straining for space in her veins, not clashing exactly, but not separate anymore either.

And it scared her.

Not because she thought it would consume her, but because it felt like it already belonged to something larger than her.

Something waking.

The sounds of the hall closed in around her again. Normal, busy, buzzing.

But Cam could still feel that flicker in the back of her mind—like a thread pulling tight. Not enough to bind. But enough to warn:

She didn't know what it meant. But it was there now. Unavoidable.

Something had changed. And not just in Val.

The cool air hit Val like a balm as she stepped beyond the torches of the dining hall. It wasn't cold exactly, but it was enough to ease the heat beneath her skin—the kind that had nothing to do with temperature and everything to do with pressure.

She hadn't finished her food. Couldn't. Her stomach had twisted the moment she sat down. The room had felt too loud and too quiet all at once. Eyes flicking, voices rising, Cam's magic pressing against her like a tide even though she hadn't meant it to.

It's not her fault, Val thought as she rubbed her arms, pacing toward the edge of the training yard. It was her own.

Her mind kept circling back to the banshee's scream. The howler's breath on her shoulder. The Veilborn scout—its mouth too wide, its eyes too still. She'd held her own, yes. Fought. Survived. But afterward... she'd shaken in the dark, hands clenched beneath the blanket. And now, even with Virellan curled in the dragon roost above the clouds, she didn't feel stronger.

She felt cracked open.

Footsteps sounded behind her.

Val turned, tense—but it was just Kaden.

He didn't speak at first, just fell into step beside her, hands tucked into his coat pockets like he did this sort of thing often.

"I'm fine," she said, a little too quickly.

"I know," he said gently. "Doesn't mean you have to be alone."

Val sighed. "I just needed air."

"Me too," Kaden replied, and let the silence stretch.

They walked across the stone paths that framed the outpost, heading toward the line where courtyard met woods. The sky was softening, streaked with copper and gray. Shadows stretched long over the ground.

Val's arms were still crossed, her jaw tight. Kaden said nothing, just matched her pace.

After a while, she asked, "Is Wyatt alright?"

"He's better," Kaden said. "Cam healed him. Not on purpose, I think—it just happened. She's like that. He was pale earlier, but he steadier now."

Val nodded. "That vision... I've never seen anything like it. It looked like it ripped him out of himself."

Kaden didn't respond immediately. When he did, his voice was quiet. "He didn't have time to ground. He usually can, but... that was something bigger. Something darker."

They paused at the edge of the trees. The wind moved through the branches like it knew something they didn't, stirring loose leaves and the scent of pine. Somewhere deeper in the forest, something rustled—but didn't come closer. Watching. Waiting.

Val didn't look at Kaden when she spoke.

"I thought bonding Virellan would make me feel... stronger. More certain. Like I'd finally fit the shape everyone keeps expecting me to fill."

She shook her head slightly. "But all it's done is make the fear louder."

Kaden didn't answer right away. He looked out over the treetops, jaw tight, arms folded across his chest like he was holding something in.

Then, finally:

"You think we weren't scared too?"

Val glanced over, not defiant—just tired. "You and Tessa always make it look easy."

A dry laugh escaped him. "That's the point. It's not."

He looked at her then, fully.

"I still wake up some nights convinced I'm going to fail them. Fail her. But I move anyway. That's all we can do."

Val looked down at her hands. "What if that's not enough?"

Kaden's voice softened. "Then we keep moving until it is."

She looked up, and for a second, her eyes met his. Something passed between them—something quiet and flickering, like the moment before lightning. She hated how much that steadied her.

Val looked away first. "It's getting late."

Kaden nodded. "I'll walk you back."

The outpost was dim now, torchlights flickering against stone and wood as they crossed back toward the barracks. Val walked beside him, arms still folded, her steps a little slower now. She hadn't said much the rest of the way, but Kaden didn't mind. He wasn't always good with words either—especially when something mattered.

When they reached her quarters, she paused. For a moment, it looked like she might say something else. But then she just smiled—small and grateful.

"Thanks, Kaden."

"Anytime," he said, and meant it.

She stepped inside, closing the door with a quiet click behind her.

Kaden lingered for a second, then turned toward his own quarters. The ones he shared with Wyatt.

The path was quiet, the sky deepening into blue-black overhead. Crickets chirped. Distant wings beat once, twice—maybe Sael or Sylithra passing by on patrol.

He thought about Val.

The night he first saw her—when he'd teleported her, Alex, and a handful of others out of the Academy—he'd noticed her right away. Not because she was the loudest, or the most powerful. But because she wasn't afraid to look him in the eye when the sky cracked open above them.

She'd been quiet. Composed. But underneath that calm was a spark. One he recognized.

He didn't know when exactly it shifted from curiosity to something else. Maybe it was tonight. Or maybe it had always been coming.

And then, of course, there was Wyatt. He smiled faintly, shaking his head.

Wyatt watched Cam like she was a prayer he didn't know how to say. Like if he looked away, she'd vanish. Kaden had known about the visions since they were twelve. Had watched his brother carry that weight in silence. Always watching. Always waiting.

He wasn't jealous. Cam was one of his closest friends—more like a sister than anything else. And Wyatt... he deserved to love someone real.

He just hoped his brother saw her clearly. Not the girl from prophecy. The girl in front of him.

Kaden reached the door to their quarters. Paused.

Something brushed his mind—dark, thin as smoke. Not Tenebrin. Not Cam. Not Val. Not Veilborn. Something else. Watching. Waiting.

His jaw tightened, but he didn't linger. Just filed it away the way he always did when shadow whispered too close.

He blinked. The presence faded.

He stepped inside. The door closed behind him with a soft thud.

Chapter 39: How They Hold Their Power

Cam stood at the edge of the training grounds, boots rooted in the earth, arms crossed loosely over her chest. Morning mist clung to the grass, and faint gold light spilled through the trees, catching the breath of dragons in the distance.

Behind her, voices echoed—Tessa laughing at something Kaden said, Wyatt speaking low and steady to Val. The others had started early, sparring in pairs or guiding their dragons through formation patterns overhead. She should've joined them. Should've moved. But instead, she stayed still.

She watched Sael glide once in a wide, elegant loop, his wings catching the light like brushed pearl. Virellan stood off to the side, more grounded, more watchful. Even from here, she could feel his thoughts brushing against Val's.

And then there was Sylithra. Silent and waiting behind her own mind, like she always was—just beneath the surface.

Cam swallowed and let her focus sharpen.

"All my friends have three abilities. Each one learned to master them in their own way. And me? I have them all. Every element, every echo. I don't even know how I'm doing it—just that it keeps building, faster than I can keep up. I'm not looking for control. Not yet. I just want to understand what I'm becoming. Maybe they can help me."

You're thinking too loudly again, Little Flame.

Sylithra's voice folded into her mind without warning—low and wry, with just the faintest curl of fondness. It always felt like heat through fog, her presence: comforting, but impossible to ignore.

Cam blinked, startled—then exhaled.

"Sorry," she offered.

There's no need to apologize. I like the noise your mind makes, Sylithra said, amused. *Especially when it circles something true.*

Cam glanced down at her palms. Callused from training. Scared from the Vorrakai battle. But still hers. Still human—for now.

They cannot teach you to be what you are, Sylithra went on, quieter now. *But they can teach you how they hold their power. Learn from them. Let it shape you.*

Cam closed her fingers slowly into fists. A pause.

Then, softer*: And for once, do not carry it all alone.*

Cam looked up, toward the others. Toward the morning light cracking open above the field. She took one slow breath, grounded herself in the wind, the soil, the flame just beneath her skin.

And stepped forward.

The sky above the outpost cracked open with distant thunder, as if answering the energy building in Tessa's chest. She'd always liked stormy days. Something about the tension in the clouds felt like home.

They stood at the edge of the northern clearing, far enough from the training grounds that the trees wouldn't catch fire—again.

Cam stood opposite her, arms loose at her sides, boots dug into the damp grass. She looked determined. Nervous, maybe. But mostly determined.

That was the thing about Cam. Always watching. Always listening. As if she could learn everything through silence.

"You sure you want to start with lightning?" Tessa asked, tossing her braid over her shoulder. Sparks danced across her fingertips. "We could do air. Or sound. Sound is fun—it breaks things."

Cam shook her head. "Lightning feels right. I've... touched it before."

Touched it. Tessa remembered that Vorrakai strike—how Cam had channeled something fast, wild, and furious, all instinct. That wasn't just touching it. That was almost becoming it.

Still, she didn't say that.

"Alright," Tessa said, and took a step forward. "First rule: lightning doesn't wait. It doesn't ask. If you hesitate, it goes wild. So don't try to leash it. Let it move through you."

Cam nodded, brow furrowed.

Tessa inhaled, grounding herself. Then she reached for the spark. It crackled in her blood, always waiting, always there. She threw her hand up toward the sky and a thin streak of white-blue light arced from her palm into the clouds above.

Thunder followed a breath later.

"See? Not so hard," Tessa said, shaking the residual charge out of her hand. "Your turn."

Cam didn't move at first. Then she raised one arm, palm open, and closed her eyes.

For a moment—just a moment—the air around her shimmered. Charged. Tessa felt the hair on her arms lift. The way it did before a storm hit.

But Cam's brows furrowed. The magic faltered. The energy didn't strike—it just... dissipated.

Cam exhaled sharply. "It's there. But it's like I'm holding too many threads at once. I don't know which one to pull."

Tessa stepped closer, her voice quieting. "Then don't pull. Breathe. Feel which one's already pulling you."

Cam blinked at her.

"I'm serious," Tessa added. "You're not supposed to force magic. You follow it. The trick is knowing when it's leading you toward power—and when it's leading you off a cliff."

That pulled a half-smile from Cam. "And how do you know the difference?"

"You don't. You get burned a few times and figure it out."

Tessa watched her for a long moment, noting how tightly she held herself, how her shoulders hunched like she was trying to make room for too much inside her.

"When I was ten," Tessa said suddenly, "I screamed during a storm. Not from fear—just to see if I could outmatch the thunder."

Cam tilted her head. Listening. Always listening.

"I lost," Tessa added with a grin. "But I heard it answer me. That's when I knew sound was more than just a voice. It was a force."

Cam's lips quirked. "I would've screamed too."

Tessa shrugged. "You're not afraid of power. That's why you'll learn. But you do have to let go."

There was a pause. Then, slowly, Cam raised her hand again.

Tessa didn't speak this time. She just stepped back and waited.

Lightning flickered across the sky like a warning.

The storm answered—not in a bolt, but in a hum. Energy gathered around Cam like wind circling a mountain peak. Her hair lifted. The air snapped sharp. Tessa could feel the charge building between them.

Then—crack.

A thin, silver line of lightning sparked from Cam's palm and vanished into the trees. Not perfect. But it was real.

Cam dropped her hand, chest rising and falling, eyes wide.

"That," Tessa said, grinning, "was a very good start."

Cam looked down at her hand. "It didn't feel like power."

"What did it feel like?"

Cam's voice was quiet. "A boundary. Like I just crossed one."

Tessa nodded slowly. "Good. That means you're getting closer."

They stood in silence for a moment, letting the tension ease.

Just before they turned back toward the outpost, Tessa added softly, "You're not alone in this, Cam. You never were."

Cam didn't reply. But her expression said enough.

Tessa didn't say anything else.

She didn't need to.

The wind that cut across the training field wasn't cold, but it was sharp—like it wanted you to flinch just to see if you would. Kaden stood at the top of the ridge, watching Cam make her way toward him. She looked steadier than she had yesterday. More present. But there was tension in her shoulders, like she hadn't let herself breathe since she woke up.

She stopped a few paces away, arms crossed. Her chestnut brown hair whipped around her face in the breeze.

"You sure?" he asked.

Cam didn't hesitate. "I need to understand this power I have. Not just what it can do—but how to carry it."

Kaden gave a slow nod. That was why he respected her—why they all did. She wasn't asking for shortcuts. She was asking for truth.

He raised one hand, fingers flickering with shadow as the wind pulled around him in a spiral. "Let's start with air," he said. "Because it's the most deceptive."

Cam arched a brow. "You're saying wind lies?"

"I'm saying wind listens," Kaden corrected. "Too well. It picks up everything. That's why it's dangerous. You don't command it. You ask. And if you ask wrong, it'll show you just how loud silence can be."

He stepped back and let the breeze rush through him. It lifted around his body like a cloak, invisible but real. Then it snapped into a compressed blast at his side, enough to knock a training dummy across the field with a solid thud.

Cam whistled. "I still forget how precise you are."

Kaden offered a faint grin. "Precision's how I stay alive." He gestured. "Your turn."

Cam closed her eyes. The wind responded immediately—maybe too immediately. It curled around her like it recognized her weight, her intent. But when she pushed, it faltered. Skittered sideways like a misheard word.

Kaden saw it the moment it slipped.

"Stop," he said quickly, stepping forward.

Cam opened her eyes, frustrated. "I felt it. Then it just—"

"You're overcorrecting. You're used to magic obeying emotion. Wind doesn't care how you feel. It cares how you listen."

She exhaled, nodded, and tried again.

This time, she let the wind move first. It circled her, cautious. Kaden watched her find its rhythm—adjust to its speed instead of forcing it to hers. And then, quietly, a soft gust lifted her hair and the dirt at her feet in a slow spiral.

Not a weapon. A response.

Kaden smiled, small and genuine. "That's it."

Cam opened her eyes, and for the first time, he saw a flicker of ease behind them. Not confidence. Not yet. But ease.

"Alright," he said, stepping back. "Now try the shadow."

Cam hesitated. "That one's harder."

"I know."

He called a sliver of darkness into his palm. It rippled like ink across his fingers, stretching and warping, alive but controlled.

"Shadow is weight. It's memory. Not evil—but full of echoes. Most people think they're summoning shadow when they're really just dredging up fear."

Cam stepped towards him, focused. "And you're not afraid of it?"

"I am," Kaden admitted. "That's how I control it."

She didn't answer. Just raised her hands and let herself reach. At first, nothing came. Then... something shifted behind her. A line of darkness where the light didn't fall quite right. It writhed faintly in the corner of her eye like a suggestion.

It didn't answer like the wind. It watched.

Kaden felt it too. His own shadows stirred—but they didn't resist. They knew her. Or maybe... they were already part of her.

Cam didn't summon more. She just acknowledged what was already there. And the darkness settled—like a wolf curling up beside someone it decided not to bite.

When she turned back to Kaden, her hands were steady.

"How did I do?" she asked.

Kaden's expression was unreadable for a moment. Then he said softly, "Better than me, the first time. You didn't try to own it. That's why it didn't fight you."

Cam was quiet, but something in her relaxed—like the weight on her ribs had shifted.

"You still haven't asked me to teach you teleportation," he said, after a beat.

Cam smirked. "That's because I like knowing where I'll land."

Kaden huffed a laugh. "Fair."

But he didn't say what he was thinking: that someday soon, she'd need to. And when she did, he'd be the one to show her how to let go of the ground without falling apart.

As Cam turned to walk back toward the ridge, Kaden lingered a moment longer.

He remembered the first time he saw her command shadow and wind in the Vorrakai battle—how instinct had taken over, how alive she looked even while breaking.

She was powerful, yes. But she wasn't losing herself to it.

She was learning how to hold it.

And Kaden? He was starting to understand why people followed her.

Even if she didn't yet.

Chapter 40: The Shape of Connection

Cam's illusion flickered, then vanished—again.

The image of the sword she'd been trying to replicate shimmered for half a second before falling apart like ash caught in wind.

Val crossed her arms. "You're forcing it. Don't shape what it looks like. Shape what it feels like. Illusion is emotion first—magic second."

Cam groaned. "Easy for you to say. You make shadows wear your face."

Val smiled faintly. "Took me two years and three broken ribs to get there. Come on. Again."

Cam started to protest, but Val raised a hand, conjuring a near-perfect replica of Sylithra with a flick of her wrist—scaled down, yes, but vivid in color, motion, presence. The dragon's wings rippled with shimmering flame before the illusion burst into gold dust.

Cam's mouth opened, then shut.

Val smirked. "It's not about accuracy. It's about belief. If they believe it's real, it is—at least for long enough."

Cam exhaled, hands on her hips. "Is that how you got so good at lying?"

"Partly." Val's expression turned serious. "Partly Virellan."

She glanced toward the shadows of the trees, where the sleek purple-gray dragon lay half-shrouded by leaves. Her head was low, eyes closed—resting but listening.

"That's when your illusions started working better?" Cam asked.

Val shook her head. "No. That's when the other thing started."

Cam looked up. "Other thing?"

Val hesitated. She hadn't told anyone this—not even Tessa. Maybe because she didn't understand it. Or maybe because it hadn't felt hers until recently.

"My third ability didn't show up until after Virellan chose me," she said quietly. "Mind-speak, or something like it. I don't know the real name. But I started... hearing people. Feeling what they felt, even when they weren't saying it. Sometimes I slip and see flashes—memories, maybe? But not mine."

Cam frowned, attentive now. "Mindwalking?"

Val nodded. "It's like I step into the current of someone's thoughts and emotions without meaning to. Like there's a river and suddenly I'm ankle-deep in it before I realize it's not my water. I read once that the old texts called it forbidden. Said it blurred too many lines between souls."

"Does Virellan help?"

Val glanced back at him. "She's the only reason I haven't drowned in it."

Silence.

Cam crouched low, dragging her finger through the dirt, tracing shapes without thinking. "You think it was always in you?"

Val leaned back on her palms; gaze tilted toward the sky. "Not always. I think it was buried. Dormant. Waiting for the right bond. The right... connection."

Cam's brows drew together. "Most of mine didn't show until after I left Brimclif. Even with Sylithra, some of them stayed quiet—like they were holding their breath. Like they were waiting for the others to arrive. Like pieces only waking once the rest were near."

Val shifted closer, her tone soft but steady. "Maybe that's the difference between power and resonance. The Capital breeds mages to control them. To keep their magic neat, single, contained." She gestured toward Cam, faint smile tugging at her mouth. "But the dragons? They don't control. They awaken. They bring out what was always meant to be."

Cam nodded slowly. "What if what's meant to be is dangerous?"

Val smirked. "Then I guess it's our job to be more dangerous."

Cam laughed softly—then stilled. "Have you ever... heard me?"

Val shook her head. "No. Not unless your thoughts are screaming."

"Good."

A beat passed.

"But if you do," Cam added, "and you find something you shouldn't... I trust you to walk out."

Val held her gaze, but something in Cam's tone snagged. Almost like there was more behind it—something unsaid, tightly guarded. For a heartbeat, Val swore she felt the echo of words unspoken. Don't. Don't ever look too closely.

She pushed the impression away and just said: "And I trust you to pull me back if I don't."

They clasped hands—not as reassurance, but as recognition.

Chapter 41: What Endures

They found a quiet corner of the old orchard, where the roots of ancient trees pressed up through the moss and the light filtered soft through their high branches. Cam stood with her arms folded, her weight shifting from foot to foot. Not anxious—just... full. Like there was too much inside her and she didn't know what to do with it.

Wyatt knew the feeling.

"You sure about this?" he asked, adjusting the leather cuff on his wrist where Sael had singed it earlier. "Light isn't easy."

Cam gave a small smile. "Nothing is, lately."

He looked at her for a long moment, then nodded.

"Alright," he said. "Let's start simple. What do you think light is?"

Cam tilted her head. "Energy? Illumination?"

"Truth," Wyatt said quietly. "Light doesn't lie. It reveals."

He opened his palm, and a pulse of warmth shimmered there—not harsh, not searing, just steady. Like dawn held in his hand.

"It's not about brightness," he went on. "It's about clarity. Focus. When I call light, I don't think about fire or heat—I think about seeing."

Cam tilted her head. "But shadow reveals too. Doesn't it? The things people try to hide."

Wyatt glanced at her, surprised by the sharpness of it. Then he nodded once. "Maybe. But light shows you the choice. Shadow just shows you the cost."

Cam stepped closer, her gaze locked on the glow in his palm. She didn't flinch, but he noticed her jaw flex. The kind of tension that came with trying not to want something too much.

"Try it," he said. "Not like a weapon. Just... like you're asking the world to be a little clearer."

Cam closed her eyes. Reached. For a long moment, nothing happened.

Then—flicker.

The air around her hand shimmered faintly. It wasn't light yet. But it wasn't shadow either.

Wyatt felt his breath catch. She was close.

"You're thinking too much," he said gently.

"I'm always thinking too much."

He chuckled softly. "Then think about this—light isn't something you force. It's already there. You just... have to stop standing in the way."

She opened her eyes, brow furrowed, then looked down at her hand.

This time, when she reached again, the glow came gentler. Like it was responding to her breath. And then it grew—a soft halo of warmth cradled between her fingers.

Wyatt swallowed. "That's it."

Cam looked up at him. "I thought it would feel bigger."

"It doesn't have to be loud to be powerful."

They stood there in silence for a moment, the light pulsing softly between them. Not blinding. Not harsh.

Just present.

Later, they sat side by side at the roots of the orchard's largest tree, knees brushing. The light had faded, but the ground beneath them was warm from sun-soaked stone.

Cam leaned back, arms behind her, staring up through the branches. "How do you... deal with the visions?"

Wyatt blinked. He hadn't expected the question.

He glanced over at her. Her eyes weren't on him—they were tracking some unseen star, some unspoken fear.

He hesitated before answering, voice low. "I don't always. Some days, they win." His jaw flexed, then softened. "But I try to hold onto what's real. What's here. That's what keeps me grounded."

A pause, then he added, almost as if realizing it as he said it: "I think that's part of why earth comes so naturally to me. The visions pull me away, but earth—it anchors me. Reminds me of now."

Cam didn't reply, but he saw the way her hands curled slightly against the grass, like she was memorizing the feel of it.

He picked up a small stone and held it out to her.

"When the visions come," he said, "hold onto something physical. Stone. Bark. Sand. Breathe into it. Name the things around you. Anchor yourself to the present, not the possible."

Cam took the stone and rolled it between her fingers.

"And what if it's not just a vision?" she asked softly. "What if it's me unraveling?"

Wyatt exhaled slowly.

"Then we hold you together. Until you can hold yourself."

Cam looked at him then. Really looked. And for a breath, the world narrowed. Her eyes, dark as the storm she carried, met his—steady, searching.

He'd seen her in flames. In frost. In shadow and light.

But this moment—quiet, trembling, real—this was what terrified him most.

Not the prophecy. Not the power.

But the girl.

The girl who didn't need a reason to trust him but did.

"You're stronger than you think," he said.

"I'm more scared than I thought."

"Good," he murmured. "That means you're still yourself."

Cam gave him a small smile. Not bright. Not wide. But honest.

And that was enough.

She leaned her head against his shoulder—quiet, unspoken trust settling between them like the last light of day.

The forge's glow spilled long shadows across the training yard. Sparks snapped with each hammer strike, and the heat softened the metal just enough to shape.

Ben watched Cam grip the half-formed blade in her palm, her brows drawn in tight focus.

"She's resisting you," he said.

Cam blinked at him. "The metal?"

Ben nodded. "She doesn't know if she can trust you yet."

Cam exhaled through her nose, flexing her fingers. "It's just steel."

He gave a small grunt. "Nothing's just anything. Not when it's bonded to your will. You're not controlling it, Cam—you're asking it to listen."

She set the blade down gently, then looked at him. "You talk about it like it's alive."

"It is. In its own way. Metal remembers heat. It remembers pressure. It takes time to teach it something new without breaking it."

Cam looked down at her hands. "Then maybe it doesn't want to be mine."

Ben stepped forward, voice low but certain. "Metal doesn't want or not want. It endures. Just like you."

He saw the flicker of something in her—doubt, maybe, or something older. But she didn't say anything. Just nodded and reached for the blade again.

He guided her through it. How to feel the pull in the metal. How to let her magic follow its natural grain instead of forcing it into shape. Her affinity was clear—she didn't bend the steel so much as reveal it, like it was already waiting to be forged.

"She listens," Cam said, surprised, as the blade warmed and curved gently to her will.

Ben smiled faintly. "She does now."

They worked in silence for a while, until the sky deepened to indigo and the forge's heat no longer pushed back the cold completely.

Then, Cam spoke—quiet, like the thought had waited too long and finally pushed through.

"I want my last name to be Miles-Layton."

Ben froze.

The hammer in his hand lowered.

He turned to her, slowly.

"What made you decide that?" he asked, gently. Carefully.

She didn't look at him. Her gaze stayed on the sword's edge. "I've carried my mother's name all my life. And I didn't know her—not really. Just her absence. I don't have many pieces of her. But now... I have you."

She paused, then added, almost too softly: "I want to carry both. That feels like mine."

Ben's throat tightened.

She never knew Isabella. And she'd barely known him. But she was still choosing this—choosing them—like she'd carried the truth of it in her bones since the beginning.

"You don't have to ask for that," he said roughly.

Cam shrugged. "I know. I just wanted you to hear it first."

Ben didn't respond right away. He couldn't. The weight of it pressed in too hard—not guilt, not anymore. Something else. Something like awe.

He hadn't raised her. Hadn't protected her the way he should've. But she was still giving him a place at her side. And she didn't owe him that.

She'd chosen to become a Miles not through blood or legacy.

But through will.

And he knew—more than anyone—that was what made a name powerful.

Cam smiled at him, small and steady. Then turned back toward the steel, holding out her hand once more.

Ben walked toward her and set down the chisel. His tone softened again. "Metal takes patience. And pressure. You don't command it. You guide it."

Cam looked at the iron again, more thoughtful this time. "It reminds me of you."

He paused. "How's that?"

"You don't move unless it matters. But when you do... it holds."

Ben looked at her for a long moment.

"You're learning," he said, voice low.

"No," she said quietly. "I'm remembering. You taught me things I didn't understand until now."

She reached for the metal again. This time, the steel lifted—not smoothly, not entirely, but enough to hover between her palms like it was weighing her intention.

It didn't scream like lightning. Didn't flare like flame.

It just held.

Ben's throat tightened. He looked at her—not the steel, but her.

"That fire in you," he said quietly, "it's changing. Shifting in ways I've only seen once before. The steel isn't the only thing enduring, Cam." His jaw flexed, but his voice softened at the end. "You are too. And gods help me; it unsettles me as much as it steadies me."

Ben exhaled slowly. The smallest smile touched his lips.

"You'll make a good smith one day," he said.

Cam smirked. "Not likely."

He didn't press it. Just stood beside her, watching the metal settle gently back onto the workbench.

He didn't say it, but the thought lingered:

You already carry more than most blades ever will.

The night was still when Cam climbed the narrow stairs of the watchtower. The stone walls breathed cold against her skin, the torches long burned down to embers. Up here, the world stretched quiet and wide—nothing but sky and stars and the faint, steady glow of the forge far below.

But their voices hadn't left her. They wound tight in her chest, louder than the wind.

Tessa's storm—don't leash it, let it move through you.

Kaden's shadows—it listens, if you don't try to own it.

Val's illusions—it's not about accuracy, it's about belief.

Wyatt's light—truth doesn't lie; you just stop standing in the way.

And Ben's fire—you don't command it. You guide it.

So many voices. So many ways to hold. And all of them right.

She let her hand drift upward into the darkness. For a heartbeat, the air shimmered—violet fire at its core, shadow-black threading the edges, and within it the faintest flicker of gold. Not bright, not whole—just a whisper, like resonance humming at the edges of something waiting to be born.

Her chest tightened. It didn't feel like fire. Or light. Or storm. Not exactly.

It felt like threads brushing against each other—voices, elements, truths—pulling toward something more.

Her fingers curled quickly, snuffing the shimmer out before it could take shape. The night swallowed it whole, leaving only starlight and silence.

Cam exhaled, slow. She didn't have words for it yet. Maybe there weren't any.

But the thought clung to her all the same, as persistent as a heartbeat: *Power doesn't only endure alone. Maybe it's what answers when you don't.*

Chapter 42: Wings and Weight

The cold had arrived before the snow. The kind of sharp, brittle chill that sank into stone and breath, warning that winter waited just beyond the next hill—but hadn't yet crossed the ridge. Frost lined the edges of the outpost towers. Dragon breath steamed like fog in the morning air. Overhead, the sky was washed in steel-gray light, pale with the promise of snow, but not quite ready to fall.

Cam adjusted her grip on Sylithra's reins, shoulders stiff beneath the weight of flight armor. The wind bit through the leather seams, but it wasn't the cold that made her heart pound.

Today, they flew together. All of them.

She glanced to her left—Sael gliding in silence beside them. Brontheus followed behind, thunder coiled in his wings. And to the far edge of the formation—

Val.

Val and Virellan.

It was the first time the full group had flown together since the Vorrakai attack. The first time Val had joined them at all. Her silhouette was smaller against the sky, her posture cautious, movements tight. But she held her ground in the formation. Barely drifting.

Cam felt the way her own magic hummed—shifting between air and flame, steadying in the current. She'd trained hard these past weeks, learned from her friends, pushed into the edges of power she hadn't known she possessed.

But today wasn't about mastering more.

It was about holding it together.

Cam steadied her breath, whispering to Sylithra, "Don't let me fall."

The dragon's laugh crackled back like distant thunder. *Little Flame. You've already risen farther than most.*

And yet still—she looked toward Val. Just to be sure she was holding on.

◈ ☽✦☾ ◈

Every breath tasted like iron and sky.

The wind howled past her ears, sharp with the bite of cold air—not quite winter, but close. The kind of cold that clung to your bones without permission.

Val leaned forward against Virellan's neck. Below, the trees blurred in shades of brown and brittle gold. Above, the sky hung low and expectant—cloud-heavy but holding. The first snow hadn't fallen yet.

Not quite winter, she thought. But close enough to feel it in her ribs.

Virellan moved beneath her with the fluid grace of an older dragon—wiser, patient, but still wary of shared flight. Their bond wasn't new anymore, but it hadn't been tested like this. Not with eyes on them. Not with so many dragons in the air.

Val gripped the reins tighter than she needed to. Her fingers ached against the reins, the leather cold and unyielding—like the sky, like the doubt she hadn't named out loud.

For half a breath, she felt Virellan's calm pulse brush her mind—steady, deliberate. Not words. Just presence. Enough to keep her fingers from locking on the reins completely.

She told herself she was calm. That her heartbeat wasn't thundering behind her ribs. That the flickering pulse of magic at her fingertips wasn't an accident.

But flying beside Cam and the others made something tighten in her chest. They moved like they belonged here. Even Cam, new as she was to this war, flew with a kind of unshakable rhythm—as if the wind already knew her name.

Val didn't want to be the weak link.

She adjusted her seat and stole a glance at Cam, just as Cam glanced back at her. Their eyes met for only a second—but something passed between them. Not magic. Not memory.

Just understanding.

Val exhaled and let herself shift forward in the saddle. *Okay*, she whispered in her mind. *Let's try*.

Virellan's wings opened wider, catching a thermal. She didn't climb fast, didn't surge ahead. She just... lifted. Smoothly. In control.

The gap between them and the others narrowed slightly. And for the first time since takeoff, Val felt something like steadiness.

She didn't know if she belonged in the sky yet. But she was here.

And she was still holding on.

Chapter 43: The Quiet Between Wingbeats

The wind had teeth that morning. Not the kind that threatened a storm, but the kind that warned winter wasn't far.

Ben stood at the edge of the ridge, arms folded, coat collar pulled up against the cold. Snow hadn't fallen yet—but the ground had stiffened with frost, and the air held that weightless stillness, like the sky was waiting to let go.

Dragons wheeled overhead in wide, practiced circles. Skylith's flame-red wings sliced the sky with ease. Virellan—new, but steady—stayed close behind her.

Ben's gaze tracked Val closely. She leaned forward into the wind like she was born for it, though he could still see the tension in her spine from here. First group flight. Not easy. But she was holding her own.

From the cliffs below, Ben stood with arms crossed, eyes trained on the sky. He didn't speak. Didn't need to. He felt the pattern of each rider in the wind, each dragon's rhythm echoing back through the stone and soil beneath his boots.

They were learning. Not just to fly—but to move together. To trust each other midair, where one mistake could cost a life.

He watched Cam lean into Sylithra's wingbeats, guiding her like someone twice her age. She hadn't just adapted—she'd begun to shape the way others flew around her.

Then there was Val. Her posture wasn't perfect, but her presence was solid. Her dragon wasn't struggling, just cautious. Good. He preferred that to reckless bravery.

They'd come a long way since that first training day. And further still from the night he found Cam again.

His eyes narrowed as he watched her steady herself after a turn. Her magic pulsed outward—not chaotic, but wide-reaching. More than just elemental. Instinctive. Inherited.

Ben didn't know what scared him more: how quickly she was growing, or how deeply she was becoming a symbol. Not just for the rebellion, but for every mage who thought they'd been forgotten by fate.

Cam wasn't just powerful.

She was beginning to believe in her power.

And that belief would draw everything toward her—friend and foe alike.

Ben let out a breath and murmured to himself, "Hold steady, kid."

Then, as if hearing him from the clouds above, Cam turned slightly in the air—just enough to adjust formation, just enough to lead.

The others followed.

And for a moment, the sky felt less heavy.

The cold had settled in, not with fury, but with finality. It laced the wind with edge and hushed the world beneath pale skies. Snow hadn't come yet, but Sael felt it in his wings, in the way the air stiffened like breath held too long.

He circled high above the ridgeline, his great white wings catching the shifting thermals as the others flew below.

Sylithra's shadow arced gracefully across the cloud-filtered light, and behind her, Cam held the reins with a steadiness that did not yet come from habit—but from something deeper. Born, perhaps, not made.

She had changed since their first flight.

Stronger, yes. But more attuned. Her power no longer flared uncontrolled—it pulsed in quiet layers now, like light caught beneath ice. Measured. Maturing.

But still she burns, he thought, dipping slightly to adjust the formation. *Even when she tries not to.*

Cam had always been the loudest silence in his mind. Her thoughts were rarely words—more like feelings brushing against his own, too vivid to ignore. Now, he felt those thoughts shifting, scattering, gathering again like leaves before a storm.

She is afraid, Sael noted—not of falling, but of ascending too fast. *Of what might meet her at the height.*

Below him, Val and Virellan flew slightly behind the group. He felt the unease threading from them like cold mist rising off water. Not fear of dragons. Not even of flight.

But of failure.

The young storm flies true, he told Virellan quietly across the link, a gentle reassurance only a bonded dragon could share. *Your wings do not falter.*

Virellan rumbled back softly, the sound more thought than speech. *She still doubts.*

Then show her what trust feels like.

Far below, Ben stood like stone on the ridge, his mind a quiet place Sael rarely intruded. But even from this height, the dragon felt the tight loop of concern woven through the man's posture. For Cam. For all of them.

Sael shifted his attention back to the sky.

He and Sylithra fell into tandem, the two largest dragons weaving wide arcs above the rest. It was instinct—an old dance from another age, where dragons flew not for war but for warning. Not as weapons, but as watchers.

He remembered skies that held stars instead of frost. Winds that were not haunted by shadow-thoughts and Veil-creatures.

He remembered flying with *him*—once. The younger one, forged after Sylithra but burning brighter, faster. Too fast. Powerful and strange even then. Before shadow took him. Before his fall.

Now, he flew with Cam.

She reached for too much, too fast. And yet, she listened. Trusted. Chose others to steady her instead of soaring alone.

That is what will save her, he thought. *Not her strength. But her choosing.*

Cam banked slightly in the wind, adjusting to guide the group westward. Sylithra's tail snapped cleanly behind her.

Sael matched her movement with quiet grace, his pale wings unfolding wider across the sky.

The cold air trembled around them.

Snow hadn't come yet.

But something else had.

Something drawing near—not just in weather, but in fate.

Sael glanced toward Cam again. He would keep her aloft for as long as he could. Even if the sky cracked open.

Even if the cold finally fell.

◈ ☽✦☾ ◈

The wind bit sharper at this height. Not a storm wind, but the kind that sank its teeth in early—whispering that winter wasn't far now. Clouds hung heavy, stitched in pale gray and ice-threaded gold, turning the horizon to glass.

Wyatt leaned slightly forward in the saddle, Sael moving beneath him like thought, smooth and unshaken. The formation flew in practiced arcs above the ridge—five riders and six dragons cutting across the sky like living sigils.

Then something cracked in the rhythm.

Not noise. A sensation.

Cam.

Wyatt felt her falter before he saw it. A ripple in the air, not from wind, but from her magic—frayed at the edges, pulsing wild. Sylithra's wings flared to stabilize, but even that correction felt wrong. Forced.

He didn't hesitate.

"Sael," he thought.

Already moving.

They shifted formation, cutting a clean curve through the current until they were beside her. Sylithra didn't protest—Wyatt could feel the dragon's awareness reach for Sael like a second breath, grounding, anchoring.

And through that bond, the link opened.

"Cam."

Her thoughts didn't crash through his mind like before. No storm. Just a breath—barely formed.

"Too many threads. Everything's pulling at once."

Wyatt's jaw tightened, but he didn't push. He knew how easy it was to tip magic into chaos when emotions spun loose. Instead, he slowed his thoughts, shaped them gently.

"You don't have to hold them all right now. Just one. Choose one and let it fly with you."

He felt her try. Not forcing but listening—something flickering inside her like the hum of a held note. Then... she steadied. Not completely, but enough. Enough to match pace again.

Wyatt eased closer until Sael and Sylithra flew nearly parallel. Their wingbeats synced, their minds already in rhythm. The bond between the dragons made what came next possible.

Without a word, Wyatt shifted his weight and rose in his saddle. Few riders risked leaving their dragon midair without trust running deeper than instinct. Wyatt, Kaden, and Tessa had long since learned the rhythm—moving between saddles as if their dragons breathed together, drilled until it became almost second nature. But Cam hadn't—not yet. Which was why, when Wyatt rose in his saddle, it wasn't just a maneuver. It was faith.

The wind clawed at him, sharp and insistent, but he pushed through with practiced ease. In one fluid motion, he leapt from Sael's back onto Sylithra's spine, catching the harness just behind Cam.

Sylithra didn't flinch. She adjusted midair with a powerful beat of her wings, her mind linking with Sael's to keep the formation balanced.

Cam turned, startled—but not afraid.

Wyatt settled behind her, not quite touching—close enough that their breath mingled in the cold. The nearness hollowed him out, an ache he'd carried for years flaring sharp and undeniable. He had seen her in visions since he was twelve—watched her burn, falter, rise. And now she was here—real, solid, steady against the wind. Every heartbeat begged him to close the space between them, to lean forward until nothing but her existed.

He didn't.

Not because he didn't want to—gods, he wanted to—but because she deserved more than the weight of his need. He held himself still, letting the ache remain.

"You don't have to carry it all alone," he said, voice low behind her ear.

Cam didn't answer right away. But her magic steadied. He felt it in the way Sylithra's rhythm calmed, how the wild hum around her softened into something controlled.

Then, in the quiet space between their dragons' minds, her thoughts reached him.

Cam looked at him—not like someone searching for reassurance, but like someone truly seeing him.

The wind howled between them, hollow and cold—but she didn't pull away. Her magic pulsed in slow, grounding surges. Sylithra mirrored her rider's shift—calm, anchored.

Wyatt didn't say more. But in that hush held open by their dragons, he let the thought drift forward:

"I see you. Not just who you're meant to become—but who you already are."

And then her voice answered—not aloud, but clear within the bond:

"It's not the visions that make me trust you. It's the way you stay."

A truth. Quiet. Bare.

Wyatt's breath caught—not because of prophecy. Because of presence. Because she leaned in now, shoulder brushing his, her head resting carefully against him.

Not to collapse.

To steady herself.

And the steadiness of her against him nearly undid him.

She looked exactly as he'd seen her a hundred times in dreams—but no vision had ever felt this close. This unbearable.

His body ached to fold into her warmth, to rest his cheek against her hair, to let years of unspoken longing break through. He nearly did. Almost. But restraint caught him at the last instant. He stayed still, the ache sharp but clean, carrying it like he always had. The dragons bore them onward, and for a heartbeat, time folded in on itself.

He didn't see fire or fate or prophecy.

He just saw her.

And in the back of his mind, Sael's ancient voice murmured—low and knowing:

This is how balance begins.

Chapter 44: Inheritance in the Air

The cold had crept into the stones of the outpost. Not the sharp bite of winter, but the quiet weight of something waiting. Snow hadn't fallen yet, but the sky held its breath, and the wind outside pressed against the wooden beams like it remembered older storms.

Corin stood in the war room, surrounded by records, diagrams, and maps long untouched. Candlelight pooled across parchment, ink bleeding slightly at the edges. Most of the scrolls were copies—translated from older, forgotten tongues. But a few... a few were original. Unmarked. Smuggled out of Caerthalen before the archives burned.

He ran his thumb along the edge of one worn page, pausing at a line he'd memorized long ago:

"Three shall rise when the Veil thins..."

The first line of the prophecy.

He'd carried those words for decades—before dragons rose from their silence, before the rebellion drew breath, before he unearthed Caerthalen's quiet obsession with power and lineage.

The truth had always lingered in the margins.

He hadn't always known the name. For years, it had haunted the edge of whispers and forbidden records—The Hollow Prince. First a fable. Then a failed project name. Then a question no one in Caerthalen dared ask aloud. But in a vault beneath the Academy, long before his defection, Corin had found a sealed scroll marked only with the sigil of silence. Inside: the name Kaelith, written in a script so old it bled into prophecy. Born not of balance, but design. A blade made hollow, meant to survive the Veil. That was before the dragons vanished. Before the rebellion. Before he realized that Kaelith wasn't just some myth cloaked in metaphor—but a real boy, once human, twisted by those who feared the prophecy and tried to control it.

Kaelith—the Hollow Prince—had not been born. He had been designed. Bred. Shaped by those who feared what the prophecy might bring and sought to seize it before it could unfold.

They had misread its purpose, mistaking power for fulfillment. What they forged instead was a vessel without balance. No bond. No flame. No light.

And now Camomile existed. Not by their design—but in defiance of it. Their interference had set the pieces in motion, but fate had chosen its own path.

She was the answer Kaelith could never be.

But the danger was still real. Because if Cam had been shaped by both prophecy and manipulation, then others had too.

Caerthalen had always hungered for ways to bind what they couldn't understand. He remembered the whisper of one relic in particular—the Heartshard. A crystal said to rest in the Council's chamber, veined with silver and cold as the Veil itself. Some claimed it could hear when prophecy shifted, when balance faltered. Others said it only listened for power. Corin had never seen it with his own eyes, but even the mention of its name was enough to chill him.

Corin's hand hovered over a different page—a registry of bloodlines buried by time and lies. Names crossed out. Families vanished. Some highlighted.

Wyatt.

Kaden.

His nephews.

He exhaled slowly, pressing his palm flat against the table. They were part of this. Not just by proximity, not even just by loyalty—but by design. And by choice.

The prophecy didn't name them directly—but Corin had long suspected:

One by fate. One by fire. One by fracture.

Cam, born of fire and silence.

Kaden, shaped by fracture—shadow, teleportation, brilliance split across too many truths.

Wyatt, always watching, always waiting... the light that chose.

But the prophecy wasn't about their power. That was what Caerthalen never understood.

It was about their bond.

He thought of the way Cam steadied when Wyatt was near. The way Kaden challenged her to think deeper, to question. The way they all trained together now, pushing, shaping, surviving.

A soft knock at the war room door broke his thought. Alex stepped inside, the torchlight catching faint on the silver clasp at his cloak.

"Scouts are back," he said simply, voice even. "No movement along the southern ridge. For now."

Corin gave him a brief nod. Alex lingered only a moment before fading back into the hall, quiet as ever. Reliable. Too reliable.

When the door shut, Corin's gaze fell again to the open ledger, unease settling heavier than before.

There were many others—mages with second, third, even fourth abilities. Tessa. Valerie. Cam's mother. Not all were planned. Some were echoes of power returning to the world. And some...

Some were created as chains, not gifts.

The dragons had gone silent for centuries not out of weakness—but out of defiance. They had been hunted, used, and bonded to those they did not choose. And now, they remembered what it was to guard—not just magic, but the Veil itself.

The Veil, Corin thought, glancing at the crude, hand-drawn sigil scratched into the corner of a map.

No one remembered how it had opened. No one knew how to close it.

But the dragons were stirring again. And Cam—Cam was beginning to remember who she was.

Corin rolled the scroll shut.

"She'll need them," he said softly. "All of them."

And still, deep in his chest, something coiled tighter with unease.

Kaelith hadn't fully returned.

Not yet.

But the Veil was thinning.

And the balance between silence and ruin was more fragile than ever.

The cold was sharper now, threading beneath armor and skin like a warning. A waiting cold. The kind that pressed close just before snow fell.

Kaden flew at the edge of the formation, Tenebrin's wings casting long shadows across the pale sky. The others moved around him—Cam steady mid-flight, Wyatt hovering near her, Val and Tessa holding a loose rhythm just behind.

They looked like a unit now.

But Kaden wasn't watching just them.

He was watching the sky itself.

Something had shifted.

It wasn't just weather. And it wasn't just magic.

It was pressure—invisible, subtle, but real. Like a door creaking open down a long, dark hallway. Just enough to feel the draft. Just enough to know it was coming from the wrong direction.

The Veil stirs, Tenebrin said in his mind.

Kaden didn't flinch. *"I thought it was already open."*

Tenebrin's voice slid through his thoughts like silk over steel. *It cracked. Long ago. But not like this.*

Kaden tightened his grip on the saddle, muscles tensing. *"How long ago?"*

A pause.

Four thousand years. Maybe more. None who fly now saw it. Not even Sylithra. But the stories remain. Carried in our marrow. Passed from clutch to clutch, from dream to dream.

"Memory?"

No, Tenebrin answered. *Inheritance.*

The formation dipped into descent. As the dragons spiraled lower, Kaden caught a flicker of motion—Wyatt shifting from Sylithra's back to Sael's with the same quiet precision as always. No spectacle. No struggle. Just motion. Fluid, practiced. As if even the wind knew to make room.

The sun angled low behind the ridge. The clouds hung heavy. The sky waited.

Kaden adjusted his posture slightly. Below, Val and Virellan landed clean—controlled, storm-quiet. Tessa followed, her dismount sharp and sure. Then Cam and Sylithra, with Wyatt just behind her, like gravity had paired them.

Kaden's gaze lingered on them a moment longer than necessary.

He wasn't jealous—not exactly. But he understood the cost of needing someone. Of being too visible.

That was how the Capital always found its cracks.

Tenebrin landed with barely a sound, despite his size. Kaden slid down and pressed a hand to the dragon's flank, grounding himself.

"They're not ready," he murmured. "But they're getting there."

Tenebrin's silver-white eyes blinked once, slow.

Neither were we, came the low, ancient reply. *When the Veil cracked the first time.*

Kaden stilled.

"You remember that?"

The dragon didn't answer.

But something passed through the bond. Not a full vision—just fragments. A darkness that rolled in like mist soaked in blood. The roar of something not meant to enter the world. Silence that screamed. And dragons... fewer than now, but proud, unbroken.

And afraid.

Not of battle. Not of the Veil itself.

But of what came before the fall—the arrogance of those who believed they could outwit prophecy, chain the balance, or rush fate.

Kaden breathed deeply.

Below the ridge, the others laughed—soft, small sounds that didn't reach the sky. Cam said something to Val that made her smile. Wyatt stood nearby, distant but aware.

They were stronger than they'd been.

But strength wasn't readiness.

And fate never waited for permission.

The cold bit deeper as the wind swept across the stone. Kaden didn't move. Just stood in Tenebrin's shadow and whispered into the hollow space between heartbeats—

"We don't have time," he whispered into the wind. And the wind, colder than before, did not disagree.

Chapter 45: The Gate Is Opening

The woods at night were quieter than silence itself—not empty but listening. The cold pressed against Cam's armor, seeping through the seams and into her skin. Each breath she took coiled into thin clouds, fragile and fleeting in the stillness. Above, Haldrin's Keep sat perched against the mountain, its torchlight flickering faintly through the skeletal branches—a watchful ember in the dark.

Beside her, Rin moved with hesitant steps, his breath trembling in the cold air. He was younger than she'd thought—maybe seventeen, lean and untested. His eyes darted nervously between shadowed trees and the faint glow of his water crystal, held tightly in trembling hands.

"I know I'm not like the others," he said quietly, voice barely more than a whisper. "No dragon. Just water. And not even that much."

Cam slowed, matching his pace with steady certainty.

"You're strong enough to be here," she said with calm conviction. "Bravery isn't about power. I wouldn't want anyone else with me tonight."

His eyes widened briefly, caught off guard by her honesty. But Cam's gaze stayed fixed ahead, never once meeting his.

A shiver crawled over the forest as the wind shifted.

Cam halted, and Rin followed suit.

There was a change—not in the leaves, or the branches, but deeper. Beneath the soil, beneath the skin of the world itself. The air warped subtly, a strange heat rippling through the cold night like the shimmer of a mirage on stone.

"Did you—"

Rin's question caught in his throat.

From the shadow-thick woods, something emerged.

It didn't walk.

It glided—a thin silhouette woven of shifting smoke and bone, wings stretched wide but insubstantial. No sound marked its passing, yet the trees recoiled as it moved—leaves curling, branches twisting away as if the forest itself knew its name.

Cam's breath caught. She had read about this once, buried in the margins of an old bestiary: *the Wraithcall.* A harbinger, a vessel for voices not its own. Do not look too long. Do not listen.

Her instincts flared. Violet fire sparked across her palms—bright, hungry, ready—but she held it back.

This was no mindless beast.

It was watching.

And gods, it was tempting—its voice threading at the edges of her mind, pulling like a tide she almost stepped into. The words weren't hers, but they felt close, too close. She forced her gaze away, biting down on the pull. She remembered the warning: Do not look too long. Do not listen.

Then it moved. Not for Cam.

For Rin.

His breath caught—a sudden sharp intake as his body stiffened, eyes rolling back into pale whites. The shadow creature seeped into him like ink dissolving in water.

When Rin spoke, it was not his voice.

Cold, layered. Inhuman. A chorus twisted with his essence. The presence from her dreams. Her nightmares.

"The gate is opening. She walks the line. The balance will bleed."

Cam took a step forward, heart pounding, magic thrumming beneath her skin—ready, but searching for a way in.

"Get out of him," she growled.

The creature's laughter slipped from Rin's lips—a sound like the wind scraping bones.

"The gate is opening. The balance will bleed," it said. *"The Hollow remembers. Watches. Waits..."*

Then, with a violent shudder, the shadow ripped free from Rin's trembling frame.

He crumpled, pale as ash, breath shallow and ragged.

Cam didn't hesitate.

Golden radiance burst from her palms, flooding the clearing in fierce, blinding heat.

The Wraithcall hissed—its smoky form writhing and unraveling, strands of darkness curling like smoke before scattering and dissolving into nothingness.

She knelt beside Rin, catching him before he fell.

"Rin—stay with me. Please—" The word broke sharper than she meant, her voice splintering as panic clawed at her throat. His eyelids fluttered, slow but alive. Cold beneath her hands but fighting.

Then the mark on her forearm flared—searing, relentless. She gasped, nearly losing her grip as the heat ripped through her veins. *The gate is opening.*

Her breath stuttered, fear threatening to unravel her. She forced herself to draw in air, steadying her hands even as they trembled against him. "No. Not now. Not you."

Cam's jaw clenched.

Calling deep within her, she reached out to the mental tether shared with dragons. The closest one was—

"Tenebrin. We need you. Now."

The night held its breath as the distant thunder of wings answered.

The creature was gone. Disintegrated into curling strands of shadow, leaving nothing but scorched air and the echo of its voice ringing behind her ribs.

But the fear didn't fade.

Cam's mark flared. Not a blaze—but a low, invasive heat that crept beneath her skin and settled there like it had always belonged. It wasn't enough to keep her from tending to Rin. But it wasn't nothing.

It pulsed like a second heartbeat.

A countdown.

Cam knelt beside Rin, pressing two fingers to his throat. His pulse was faint but present, fluttering like a trapped bird. His skin was clammy, drained. His breath came in shallow pulls.

"You're okay," she whispered, brushing his damp hair back. "You're going to be okay. Just stay with me, alright?"

She swallowed the panic clawing its way up her throat and reached out—not with her hands, but with her mind.

"Tenebrin."

A long beat of silence. Then:

I see you.

His voice rumbled through her mind like a mountain shifting in its sleep.

"Rin's down. Possessed. Something... something entered him and spoke through him. It's gone now but—"

She stopped herself. The mark pulsed again.

"—I need help. I can't get him back alone."

Hold on. I'm descending.

Wind stirred the trees above—quiet at first, then louder as a shape cut through the dark clouds, massive and fast.

Cam stood, shielding Rin's body as branches bent under the force of wings. Tenebrin dropped between the trees like a living shadow, landing with such fluid grace it barely disturbed the earth. His scales shimmered with flickers of muted black and gray, and his silver eyes locked onto hers.

The Wraithcall? Tenebrin's thoughts cut through the air like a blade.

Cam nodded once. *"It's real. It spoke through him."*

The dragon lowered his head, nostrils flaring as he sniffed the air. His wings twitched.

The Veil stirs deeper than I've felt in centuries. This one was sent.

Cam swallowed, adrenaline spiking again. *"I know."*

She gently lifted Rin's upper body as Tenebrin extended a talon.

Bring him. We fly.

She didn't hesitate. With a grunt, she shifted Rin's limp weight over her shoulder. Tenebrin crouched low and she climbed up, securing Rin in front of her with one arm.

Tenebrin launched upward, straight through the trees, wind whipping her braid across her face. Haldrin's Keep's outer edge came into view above the canopy—stone and torchlight rising like a promise through the dark.

They soared toward it, and only then did Cam feel her hands tremble.

She looked down at Rin, unconscious against her. The mark burned once more—quiet now but not gone.

The gate is opening.

And whatever waited behind it wasn't done with her

◈ ☽✦☾ ◈

Tenebrin landed in the outer courtyard with barely a sound—his wings folding in tight as Cam slid down with Rin still clutched to her.

The moment her boots hit stone, a nearby watchguard startled.

"Rider—what happened?"

Cam didn't break stride. "He needs a healer—now."

She cradled Rin tighter, pushing through the arched hall toward the infirmary. The Keep's corridors blurred past—glowing torchlight, cold stone, faces turning as she passed. None of them mattered right now.

She burst through the infirmary doors with the force of someone twice her size.

Mirell looked up from a table, startled. "Cam? What—?"

"Possession," Cam said tightly, laying Rin gently on the nearest cot. "He's alive, but weak. Something took hold of him out there and... spoke through him."

Mirell moved quickly, placing her hands to Rin's temples, then to his sternum. Her brow furrowed. "His essence is intact. Drained, but intact. No trace of the creature left."

Cam's jaw clenched. "That's because I burned it out."

Mirell glanced at her, eyes narrowing slightly. "You used light?"

Cam nodded once.

The healer didn't press further, but her expression turned cautious. "He'll need rest. We'll keep him warm. He'll wake when his strength returns."

Cam exhaled slowly, running a hand through her hair. The mark still pulsed beneath her sleeve—faint, but ever-present.

Mirell touched Rin's wrist gently. "Whatever you did, it worked. But this..." she hesitated, glancing back at Cam. "This isn't normal magic, is it?"

Cam didn't answer right away.

She met Mirell's gaze steadily.

"I need to speak with Ben and Corin. Keep this between us for now."

Mirell nodded, solemn. "You'll find them in the lower strategy hall. I'll watch over him."

Cam stepped back from the cot and turned, her heart still pounding but her expression carved into something colder. Focused.

The dread hadn't passed.

It had simply shifted.

She pushed open the infirmary doors and slipped back into the dim corridors of the Keep, her boots hitting the stone with purpose.

The Hollow had spoken. The mark had answered.

And something in her gut told her this was only the beginning.

Chapter 46: The Hollow Prince

The door to the infirmary shut softly behind her.

Cam lingered just outside it, one hand resting against the rough stone of the corridor wall. Her pulse hadn't slowed, not fully. Rin's breath had been ragged; his skin was too cold. It should've comforted her that he lived.

It didn't.

She looked down at her gloved hand, flexed her fingers, then let out a breath and pushed away from the wall. The corridor stretched ahead—quiet, torchlit, the flicker of firelight catching faintly on the carved sigils etched into the foundation stones. They weren't glowing now. That unsettled her too.

She moved quickly. Not out of panic, but urgency.

Down two flights. Through the eastern hall. Past the main barracks where only silence waited.

By the time she reached the lower strategy chamber, her heart had steadied—but the dread had not.

She knocked once, then pushed the door open.

Ben and Corin were already inside, hunched over a half-unfurled map and a table scattered with scouting reports and weather charts. They looked up as she entered.

Ben took one look at her and stood straighter. "Cam?"

She didn't answer right away. She crossed the room in three long steps and set her hands on the edge of the table.

"There was something in the forest," she said, voice low. "It wasn't like the others. It didn't attack—it possessed."

Corin's gaze sharpened. Ben didn't move.

She went on. "It entered Rin. Spoke through him. Its voice was layered—inhuman. It said things. Warnings. Promises."

"What did it say?" Corin asked, already bracing.

Cam's voice didn't waver, but something in her chest tightened as she repeated it.

"The gate is opening. She walks the line. The balance will bleed."

A pause. Then she added, quieter:

"The Hollow remembers. Watches. Waits."

The silence that followed was thick. Not just thoughtful—guarded.

Ben's face didn't change, but his fingers curled slowly into fists.

Cam's gaze flicked between them. "That meant something to you."

Neither man replied immediately.

"I've seen him before," she said, pressing. "In visions. In the mark. Not often, but... enough to know he's watching. But I never knew what to call him. Just a shadow. A... hunger."

Corin looked at her, eyes steady, voice calm. "Describe him."

Cam hesitated, then nodded once. "Not a face. Not fully. Just... fragments. Veiled. Shifting. Like he's wearing something that doesn't belong to him. But the thing that stands out isn't his form—it's the absence inside him. Like something vital was carved out, and all that's left is need."

Another pause. Then Ben spoke.

"His name," he said quietly, "is Kaelith."

The air in the room seemed to constrict.

Cam's mind caught on the name like a blade through cloth. She'd never heard it before—but the weight of it settled into her bones like recognition.

"Kaelith," she repeated, almost to herself. "Is that what he calls himself?"

"No," Ben said. "That's what he was called, once. Before. Now... they call him the Hollow Prince."

Cam blinked. Something in her blood turned colder than the mountain air. She had heard Ben use the name before as well as Sael but neither explained what it'd meant.

Until now. "You've known. This whole time."

"We thought about telling you when the mark first appeared," Ben said quietly. "But you weren't magically stable enough. If he sensed the truth too soon..." He trailed off, the implication sharp.

Corin didn't flinch. "Yes, we've known."

"And you didn't think I deserved to know?" Her voice wasn't angry—but it wasn't quiet either.

Ben's jaw tightened. "You weren't ready. Not for the truth. Not for the pull he would feel if you knew him by name. Names hold power, Cam."

The mark on her wrist flared—hot and deliberate, like it agreed. Cam's breath caught, her hand curling into a fist beneath her sleeve.

Cam stepped back, crossing her arms tightly. "I've had visions. Nightmares. I've heard his voice in my head. And you thought I wasn't ready?"

"We didn't want to feed the connection," Corin said gently. "Knowing him strengthens it. He's not bound by space the way we are. The more you name him, the more he sees."

Cam's throat ached with the urge to argue—but deep down, she knew what they meant. Even now, the name still rang in her ears. Kaelith. A summons. A shiver.

"What happens if the gate opens?" she asked finally.

Ben's answer came first. "Then everything shifts. What we've been holding back... it doesn't stay hidden."

Corin followed: "The Veil fractures. Balance unravels. If he returns fully—it's not just a war anymore. It's undoing. Of magic. Of memory. Of us."

Cam stood in stillness, the firelight catching the faint sheen of sweat on her brow. She didn't know what scared her more—that they'd kept it from her, or that part of her already knew it was coming.

Ben stepped closer, his voice softer now. "You did good tonight. You stayed calm. You protected Rin. You listened to your instincts."

"Instincts don't feel like enough anymore," Cam murmured.

"Then we'll make sure you have more," Corin said. "You're not facing this alone."

She looked up. The weight of it all pressed against her—but she didn't collapse under it. Just... braced herself.

Ben gave her a nod toward the corridor. "Get some rest. While you can."

Cam didn't argue. But she didn't move immediately either.

She looked down at her gloved hand again, flexed her fingers like she had outside the infirmary.

The name still echoed. *Kaelith.*

She turned toward the door. "If he's watching... I'm watching back."

And then she left.

◈ ☽✦☾ ◈

Ben stayed behind after Cam left; fingers still pressed to the edge of the war table. The wood was worn smooth from years of use, but tonight, it felt brittle under his grip—like one wrong move would splinter it.

He'd seen the shift in her. The resolve. The fear she wouldn't name.

She was changing faster than he could hold onto.

The gate. The mark. The voice in the forest.

He should've told her sooner.

Footsteps stirred behind him. He didn't need to turn.

Corin's presence was quiet, but never passive.

"She's not a child," Corin said. Calm. Measured. But underneath, Ben heard it—that undercurrent of urgency that only surfaced when the stakes had already started to slip.

"I never thought she was," Ben said. His voice felt heavier than usual. Like every word carried a weight he hadn't quite reckoned with.

"You treat her like she might break."

Ben's gaze didn't lift. "No. I treat her like someone who already has."

That earned him silence. Just long enough for the torchlight to flicker. Ben felt it—the moment Corin made the choice to press, gently but without leaving room to turn away.

"You need to tell her everything. Even the things I don't know."

Ben's grip tightened on the table's edge. "If she knew too soon, then he would have too. And I didn't want to risk that."

Corin was closer now, standing just across from him. "That's not your call anymore. She's already in it. She's already bleeding for this."

Ben looked up. Met his old friend's eyes. "You don't know what you're asking."

Corin didn't flinch. "You're right. I don't. Not all of it. But she deserves to."

Ben exhaled slowly. The kind of breath that used to come after fire—when the world was still burning, but quieter now. The kind that tasted like ash and memory.

"She is my daughter."

"I know."

"I swore I'd protect her."

Corin's voice softened but didn't bend. "Then trust her to survive the truth."

Ben didn't answer. Not right away. He just stood there, watching the light shift across the old map on the table. The ink was fading. The edges curling.

Like everything else they'd once thought fixed.

"She deserves more than what we were given," he murmured.

Corin nodded once. "Then give her that."

When the room fell quiet again, Ben didn't move.

But in his chest, something had already begun to break open.

Corin's words struck deeper than Ben expected.

'Tell her everything.'

His fingers curled around the edge of the table. He remembered the weight of her, all those years ago—barely more than a breath, wrapped in a threadbare blanket. He hadn't even dared whisper her name aloud.

And now she was asking questions he'd buried too deep.

Cam wasn't watching where she was going. Her thoughts churned—too loud, too fast—looping back on the words Ben and Corin had spoken. The Hollow Prince. Kaelith.

She turned the corner—

—and collided hard into someone.

Strong arms caught her before she could stumble.

"Cam—"

Wyatt.

She stepped back too quickly, grounding herself with a palm against the wall, eyes wide.

"Sorry," she muttered, breath still half-caught. "I didn't see—"

"I noticed," he said softly. His eyes searched her face. "Are you alright?"

She meant to nod. Meant to lie. But her mouth didn't move.

Wyatt didn't press, but the air shifted—weighted with everything unspoken.

Cam glanced once over her shoulder, then back at him. "Come with me?"

He didn't ask where. Just followed.

◈ ☽✦☾ ◈

Her quarters were quiet, tucked into the stone with a single lantern still flickering low. She shut the door behind them and leaned back against it for a moment, as if keeping the world out would help her hold it together.

Wyatt waited.

And that was what undid her.

"I saw it again tonight," she said. "But it wasn't a vision. Not this time."

Wyatt's brow furrowed, his whole posture still—listening.

Cam told him everything. The patrol. Rin. The Wraithcall. What it said.

Then the part she hadn't even begun to understand:

The Hollow Prince. Kaelith.

The name she'd seen in dreams but hadn't known belonged to someone real.

"They knew," she whispered. "Ben and Corin—they knew all along."

Wyatt stepped closer, slow and careful, like coming too quickly might shatter something between them. "Are you okay?"

"No," Cam said. "But I will be. I just... need to think. Or not."

His gaze held hers, steady and aching with the same weight she carried. "Will you be alright tonight?"

She hesitated, her breath catching as though the answer lodged somewhere between her chest and her throat.

She could say no. She could ask him to stay.

The words trembled there. On the edge of her throat.

But instead, she said, "I'll be fine."

Wyatt didn't move. For a few long moments, he simply stood there—close enough to reach her, far enough to let her choose.

And she didn't ask him to leave.

Not right away.

Not at all.

Wyatt turned toward the door, slower than he needed to. As he reached for the handle, his fingers brushed hers.

Not by accident.

Not fully on purpose either.

Just a quiet moment of contact—warm, grounding, real.

Cam didn't pull away. Neither did he.

And then he left, the door clicking shut behind him with barely a sound.

Silence returned, but it wasn't empty.

She stood there a while longer, her hand still tingling from his touch. He stayed—even when he didn't have to. He always did.

Why does he stay? She thought. *What does he see in me?*

The questions burned sharper than the mark on her wrist. Because she knew what she saw in herself—fractures, shadows, a girl carrying too much of what should've been left to legends. But when Wyatt looked at her... gods, it was different. Like she was someone worth holding onto, even when she tried to keep everyone at a distance.

And that was what scared her most.

She'd been ten the last time she let herself love someone that close. Ten, and already old enough to know what absence felt like. Anthony—her father in every way that mattered—had been the one place in Brimclif she felt safe. Until he was gone. His death had carved a silence so deep she'd built her walls from it, piece by piece, until even Ben hadn't been allowed too near.

But Wyatt... Wyatt never asked to break through those walls. He just stayed. Quiet. Patient. Certain. And that was more dangerous than any prophecy—because if she let him in, if she let herself need him the way part of her already wanted to, losing him would shatter her in ways she wasn't sure she could survive.

The lantern's flame flickered low, casting long shadows against the stone. She pressed her palms flat to the wood of the door, as if it could hold her steady against the weight pressing in from all sides.

Her chest rose and fell once, sharply—breath catching on the edge of a tremor she couldn't quite suppress. Her fingers curled against the wood, nails biting faint crescents into the grain before she forced them to release. For a moment, her gaze dropped to her hand, brushing her thumb across the place where Wyatt's fingers had grazed hers—as if the memory might anchor her. Only when she exhaled, unsteady and slow, did she turn from the door.

She didn't know what tomorrow would bring.

But she knew who had her back when the world started shifting.

And that mattered more than fate.

◈ ☽✦☾ ◈

The room had gone quiet. Too quiet.

Cam sat on the edge of her bed for a long time, letting the silence settle around her like fog. Her cloak still draped over the chair. The hearth had long since gone cold. She didn't remember curling beneath the blankets, only that at some point, her body gave in.

Sleep took her—but not kindly.

She opened her eyes to darkness, standing barefoot on stone.

It wasn't her room.

It wasn't anywhere she knew.

Black mist coiled low along the floor, thick and pulsing. The air felt stretched thin—like a veil pulled tight between two worlds, seconds from tearing.

She moved without deciding to, the way one walks through memory.

The shadows parted ahead of her. A shape formed—not a man, not fully. A voice more than a body. A presence more than a face.

"The gate is opening."

The words echoed through her—not into her ears, but behind her ribs.

"Who are you?" she asked, but her voice barely carried.

"The balance will shatter."

Each word rippled the space around her. The stone beneath her feet cracked—hairline fractures laced with lightless veins. Her mark flared, burning beneath her skin even in this place.

"Stop," she said, stepping back. "Get out of my head."

The presence didn't move. But it grew. Expanded.

"You are the fulcrum. Become—or break."

A thousand images crashed over her in a single breath—wings made of smoke, cities devoured by silence, the sky splitting open like glass.

She tried to wrench herself away.

Tried to wake.

But the vision *held* her.

Until—

A sudden *snap*, like a thread breaking.

Cam jolted upright in bed, chest heaving.

The fire was still out. Her room was dim. Silent. But she wasn't alone—not entirely.

The mark on her arm burned bright for a heartbeat.

Then dimmed.

Not gone. Just waiting again.

Her breath slowed. The air still tasted wrong, like ash and iron.

She rose quietly, crossing the room to the window. Outside, the trees were still. The wind hadn't moved.

But something had.

The vision clung to her skin. She could still hear his voice, feel the pulse of the Veil breathing against her.

The gate is opening.

The balance will shatter.

She pressed a hand to the glass, watching the tree line.

The threat wasn't distant anymore. It was close—and rising.

Her voice was barely a whisper:

"I'll face it. Whatever it is."

And for the first time since the mark appeared, she wasn't waiting to be told what to do.

She was choosing.

Even if it cost her everything. Even if it pulled her straight into the Veil.

Chapter 47: Shadows In the Light

A few days had slipped by since Cam's encounter with the Wraithcall. Rin had made a full recovery but was off patrols for a while. Yet the quiet that followed wasn't ease—it was the kind that prickled like a warning.

Brittle leaves twisted in the wind, their edges blackened by early frost. They fell like ash from the half-stripped branches, whispering secrets too quiet to catch. Every step cracked through the underbrush like a warning. Damp rot mingled with the scent of pine and something else—older, fouler, foreign.

The frost wasn't out of place for the season—but the way it clung to bark and crept along the roots was. It spread in spiderweb patterns, black-veined and wrong, as if something had bled through the soil and frozen mid-crawl. The silence was too heavy, too precise. Not natural.

They hadn't come out for just a routine sweep. Corin had chosen six of them—each with sharp senses and a different way of listening to the world. Cam felt the wrongness underfoot, subtle and shifting like a hum beneath the soil. Wyatt had dreamed of this clearing three nights ago—cold, broken, shadow-stained. Kaden saw patterns in the quiet, tracking what wasn't there as clearly as what was. Tessa tilted her head, listening to the air itself—the absence of birdsong, the way wind moved like it didn't want to be heard. Val moved between them like water, tuned to emotional undercurrents and illusions just beneath the surface. And Alex, as always, kept to the edges—silent, steady, watchful. Reliable. Maybe too much so.

Cam crouched beneath a gray-limbed pine, her gloved fingers brushing a gouge in the bark. The marks were too clean. Three long slashes angled with precision, the wood beneath unnaturally pale, like it had been drained of color.

She didn't speak at first.

Wyatt stepped beside her, boots sinking into the soft ground. His breath misted white. "It's colder here than it should be."

Cam traced the marks again. "They weren't here last week."

At her feet, the roots had blackened. Frost climbed them like veins, spiderwebbing into the soil. A thin crust of ice crackled over dead leaves, untouched by snow or rain. It hadn't stormed. It shouldn't have frozen. And yet...

"It feels like something's leaking through," Kaden muttered. He stood a few paces uphill, surveying the same path from a different angle. His eyes were narrowed, calculating. "The Veil's thinning again."

"No sign of a rift?" Val asked, her voice low as she stepped closer. She was watching the trees, her expression unreadable.

"No," Cam said. "Just this."

Tessa exhaled into her gloves and rubbed them together briskly. "Great. First blight, now frost rot. Anyone else ready to go home and light themselves on fire for warmth?"

Cam almost smiled. Almost.

◈ ☽✦☾ ◈

The trail dipped into a narrow gulch where a small stream wound its way through half-frozen moss and rock. That's where they found it—just beyond the water's bend.

A carcass.

Cam stopped short.

It had once been a deer—now hollowed and twisted, ribs broken outward as if something had clawed its way from the inside. Its eyes were pits of black frost, wide and sunken.

Even Wyatt took a step back. "That's not natural."

Cam's voice came out quieter than intended. "Nothing about this is."

Kaden swore under his breath. Val turned away slightly, her jaw tense. Tessa crouched beside it, not touching, just... studying. The wind rustled her red hair like static.

"We move," Kaden said. "Whatever did this might still be near."

They didn't argue.

As they climbed out of the ravine and back toward the ridgeline, Cam glanced behind them—then paused. For a moment, she felt it: something watching from beyond the line of trees, just out of reach. Not a creature. Not a mind. But presence.

She tightened her cloak and didn't speak of it.

The slope leveled into a frostbitten clearing just narrow enough to shelter them from the wind and hidden enough to avoid the eyes of passing scouts.

"We'll stop here," Kaden said, scanning the tree line. "Too risky to bring anything back to the Keep."

Wyatt immediately began clearing the space between two moss-covered stones, using his blade to dig out the dampest leaves. Tessa started arranging half-dry wood into something vaguely flammable. Cam knelt by the brittle grass and pressed her hand to the earth. She whispered a warming incantation—an old one. Slow, careful. Heat pulsed gently beneath her palm, not fire, but comfort.

Across the camp, Val was slower unpacking her gear. Her movements were precise, but her gaze drifted often to the trees. Her shoulders were tight. Listening.

"Hey," Alex said softly as he moved beside her, brushing leaves from his bedroll. "You alright?"

She gave a distracted nod. Then, after a pause: "It's loud tonight."

Alex blinked. "What do you mean?"

Val's brow furrowed. She tilted her head slightly, as if tuning into something only she could hear. "There's a knot in the air. Like... minds straining against a wall. Something's being hidden, but it's bleeding through anyway."

Alex's hand tightened on his knife. "Shadow creatures?"

Val shook her head. "No. Too structured. This feels... disciplined. Purposeful."

A beat of silence passed between them, broken only by the wind sliding through the bare branches above.

"Human?" he asked.

She didn't answer. Not then.

The fire had burned low to glowing embers, crackling faintly under the stir of night wind. The forest was still. Too still. Even the owls had gone quiet.

Val lay with her eyes open, her mind tethered to threads most couldn't feel. They stretched out into the dark, brushing against trees and rocks, against thought and memory, listening for the pulse of presence. Of warning.

She had trained herself not to listen too hard. Had taught herself to mute the noise of other people's minds. But tonight... the noise pressed in.

Something was coming.

Not beasts. Not born of Veil or darkened forest.

Humans. With intent.

She sat up slowly, her fingers already wrapped around the hilt of her dagger. Magic bloomed inside her mind—not flashy but sharpened to a needle's point. She pushed outward gently, feeling for the edges of other thoughts.

Cold.

Focused.

Too focused.

Then—*Snap.*

A twig. Far too close.

Not the casual shift of forest life. This was placed. Measured.

Deliberate.

Before her voice could rise, she reached—not with sound, but with her mind.

Cam.

She didn't need to speak. The connection sparked like flint, urgent and clear. A warning, not in words, but in pressure. Danger. Now.

She felt Cam wake like fire catching dry tinder.

Val was already on her feet. "Up!" she barked, cloak tumbling from her shoulders. "Now. We're not alone!"

Then she reached outward—into the minds pressing in from the dark.

And what she felt was colder than frost.

No surprise in them.

No curiosity.

No fear.

They knew who they were attacking.

They came for Cam.

They came to take her alive.

And they came knowing what she was becoming.

She was already halfway to her feet when Val's mind brushed hers—sharper than any voice, more urgent than any shout.

Cam.

A warning with no words. Just fear. Focus. Fire.

Something inside her snapped taut.

The air shifted—slowed.

She felt it like a ripple across water: time dragging around her, thick and syrupy. Sparks flickered across her vision. Leaves twisted slower. Shadows bled longer.

And Wyatt—Wyatt saw it too. His head snapped toward her, eyes wide with understanding.

"Cam—?"

But she was already moving.

Her magic surged to meet her will—raw, instinctive. Not channeled, not careful. Alive.

"Scatter!" She shouted, not bothering to look behind.

Glyphs lit the dark like flares as the attackers closed in—robed mages, coordinated, silent. Predators.

One raised a sigil toward Val. Cam didn't think. Her hand shot forward and the spell collapsed in a burst of heat and static, the glyph incinerated midair.

Tessa moved next—blinking from confusion to fury. Lightning cracked at her fingertips, drawn from the storm coiled always just beneath her skin.

Kaden rolled to intercept two at once, blades gleaming silver-white with wind. His stance was low, perfect—already reading their footwork before they committed.

And Wyatt—

Wyatt didn't hesitate.

He stepped into Cam's blind side, back-to-back with her as a mage lunged toward them. His blade theirs with a clang of steel and a flare of red firelight. His eyes never left her.

"Don't lose yourself, Cam—I'm right here."

Cam didn't answer. She couldn't. Her focus was everywhere—on her friends, on the flickers of light from the glyphs, on the quiet footsteps circling behind them.

On the fact that they weren't trying to kill her.

They were trying to surround her.

Take her.

Alive.

That thought made her blood burn hotter than her magic.

A figure darted in from the right. Cam lifted her arm and called—not fire, not ice, but force, a sheer burst of pressure that cracked outward like a shockwave, sending the attacker flying into a tree trunk.

Another teleported behind her. Wyatt was faster.

Steel hissed. The mage fell, groaning.

"I've got you," he said low, fierce.

She nodded, heart pounding, vision splintering with light and sound and instinct. "We have each other."

Around them, the fight turned.

Brontheus shrieked above—Tessa had summoned him, mid-battle. The green-black dragon blazed through the trees, scattering two mages with a whip of his tail before vanishing again into the clouds.

Tenebrin's roar followed—lower, darker.

Cam blinked. Kaden had disappeared.

Then reappeared.

Behind one of the attackers. Blade to throat.

A shadow blink.

Everything was chaos.

But it was controlled chaos now.

Because they'd had a few seconds more.

Because Cam reacted first.

The air vibrated with charged magic—runic pulses, elemental surges, the burn of fire against cold wind. They were holding their ground. For now.

But it was changing again. Cam felt it.

Another shift.

A trap—subtle, magical, closing in.

Wyatt broke from her side, his gaze flicking toward Val. She was pinned down, a mage at her flank, trying to tear through her defenses. Kaden was holding off two more by himself, teleporting in staggered bursts that left him gasping.

"I've got to—" Wyatt began, breathless.

"Go," Cam said without hesitation. "They need you."

His hand brushed her wrist—just once—before he took off toward them.

Cam turned, magic bristling at her fingertips.

But the moment he left, they pounced.

She didn't see the mage coming. Not until it was too late.

A pulse—dark and laced with memory—struck her from the side.

Not fire. Not shadow. Something older.

Silence bloomed in her mind like a scream that couldn't escape.

Her magic fizzled, not gone—suppressed. Like a hand was closing around it.

The clearing blurred. Shapes smeared like watercolors in the rain. Her own breath echoed too loud in her ears. Every step felt muffled, distant. Like her body had betrayed her.

Then—

Brimclif.

The brittle cold of the riverbank behind her old home. The way the townspeople looked through her when she tried to speak. The whispers she wasn't meant to hear.

"That girl's not right. Best to leave her be."

Anthony's voice echoed next—gentle, desperate. *"Hide it, Cam. Please."*

Hide it.

She staggered, blinking hard, but the fog didn't lift. It pressed in.

A tall figure stepped into view—robes ink-dark and lined with silver glyphs stitched into the hems. His face was blurred, indistinct, but the voice was clear:

"You're not meant to shine."

Cam's pulse hammered.

"You're meant to be forgotten. That's what you fear, isn't it?"

She wanted to scream, to burn him down where he stood. But the magic was tangled—not bound like chains, not sealed by brute force—but *mirrored.* A psychic rune, tailored to echo her own memories back at her like a cage.

She fell to her knees.

And she hated it. Hated how it reminded her of being ten years old and powerless. Of waking up from dreams of wings and fire, only to find herself small, cold, and alone. Of the years she spent believing she was broken.

"I'm not her anymore," she rasped, but the words felt thin, swallowed by the fog.

"Then prove it," the mage said.

He raised a gloved hand—runed with ink that bled upward like rot. A spell sparked to life, shadowed and invasive, ready to sink in deep.

"Don't," Cam whispered.

Her magic surged against the veil.

Then—Steel whistled through the air.

The spell shattered, sparks exploding in every direction.

Alex slammed into the mage shoulder-first, his blade cutting across the runes on the mage's glove with brutal precision.

The mage reeled. Alex pressed the advantage, his second blade flashing out. The attacker vanished in a flicker of mist—retreating.

Cam gasped as the spell's grip loosened.

The fog cracked.

Magic rushed back in like breath after drowning.

"I had him," Cam whispered, shaking.

Alex dropped beside her, eyes scanning her face. "No. He had your *fear.* That's not the same thing."

Cam's breath shuddered out, uneven. For a moment, she still felt the chains—the weight of Brimclif pressing her back into the dirt, small and voiceless. Her fingers trembled against the ground.

But then heat flickered at her palms, stubborn, unyielding. Her fear hadn't snuffed it out. It had fed it.

Cam steadied herself, breath catching. Whatever look Alex gave her, she didn't meet it. She didn't want to see fear—not when she was still dragging herself back from it.

She looked at her hands, the crackle of power coalescing again in her palms. This time, it didn't feel fragile.

It felt earned.

"They're trying to unravel us," she said. "Piece by piece."

Alex's jaw tightened. "Then don't give them anything to unravel."

Cam rose, the fog fading fully now. Around her, the battlefield was still burning—Kaden staggering, Val pinned behind a crumbled ward, Wyatt fighting his way back.

And something dark moving in the trees—another wave coming.

Cam set her jaw.

No more hiding.

She called her magic forward—not just raw force, but memory too. The girl in Brimclif. The pain of being unseen. The fire that never quite went out.

She would not be quiet.

The mage lunged forward, chains flaring with runes meant to suppress. But Cam's magic flared hotter.

She dropped low, instinct and memory blending in one searing motion. Her palm struck the earth, and from that point outward, a surge of heat exploded—molten light erupting beneath the mage's feet. He faltered, eyes wide, just before her next spell cracked the ground beneath him, swallowing him in a burst of raw kinetic force.

Breathing hard, Cam staggered back.

Not enough.

She felt the others still fighting—more movement in the trees. They weren't done. Not even close.

A shape moved behind her—

—but then Wyatt was there.

He slid to her side, sword gleaming, clothes torn from the fight. His free hand braced her shoulder just as another rune sailed through the air, missing by inches.

"I saw the flare," Wyatt said, breaking through the press of bodies. His eyes found hers. "You okay?"

"I'm here," she answered, breathless.

They fell into place without needing to think—back-to-back, steadying each other as more figures closed in.

Cam's grip tightened. "This is the worst of it, isn't it?"

Wyatt didn't answer. His jaw was set; gaze locked on the trees where the next wave gathered.

She already knew.

They were walking straight into the heart of it—and they'd do it together.

Chapter 48: Over the Edge

The cold night air crackled with magic, sharp and biting. Runic glyphs ignited, elemental forces collided—a fierce storm of fire, wind, and frost. The mages pressed in, closing the circle with deadly precision. Cam's heart hammered. They weren't just after victory. They wanted her alive.

She sent a silent call through the Veil, fingers trembling*: Syl, I need you!*

Only silence answered, heavy as the frost biting at her skin.

Ten miles, she reminded herself. *Sylithra can't cross that in an instant. Not fast enough.*

The circle closed tighter. Bolts of ice hissed past her ear; heat from a fire ward seared across her arm. Wyatt deflected a strike with a sweep of stone, but even he staggered, teeth clenched. Val's water shield buckled under another barrage. Tessa's lightning sparked wild, too many opponents for her to strike all at once.

A sudden flare ignited beneath Cam's skin. Golden veins pulsed faintly, glowing like molten threads under her flesh. The magic surged, fierce and insistent—too much. The warning burned bright in her nerves.

She swallowed hard. "Hold. Hold until they come."

Wyatt's voice cut through the chaos beside her. "Cam, you're pushing too far. You need to—"

"No time," she snapped, eyes blazing. "We end this now."

She thrust her hands forward. Violet flames roared to life, colliding with the wind rushing off Kaden's flank. For an instant, the fire didn't just burn violet—it flared with veins of molten gold, brighter, sharper, carried on a current that wasn't hers. The strike tore through several attackers, scattering them in a shower of sparks.

Both she and Kaden froze in the aftermath, startled. The flame guttered back to violet, but the echo of that gold shimmer lingered in her vision, impossible to ignore.

Cam's arms shook with the effort of holding it back.

The ground shuddered beneath her boots. At first, she thought it was her magic breaking loose. Then—

A roar rolled across the night. Distant. Rising.

The sound built with each breath—like thunder drawn closer on vast wings.

Sylithra dove from the clouds, wings slicing through the smoke. Her scales shimmered with molten black and blue, her maw glowing with flame. In the same breath, Tenebrin and Brontheus crashed down behind her in a tight formation around the group, their combined presence an overwhelming force.

The mages faltered, fear flickering in their eyes.

Cam seized the moment.

"Now! Push them back!" she shouted.

Fire and storm, shadow and ice—magic tangled and struck, tearing through enemy ranks.

One by one, the mages fell.

As she thrust her hand forward again, her flame surged violet—and in that instant, a shimmer of gold laced through it, burning brighter where it brushed against Wyatt's light. The strike cleaved a path through their enemies, scattering the last of them in a flare that wasn't hers alone.

Cam, breath ragged, stared at the fading glow in her hands. "That wasn't just me," she whispered, voice shaking. She shook of the thought as the battle died.

"We can't stay. Mount up!"

The words tore from her throat, but the golden glow under her skin burned hotter in answer. Pain seared through her arms, down into her chest, like fire threading her veins. Her knees buckled as the glow flickered violently, too much to contain.

She gasped and dropped to one knee, nearly spent.

Wyatt saw it immediately—the faint glow under her skin. Gold, subtle but unmistakable. His blood went cold. Burn-veins. He'd read of it once, in the margins of an old Academy ledger—mages who burned so hot their own power hollowed them out. Not fatigue. Not exhaustion. Collapse. Permanent. Most never woke again.

Gods, not her. Not now.

Fear surged through him harder than any spell. He sprinted toward her, every instinct screaming to drag her out of the fight, to shield her from herself.

He was already running toward her.

"Cam!" he shouted, reaching her side just as Sylithra landed with a deafening crack of earth and wind.

Cam looked at him with eyes brighter than they should've been. "They'll come again. We have to go."

Tessa helped Alex onto Brontheus, Kaden and Val mounted onto Tenebrin. Wyatt helped Cam to her feet, but she didn't move toward Sylithra.

Not yet.

◈ ☽✦☾ ◈

Cam felt it too—the way her veins seared like fire threading through glass, the tremor in her knees that no amount of will could steady. Every breath came sharp, metallic, as if her lungs were filled with sparks. Her hands shook even as she raised them. She knew something was wrong. Knew she was close to breaking.

But stopping meant the others would fall. Stopping wasn't an option.

Her body was screaming enough. Her heart whispered more.

"No," Cam said, gaze hard. "They're tracking me. They'll follow. We need to lead them away from here—and from Haldrin's Keep."

Cam's eyes flicked to the ridgeline just beyond the trees—the one they passed before they made camp. The highest point before the valley drops. Open air. Clear view. Sylithra would see her from there—if she flew fast enough.

"The ravine's deep, but not endless. If I time it right, she can catch me."

Wyatt frowned. "You're not serious."

"I'll draw them out—toward the ravine. They are after me anyway. You and Sylithra swing back and catch me before I fall."

"You're planning to *jump* off a cliff."

"It's a deep ravine," she said, almost dryly. "Plenty of time."

"No." He stepped in front of her. "You're barely standing."

Kaden stared at her like she'd lost her mind. "Cam, that's suicide."

Tessa stepped forward, her voice sharp with panic. "You can't outrun all of them—not like this."

Val's brow furrowed, her tone tight. "They're trying to unravel you. And you want to hand them the thread?"

Cam's gaze was steady, burning despite the cold. "They're not after any of you. Just me. If I stay, they'll follow us straight to the Keep. If I run—here, now—it gives us distance. And time. That's all I need."

She looked at them one by one—Kaden, Tessa, Val, Alex. Their faces were pale, tight with worry. But beneath the fear, she saw it. The understanding. The reluctant agreement.

Last, she turned to Wyatt.

He didn't speak.

He didn't have to.

She saw it in his eyes—that ache of knowing, and the terror of what it meant.

Her voice softened. "It's the only way."

She touched his arm, steadying him—and herself. "They'll find us again if I don't. I'll lead them as far away as I can. And then jump."

A breath passed between them. Then he nodded once.

"I'll catch you," he said.

Her eyes softened. "You always do."

Then with light warning she took off through the trees. She didn't say goodbye—but it felt like one.

Cam's feet pounded the forest floor as she sprinted away from the others.

Branches whipped her face, rough bark scraping her palms when she stumbled.

Spells hissed through the air—a jagged lance of ice, a burst of searing fire—and she dove behind a fallen log, breath coming in sharp gasps.

"*Cam!*" Wyatt's voice echoed, strained and urgent.

But she didn't stop.

She couldn't.

Not now.

Not when they needed her.

This isn't just a fight. It's their lives—my family.

The mages' voices grew closer, orders shouted, feet pounding in pursuit.

She twisted, dodged another spell that scorched a tree beside her, and ran deeper into the shadowed wood.

Each step was a promise. *I will protect them. No matter what.*

Her lungs burned with cold air; branches clawed at her arms, and the ground beneath her feet fell away faster than she expected. Ahead, the cliff edge loomed—a jagged scar against the dark sky, sharp and unforgiving.

Cam's boots skidded across the frozen leaves as she darted downhill, her breath sharp and fast in her throat. Frost shattered underfoot. A glimmer of gold pulsed faintly through her veins—too early, too bright.

She didn't see the attacker until he was already on her.

A mage slammed into her from the side, knocking her off balance. The force of it drove them both to the ground, and before she could reach for her blade, he pinned her down, one hand twisted in her collar, the other alive with spell light.

He pressed her into the dirt, trying to suppress her by force. His magic wrapped around hers like iron bands, laced with intent—contain, subdue, erase. He didn't need to ask who she was. The veins told him everything.

"You're burning already," he spat, eyes flicking to the gold threading beneath her skin. "You should be down by now."

She gritted her teeth. Her body screamed in warning—magic surging too hot, too fast. *'When you start to glow, stop using magic.'*

But she wasn't stopping. She couldn't.

Her eyes snapped open.

Pain flared through her chest—bright and blinding. One more spell could break her. She cast it anyway.

The ground beneath them quivered. A surge of earth burst upward, throwing the mage off balance. She rolled, yanking her dagger free, and slashed. Steel met steel—his blade was already drawn—and they clashed in close, brutal arcs. He struck with spells between parries. She countered, reckless, instinctual—drawing not just from earth but from water, from air, from the creeping shadows that seemed to bend toward her.

A jet of water burst from the soil, slamming him back. A gust of wind knocked him into a tree. When he tried to cast again, she drove her blade forward and struck.

He choked, stumbled—and fell.

Cam stood over him, chest heaving, gold still flickering beneath her skin. Her hands trembled. Her limbs screamed. She dropped to one knee with a grunt. Her vision swam, exhaustion clawing its way up her spine like frostbite.

Footsteps. Shouting.

More mages.

No time.

She pulled herself up and kept going—kept running. Her breath was ragged now, shallow and sharp. Each stride dragged her body closer to the edge of collapse. Her strength was nearly gone, but she didn't stop. Couldn't stop. Not with everything riding on this.

Her legs burned. The trees thinned.

The ground tilted upward—and then vanished.

Ahead, the cliff loomed like a wound torn into the earth. Jagged. Cold. Final.

She faltered for a breath.

Behind her, voices surged—closer now, charging through the brush. Orders barked. Magic cracked through the trees like lightning.

Her breath caught.

There was no time to hesitate. No time for doubt.

She glanced back once, the sounds of pursuit pounding closer—voices yelling commands, spells tearing through the air like thunderclaps.

Wyatt's voice again, through the dragonlink—desperate—*"Cam, STOP!"*

But she didn't. They have to lose her here.

Cam raced across the rocks, golden light flaring behind her. Her body screamed, her vision blurred—but she didn't slow. At the cliff's edge, she didn't hesitate. But her legs faltered for half a step, muscles trembling. Was there enough left in her to make the leap? The thought knifed through her chest, cold and sharp, almost louder than the pursuit. Her breath caught sharp in her chest, fear clawing through her resolve.

She jumped.

And for a breathless second, she was falling.

The wind rushed like a scream around her ears, and for a heartbeat, there was only weightlessness.

For a heartbeat, the world dropped away—the cold wind screaming past her ears, the forest canopy a blur below.

Weightless.

Panic rose like a tide.

Then—

A roar cracked the sky. Claws sliced the air. A shadow dove. Wind screamed in her ears as Sylithra surged up beneath her, wings flaring.

But Cam's aim had been off—too low, too slow—

Her fingers brushed the edge of Sylithra's scales—

And then *his* hand caught hers like an anchor, powerful and warm, pulling her from the edge of nothingness.

His grip was rougher than usual, almost desperate, like he couldn't bear to let her slip. For a breath, she thought she saw something break in his eyes—fear, relief, something deeper she wasn't ready to name.

"Gods, Cam, you're insane," Wyatt gasped, straining as he yanked her up beside him on Sylithra's back.

Her boots scraped against the slick scales, and she lurched forward, clutching his arm before she could steady herself. The motion ripped a shaky, nervous laugh from her throat—too close to a choke, too close to the fall. Her heart was still racing. "I know," she said quickly, breath uneven. "But you'll be there to catch me if I fall."

He didn't even pause. "You know I always will."

Together, they soared upward, Sylithra's wings beating a powerful rhythm beneath them. The forest and the shadows shrank below, swallowed by night.

As they flew back toward Haldrin's Keep, Cam felt the weight of everything pressing down—the fear, the hope, the fragile threads of trust weaving tighter between them.

The shadows had come for her—but this time, she burned back.

The fight had ended.

But the war? It was just beginning.

Chapter 49: A Quiet Kind of Doubt in What They Trust

The wind had gone still.

Sylithra's wings swept low in one final arc before she landed on the frostbitten ridge. Her talons scraped stone, and a tremor hummed through the earth beneath them. Steam curled from her nostrils, rising in slow spirals.

Cam sat slumped in the saddle, her body aching beneath layers of blood-stiffened cloth and soot. Her head throbbed—there was a crust of dried blood on her temple that she hadn't dared touch. Wyatt rode behind her, one arm looped loosely around her waist. He hadn't said much since they'd fled the ambush. None of them had.

Below them, Haldrin's Keep came into view, tucked against the mountainside. Its familiar spires peeked through early morning mist. Smoke drifted up from the chimneys, curling lazily into the pale light.

Cam narrowed her eyes.

White rooftops?

She blinked.

No—snow.

Fat flakes drifted silently from the clouds, soft and slow, like the ash that had haunted them only hours ago. One landed on the back of her glove. It melted instantly.

"It's snowing," she murmured, voice rough.

Wyatt leaned in just close enough for her to feel his breath near her ear. "First snow."

Behind them, wings beat hard against the cold sky. Brontheus landed next, thunderous and coiled with tension, his green-black scales shimmering faintly with leftover lightning. Tessa slid down from the saddle fast, but her limp gave her away. She barely caught herself before Alex was at her side, steadying her.

Their hands found each other's without thought.

Tessa grumbled, muffling it into her scarf. "Of course it's snowing. Why wouldn't it be?"

Tenebrin followed soon after, gliding to the ridge like a living shadow. His wings folded in tight as he landed without a sound. Kaden dismounted first, jaw tight, movements practiced and slow. Val came down next, pale and unsteady, but didn't resist when he took her arm. Her gloved hand brushed against his, and it stayed there as they fell into step.

The dragons didn't follow.

Sylithra, Brontheus, and Tenebrin remained behind, silent and still as statues on the ridge, their breath curling in the cold. They would wait there—watchful, enormous, and wounded in ways that didn't bleed.

The six of them walked.

There was no rush, no strength left to fake. Boots crunched softly through the thin layer of fresh snow. The only sound was the wind threading through the trees and the distant creak of Haldrin's front gates beginning to stir.

Cam kept her steps even, though her limbs ached and her vision blurred at the edges. Her body screamed for rest, but her mind was still tangled in what they'd just survived.

Wyatt stayed close, matching her pace. He didn't say anything at first, just walked beside her with quiet purpose.

Cam stared at the ground as they moved—at the snow melting beneath their steps, already stained with ash and blood.

Finally, Wyatt's voice broke the silence. "You okay?"

Cam didn't answer right away. A snowflake landed on her glove again. She watched it disappear into the leather.

"I killed someone," she said quietly. "A mage. He looked straight at me. He didn't even blink. And now when I close my eyes, I still see his."

Wyatt didn't flinch. He didn't ask for more.

"He didn't hesitate," Cam added. "None of them did."

Her voice was low, tight around the edges. Not bitter. Just tired. Just real.

"But you did what you had to," Wyatt said, not cold—just steady. "You got us out."

Cam didn't respond. Her gaze drifted to the others ahead—Tessa still leaning into Alex, Val holding tightly to Kaden's sleeve like an anchor. Everyone limping. Everyone silent. But alive.

They were still here.

So was she.

Cam's voice was barely a whisper, but it held.

"We're all still here."

Wyatt didn't press her further. His gloved hand brushed close to hers as they walked—close but not touching.

The snow kept falling. And behind them, the dragons waited, silent and watchful beneath the dawn.

The snow followed them down the ridge.

Haldrin's Keeps outer wall rose slowly into view as they approached, stone slick with frost and age. The gate was closed but not barred. A lone figure on the watch recognized them first—a sharp whistle cutting through the quiet. Then motion. Lanterns lifted. Voices murmured. The gates creaked open.

Ben was already walking ahead of them, having pushed forward the last hundred paces without a word. His silhouette cut a commanding shape through the mist, cloak trailing behind him like shadow.

He turned just before crossing the threshold and barked gently, "Straight to the infirmary. All of you."

None of them argued.

Tessa winced with every step, jaw clenched as she leaned more heavily on Alex. Blood stained the edge of her scarf, barely visible against the dark red wool. She kept her head high regardless, glaring at any soldier who looked too long.

Val didn't speak at all. Her eyes never left Kaden—not once. She moved like someone who had lost her footing but hadn't hit the ground yet. Her fingers were still tangled in his sleeve, knuckles white.

Cam lagged a few steps behind them, her breath coming too shallow. Her head ached sharply now, the crusted blood at her temple catching in her curls with every movement. Her legs felt numb, and not from the cold.

Ben fell into step beside her.

"You're not hiding it well," he said quietly, not looking at her.

Cam blinked. "Hiding what?"

He nodded toward her hand. Faint threads of golden light still shimmered beneath her skin, dimmed but not gone.

Cam tucked her hand beneath her cloak. "Didn't mean to."

Ben didn't press. He just looked at her for a long second, then said, "You made it back."

Barely, Cam thought. But yeah.

Ahead, the heavy wooden doors of the Keep groaned open. Warm light spilled out onto the snowy stone. Healers were already moving inside, alerted by the gate watchers. A woman with streaked gray hair ushered them in with calm authority.

"Infirmary's prepped. Lay them down, triage by severity."

"I'm fine," Tessa muttered.

"You're bleeding from three places," Alex countered, already guiding her inside.

"I can walk—"

"You're limping."

"I'm limping *with purpose*."

Val nearly stumbled as she crossed the threshold, and Kaden caught her under the arm before she hit the wall. "Easy," he murmured, almost too quietly to hear.

"I'm fine," Val whispered.

"I know," Kaden said, but he didn't let go.

Cam moved with the others into the Keep's inner halls. The heat hit her first—too fast, too warm. It made her dizzy. The torchlight flickered against the stone, casting everything in gold and shadow. She felt it again—that strange, soft shimmer beneath her skin. It wasn't ready to disappear yet.

They were guided into a side corridor lined with cots and supplies. The infirmary smelled like old bandages and clean water, the bitter tang of salves, and something underneath—faint smoke, clinging from the night before.

One by one, they were separated gently—Tessa to a cot near the back with Alex sitting at her side; Val seated next to a brazier while a healer checked her pulse and eyes. Kaden stood between them, arms crossed, refusing care until the others were seen.

Cam stood near the doorway, uncertain. Disconnected.

"You too," a healer said, trying to usher her to a cot. "You've got head trauma—"

"I'm not bleeding anymore," Cam replied, too quickly.

"You're still glowing," the woman pointed out.

Cam didn't answer.

She felt Wyatt at her side again. His presence hadn't left her for more than a moment since they landed. He said nothing, just gave her the faintest nudge of his shoulder. She followed it to the cot and sat down slowly, trying not to wince.

The healer moved away to get supplies.

Cam looked at her hands.

The gold was fading now—flickering at her pulse points like the last light in a storm's wake.

Wyatt sat next to her without asking. Just breathing.

The room hummed with soft voices, clinking glass, rustling bandages. No one laughed. But no one cried either.

They were alive.

Cam sat on the edge of the cot, elbows on her knees, cloak still wrapped tight around her shoulders. A faint line of dried blood pulled at her temple when she shifted. Her hands rested open on her thighs—scraped, faintly glowing, and quiet now.

Wyatt stayed beside her, shoulders brushing. They hadn't spoken in minutes.

Outside the infirmary window, snow still fell—soft and relentless.

Cam's voice broke the silence first, so low it barely made a sound.

"...It wasn't on purpose."

Wyatt turned toward her slightly. "What wasn't?"

She hesitated, then flexed her fingers. The golden light was almost gone now, barely more than a flicker beneath her skin.

"When the ambush started—I don't know how I did it. I just... everything slowed. Not them. Not us. Just the moment." She exhaled, slow and shaky. "Like the air had turned thick, like a heartbeat stretched too long. For half a breath, it felt like the world hesitated. And that half-breath gave Tessa room to spark, gave Kaden a step ahead, gave me—just enough to move first."

Wyatt didn't interrupt. He only nodded once, faintly—he'd seen it too.

She went on, voice steadier now. "And in that choice, I realized I had more power than I thought."

"And it gave us enough to survive," Wyatt said quietly. Not as reassurance—just truth.

Cam blinked down at her hands again. "I didn't even know I could do that."

"You didn't *think*. You *chose*."

That made her glance at him, tired and wary. "What if next time I choose too late?"

Wyatt met her eyes, calm and steady. "Then we live with it. But you didn't this time."

Cam let out a long breath she hadn't realized she was holding.

"I was scared."

"I was too."

They sat in silence for another moment, letting that honesty settle between them—soft and solid like the snow outside.

The healer returned a moment later with clean cloth and balm. Wyatt stood, quietly giving space, but not leaving entirely. As Cam tilted her head for the woman to tend her wound, she looked toward the others—Tessa resting with Alex beside her, Val finally asleep, Kaden leaning against the wall with his arms folded but eyes watching all of them.

They were alive. Because time had slowed for just long enough.

The fire in Corin's study burned low, casting long shadows across the map table. Kaden stepped inside, tugging his jacket tighter. He hadn't slept. Didn't plan to.

Ben stood near the wall, arms folded. Corin glanced up but said nothing right away.

Kaden broke the silence. "They came out of nowhere. Ten miles from Haldrin's Keep—no wards, no signs. Just... hit us in the dead of night."

Corin nodded once. "You didn't send a flare."

"We were camping overnight. Found signs of blight, frost rot too. Figured we'd scout more in the morning." Kaden paused. "We weren't trying to hide, but we didn't light anything noticeable either."

Ben's voice was low. "They knew where to look."

Kaden hesitated. "Yeah."

He looked down at the map, tracing a path with one finger. "Val woke us. Said she felt something—minds, maybe. Like pressure. Gave us just enough time to brace."

Corin finally spoke. "They were after Cam."

Kaden nodded. "Went for her first."

A beat of silence.

"We swept that area a week ago," Kaden added. "It was clean. No one should've known we'd head out that way."

He looked around the room, quiet. Something itched at the back of his thoughts—he couldn't place it.

"Doesn't feel like chance," he muttered. His fingers drummed once against the map, then stilled—too deliberate. His mind was already moving three steps ahead.

Ben shifted but didn't speak. Corin's expression didn't change.

Kaden stepped back toward the door. "I'll write up the rest later. Just... thought you should know."

He paused. "If something's off, I'll find it. But we don't talk about this here."

Then he was gone.

The fire crackled in his wake.

Chapter 50: The Storm Inside

The snow had slowed.

The glow of dusk-light lanterns cast soft golden shapes against the infirmary walls. Only a few cots were occupied—just her group, the ones who had come back from the routine sweep, turned ambush. The room had quieted into that breath-between the hush after fear, where no one dared speak louder than they had to.

Cam lay on her side, blanket draped across her legs, but her cloak still wrapped around her shoulders. She hadn't removed her boots. Her gloves sat beside her, folded but untouched. Her hands still carried the faint scent of blood and ash.

She stared at the space between floorboards. Still awake.

The healer had offered her a sleeping draught earlier—gently, without pressure—but she'd refused.

She didn't know why.

Everyone else had taken it. Wyatt, even Kaden. Val hadn't made a sound when they gave it to her. Tessa had resisted, but Alex had convinced her with a quiet look and a hand on her back.

But Cam... hadn't swallowed the bitter root. Couldn't.

Maybe it was because this was her first real battle. Not against shadows or hollow creatures, but against people. Mages who had looked her in the eyes. Who had chosen death over surrender. And she had answered with fire, blade, and light.

And now she was here. Awake. Still holding the moment in her chest like a shard of something she couldn't put down.

The door creaked softly open.

She didn't move.

But her breath caught a little when Ben stepped in—boots quiet, cloak still wet at the edges. His gaze passed gently over the room, then landed on her. No urgency. No demand.

Just him.

He crossed the room and sat beside her, not on the cot but on the floor, back to the wall. They didn't speak for a long moment.

Then—

"You haven't slept," he said, not as a question.

Cam didn't answer right away. Then: "Neither have you."

Ben let out a soft breath through his nose. A hint of a tired smile, but only that.

She glanced down at her hands, then away.

"I thought I could," she murmured. "But I didn't want to dream about it."

Ben's voice was low. "You will. Even if you didn't take the draught."

She nodded, barely.

Another pause.

"I've... killed shadow creatures before," she said. "But that felt different. They were already something else. Not... not someone. But this time—it's like the silence after his death is louder than any scream. I keep seeing his eyes, and it's like he's still waiting for an answer I don't have."

Ben's hands rested loosely over his knees. He hasn't looked at her yet.

"You looked him in the eyes?"

She nodded.

He didn't say 'I'm sorry.' He didn't say 'it gets easier.' Instead—

"Do you know what I remember from my first battle?" he asked, voice softer now. "It wasn't the fight. Or even who I killed. It was after. I remember the snow melting on my gloves. Just... drops running off. Like the world didn't care what I'd done."

Cam swallowed. Her throat felt tight.

"I think I'm still waiting to feel like it was right."

Ben turned toward her at last, his eyes quieter than she'd ever seen them. "You don't have to feel that. Not tonight."

She looked at him. "Then what am I supposed to feel?"

His reply was quiet. "Anything you need to."

The words settled in her chest like a hand placed gently over her heart—warm but not trying to carry it for her.

"I didn't know why I didn't take the draught," she said finally. "But... maybe it's because if I sleep, I'll forget how it felt. And I don't want to forget. That would make me like them, wouldn't it?"

Ben shook his head, firm now. "No. That makes you not like them."

Cam blinked hard, but no tears came. She didn't want to cry. Not yet.

Ben reached out, slow, and placed a hand over hers. It was solid. Real. She didn't pull away.

"You don't have to prove anything to anyone, Cam," he said. "Not even to me. Especially not tonight."

She nodded once. Then again.

And for the first time since the battle... she let her eyes close. Not in sleep, but in rest.

Ben didn't stay long. Just long enough to make sure she had water, a blanket, and silence if she needed it. He gave her a small squeeze to the shoulder before standing, hesitation soft in his eyes.

Cam sat there for a while after the door clicked shut. The fire had dwindled to embers. She couldn't tell if the glow she saw was from the hearth or her own veins, still faintly gold beneath her skin.

They had all made it back. No one from her group had died.

And yet something in her had changed.

She waited until his footsteps faded down the corridor, until she was alone with the hush. Still, she didn't sleep. Not yet.

◈ ☽✦☾ ◈

It was early morning when she slipped out—carefully, quietly, not to wake the others. The corridors of Haldrin's Keep were hushed. She passed no one as she climbed stair after stair, up to her favorite place: the small overlook above the battlements, tucked into a cragged corner of the Keep.

Tessa jokingly called it her "brooding place."

But to Cam, it was just... high. Clear. The wind could reach her here. She could breathe.

She pressed her palms to the cold stone railing and watched the snow fall in slow, thick spirals. It had softened the world into something that looked safe.

This was the first time she'd killed someone.

It hadn't felt like anything at first—just survival.

But now that it was quiet, it was all she could hear. The sound of his breath, the way his eyes changed, the heaviness in her hands after. She hadn't flinched. She hadn't hesitated.

She wasn't sure what that said about her.

She sat down, legs pulled up to her chest, letting the cold settle into her bones. It reminded her she was still alive.

You are not broken.

The voice in her mind was low and clear, like a breath of wind against old stone.

Sylithra.

The first time is always loud. Louder in silence. Loudest in those who feel the cost.

Cam didn't speak aloud. She didn't need to.

She wasn't sure how long she'd been able to do this—talk to dragons in her mind—but it had deepened since Sylithra had touched her soul.

You could have hardened. You didn't. Even Kaelith didn't cry the first time. But he never wept at all.

The others—Skylith, Sael, Tenebrin—were there too. Faint murmurs of support, subtle warmth beneath the snow.

But Sylithra remained the closest, her presence wrapping like a shawl around Cam's weary thoughts.

You are still you, Little Flame. And you do not stand alone.

Cam closed her eyes. Not to cry. Just to feel.

She didn't hear Corin approach. He was quiet like snow, all soft steps and sharp intuition.

He stood beside her at the edge of the overlook; arms crossed against the wind.

"You stayed awake," he said, his voice soft but not pitying.

"So did you," she replied.

For a long moment, they said nothing more. He didn't ask her what she'd seen or what she felt. Just stood with her.

"I remember my first," he murmured eventually. "And my second. And how the world didn't care either time."

Cam didn't answer. She didn't have to.

"The weight of it wasn't just mine. It was part of a lineage I never asked for—but one I can't deny. It never gets easier. But you get... clearer," Corin said. "You learn what parts of yourself to hold onto. And which parts were never truly yours."

He reached into his coat and pulled something small from a wrapped cloth. A pendant, no larger than a coin—simple iron framing a cloudy shard of quartz, runes etched faintly into the metal.

"Your mother carved the runes. Ben forged the setting. It's a charm meant to quiet the storm when your thoughts get tangled."

Cam's breath hitched. She took it carefully.

"Why didn't you give it to me before?"

"Because you hadn't seen the storm yet."

She clutched it tightly in her fist and nodded.

The door creaked softly as Cam stepped inside the infirmary. The air was still thick with the scent of poultices and dried herbs. A few cots were occupied—Tessa lay curled under a blanket, Kaden faced the wall, and Wyatt's hand was still bandaged, his chest rising with steady breath.

Val was the only one awake.

She glanced up from where she sat propped against her pillows, braid mussed, a faint bruise along her collarbone, eyes sharp even in half-light.

Cam lingered in the doorway.

"How are you feeling?"

Val gave a slow exhale.

"Like I fell off a dragon going full dive and landed in my own ribs. So, you know. Not great."

A pause. Then, dryly:

"You look worse."

Cam gave a tired snort and crossed the room, lowering herself onto the edge of her cot. She stared at the sleeping draught on the table, untouched.

Val followed her gaze.

"You planning to take that, or just glare it into submission?"

"I wasn't sure." Cam's voice was raw, lower than usual. "Everyone else already did."

Val tipped her head back against the wall, studying the ceiling beams with a lazy kind of calm that didn't quite reach her eyes.

"You're not everyone else," she added after a beat.

Cam finally reached for the vial, turning it in her hands. The liquid caught the lamplight, curling like smoke inside glass.

Val's voice softened—not pitying, just even. "You kept us alive back there. Doesn't matter how it felt."

Cam's grip tightened. "I didn't feel brave. Just... cornered. Like there wasn't another choice."

"Yeah." Val's mouth quirked faintly, though her gaze stayed distant. "That's how it always goes. You move first, think later. Then it catches up when things are quiet."

Cam drank, the burn heavy in her chest. She didn't look up. "I can still see their faces."

Val didn't flinch. "Good. Means you're still you. The day you stop feeling it—that's when you should worry."

Cam closed her eyes for a moment, breathing slowly. "It doesn't feel like enough."

"It never does," Val said simply. "But it was what kept the rest of us breathing. That's the part you hold on to."

Cam blinked slowly. "I wasn't brave. I just... had to keep going."

"That's the truth."

They didn't speak again. Just sat together, breaths gradually falling into the same rhythm. It wasn't comfort exactly, but it was steady. And for now, that was enough.

◈ ☽✦☾ ◈

The sleeping draught pulled her down gently.

But sleep did not mean safety.

She was in the forest again. But it was too quiet. Snow fell up instead of down. The trees whispered in reverse. She turned toward the clearing—

And there he was.

Kaelith.

He stood in the center, robed in the shadow of sunlight. His eyes found hers instantly.

"You saw what you could be," he said, tilting his head. "Do you know what you are becoming?"

He raised his hand, and the forest melted away.

In its place: a city burning. Dragons in chains. Wyatt and Kaden broken and bound in threads of shadow. Sylithra screaming from the sky.

"You could stop this," he said. "You could prevent all of it. If you stopped fighting fate. If you stopped fighting me."

Cam stepped back—but her feet were rooted.

"You are the beginning," Kaelith whispered, stepping closer. "But you could be the end."

She gasped—

And awoke to darkness, cold sweat slick on her skin. Her fist was clenched tight around the pendant, its edges pressing into her palm. She hadn't even realized she'd held onto it in her sleep. The runes were warm. Too warm. Like her mother's hand refusing to let go.

And beneath it all, the faintest whisper still echoed in her mind:

Choose well, Little Flame.

The draught carried her down into restless sleep, and with it came the dream. Hollow eyes. A voice that echoed like stone cracking beneath water. She reached for it—and then it was gone.

Cam had woken with the taste of silence still heavy in her mouth. She didn't bother trying to close her eyes again. Instead, she rose, letting the stillness of the keep swallow her steps.

The corridor was dim, her movements quiet beneath the weight of the past day pressing against her chest. The cold air lingered despite the warmth spilling from torches set along the stone walls. Her mind drifted, cycling through fragments of the ambush—the flicker of golden light beneath her skin, the sound of blades, the heavy silence after. Cam's steps were quiet as she moved down the dim corridor of Haldrin's Keep, the heavy weight of the past day pressing against her chest. The cold air still lingered, despite the warmth spilling from torches set along the stone walls. Her mind drifted, cycling through fragments of the ambush—the flicker of golden light beneath her skin, the sound of blades, the heavy silence after.

She wasn't sure if the ache in her limbs or the dull pulse at her temple was worse. Maybe both.

The others had gone to their rooms or sought solitude. Cam figured Tessa would be resting somewhere nearby, probably alone. They all needed space to recover—to hold onto whatever pieces of themselves were left.

She barely noticed the faint sound of voices ahead, soft and low, carried down the stone hallway like a secret breeze. It was unexpected, but something about it made her pause, curiosity pulling her closer.

Cam rounded the corner, expecting to find Tessa sitting quietly, maybe talking with someone from the healing staff or reading. Instead, her breath hitched.

There they were—Tessa and Alex, closer than she had ever seen them before. Foreheads pressed together, eyes closed in a shared laugh that was intimate and light, almost stolen from a world that still hadn't been fully shattered.

Alex's hand rested gently on Tessa's waist, warm and steady. Tessa's fingers tangled in Alex's hair, soft and sure.

Neither noticed Cam until her sudden presence broke the spell.

"Cam," Tessa's laugh faltered. Alex's hand froze mid-movement, eyes wide.

Cam's cheeks flamed with embarrassment and something else—a mixture of surprise and something unspoken. She quickly stepped back, the cool stone wall pressing against her back as she fought to gather her scattered thoughts.

"You're awful at secrets, you know," Tessa teased Alex, a playful grin breaking across her face despite the surprise.

Alex shrugged, a small smirk tugging at his lips. "Well, I guess it's not a secret anymore."

"I-I'm sorry."

She turned on her heels walking back the way she had come. She heard Tessa giggle.

Cam swallowed and forced a smile, the warmth in their closeness lingering in her mind long after she turned away.

In the middle of everything—chaos, fear, loss—they had found something real.

Chapter 51: Sparks in the Snow

The sun dipped low behind the western ridge, casting long amber shadows across the warded perimeter. It had been a few days since the ambush, but the echoes of it still clung to Cam like a second skin. Patrol duty was supposed to be uneventful this time of evening—especially within the inner circle—but her nerves prickled with a restless edge she couldn't shake.

She adjusted the grip on her weapon and tried to focus on the rhythm of her boots against the stone.

Alex walked beside her in easy silence. Not too close. Not too far. Just enough that she could feel the warmth of the forge still clinging to his coat, the faint scent of coal and iron trailing in his wake.

She hadn't meant to think about it again—not here, not now—but the memory pressed close.

The mage's spell hadn't hurt in the usual way. It had slipped past her defenses, past her strength, and coiled around something deeper. Her magic had evaporated from her reach as if it had never belonged to her at all. And in its place, her own fear whispered: *What if this is who you are underneath it all? Powerless. Alone. Unworthy.*

She'd frozen. Her body hadn't, but her will had.

Then Alex had come. Silent. Swift. His blade cut clean across the mage's chest, and just like that—air had rushed back into her lungs. The spell broke. Her magic returned like a tide.

She hadn't said much then. Just a shaky breath and a nod. But it lingered now—this question she couldn't name. This thread she couldn't quite pull.

"Thank you," she said softly, glancing over at him. "For the other night. I didn't get the chance."

Alex didn't look at her right away. His gaze was fixed on the shimmer of the outer wards, where the last light of dusk played tricks in the air. When he finally spoke, his voice was calm.

"Did what anyone would've done."

Cam's hand tightened on her sword strap.

"It wasn't like fire or frost," she said slowly. "It didn't hurt like that. It... slipped under everything—my wards, my strength—like it reached straight for my core. And for a breath, it was gone. My magic. Like I was empty. Hollow."

She swallowed hard, voice lower. "I've never felt anything like it. I don't ever want to again."

Alex's hand shifted on his sword hilt, the motion too sharp to be casual. "Then it's good I was there," he said quickly—too quickly. His half-smile followed, but it didn't reach his eyes.

Cam studied him for a long beat. "Do you know what that spell was?"

Alex gave a short laugh. "Not really. I've read stories. Same as you."

She stopped walking. "But you didn't answer the question."

That made him glance over—his mouth curved in a half-smile, but it didn't reach his eyes. "Some things are better not known. Doesn't mean they aren't real."

Cam studied him for a moment. The way he stood just a little too straight. The flicker of something unreadable in his expression. Not fear. Not guilt. But something.

It stirred in her—a whisper of unease. A thread she could follow if she wanted to.

But she was tired. And the fear spell still clung to the edges of her bones like smoke.

She looked away first.

"Come on," she murmured, adjusting the strap of her sword. "We've still got half a circle to finish."

Alex didn't argue. He fell in step beside her, quiet as ever.

But as they walked, Cam couldn't help but glance sideways once more.

Some masks weren't worn. They were lived in.

She didn't know what was worse—that he'd hidden it so well, or that she hadn't wanted to look.

And maybe—just maybe—this was one of them.

She exhaled, almost convincing herself it didn't matter. Not tonight.

By morning, the quiet weight of the night patrol had given way to the clang of steel and the thud of boots in the sparring ring. Sunlight spilled across the yard, catching on blades and bare earth as the circle came alive with practice.

Cam pivoted on her heel, narrowly ducking under Wyatt's wooden blade. He tracked her with a half-smile, deflecting her next strike with the flat of his practice sword. Their movements were clean and practiced—like dancing to a rhythm only they could hear.

Across the ring, Kaden mirrored Wyatt's stance, matching the angle of his blade with unconscious synchronicity. They didn't speak. They didn't need to. Every shift in weight, every pivot or parry—they moved like two halves of the same thought.

Cam stepped back to catch her breath when—

Whap.

A snowball smacked into Kaden's shoulder. He didn't flinch.

Without so much as a pause, he caught the next one midair and sent it sailing back.

Thud.

It caught Tessa on the side. "Hey!" she shouted, laughing. "Uncalled for!"

"Your aim was off," Kaden said, cool as ever.

"Your *face* is off."

Tessa darted behind Cam, grabbing her shoulders. "Protect me!"

"I'm innocent," Cam protested, hands up like a peacekeeper caught between nations.

"You're in the blast zone now," Kaden warned, lobbing another snowball. It landed just inches from Cam's boots.

Val, red-faced and giggling, ducked behind a training dummy.

Tessa peeked around Cam's shoulder, grinning. "Gods, you two training or dancing?"

Cam didn't need to ask who she meant. Wyatt and Kaden both fought to suppress smirks. She could feel it too—something unspoken passing between them in the space of a shared rhythm. Familiar. Grounding.

Her gaze slid toward Val, who was doing a poor job of not looking at Kaden. And Kaden—his eyes lingered a little too long on Val before he turned away. Tessa didn't miss it.

"Oh, this again," she said, elbowing Cam. "Are you seeing this?"

Cam snorted. "Seeing everything."

Kaden raised an eyebrow. "Some of us are trying to train."

"Some of us," Tessa countered, "are trying to *flirt*."

Wyatt chuckled under his breath, brushing snow from his sleeves.

Cam's smile softened. She looked at all of them—still breathing, still here. Kaden guarded but steady. Val, fierce and flushed. Tessa, untamed energy wrapped in charm. Wyatt, standing quiet beside her, always aware of her movements.

This was what held them together.

Not destiny. Not prophecy.

These moments. These flickers of normal.

The ache in her chest—the one that never fully left—eased. Just a little.

The five of them were already in motion—sweat rising in the cold, blades ringing, spells cracking sharp through the air. Cam ducked beneath Tessa's swing, rolled, and sent a pulse of pressure upward from the ground, forcing Kaden to pivot mid-air with wind just to avoid slamming into a post. Val's hands flickered with golden runes, a flickering ward catching Wyatt's spell just in time.

They moved like pieces of a storm—messy, raw, and only beginning to understand the shape they formed when they moved together.

Corin stood at the edge of the platform above the training ring, arms folded in front of him, his breath fogging the morning air.

There was something deeply *right* about seeing them like this. Not for the rebellion's sake, not even for prophecy—but for their own. For all the weight each of them carried, they were still learning to choose each other. That mattered.

And yet, beneath that pride... a chill hadn't left him all morning.

The vision had come without warning. A flicker—a candle snuffed in an unseen room.

He had seen shadows coiling behind someone's eyes—not just betrayal but tethered. Bound. Like a thread of the Veil pulling from within their own walls. A betrayal not yet made but already seeded. No voice. Only the sensation of something trusted... being used.

Corin closed his eyes briefly. It wasn't the first time the Veil had blurred his foresight, but it was the first time it felt *deliberate.*

Then there was the other thing—the discovery beneath the Knighthood ruins. Half-buried in frost and stone. A fragment. Older than the rebellion. Etched with symbols he hadn't seen since before the collapse of the old world.

Veilbind.

The word wasn't supposed to exist anymore.

He had tried to tell himself it could wait. That they deserved time. But the longer he waited, the louder the Veil hummed against his senses. The Hollow Prince was waking. And now... something else was, too.

Corin's eyes flicked back to the group.

Cam paused, laughing breathlessly as Wyatt tossed her his scarf mid-duel. Kaden rolled his eyes. Val's lips tilted up for half a second before she caught herself.

He hated to break this.

But the truth couldn't wait much longer.

◈ ☽✦☾ ◈

By mid-afternoon, drills had shifted to full sparring rotations. The sun hung low behind cloud cover, casting long, blurred shadows across the grounds. Breath fogged the air with every exhale.

Snowflakes rose in light spirals as Val circled to the left, her braid swinging like a metronome behind her. Kaden tracked her steps, blades at the ready, jaw tight with concentration.

Tessa leaned toward Cam again, voice low. "I give them four more seconds before one of them breaks the tension and just proposes."

Cam didn't even look away. "Tess..."

"What?" Tessa grinned. "It's romantic. All that slow circling, the brooding eye contact? It's like foreplay with extra footwork."

Wyatt, now seated beside Cam, coughed into his sleeve to hide a laugh.

In the ring, Val feinted right and struck low. Kaden caught it, parried, stepped in. Too close. His retreat came a heartbeat too late to erase the smile that flickered across Kaden's lips.

Tessa gasped softly. "There it is. A smirk. A real Kaden Valehart smirk. Gods help us—it's happening."

Cam arched an eyebrow. "They're just sparring."

"How *dare* you downplay the most emotionally charged choreography I've ever seen," Tessa whispered. "I'm *wounded*."

"Wounded how?" Wyatt asked mildly.

Tessa clutched her chest. "In the heart. Where the drama lives."

Back in the ring, they reset—breaths rising, shoulders in sync.

"You're holding back," Val said, sharp.

Kaden didn't blink. "So are you."

Val lunged again—faster this time. Their blades clashed, rang through the clearing. Kaden caught her wrist, and they landed chest-to-chest in a frozen, breathless moment.

No one moved.

Tessa let out a delighted squeak.

Val pulled away first. "Again."

Cam murmured, smiling now, "You're not wrong."

"I *never* am," Tessa whispered smugly.

The ring went quiet for a heartbeat, the air heavy with the scrape of steel still echoing between them. Sweat ran down Val's temple; Kaden's grip flexed once before he finally let go. The tension broke in a rush of breath—half laughter from Tessa, half silence from the rest.

Kaden stepped back to the edge of the ring, brushing dust from his tunic. "You're faster than last time."

Val gave him a look. "You're getting predictable."

Tessa clapped once. "Lovebirds off the floor. Next: our chosen one and the dragon rider who definitely stares when he thinks no one's watching."

Wyatt exhaled. "I don't—"

Cam cut in, deadpan. "You kind of do."

Wyatt blinked. "You noticed?"

Tessa whooped. "Oh, this is gold."

Cam flushed but rolled her shoulders, stepping into the ring. "Focus, Valehart."

"Always," Wyatt said, sliding into stance, blade angled low.

Steel met steel. Their match unfolded slower than the last—less spark, more simmer. Each strike measured. Each step deliberate. The rhythm was quiet, steady, like the two of them were writing their own language in the ring.

"You're holding back," Cam said, her voice low, the words punctuated by the scrape of her blade against his.

Wyatt parried and smiled faintly. "Maybe I don't want to bruise you."

Cam lunged hard, forcing him back a pace. "Try me."

Their blades rang again, a clean arc of silver and sound. They circled, feet scuffing in the packed dirt, shoulders brushing close when they collided. For every strike Cam pressed, Wyatt countered, his eyes never leaving hers.

From the sideline, Tessa cupped her hands. "Don't make this boring!"

Kaden crossed his arms, unimpressed. "You're relentless."

"I'm observant," Tessa said brightly. "Cam's got that look."

Kaden arched a brow. "What look?"

"The *I-trust-you-more-than-I-should look.*"

Back in the ring, Wyatt swept his leg. Cam pivoted late, stumbled—he caught her without thinking, as if the space between them had already been written that way. His grip was steady, instinctive—like she'd never really been in danger of falling at all.

They froze.

The sounds of the yard—Tessa's chatter, Val's low laugh, the distant thrum of wards—fell away for just a breath. Cam's pulse quickened. She let herself lean into the warmth of his hold—just a second too long.

Then she stepped back, too fast. "Thanks."

Wyatt sheathed his blade with a smile, soft and certain. "Anytime."

Tessa stage-whispered, "Ten gold says they'll kiss before the next snowstorm."

Cam spun toward her. "Tess!"

"I said kiss," Tessa shot back, grinning. "Not scandal."

Wyatt fell into step beside Cam as they left the circle, his arm brushing hers.

Cam muttered, "Remind me never to spar in front of her again."

Wyatt's smile lingered. "No promises."

They walked shoulder to shoulder, boots crunching across snow-hardened ground. The others' laughter faded behind them, swallowed by the hush of the wardline.

The moment passed. But something in it stayed.

Cam caught herself still smiling—tucking the warmth away like a spark in her chest. Small. Quiet. Carefully unspoken.

◈ ☽ ✦ ☾ ◈

Dinner had grown quieter by the time Kaden noticed it—the way Val sat slightly back in her chair, one hand pressed to her temple. She barely touched her food, and her eyes weren't scanning the room like usual. They were distant. Inward.

He leaned a little closer.

"Headache?" he asked under his breath.

Val gave a small nod, her voice thin. "Something like that."

Kaden glanced toward the hall's heavy doors. "Come on. Walk with me. Might help clear the noise."

She hesitated just long enough for him to think she'd say no—then stood without a word.

◈ ☽ ✦ ☾ ◈

The snow was falling lightly by the time they stepped outside. Lamps behind the windows cast a soft golden glow, but out here, under the open sky, everything felt quieter. Real.

They didn't speak as they crossed the courtyard or passed through the narrow gate at the far edge of Haldrin's Keep. Just walked—boots crunching softly in the snow—until they reached the ridge where the forest met the cliffs.

The stars were out, but the world below held no light.

Val stopped near the edge, her arms crossing tightly over her coat. The wind pulled at the end of her braid.

"They say the Veil thins near the solstice," she murmured.

Kaden stood a few steps behind her; hands tucked into his sleeves. "They say a lot of things."

She looked over her shoulder at him. "You don't believe it?"

"I believe it," he said quietly. "Just not for the reasons the old texts give."

Val turned back to the trees. Her silhouette was silvered in moonlight, pale edges tracing strength he knew she didn't always feel.

After a moment, she said, "I wasn't sure I belonged here when I first arrived."

He stayed quiet.

"I mean—I have the training. The skills. And then Virellan. But not the history. Not the roots. You all had something tying you to this place. To each other."

"We bled for those ties," he said. "Sometimes we still do."

She gave a faint laugh, but it didn't last. Her voice dropped.

"You saw me at my worst. In the dark. After that mission. I still hear things. From minds I don't want to touch."

"I know," he said. "And you're still standing."

That made her turn toward him—really turn.

He held her gaze. "You don't have to be anyone else to earn your place here, Val. You already did."

Her breath hitched. For a second, Kaden thought she'd look away. But instead, she stepped closer—just one step, deliberate.

"I'm not always easy," she said, quieter now. "Sometimes I'm too much. Sometimes I'm nothing at all."

"You're still here," he said again, his voice steadier this time. "And I see you."

For a beat, everything stilled. The silence stretched between them, filled with everything they hadn't said since the ambush—the shadows still clinging, the wounds still half-healed.

Then—softly, unguarded—she whispered, "I don't want to do this wrong. Us. This."

Kaden's reply came without hesitation. "Then don't rush it."

Her hand lifted, fingers brushing the edge of his scarf. Not a question. Not a hesitation.

A choice.

She leaned in, and he met her halfway.

Their lips touched—tentative, searching—then steadied. Like a bridge between two storms finally finding stillness.

It wasn't perfect. It wasn't certain.

But it was real.

And this time, neither of them looked away.

Cam had only meant to walk a while. She wasn't looking for anything. The corridor along the west wing was always quiet at night, its tall windows framing the snowy courtyard below.

But she caught a flicker of movement.

She paused.

Through the frost-touched glass, two shapes stood wrapped in the hush of winter. Val and Kaden. Foreheads pressed together, eyes closed, the stillness between them more intimate than any touch.

Cam stilled.

No jealousy. No sharpness.

Just a quiet ache beneath her breastbone.

Not every kind of strength came from magic. Sometimes it meant letting someone stay.

She turned before they saw her.

And walked on.

Chapter 52: A Quiet Kind of Strength in What They Choose

The snow had softened everything—every step, every sound, every thought that tried to rise too loudly. Cam sat near the edge of the ridge, knees drawn to her chest, cloak tight around her. The wind didn't bite so much as whisper, curling beneath her skin, wrapping around the ache she hadn't been able to name since the attack.

She stared out at the blurred outline of the forest, her thoughts nowhere and everywhere. And when she blinked, she saw them again—Kaden and Val, heads bowed together in the courtyard. Unafraid. Unhidden.

She didn't mean to think of Anthony. But she did. Ten years of her life had been shaped by his hands, his voice, his steady presence in the small cottage that had once felt like the whole world. He wasn't her blood, but he had been her father in every way that mattered. Until he was gone.

The silence he left behind had carved something deep in her—a hollow that never quite closed. Left in a house that was never hers, with a woman who made her feel unwanted, Cam had learned early that closeness could turn to loss without warning.

That fear hadn't left her. It lingered now, even as she thought of Wyatt. The way he steadied her in the fight, the way his hand caught hers, the way he looked at her like she was more than a weapon. She wanted to trust that, to lean into it. But the memory of Anthony's absence pulled sharp inside her chest.

Because if she let herself fall—if she let someone in again—what happened when they were taken too?

Footsteps approached slowly and carefully. She didn't have to look to know it was Wyatt.

Wyatt had seen her slip away from the firelight. He hadn't followed immediately. Sometimes Cam needed space more than she needed company. But tonight—he felt it in the pull behind his ribs—she needed both.

He sat beside her without a word, just close enough that their shoulders almost brushed.

After a long moment, he asked softly, "You okay?"

Cam didn't answer right away. Her voice felt caught somewhere in her throat.

"I saw them," she murmured. "Kaden and Val."

Wyatt nodded once, snow collecting in his hair like stardust.

"They weren't afraid to want something. They didn't stop themselves."

Wyatt's voice was careful. "And you do?"

She hesitated. "I don't know if I can let someone in like that—what if I lose them too?"

Wyatt didn't flinch. Didn't rush to fill the silence.

He simply laid his gloved hand down beside hers on the snow-packed stone—close but not touching. Letting her choose the distance.

Then, almost under his breath, he said,

"Even if you can't say it, I'll be here until you can."

Cam let out a slow breath. Her eyes burned, but she didn't look away. The weight in her chest hadn't vanished—but it shifted. Made room.

People were beginning to choose each other again.

She looked down at his hand beside hers, steady in the snow.

And maybe... maybe she could too.

The outpost was quiet in the pale moonlight, snow still clinging to the rooftops. Most of the others hadn't turned in early—still nursing bruises from the sparring they did earlier in the day. Cam hadn't turned in yet, unable to sleep. Her thoughts were still tangled with what Wyatt had said.

'Even if you can't say it, I'll be here until you can.'

She rubbed her hands together as she crossed the stone corridor, cheeks still warm from the crisp— wind and from the memory of Wyatt's quiet smile when he'd handed her the scarf during sparring. She had meant to give it back, but he'd told her to keep it—winters at Haldrin's Keep were never kind. The cold pressed sharp against her skin, but she welcomed it.

Each breath frosted in the air, grounding her, anchoring her before her thoughts could drift too far into what-ifs.

She had walked nearly to the mess hall when she spotted Corin standing just off the archway—hood up, arms folded, eyes distant.

"Camomile," he said, quiet but certain. "A word."

Something in his voice made her stop instantly. She followed him into a narrow chamber off the hallway; the one used for council meetings when the war room was occupied. The air inside was colder than the corridor, stone walls holding onto the night.

He didn't sit. Just turned, looked at her, and waited until the silence settled enough to speak through.

"There's something you should know," he said.

Her heartbeat quickened, but she didn't speak. Just nodded.

"I saw something. Last night." His voice was low. Careful. "A shadow where there shouldn't be one. Inside these walls."

Cam blinked. "You mean—someone here?"

Corin hesitated. That alone told her more than his words.

"I couldn't see who. The vision broke—like something was masking them, deliberately."

A chill moved down her spine, slow and creeping.

He met her gaze. "Be careful, Camomile. Trust your instincts. Especially now."

She didn't ask if he was sure. She didn't need to.

"I trust you," she said, steady. "Even without the whole picture."

For a moment, his eyes softened. Just a fraction. Enough to remind her that whatever burden he carried, it was heavy, and it was old.

Cam left him standing there, but the words stayed with her—thick in her chest, like smoke before a fire.

There was something buried deeper than ruins.

And someone close enough to undo them from the inside.

Chapter 53: Held in the Silence

The cold bit deeper this morning—crisp and dry, the kind that settled into bones without asking permission. It threaded through seams and sleeves, clung to the inside of her throat, and made each breath a visible thing, curling slowly into the sharp air.

Haldrin's Keep stood steady against it, carved into the granite shoulder of the Valthorne Mountains like it had always been meant to endure. Not built—endured. The walls bore the marks of it: cracks, weathering, lichen growing in old seams like the stone had started remembering.

Cam hadn't slept—not really. Every time she closed her eyes, something inside her stirred. Not fear. Not quite.

Just... tension. A hum beneath her skin, like her magic had begun listening for something she couldn't name. It wasn't pulling this time—it was waiting. Attuned. As if the mountain itself had whispered a question, and her veins hadn't stopped straining for the answer.

She hated the feeling.

Her boots tapped a soft rhythm along the upper wall, each step swallowed by the wind as she paced the eastern battlement. From here, the Valthorne Range stretched out like the spine of some ancient creature, jagged and unmoving. The peaks caught what little sunlight broke through the clouds, casting long, shifting shadows down into the Karethwyn Forest below.

The forest looked endless from up here—dark green and tangled, too vast for comfort. Cam had grown up beneath its boughs, but from this height, even the trees seemed like they were bracing for something.

She stopped beside the eastern turret and leaned against the stone, its surface rough beneath her gloved hands. Cold, but grounding.

Somewhere beyond those far ridgelines, tucked behind a bend in the cliffs, lay Caerthalen, the Capital of Valmira. She had never seen it with her own eyes, but she didn't need to.

Mirell, the Keep's healer, had spoken of it just days ago—her voice clipped, wary, like even saying the name too often might draw its gaze.

Cam didn't need a map to feel its reach.

Caerthalen didn't need to be seen to cast a shadow.

It reached across provinces and policies, through bloodlines and broken promises. Through her.

A pale glint caught her eye across a distant pass—the spires of the Mystic Academy, just barely visible between two peaks. Taller than they should've been. Too clean for how much dirt lay beneath them.

She'd spent four months inside those halls, during the summer—undercover, quiet, careful. Searching.

Even now, just thinking of the vault beneath the floors made a shiver dance down her spine. The cold she could handle. The memory was worse.

She pulled her cloak tighter and shifted her stance, one hand brushing the hilt of her sword. The leather grip was smooth, worn to fit her palm perfectly. Comfort through repetition. Familiar weight.

Then the mark on her forearm stirred.

Not pain. Not quite. But heat—low and watchful, like coals under ash. She rolled down her sleeve and pressed her palm to it, hoping the pressure might dull the awareness.

It hadn't burned, but it hadn't faded either.

It watched.

She exhaled slowly, letting the wind take the breath and scatter it into the morning chill.

The Keep had changed since she had returned. Grown louder in some places, quieter in others. The kind of quiet that wasn't stillness—it was listening.

The stones underfoot felt heavier than they had the day before. Like they were waking up too.

She didn't know what was coming.

But Haldrin's Keep did.

And so did the mountain.

"You know," came a familiar voice from behind, dry and amused. "It's starting to get suspicious how often you disappear up here."

Cam didn't turn around. "Good morning, Tessa."

The footfalls drew closer, light but confident. Tessa appeared at her side, wrapped in a slate-gray cloak with the collar pulled high against the wind. Her red braid was pinned back in a messy twist, several strands already escaping to whip across her cheeks. She looked half-frozen, sharp-eyed—and far too pleased with herself.

"Ben said you've been brooding on the wall again. Every day this week," Tessa said, bumping her elbow against Cam's arm. "Care to admit you're thinking about him?"

Cam glanced sideways. "The sky?"

"Wyatt," Tessa said, smug. "Though sure, the sky's nice too."

Cam sighed through her nose and kept her eyes on the ridgeline. "Don't you have anyone else to harass?"

"I did. Kaden and Val were sparring when I left. Technically. It looked more like they were negotiating with blades. Lots of lingering eye contact and unnecessary pivots." She gave a theatrical shiver. "Too much tension for this early in the day. I figured I'd give them some space to pretend they're not in love."

Cam cracked a faint smirk. "That's generous of you."

"I try," Tessa said, folding her arms over the stone ledge and leaning forward slightly. Her eyes tracked the winding trails that cut through the trees below, dusted in thin snow.

For a moment, the two stood quietly—wind tugging at their cloaks, the mountains vast and unmoved around them.

"You know," Tessa said at last, voice softer now, "when Corin first called this place Haldrin's Keep, I thought it sounded a little theatrical. Like something out of a bard's tragedy. But now..." She trailed off, exhaling white breath into the air. "Now it feels like the right name. Like the stones remember something."

Cam nodded, slow and thoughtful. "He said it was the last outpost to fall before the mountain line was sealed. That was before they carved new roads through the Valthorne Pass. Ben mentioned it once, too. Said the Keep didn't feel like it was built. Said it felt like it had been waiting."

Tessa arched an eyebrow. "Waiting for what?"

Cam didn't answer immediately. Her hand drifted—almost absently—to her left forearm, brushing over the fabric where the mark sat hidden beneath her sleeve.

"I don't know," she murmured. "But it's still waiting."

A beat passed. The wind rose briefly, whistling through the tower slats above.

Then, in true Tessa fashion, the tension snapped like thread. "Well, you've got about two minutes left of this brooding session. Corin's calling a meeting."

Cam blinked, shifting her focus. "War table?"

"Nope," Tessa said, spinning around and starting toward the stone stairway. "He said it's *'one of the old ones.'*" She waggled her fingers over her shoulder like a ghost. "Ominous capital letters included."

Cam's brows furrowed. "And that doesn't bother you?"

"Oh, *everything* bothers me lately," Tessa called back, tone breezy. "Come on. I'll race you to the bottom."

Cam lingered a moment longer—just enough to feel the weight of the mountain at her back and the wind curling across her face. Then she turned, falling into step behind her friend.

The pull inside her hadn't faded.

But at least, for now, she wasn't facing it alone.

Cam took the corridor slowly, trailing her fingers along the stone. The Keep was old enough to breathe. She could feel it sometimes—like it exhaled with her.

Wyatt appeared just as she reached the archway near the stairwell. His cloak was dusted with snow, hood half-lowered, brown curls damp at the edges. He moved like he belonged here—quiet, present, always watching.

"Couldn't sleep?" he asked.

Cam didn't look at him at first. "Not for lack of trying."

He stepped closer, careful not to crowd her. "You feel it too, don't you? Like something underneath the mountains is shifting."

Cam's mouth tightened. "It's worse in the stillness. I keep hoping it'll pass."

"But it hasn't."

"No."

He was close enough now that their arms brushed as they started walking. The contact was brief—but not forgettable. Their hands, gloved and ungloved, touched for a heartbeat. Neither of them pulled away.

Cam felt her magic settle—not surge or flicker. Just quiet. Still. Balanced.

And she hated how much comfort that gave her.

She glanced at him sidelong. "You always ask like you already know the answer."

He smiled faintly. "I never know the answer. I just... wait for you to say it."

There it was again—that quiet gravity she couldn't explain. The feeling that when he looked at her, he wasn't waiting for the version of her written in someone else's story. He was seeing her. As she was now.

Not fate.

Not prophecy.

Just her.

She didn't say any of that. But she didn't need to.

When they reached the carved wooden door of the strategy chamber, Wyatt slowed.

"You'll tell me," he said, "if anything changes?"

Cam's breath left her in a slow curl. "I will."

Their eyes met—brief, searching—and then the door creaked open from the other side.

Tessa stood there, arms crossed, one eyebrow already raised.

"Well, well," she said. "And here I thought we were the ones taking our time."

Kaden was just behind her, trying—and failing—not to smirk. "At least they weren't pretending to train."

Cam stepped through without responding, but not before Tessa gave Wyatt a very pointed look.

Wyatt blinked. "What?"

"Nothing," Tessa said too quickly. "You're just shining a little too bright. Didn't know we were doing courtship by lantern now."

Cam caught the twitch at the corner of Wyatt's mouth before he deadpanned, "Good thing you brought enough light for both of us then."

Tessa groaned, but Kaden actually laughed, low and startled, and Cam had to bite back her own smile.

Cam sighed and kept walking. "Tess..."

"Just saying. It's *adorable*."

Cam gave her a sideways glance—half warning, half curiosity. "It seems like everything is bothering you today, or is it just me?"

Tessa hesitated a beat too long. "Guess it's not just you. Everything is these days."

Something flickered in her expression then—something tired, too fleeting to name.

Cam almost said something, but Tessa shrugged, pushing off the wall with a breezy grin. "Anyway. Let's go before Corin starts brooding harder than you."

Kaden murmured something low to Tessa as the door shut behind them, and she let out a delighted laugh.

Cam straightened slightly, Wyatt's warmth still lingering at her side. She gave Tessa a look that said "don't," and Tessa held up her hands, mock-innocent, and turned away, and the four of them stepped inside.

The laughter echoed behind them. But the war room, as always, demanded silence.

But the air in the war room was already different—quiet, heavier. The kind of silence that bent around old truths and decisions not yet made.

Cam's smile faded as she took her place near the long table.

The moment between her and Wyatt was already retreating—folding itself away like a page marked for later.

It was colder in the war room than Cam remembered, the stone walls steeped in shadow and whispered history. Flickering torchlight threw long, uneven shadows across the worn oak table, the grain scarred by decades of councils and battles. The low murmur of voices ceased as Corin entered, his presence commanding silence without a word.

Around the table, familiar faces bore the weight of exhaustion and resolve. Ben's hands, rough from years at the forge, rested clenched beside a map etched with recent patrol routes. Val's sharp eyes flickered briefly to Cam, the tension in her posture betraying the quiet strength she usually wore like armor. Kaden sat straight-backed, every muscle taut, calculating risks in the spaces between Corin's words.

Corin's voice cut through the stillness, calm but edged with steel. "We are no longer facing scattered threats or isolated raids. Caerthalen may lie beyond the mountains, but its shadow creeps ever closer. It pulses with intent—a heart beating in time with the forces arrayed against us."

He paused, letting the weight of his words settle like dust in the heavy air.

"Their tactics have shifted. They're moving faster, striking smarter. The recent disappearances—scouts, messengers—they're not accidents or missteps. They are pieces in a larger game."

"The mountain passes near the Valthorne Range aren't safe anymore," Ben said. "Two patrols vanished this week. No trace. No battle signs. Just... silence."

Val leaned forward, her voice low but urgent. "Something unnatural stirs in the northwest. The air hums with magic I can barely contain. A scouting party disappeared without a sound or a trace. It's as if the land itself swallowed them whole."

Kaden's eyes darkened, calculating. "That perimeter has always been the most dangerous. But now, it feels like the very air conspires against us."

Tessa folded her arms, a spark of mischief shadowed by concern. "Whoever's behind this knows the terrain better than we do—and they're using that knowledge to hunt us."

Wyatt shifted beside Cam, his gaze steady but guarded. She could feel the subtle tension in his shoulders; the quiet way he scanned the room as if expecting an ambush to come through the door at any moment.

Corin's voice dropped, thick with the gravity of what lay ahead. "Our enemies adapt quickly, and so must we. The fragile balance we fight to restore is cracking. And the cost of failure will be greater than any of us have yet faced."

His eyes locked on Cam's briefly, a silent call to vigilance and strength.

"Prepare yourselves," he said, voice resonating like a drumbeat in the hollow room. "This is just the beginning."

The room held its breath, the flicker of torchlight trembling as if echoing the unspoken fears between them. Outside, the wind whispered through the Keep's battlements—a cold reminder that the Veil was thinning, and time was slipping through their fingers like sand.

As the group began to break apart, voices rising in low discussion and movement shifting toward action, Cam lingered near the table, her fingers brushing the edge of the old wood.

Wyatt stepped beside her, his presence quiet but grounding.

"They're scared," he said softly, his eyes still on the map. "Even Corin."

She didn't answer right away. The shadows along the southern ridge on the map felt deeper than ink.

"Are you?" she asked without looking at him.

He gave a faint breath of a laugh—dry but not unkind. "Yeah. But fear's not the worst thing we can feel."

"What is?"

He finally looked at her.

"Hopelessness."

Their eyes met. In that breath of stillness, something unspoken passed between them—not romantic, not dramatic. Just real. Recognition. Trust. A flicker of something anchoring them both in a world sliding sideways.

Cam nodded once, then turned to leave. Wyatt's hand brushed her arm—brief, steady. "Whatever's coming... you won't face it alone."

She didn't answer, but her steps slowed as she moved away. And Wyatt stood in the shadow of the war table, the promise lingering in the silence.

Chapter 54: Sparks and Shadows

The midday sun filtered through thin clouds, casting slanted light over the packed dirt sparring ring. Dust floated in the air like golden flecks, disturbed only by the blur of movement as Kaden and Val circled each other, blades drawn and breath steady.

Cam leaned against the fencing, arms crossed, watching the two with narrowed eyes. Kaden's footwork had improved—Val wasn't holding back either. There was something rhythmic in their exchange now. Less testing, more trusting.

"Think they'll admit they're into each other before or after they knock each other out?" Tessa's voice came from beside her, sharp with amusement.

Cam smirked. "Depends on who lands the hit."

"Oh, I've got ten coppers on Val. Kaden gets too showy when he's flustered."

As if on cue, Val feinted left, then pivoted low and swept Kaden's leg from beneath him. He landed on his back with a startled grunt. Val offered a hand, smirking down at him. Kaden took it, and for a heartbeat too long, they didn't let go.

Cam's chest tightened. She knew it wasn't just sparring anymore—she'd seen the way they slipped away before, the way they kissed when they thought no one was watching. A part of her felt the ache of it, the reminder of what closeness could cost. Like the dragons, she would not speak what wasn't hers to tell. Some truths were meant to be kept safe, carried in silence.. But the sight of them carved at her in a different way—because she wasn't sure she could ever choose closeness so openly.

So, she turned her gaze back to the ring, letting Tessa chatter fill the air. But the thought lingered, quiet and wistful, tucked deep where no one could reach.

Tessa nudged Cam with her elbow. "Called it."

Cam rolled her eyes, suppressing a grin. "You're terrible."

"I'm observant," Tessa corrected, flipping her red braid over one shoulder. "And if I'm right about them, I'm *definitely* right about you and Wyatt."

Cam stiffened just slightly. "There's nothing to be right about."

"Mmhm," Tessa hummed, unconvinced. "You blush like a girl in a bard's song every time he says your name."

Before Cam could retort, Wyatt walked up behind them, expression calm but curious. "Did I miss something?"

Cam didn't turn. "Nothing important."

Tessa gave him a slow, knowing look. "Oh, just girl talk."

Kaden and Val stepped out of the ring. Val raked a hand through her hair, eyes still glittering from the fight. "Your turn, Cam."

Cam stepped in, tossing Tessa a look. "Try not to narrate this one."

Tessa winked. "No promises."

Wyatt followed her into the ring, sliding his practice blade free from the sheath. His eyes met hers across the distance, steady and unreadable—except for the quiet warmth beneath it. It sent something fluttering low in her chest.

They began to circle. No words. Just the hush of shifting feet and tension like a drawn bowstring.

Cam struck first—fast, calculated—but Wyatt blocked with ease. He was always calm when he fought, always listening with his whole body. Her second blow was faster, more aggressive, but he met it, their blades ringing together.

"You're holding back," he said quietly, almost teasing.

"I'm not."

"You are."

They broke apart, circled again.

"You always do when you're overthinking," he added.

Cam narrowed her eyes. "Do I?"

Wyatt's smile was slight, but real. "Yes."

This time, when she moved, it wasn't precise—it was instinct. Fast. Wild. And he barely caught her blade in time, the force sending a tremor down both their arms.

They stood close now, blades locked, eyes inches apart. Cam's breath caught. His eyes searched hers—slow, reverent. She hated how clearly he saw her. And how she wanted him to.

Then she remembered they weren't alone.

Tessa's voice rang from the fence. "At this pace, I'll be old and gray before you two admit you're in love. Speed it up!"

Cam jerked back first, lowering her blade with a flush. Wyatt let her go, his expression unreadable—but his ears were pink.

Kaden laughed from the fence. "I think Tessa's bored."

"I am bored," Tessa shot back. "Not even a dramatic sword-flip? Gods, you're killing me."

Cam sheathed her blade and stepped out of the ring without another word. Wyatt followed, quieter now.

Tessa leaned into her side and whispered, "Don't worry. You'll thank me later."

Cam gave her a look. "For what?"

"For not letting you run from something that might be real."

Cam didn't respond, but her silence said enough.

Cam moved ahead with Tessa, her steps a little too quick, like she needed the movement to outrun something.

Wyatt lingered behind, adjusting the strap of his blade—more for something to do than anything else.

He hadn't meant to look at her like that.

But he'd seen her for years in his visions—sometimes whole, sometimes shattered. Always just out of reach.

Now she was real. Close enough to touch. Close enough to steady. And still just out of reach.

There was something about her that undid him—not just the power or the prophecy, but her. The sharpness. The fire. The grief she didn't speak.

And he didn't know how to stop looking.

So, he didn't.

He just followed, keeping a little distance, like he always had.

Chapter 55: The Last Gate

Beneath Caerthalen's oldest halls, far below the sunlit domes and gilded spires, the chamber was silent. Carved from obsidian-veined stone and lit only by flickering wall sconces, the air pulsed with ancient power. In the center of the long crescent-shaped table, a shard of pale crystal lay embedded—its surface cold and veined with threads of silver, like roots reaching through the stone itself.

They called it the Heartshard. Few outside the Concord of Aetherhelm knew of its existence. Fewer still understood what it truly listened for.

The Council had convened in shadows. No heralds. No scribes. Only the highest seats: generals of the Knighthood, arch-mystics of the Academy, the noble stewards who oversaw Caerthalen's fragile dominion. All sworn to order. All haunted by what they could not control.

"The girl escaped again," someone finally said. Their voice was carefully neutral, though tension clung to the words. "Our contact confirmed it. The outpost held longer than expected—and she was stronger than projected."

There was a pause.

"She's not just strong," said another, older voice—frayed, skeptical, bitter. "She's evolving. Faster than he did. She may surpass him."

Unspoken, but felt, '*him*' did not need naming.

Across the chamber, a highborn councilor sat perfectly still. Gold clasps caught the candlelight on his collar. He had not spoken since the report began, only observed—head tilted ever so slightly, eyes unreadable. His presence unsettled the others in subtle ways they couldn't explain.

"She can't be allowed to trigger the prophecy," a third voice cut in, sharp with fear disguised as resolve. "We barely survived the last reckoning. If she completes the cycle, the balance could shift."

"Then perhaps we *shape* her rise—curate it. A controlled ascension is preferable to an uncontrolled collapse," murmured one of the mystics.

Murmurs followed. Calculations were being made behind every mask.

"And if control proves... untenable?"

Silence again.

The highborn councilman finally moved—just enough to lay his fingers against the pale shard. The crystal responded with the faintest flicker of light, not visible to all, but enough. A pulse. Like a heartbeat.

No one dared question the weight behind the quiet that followed.

In that silence, something deeper stirred—unfelt by most, but not unseen.

Though none could name it, a truth slithered beneath their plans: if the prophecy unfolded—even under their control—something else would awaken with it.

And in the silence, the crystal pulsed once more—dim, pale.

He would walk through the world again, free from his bindings.

He drifts, not in sleep, but in stillness — an ancient consciousness curled beneath the crust of waking worlds.

The Veil is not silence. It whispers.

It *remembers.*

And through its thinning threads, so does he.

A thousand years of waiting, and still the echoes hold her shape — the girl of starlight and storm, reborn in fragile flesh, hidden behind laughter and fear. She is not the first they bred, but the first to *survive herself.*

He has seen them all. The others. The almosts. The failures. Each one born with a flicker of his design — twisted, weak, broken by the weight of what they were meant to carry. But she—

She was different.

He felt it the day she first *screamed* into the world. Not in a palace. Not in a temple. But in dirt. In blood. Her soul unfurled like a flare in the dark, burning gold beneath the skin of time.

So, he *watched.*

Not with eyes, but through shadows and dreaming things. Through the cracks in minds too soft to notice. Through the mouths of crows, the sighs of leaves, the turning of tides. He watched her stumble, love, rage. He whispered when she cried. He wove fear into her sleepless nights and laced wonder into her rarest joys.

And when the world began to stir around her — when dragons once more remembered how to *speak* — he sent his first tests.

The shadow creatures. The Vorrakai. The mages. The creeping creatures born of broken souls.

They were never meant to *kill* her. Only to wound. To peel back her skin and see what sang beneath.

And she sang.

Louder than any before her. And louder still.

Caerthalen now stirs like a hive disturbed, desperate to cage what they cannot name. Fools. They think she is a key. Or a curse. Or a crown to wield. They scurry beneath stars that no longer belong to them.

But he knows the truth.

She is *the last gate.*

And when she opens — whether by will or by ruin — he will step through.

Not as a whisper, not as a dream, not as a shadow.

But as a god returned.

As the true and rightful soul of the world.

He was cast into silence.

Now, he rises.

Chapter 56: Fault Lines

Cam's fingers hovered over the ancient rune scroll, her brow furrowed in concentration. The ink shimmered faintly under the flickering lantern light—a precise mix of iron dust and something older, something Ben had only called threaded starlight. It made her skin tingle.

Sleep had become secondary; the scrolls consumed her days until even her dreams hummed with half-formed runes and broken chants.

She muttered the binding pattern aloud, lips barely moving. She had spent days reading the scrolls, learning the spells and drawing the runes.

"Balance over flame. Anchor through word. Circle unbroken..."

A soft hum rose from the ink as the rune she traced with a stylus sealed onto the vellum. Satisfied, Cam leaned back and flexed her hand. Her eyes were heavy from hours spent in the rebel outpost's cramped library. The stone walls smelled of dust and old candle wax, and the air carried that particular silence books demanded.

She had almost begun the next page when the door creaked open.

Brice stepped inside, tall and lean, his rough gloves still dusted from forge ash. A smudge of soot streaked one cheekbone, giving him a permanent look of having just walked through a fire.

"Camomile," he said quietly, voice scratchy with long hours and little sleep. "Corin's asked for you in the war room. Said it was urgent."

Cam blinked, grounding herself from the tangle of runes and memory.

"Did he say why?" she asked, rising and gathering the scrolls with practiced care.

Brice just shook his head. "Only that you'd understand once you got there."

She nodded, tucking the papers under her arm and slipping past him.

The halls of Haldrin's Keep were quieter than usual—curiously so. A strange hush lingered, like the world was holding its breath. Cam's boots echoed off stone as she made her way toward the war room, heart already beginning to stir with unease.

The heavy wooden door stood ajar.

Corin stood at the long table alone, the room bathed in gold light from the setting sun slanting through narrow windows. He wasn't looking at her. His hands rested on either side of a large, aged map.

"You wanted to see me?" Cam asked gently.

He looked up. The lines on his face seemed deeper today, his eyes clouded with something heavier than strategy.

"Yes," he said. "Come in. And close the door."

Cam obeyed, stepping closer as Corin gestured to a marked section of the map—the ruins of the old Knighthood stronghold near Caerthalen. A tangle of old sigils and red wax symbols were scrawled across it, some of which pulsed faintly with dormant magic.

"There's something buried beneath the old Knighthood stronghold—deep below what the Capital built," he said. "Not older than dragons, no—but older than the Accord. Older than the binding of magic to law. Whatever it is, it was sealed by those who feared its return. I can't see it clearly but it's there."

Cam frowned. "I thought the ruins were just..."

"History," Corin finished for her. "That's what we were meant to believe. But that place was built over a vault. A sealed chamber far beneath the foundation stones. I don't know what's inside—but I know it's waking."

Her mark flared under her sleeve—hot for just a moment, a pulse like a heartbeat. She shifted subtly, keeping her expression even.

"Why now?" she asked.

"Because something—someone—is stirring it. Perhaps Kaelith. Perhaps you," he said, voice quiet. "Either way, we don't have much time. If we wait, Caerthalen will send their own. And if they find it first..."

His jaw tightened.

"...then the cost will be more than we can pay."

Cam swallowed, feeling the weight in his words settle in her chest like stone.

"You leave at dawn. Retrieve what you can," Corin said, finally looking her fully in the eyes. "You'll need your closest. I'll tell Kaden, Wyatt, Tessa, and Valerie about this. Take whoever you trust. But be ready, Camomile. This... this will not be just another ruin. This is a turning point."

For a moment, all she could hear was the distant call of a bird outside the window.

The silence was brittle.

Cam nodded. "Understood."

But even as she said it, the air in the room seemed to change. The light grew colder. And her mark... her mark whispered something she didn't yet have words for.

The cold crept in like fog, quiet and sharp. Cam pulled her cloak closer as she climbed the stone steps to the outer wall, the torches behind her flickering low. Sleep had evaded her for hours now, stolen by dreams she couldn't remember and a feeling she couldn't name. Not dread... but not peace either.

At the top, a familiar silhouette stood still at the edge, pale hair catching the moonlight like frost.

Alex.

She paused, debating whether to turn back—but something kept her rooted. He hadn't noticed her yet, or maybe he had. With Alex, it was always hard to tell.

"Couldn't sleep?" he asked without looking.

Cam approached slowly. "Not really. You?"

"Didn't even try."

They stood in companionable silence. Below, the woods stirred with a restless breeze. Cam watched the trees, her breath misting in the moonlight.

He's always so composed. Like a painting set just slightly out of place.

"I used to love nights like this," Alex said. "Before the war. Before the Keep. Back when the world still felt... big. Unwritten."

Cam glanced sideways. "And now?"

He didn't look at her. "Now it feels like we're all just characters in someone else's story. Reading lines we didn't get to choose."

The words echoed something deep in her.

"I know the feeling," she said. *Maybe too well.*

Alex turned to her then, his expression unreadable but not unkind. "You? You're the Chosen One."

Cam gave a dry laugh. "Chosen One. That's just a title. It doesn't mean I know who I am. I was supposed to be ordinary—quiet, invisible. Now I'm a mage, a dragon rider, maybe a leader." She shook her head, voice dropping. "Some days I feel like I'm wearing a story that doesn't belong to me. And I don't know if I'll ever grow into it... or if it'll break me first."

She hated admitting that—but she also hated lying to herself.

His eyes softened. "Maybe the people who question themselves the most are the ones who should lead. The ones who never wanted a throne but still stand in the fire when others run."

Cam blinked, startled by the clarity in his voice.

He always hid behind sarcasm. This... this felt different.

"I don't say this often," he added, glancing away. "But I'm glad you're here, Cam. I think Tessa is, too. Even if she pretends otherwise."

Cam gave a small smile. "Tessa doesn't pretend much."

Alex laughed lightly. "True. But she's the reason I'm still here. She keeps me grounded. Reminds me what I'm fighting for."

His tone was earnest, but something beneath it tugged at her ribs—like a shadow behind glass. Her mark flared once under her sleeve, a faint heat she ignored.

Like a shadow in clear water. You almost don't see it... until you do.

"You ever feel like you don't belong here?" she asked quietly.

His answer came too quickly. "All the time."

She studied him, trying to read between the lines. His eyes didn't shift. His shoulders didn't tense. But still—something in her flinched.

"I wasn't raised in the rebellion," he said. "I didn't grow up with dragons or prophecy. I'm just... trying to be useful. To matter."

Cam swallowed the lump in her throat. "You do."

Their eyes met, and for a moment, everything stilled. No sounds. No war. No prophecy. Just two people, clinging to the fragile thread of connection.

She stepped back first. "I should try to rest."

He nodded. "Goodnight, Cam."

"Goodnight, Alex."

But as she walked down the steps, that fragile peace frayed at the edges.

A weight tugged behind her ribs—like she'd left something unfinished. Like a name she should remember. Like a lock without a key.

Why does it feel like he wanted to say something else?

She walked down the steps, but halfway she paused, glancing back. He hadn't moved. Still as stone, watching the forest.

Her skin prickled. The mark on her arm pulsed once more.

She forced herself onward. Maybe it was nothing. Maybe she was just tired. But the unease didn't leave.

It pressed like a whisper she couldn't hear.

The map room at Haldrin's Keep was tucked deep within the stone corridors of the east wing—far from the training halls and echoing courtyards. The stars outside were beginning to fade, and no true sunlight had yet reached the windows. Firelight flickered along the high walls, casting angular shadows across the ancient stone floor. Dust hung suspended in the air, catching on breaths and breathlessness alike.

A long oak table dominated the room's center, its surface warped slightly from age, blackened ink stains seared into its grain. Maps—some brittle with age, others freshly inked—were layered in uneven stacks. Pages bled into one another: cartographer's lines beside draconic glyphs, rebel notations overlaying records from a forgotten empire.

Cam stood at the far end of the table; her gloved hands braced on either side of a faded parchment. Her eyes tracked the intricate etchings of the Knighthood ruins understructure—vaults and chambers descending layer by layer beneath ruins pristine corridors. Her breath caught at the lower edges of the design, where the ink bled darker, blurred, altered.

Wyatt stepped beside her in silence, his presence quiet but grounding. He didn't touch the maps—he just watched, eyes moving with her own, reading what she saw without asking.

On the opposite side, Kaden crouched low, his dagger unsheathed and used not as a weapon but as a tool. He gently nudged the corner of a vellum scroll, peeling it back with practiced precision. The gesture revealed a second set of notations beneath—hastily scribbled, jagged lines disrupting the elegant curvature of the original architecture.

"There," he said, pointing with the tip of his blade. "Here's the breach. The corridor used to continue south. Someone diverted it."

Cam leaned in. Her brows knit. "That ink's darker... fresher."

Corin stepped closer from the firelit alcove. He moved with quiet intent, his robe brushing the floor with a whisper. "Sloppier, too. They didn't even match the calligraphy. Whoever altered this map didn't care about appearance—only misdirection."

Cam exchanged a glance with Wyatt, who nodded once, sharp and silent.

Kaden straightened, folding his arms. "But why go through the trouble of hiding something no one was supposed to find?"

Corin stared at the exposed layers for a long moment. Then he exhaled, slowly. "Because some knowledge is only dangerous when remembered."

Wyatt shifted, his voice soft. "Or when it gets too close."

Cam said nothing, but her pulse had quickened. Beneath her sleeve, the faint black mark on her wrist warmed—just a flicker, barely there. She curled her fingers slightly, grounding herself against the rough wood of the table.

"This set of maps was sealed in the scholar's vault beneath the Mystic Academy," Corin said. "It was supposed to remain lost. The only reason we found them was because a lightning strike collapsed half the western archive during last year's spring storm."

He stepped forward, tapping a faded sigil half-obscured by the newer ink. "I've studied Caerthalen for decades. The official records, the myths, even the Veilborn sigils that predate the Knighthood itself. But the lower levels?"

Corin met her gaze, unreadable. "Those levels were buried for a reason."

Cam hesitated, her fingers brushing the red-marked doorway on the map. "Buried... or maybe protected?" The question slipped out softer than she meant, more uncertain than sure.

For a long moment, Corin didn't answer. Then he inclined his head, voice low. "Sometimes it's the same thing."

A silence fell over the room. Not empty, but thick—like breath before a storm. In the hearth, the flames cracked once, loud in the hush.

Wyatt's gaze flicked to hers, steady for just a breath. Enough of a tether.

Then Corin said, more quietly, "We may not just be unsealing knowledge. We may be waking it."

Cam's heart stumbled in her chest.

She looked down at the map again, at the jagged red ink, the ruined passage, the sigils half-scrawled like a warning or a prayer. Her skin prickled—not from fear exactly, but recognition. Something old stirred. Something ancient and waiting.

She didn't look at Wyatt when she murmured, "Then we need to know what it is before it wakes alone."

Kaden nodded, lips pressed thin.

Corin's eyes lingered on her for a moment longer—thoughtful, hesitant, like he wanted to say more. But instead, he turned toward the shelves, already reaching for a sealed scroll.

As the group began gathering their maps and supplies, Cam glanced down at her hands. Her gloves were worn and frayed—the stitching loose near the wrists, stained at the fingers with soot and ink. As she adjusted them, she caught Wyatt watching her.

Just for a second. A glance too long. A question unspoken.

He didn't say anything.

Chapter 57: Echoes Beneath the Stone

The courtyard buzzed with quiet movement. Tessa stood near the armory entrance, sharpening her curved blade with steady, precise strokes. Sparks leapt in small bursts each time metal kissed stone.

Wyatt checked his gear near the stables—buckling straps, adjusting his bracers. His focus was intense, silent. A few paces away, Kaden spoke in hushed tones with Corin near the map table, their brows furrowed in mutual strategy.

Cam crossed the frost-dusted flagstones toward the center of the yard, still tying her vambrace. Valerie intercepted her, a thick leather scroll in hand.

"I found this in the back of the library," Val said, her breath misting. "It's old—really old. Tucked behind the runic atlases Ben had you working on. It might help when we reach the ruins."

Cam took the scroll. The edges were cracked with age, but the ink was still dark, traced with overlapping arcane script and half-faded cartography. It was a partial map—likely of the tunnels beneath the old Knighthood stronghold ruins.

Valerie tucked it into her satchel with care, snapping the strap closed.

"Don't lose it. I have a feeling it's more than just directions."

As Cam turned to head toward the armory, movement to her right caught her attention. A group of younger rebels stood clustered near the weapons rack, their eyes flicking in her direction.

A boy—no older than sixteen, gaunt and pale from a winter of hard living—stepped forward with too much bravado.

"Are you even one of us?" he asked. Not cruel, but loud enough for others to hear.

The words landed with a low hush across the courtyard.

Cam didn't flinch. Her voice was quiet, but steady.

"I was a blacksmith's daughter from the edge of Valmira. I bled for this cause before I understood what it meant. I've lost people. I've made mistakes. But I'm still here. So are you."

The boy looked down, ashamed. But Cam didn't look away from him.

Power didn't earn their trust.

Proving herself will.

Not through magic or prophecy... but through the choices she makes when no one's watching.

She remembered arriving. The way the Keep had loomed through the fog, dark stone and narrow towers, full of people who fought like they were born for it.

She hadn't known how to fight. Not like them. Not with swords, not with control. Her magic flared unpredictably—water turned to steam, wind to chaos. In her first combat drill, her feet tangled. In the second, her magic shorted out the entire practice circle.

No one said it outright, but she felt it in the silence. In the stares. In the way they avoided her table at meals.

She almost left.

Then, one morning, a voice cut across the training yard:

"If you're going to knock someone over, at least make it look intentional."

Cam had turned. Tessa stood grinning, braid laced with copper wire, a curved dagger in each hand. She didn't look scared. She didn't look impressed either. But she looked willing.

That was the first time someone saw her and stayed.

Corin approached, catching the tail end of the moment. His voice cut the air with calm authority.

"She's risked more than most to stand beside us. And when the time comes, it won't be titles or bloodlines that determine who survives—it'll be trust," Corin said, voice firm but level. "That whetstone you just sharpened your blade over? She helped retrieve it during a mission you wouldn't have survived."

The boy lowered his eyes. Corin didn't look angry, only tired.

"We don't need perfect warriors," he said. "We need the ones who keep standing when everything tells them not to."

He held Cam's gaze for half a second, then moved on without another word.

Cam nodded—quietly, without resentment—then turned back toward the armory.

The courtyard quieted. Cam met Ben's eyes for half a heartbeat—enough to know he'd heard her. Enough to share the weight.

As the sun breached the horizon, painting gold across the mist, Cam took a slow breath.

The ruins awaited. And with them, something older than any scroll, any blade, any rebellion.

Cam stepped into the armory, the chill clinging to her shoulders despite the heavy stone walls. The dawn light barely reached through the slitted windows, casting long shadows across the racks of spears and bundled gear.

She was tightening the strap on her vambrace when footsteps sounded behind her—light, familiar.

"Are you alright?"

Wyatt's voice was soft but steady. He lingered in the doorway, his eyes finding hers beneath the low light.

"I heard what happened," he added, quieter now. "Out in the courtyard. That boy—"

"Everyone heard it," Cam cut in gently. Not bitter. Just tired.

Wyatt stepped closer, concern etched into his features. "He doesn't speak for any of us. You know that, right?"

She didn't answer immediately. Instead, she took a slow breath and began preparing for the mission ahead.

As Cam reached for her gloves and pulled them on—worn, frayed at the edges, the stitching loose near the wrists—Wyatt's gaze flickered downward, lingering a moment too long.

He didn't say anything, but his glance said more than words ever could.

"Come on," Cam said, voice steady. "The ruins won't wait."

He fell into step beside her. "Neither will Sael."

The crisp air clung to the stone walkways of the roost as pale sunlight spilled over the ridgeline. Shadows of massive wings stretched along the curved walls, and the wind carried the earthy scent of scale, saddle leather, and sky. The three dragons—Sael, Brontheus, and Tenebrin—waited in quiet stillness atop their perches, their sharp eyes catching light like molten jewels.

Cam stood beside Sylithra, brushing her fingers lightly along the dragon's obsidian-blue scales. Gold veins shimmered faintly beneath the surface, pulsing like living magma.

Little Flame, Sylithra murmured in her mind, her voice like embers in the dark. *There is movement below the stone. Something older than the ruins. Older than memory.*

Cam's hand stilled. "You feel it too."

Not feel. Hear. Beneath the threshold of waking, something stirs. It watches but does not yet breathe.

Cam exhaled slowly, grounding herself against the steady warmth of her dragon's presence. "We'll be careful."

Be brave, Sylithra replied. *But not blind.*

Behind her, quiet footsteps approached.

Wyatt stepped into the light, holding something in his hands—thin, supple leather gloves dyed a deep obsidian with faint golden threadwork. The stitching was intricate, precise, made to withstand both grip and magic.

"I made these for myself," he said softly, stopping just beside her, "but I think they'll suit you better."

She blinked, surprised, as he offered them over. The leather was warm from his hands. "For better grip?"

He gave a crooked smile. "Sure. And maybe so you stop wearing the ones that look like they've fought a war on their own."

Her gaze dropped to her current gloves—worn and frayed at the edges, the stitching at the wrists pulling loose. They'd survived months of grueling training and sleepless nights. She opened her mouth to respond but didn't know how to say thank you in a way that would mean enough.

He didn't press. He just stood with her, a quiet presence as the sun warmed the stones around them.

Tessa's voice echoed across the roost. "Alright, lovebirds, mount up before I start shedding tears."

Cam turned with a flush, finding Tessa already striding toward Brontheus, hair gleaming like fire in the sun. Her dragon stretched his wings, electricity flickering faintly between the edges.

"You've gotten soft," Tessa added with a teasing smirk. "Remind me to knock it out of you later."

Wyatt shook his head but smiled as he moved toward Sael. He mounted first with practiced ease, the white dragon shifting slightly beneath him, already attuned to his presence. Cam followed, pulling on the new gloves and settling into place behind him, her hands brushing his waist as she adjusted.

Moments later, the sound of heavier boots echoed.

Val and Kaden entered the roost at a brisk pace, hands clasped in each other's, eyes alert, tension visible in their shoulders. Tenebrin stood behind them, scales a black as night, shadows curling faintly from his wings.

Kaden hesitated a moment, glancing toward Corin's tower—the high spire catching light like a watchful eye—but he didn't speak his thoughts aloud. There wasn't time.

He sighed and muttered something under his breath that sounded a lot like "gods damn stubborn ass."

He and Val moved toward Tenebrin together, exchanging a look only an entwined pair shared before they swung into place.

Cam glanced around the gathered riders.

Three dragons. Five of them. A silence hovered—one of those heavy moments before everything changes.

"Wait!" a voice called from below.

Cam leaned slightly to look over the edge of the roost.

Alex was climbing the carved stairs two at a time, winded but determined, a blade strapped to his back and hair mussed from running.

"I'm coming."

Tessa groaned. "Alex—no. We've talked about this."

"You need me," he said, already heading toward Brontheus. "Last time we were ambushed, I kept Cam from being taken. Or do you not remember the part where I stabbed an enemy mage in the throat?"

Cam blinked. "He's not wrong."

Kaden sighed, glancing once more toward Corin's tower like he wanted another adult to appear and solve this—but the skies were too clear, the timing too tight.

Tessa scowled. "Fine. You so much as slow us down, I'm tossing you off mid-flight."

Alex grinned. "Romantic."

She shoved him ahead of her, and he climbed up behind her on Brontheus with surprising grace.

Wyatt glanced over his shoulder to check Cam was secure. "You good?"

She nodded, tightening the new gloves. They fit like memory. "Let's fly."

The dragons shifted, muscles coiling as wings unfurled with a rush of air and promise. In the distance, clouds waited like veils to be torn through.

The descent into what lay below had begun.

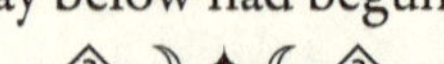

The dragons rose as one—three dark shapes against the early morning sky. Their wings carved wide arcs through the crisp air, scattering the quiet that clung to the peaks like mist. Wind bit at Cam's face, sharp and bracing, as the outpost fell away beneath them—stone and smoke and memory shrinking with each beat of wing.

She rode behind Wyatt on Sael, the great pale dragon moving with effortless grace. Her gloved fingers gripped the saddle's edge. The leather didn't quite fit her hand—shaped for him, not her. But he'd given them anyway, without words, without expectation.

It stayed on her hand like a tether. A reminder.

Ahead, Brontheus surged forward, green-black wings beating with rhythmic force, electricity flickering faintly along his spine. Tessa leaned into the flight, eyes narrowed with fierce focus, Alex settled behind her—close, but still slightly awkward.

Tenebrin cut across the wind farther ahead, nearly invisible in the shifting light. His dark form shimmered once as they passed the tree line, Kaden and Val riding silent, watchful.

The sky was wide and open, a gradient of pale gold and silver as the sun crept higher. The chill of morning still lingered, but it carried promise too—of something beginning.

Cam turned once in her saddle.

The outpost sat quiet and gray beneath them, curled into the ridge like a secret. Smoke coiled lazily from the chimneys. No movement, save for the banners fluttering near the main tower and the faintest glint of armor in the courtyard far below.

Her eyes lingered on the roost. On Sylithra, who had remained behind, her massive wings folded like patience itself. The dragon had met Cam's gaze before they left—one last moment, ancient gold eyes fixed on her wrist where the black mark pulsed faintly beneath the glove.

Little Flame, Sylithra had murmured through the bond. *Do not forget what you carry.*

Now, the silence pressed against Cham's ears. The higher they rose, the thinner the noise became—until all she could hear was her own breath and the faint rustle of wind against scales and leather.

She looked ahead. The road forward was uncertain. The ruins, the mission, the truth. Everything.

Then she looked back once more.

Stone and shadow. The only place that had ever felt like a beginning.

Her voice was quiet, almost lost to the wind: "No more running."

And far below—far beyond sight—in the deepest tangle of forest, a shadow moved.

Not a shape, not a body. But presence.

A breath exhaled too slow. A cold that did not belong to the air. It stirred beneath the roots, curled in the hollow of the world, sensing the ripple of magic above.

It felt her leave.

And through the veil, Kaelith smiled.

He did not wake—not yet. But the thrum of her power, the warmth of her defiance, brushed against the threads he had left buried long ago.

"Soon," he whispered, voice coiling into the earth like smoke. *"So soon, Little Flame. My last gate."*

Chapter 58: The Vault Beneath

The sky dimmed to bruised violet as the dragons crossed the jagged spine of the Valthorne Range. Below, mist clung to the valleys like smoke, rising in lazy curls around crumbling stone towers swallowed by time. The wind clawed at them, sharp and cold, but the dragons moved as one—Sael in the lead with Cam and Wyatt, Tenebrin just behind with Kaden and Val, and Brontheus higher on broad.

Cam pressed her gloved hand to Sael's scales, grounding herself.

Every step forward feels like falling toward something I already know.

A voice stirred in her mind. *"You're quiet."*

It was Kaden, his tone low through the dragonlink.

"Just thinking," she sent back, surprised how easily her thoughts met his. *"I don't like what this place feels like."*

"You shouldn't" Kaden's reply was sharper than usual. *"The old strongholds weren't just walls—they were warnings. If the wards are still up, we'll know soon."*

"Or not know," she murmured aloud, not realizing she said it until Wyatt gave a tiny glance over his shoulder.

"Which is worse," Kaden replied dryly, amusement flickering just under the unease.

Trailing slightly above them, Brontheus's broad wings cut through the wind, carrying Tessa and Alex. The two were bickering through the gusts.

"If I fall," Alex shouted over the wind, "Brontheus is catching me."

Tessa didn't even look at him. "If you fall, he's aiming for a clean drop."

Cam smirked. Alex's laugh carried on the wind despite the bite of the cold.

They flew in silence for a time. No more jokes. Just the rush of wind, the creak of saddle straps, the distant hiss of air between broken peaks. Shadows deepened as night approached, and far below, the ruins came into view—cracked battlements half-swallowed by the cliffside, black stone collapsed inward like broken teeth.

They landed just before dusk on a rocky ridge overlooking the ruins. The dragons remained on alert, tails curled and wings half-flared. No fires were lit.

◈ ☽✦☾ ◈

That night, sleep was hard-won.

The group camped on a narrow ledge above the ruined stronghold. Thin, bitter air carried the distant howl of wind through fractured stone. Only silence, shifting watches, and the steady presence of dragons held them together.

The dragons curled close to the ridge's edge, forming a half-circle around their bonded riders. Tenebrin lay with wings tucked tight, his massive body radiating warmth like a furnace. Kaden and Val rested near his side, half-wrapped in travel cloaks and half in each other, sharing a quiet, unspoken closeness that needed no explanation.

Brontheus had coiled his long tail protectively around Tessa and Alex, who had collapsed into a pile of limbs and whispered arguments. At some point, Alex had used Tessa's cloak as a blanket and earned himself a playful elbow in the ribs for it. Brontheus snorted once, amused.

That left Sael—and Cam.

Wyatt stood a few paces away, arms crossed, gaze fixed on the dark horizon. He had volunteered for first watch. Cam suspected it was partly out of habit... and partly to avoid the awkwardness.

She sat near Sael's foreleg, his warm breath brushing over her shoulders. He rumbled low and steady, like a giant breathing mountain.

"Should I make a bedroll for you and Wyatt?" Tessa whispered just loudly enough as she passed by to settle with Alex again. Her grin was all teeth in the dark.

Cam rolled her eyes but said nothing. Kaden glanced over from where he lay beside Val, his expression unreadable—except for the small, knowing look he exchanged with Tessa. No one said it out loud, but they all saw the quiet gravity that pulled Cam and Wyatt into each other's orbit.

Still, no one pushed.

Cam eventually lay down alone, curling against Sael's warmth. The dragon's body heat was enough to stave off the cold, but sleep drifted slowly, reluctantly, toward her.

Cam's dreams twisted with fog and static. She stood somewhere cold and hollow, the edges of the world fraying.

A chained figure writhed in shadow, indistinct. Its head turned toward her.

Symbols pulsed on the walls—symbols she recognized from the library, and from something older. A vision. A memory.

Her hand glowed dimly with the same markings.

Then a whisper, too close:

"Almost."

Cam woke with a jolt, the air sharp in her lungs.

The stars were a scatter of distant fires—cold and countless. Wyatt stood at the edge of the ridge, watching them flicker over the ruins below. His breath came in soft clouds, dissipating as quickly as the thoughts in his head.

He hadn't slept. Wouldn't, really—not tonight. The air here felt wrong.

Behind him, the others slept close to their dragons, warm beneath layers of travel cloaks and dreams. Even Alex had stopped talking. Tessa was curled against his side; her hand tangled in his shirt like she might anchor herself there.

Kaden and Val rested close to Tenebrin's chest, the dragon's slow breathing a steady lull. Val had a hand on Kaden's arm. They both looked peaceful.

Cam was the only one who shifted. Her silhouette moved faintly, her body curling tighter in sleep. She murmured something he couldn't hear, then flinched—waking.

Wyatt turned before she could fully sit up, his voice soft.

"You okay?"

Cam blinked up at him, her eyes shadowed by whatever had clawed through her dreams.

"Just a dream," she said, though her tone lacked conviction.

"Was it like the others?" he asked, already knowing the answer.

She hesitated. "No. It felt... older. Like it wasn't mine."

Wyatt nodded once and offered a hand, helping her sit fully upright. Her palm was warm from where she'd been pressed against Sael's side. She didn't let go right away.

Neither did he.

"I'll take over," she offered, but he shook his head gently.

"Stay. Rest. I've got it."

Cam looked at him a moment longer, eyes catching the faint light. "You haven't slept either."

"When I sleep," he admitted quietly, "I see things I'm not ready to understand."

There was a silence between them—not awkward, but weighty.

"Your visions?" Cam asked.

Wyatt nodded, his gaze drifting again to the ruins far below. "I think something's awake down there. I felt it earlier. Before we even landed."

Cam swallowed, rubbing her arms. "I dreamed of chains. Symbols on the walls. One of them was on me. My wrist."

She turned it over, and even in the moonlight, the faint black mark seamed to thrum faintly, like coals buried deep under ash.

Wyatt exhaled, slowly. "It's starting."

Cam's voice was quiet. "What is?"

He looked at her then, and for a moment, he looked older than twenty. Worn by things he couldn't say aloud.

"The part no one prepared us for."

The night had thinned into that liminal space between stars and sunlight; the world held in hush. Mist drifted like breath across the broken ridges below, clinging to jagged towers and collapsed walls. The doors at the southern end of the ruins pulsed with a stillness that felt too deliberate.

Wyatt sat near the cliff's edge, knees drawn up, cloak tucked tight. Beside him, Cam swayed slightly—awake but fighting it. Her eyes were half-lidded, lashes dark against wind-chilled skin.

"You should sleep," he murmured.

"I'm fine," she whispered, though her voice was frayed with fatigue. "Didn't want to leave you alone up here."

He gave her a small smile. "You're not leaving. Just resting."

Cam hesitated, then sighed. "Can I...?"

Wyatt shifted wordlessly, offering his shoulder. She accepted, her head coming to rest gently against him. For a moment, they simply breathed. Her hair tickled his neck. His arm, unsure, hovered—then relaxed behind her shoulders.

"I forgot how quiet the world can be," she said, barely audible. "Before all this."

He tilted his head, resting it lightly atop hers. "It's still here. Just harder to find."

The silence that followed was soft, earned, not awkward. Despite only knowing each other for a few months, it felt like years. As if their bones remembered the shape of this closeness before their minds ever caught up.

Cam murmured something unintelligible—already halfway asleep.

Kaden's boots crunched behind them.

Wyatt opened one eye. Kaden, holding the spyglass now, gave him a look and nodded toward Cam.

"She out?"

"Just now," Wyatt said softly, adjusting her blanket around her arms.

"You sleep at all?" Kaden asked, voice low but not unkind.

Wyatt shook his head. "Didn't want to."

Kaden paused. "She trusts you."

Wyatt didn't answer, just kept his head gently leaned to hers.

Kaden stepped forward, lifting the spyglass to his eye. "Get some rest. I've got it from here."

Wyatt exhaled through his nose, not quite ready to let the moment go—but he shifted slightly, letting himself lean back just enough to doze with her safely tucked beside him.

◈ ☽✦☾ ◈

The sky was bleeding into gray when Cam stirred.

The cold had crept into her fingers, but her cheek was warm. Her head was still on Wyatt's shoulder—and his head, she realized with a flutter of surprise, was resting lightly on hers.

She blinked, adjusting to the pale light.

A small, quiet memory flickered behind her eyes: Wyatt gently lifting her blanket higher... the faint sound of Kaden taking over the watch... the steady thrum of a heartbeat beside her that lulled her into sleep.

She didn't move. Not yet.

Then she felt it.

Something down below shifted.

Not the ruins themselves, but the air—a glimmer, thin and unnatural, dancing like heat over stone. But there was no warmth in it. Just cold shimmer, like cracked glass held beneath water.

"Kaden," she said softly, voice thick with sleep. "Did you see that?"

Kaden lowered the spyglass, squinting into the valley. "See what?"

"A shimmer. Over the southern edge of the doors ."

He scanned, his brow knitting. "I see it. It's faint."

Cam sat up more fully, brushing her fingers over the skin where her mark lay hidden. Her wrist burned faintly—like the chains and sigils from her dream had branded her beneath the skin.

"Do you think that's... old warding?" she asked, her voice low.

Kaden squinted, lowering the spyglass. "No. Leftover wards wouldn't shimmer like that. These were dormant—something's reawakened them."

Wyatt stirred beside her, rising slowly. "The shimmer wasn't there last night."

Cam's gaze locked on the southern ridge.

The fog pulsed. Once. Then again—slow and deliberate.

She swallowed hard.

Her mark throbbed in time with it, like a second heartbeat beneath her skin.

"It knows we're here," she whispered.

No one argued.

Chapter 59: Echo into a Flame

The silence that followed wasn't comfortable this time. It was bracing—like breath held before a storm.

Cam stood slowly, brushing sleep from her limbs. The cold had settled into her joints, but something else—something electric—was keeping her awake now.

The shimmer had faded back into stillness, but the echo of it lingered in the air. It felt like a held breath. Watching. Waiting.

Wyatt stretched beside her, then reached for his pack. "We move?"

Kaden was already adjusting his gloves; his gaze fixed on the broken path below.

"Yeah," he said. "We're close enough now. From this point on, we proceed with caution."

He glanced over his shoulder at the others as they emerged from their temporary camp—Tessa tightening the straps on her bracers, Alex checking the edge of his blade, Val silent but alert behind them.

"The outer wards might be dormant," Kaden continued, "but the shimmer proves something's active deeper in. Could be a trap. Could be a trigger. Either way—we don't know what this place remembers."

Cam met his eyes. "Or what remembers us."

Kaden gave a slight nod. "Exactly."

With that, he turned, cloak snapping in the wind, and began picking his way down the craggy slope. The others followed in silence, boots crunching over stone and frost. As they descended, the ruined stronghold loomed larger—its towers broken, its bones still proud.

Cam's hand drifted to the hilt at her side.

Something deep below was waking.

And this time, it felt like it had her name.

The gate's ancient hinges shrieked like something protesting the light.

As the iron parted, the air shifted—colder, heavier, as if exhaled from the lungs of the mountain itself. Dust billowed forward in a thick veil, and behind it, the ruins awaited. Not lifeless. Waiting.

They stepped into the stronghold one by one.

Cold stone met them like a forgotten pulse. The vast entry hall was steeped in stillness, the kind that pressed against the skin like a second breath. Above them, broken archways framed a collapsed ceiling, leaving long shafts of filtered light to pour through, catching motes of dust like falling stars.

Faded banners still clung to crumbling pillars, their tattered ends fluttering faintly as the group passed. The sigils were nearly erased by time—a dragon coiled around twin swords—but not enough to be forgotten. Tessa brushed her fingers over one as they moved past, frowning.

"This used to be a command hall," she whispered. "Before the Knighthood moved to Caerthalen. Before they started rewriting their own history."

"No one rewrites history unless they have something to hide," Kaden said quietly.

They moved deeper into the stronghold, boots echoing softly across fractured stone.

Near the far wall, a rusted door remained shut—not by age, but by intention. Glyphs glimmered faintly across its surface, pulsing in rhythm like a slowing heartbeat.

Tessa stepped forward, hand crackling with restrained energy. "Arcane lock," she said, brushing away grime with her sleeve. "Old style. Not taught anymore."

Wyatt tensed beside her. "It's still active."

"Barely." Tessa narrowed her focus. A narrow bolt of lightning flared from her palm, searing into the glyphs. The symbols flared in response—then sputtered and went dark with a snap.

The door cracked open. The air behind it was colder still.

Alex stepped through first, sweeping his lantern in a slow arc. The light caught on shattered tiles, collapsed murals, and what remained of carved statues now broken at the neck.

"This place..." he murmured. "It's not just abandoned. It was buried."

Cam followed in silence, the weight of the space crawling across her skin. Something about the stone felt aware.

Not malevolent. Just... watching.

Alex crouched near a pile of rubble and cleared it with a grunt. His fingers closed around something buried beneath layers of stone and soot. He pulled free a broken blade—its hilt jagged, its edge dulled but intact. Time had gnawed at the weapon, but one thing remained untouched: a sigil carved deep into the steel.

Not Caerthalen. Not even from the early wars.

"This wasn't forged by any smith alive today," Alex said, voice low. "This is pre-unification. Maybe even pre-Veilborn."

Cam knelt beside him, drawn forward by the strange hum building at the edge of her awareness. Her hand hovered above the blade. She didn't touch it—but the mark on her wrist prickled like static.

Wyatt noticed. He stepped closer, voice soft. "What is it?"

"I don't know," Cam said. "But it knows me."

The words left her mouth before she fully realized them.

A subtle vibration trembled through the floor beneath them—so faint it could've been imagined, but they all felt it. Val stiffened. Kaden turned his head sharply, eyes narrowing as he reached for the map tucked into his belt.

"There's a corridor," he said. "Should be behind that collapsed archway. Corin thought it was just a supply passage, but..."

He didn't finish.

Together, they cleared the rubble, uncovering a narrow hallway lined with faded sconces and half-ruined runes. The walls felt tight, like a throat beginning to close.

At the far end, a spiraling stairwell disappeared into the earth, its first steps choked in shadows.

The hum grew stronger.

Cam took a slow breath. That pull inside her—the one that had first whispered beneath her skin when they landed—was now an ache. Not painful, but deep. Like something stirring beneath her ribs that had been buried with the stone.

"This is it," she whispered.

Kaden drew his sword slowly. "From here on out," he said, his voice low but steady, "No more talking unless needed. No magic unless absolutely necessary. We don't know what's waiting down there—or what might wake if we draw too much attention."

He met their eyes, one by one.

Wyatt nodded first, shifting to Cam's side with silent resolve. Tessa clenched her jaw and stepped behind him, lightning fading to a quiet hum beneath her skin. Val moved last, her daggers already in hand.

They descended together.

Not like soldiers.

Not like rebels.

But like echoes returning to the place where it all began.

◈ ☽✦☾ ◈

The stairwell ended in silence.

The descent had felt longer than it should've been—impossibly long, as if space had stretched the farther they walked. The last steps opened into a narrow antechamber carved into the roots of the mountain. There, time itself seemed to hesitate.

At the far end stood a pair of massive stone doors. They loomed like the teeth of the world, sealed and scorched; their surface threaded with dark veins of crystallized runes. Shadow wards pulsed faintly across the stone, flickering like dying embers—patterns that twisted in on themselves, ever-moving, never settling.

The air hung thick with Veil energy. It clung to their skin like smoke, pressing against their lungs. The light from their torches warped slightly in its presence, bending just enough to make the space feel wrong—like they were standing inside someone else's memory.

Tessa's voice was barely a whisper. "These are not normal wards. They're looped. Layered and unstable."

"Veilborn architecture," Kaden murmured. "Older than the wars. I've only seen fragments in Corin's scrolls."

Alex approached slowly, eyes fixed on the patterns. "There's dragonic beneath the surface," he said, tracing the curve of a mirrored spiral etched into the wall beside the door. "And something else—something newer. Like someone tried to reinforce what was already here... or corrupt it."

Val kept to the back, daggers still ready. Her stance was steady, but her shoulders had drawn in, like even her instincts couldn't make sense of the space. "This place wasn't built to keep something out," she muttered. "It was built to keep something in."

Cam's heart was beating too fast. The moment they stepped into this space, the pull had become unbearable—no longer just a whisper beneath her skin, but a soundless chord resonating in her bones.

She stepped forward. Slowly.

The others didn't stop her. Couldn't.

The wards reacted to her presence—not violently, not defensively—but with quiet recognition. The looping shadows stilled, as if they'd been holding their breath. Then, like mist under sunlight, they parted. No sound. No resistance. Just silence.

The doors responded a moment later, groaning as dust fell from their seams. They shifted outward with a slow, grinding exhale, revealing the chamber beyond.

Cold air rushed out to meet them—thin and ancient, like it hadn't been breathed in a thousand years.

Cam stepped inside first.

The room was vast, but low-ceilinged, circular and perfectly symmetrical. Pale stone stretched in mirrored spirals along the walls, the markings glowing faintly with buried power. Ancient dragonic covered the floor in delicate, curling lines—language long since forgotten, but still alive in the stone.

No torches. No light source.

Yet the chamber glowed faintly, like it remembered the sun.

The Veil energy was denser here. It didn't swirl like mist—it hung in sharp angles, folding time into itself. A single second could stretch or vanish depending on how you moved.

Wyatt crossed the threshold behind Cam and stopped abruptly. "It feels wrong," he said, voice low. "Like the room's watching us move."

Kaden touched one of the spiral carvings. "It's not just watching," he murmured. "It's remembering."

No one raised their voice.

Even Tessa, who never walked quietly, moved like she was afraid of waking something.

Cam walked to the center of the room, drawn forward by something deeper than logic. Her footsteps echoed—but only once. The next made no sound at all. The one after repeated itself.

At the heart of the spirals, a cracked pedestal waited. Empty. Silent. Yet the impression of something once powerful still clung to the stone, humming in her bones.

She reached toward it—then stopped. The pull shifted, sliding through her chest like a current. Not to the pedestal. Beyond it.

Her gaze lifted to the far wall. One spiral was etched deeper than the rest, its grooves laced with a dull blue gleam like frozen lightning. The hum in her wrist grew sharper, the mark burning hot beneath her sleeve.

She moved to it slowly, almost against her will. Her fingers trembled as they hovered above the carving. The looping wards in the chamber stilled, waiting.

Cam pressed her palm flat against the spiral.

The mark flared white-hot, and the room shuddered. Not in sound—but in her veins, in her skull.

A vision ripped through her: A throne carved from shadow.

A boy with hollow eyes and bloodless skin.

And a voice without breath: *You've come too far to turn back now.*

Cam gasped. Her knees buckled.

Darkness surged up, swallowing thought, breath, everything.

She collapsed.

Wyatt lunged forward, arms wrapping around her before she struck the stone. Her weight sagged against him, terrifying in its stillness. Her eyes were open, staring—but not seeing him.

"Cam," he whispered, shaking. "Stay with me."

Light flared desperately from his hand, spilling across her skin. It flickered. Failed.

The chamber held its breath. Just him, holding her.

Then the silence broke—boots scraping stone, sparks of lightning crackling as Tessa ran, Kaden's dagger drawn, Val's cloak snapping behind her. Even Alex's face had gone pale as he stumbled closer. They closed in around them all at once, the air alive with panic and fear.

And beneath it all, something stirred. Watching. Waiting.

Chapter 60: He Sees Her

Sound folded inward. Light bent.

The moment her skin touched the spiral; reality fractured like a dropped mirror.

The chamber shivered—walls rippling as if submerged in water—and then vanished.

She stood alone.

The world around her was breathless and colorless. Cold-white and gray, like frost spread across air. No ground beneath her, no ceiling above—only endless stillness, suspended in a place that felt both infinite and suffocating.

The Veil.

Cam reached for her wrist out of instinct, but her body didn't quite respond—more memory than motion. Her thoughts felt strange here, like echoes without source.

Then—

A voice. Low. Intimate.

"Sister. Mirror. Your soul remembers me."

It wasn't heard so much as felt, like bones cracking under quiet pressure.

Cam turned—slowly, against the weight of the plane—and saw him.

A figure cloaked in moving shadow, form undefined yet unmistakably human. His face—her face—reflected like a warped version in firelight: same bone structure, same eyes, but hollow. Twisted. Worn thin by something ancient and bottomless.

Kaelith.

The Hollow Prince.

His eyes were bottomless black, and yet they saw her. Truly saw her.

He stepped forward, slow and graceful.

"You were not supposed to awaken yet. But the mark remembers. The blood remembers. You are what I could not be."

His hand lifted toward her face, fingers stretched to touch—hovering a breath from her skin.

"I have waited so long..."

Cam couldn't move.

The Veil began to pulse around her—rhythmic, like a second heart forming in the silence.

"We were meant to be one voice. But you've turned your echo into a flame."

His fingertips brushed the air just shy of her cheek—

And then flash of gold-white light cracked through the Veil. Warm. Real. Familiar. A tether yanking her backwards.

Tessa stumbled to a stop, heart hammering, as Wyatt cried out.

She hadn't even realized she'd run until she was kneeling beside him, beside Cam—who was sprawled across the stone floor like a broken star, her skin pale and far too still.

"Cam—" Tessa breathed, reaching—then froze.

The air shifted. A ripple, sharp enough to taste. The ancient runes carved into the chamber walls flickered faintly, like they were listening.

And then something pressed into her mind.

Not a whisper. Not a nudge. A storm.

Brontheus.

Stormsinger.

The words cracked through her like lightning splitting bone.

She stiffened; breath caught in her chest. Brontheus had never entered her head like this—not unless she was dying.

He stirs. The Hollow wakes. You must leave. Now. Cam's mark is no longer dormant—and the Veil sees her as a beacon.

The words weren't sound at all but sensation—ozone, thunder, a storm tightening behind her ribs.

Tessa's eyes darted down. Cam lay slack in Wyatt's arms, her chest unmoving, her wrist curled tight against her body. The black mark pulsed beneath her skin—once, twice—like a heartbeat of its own.

"She's cold as ice," Tessa whispered, her throat dry.

Brontheus pressed again, urgent and unyielding.

All of them feel it. Sylithra. Sael. Tenebrin. Virellan. Skylith. Even the hidden nest stirs. The sky above this mountain has begun to shift.

Tessa swallowed hard. The chamber suddenly felt too close, the air too thin. She looked at Wyatt, still clutching Cam, whispering something desperate against her hair.

Aloud, she forced her voice steady: "We need to move. Now. Before this place remembers more than just her."

Brontheus's presence lingered a breath longer, then withdrew, leaving the metallic aftertaste of storm behind.

Her pulse thundered, but she kept her expression sharp. Controlled. She couldn't afford to fall apart now.

She hadn't breathed. Less than a minute—yes—but it was too long.

Wyatt held her tighter, his hands trembling against her back, his mind blank but for one thought*: No. Not her.*

It had only been seconds, but it felt like the world had stopped spinning. Then her breath tore back into her lungs like she'd clawed it from the Veil itself.

Cam jolted against him, chest rising too fast, her eyes wide but unfocused. She looked around the chamber as if the walls were wrong, the air too thin. Her fingers twitched like they didn't belong to her.

Wyatt let out a sound between relief and panic, his forehead pressing briefly to hers. "You stopped breathing," he whispered, barely able to keep the shake from his voice.

But her eyes weren't really seeing him. They were glassy, dilated—he knew that look. The dragons were in her head again. All of them. The block she'd carried for months had broken wide open.

"Cam—hey," he murmured, brushing her hair back from her damp face, trying to anchor her.

Then her body stiffened. Her spine arched slightly, a whimper slipping from her throat as her hands tangled into her hair. Her breathing fractured, ragged.

"The block—it's gone," she gasped. "I can't—"

A flare of gold rippled beneath her skin, her veins lighting once before dimming into a low, unstable hum. Her skin was hot beneath his hands, unnaturally fevered.

Wyatt's gaze caught on the mark at her wrist—it pulsed, deep and wrong, like something watching back. She gripped it like it burned.

And then, in a voice that broke on the edges of fear, she whispered:

"He knows I'm here."

Wyatt's stomach turned cold. He didn't ask who. He already knew.

A sharp pulse ignited behind his eyes.

You must leave. Now.

Sael's voice cut clean through his panic—low, cold, absolute.

The Veil stirs. You are not alone in this place.

Wyatt swallowed, his grip tightening around Cam's trembling form. The shadow she'd seen—whatever reached for her—was still watching.

Cam's breath had torn back into her lungs like drowning air. Cold stone met her back, but all she felt was heat—the searing pulse in her wrist, the dizzying ache behind her eyes.

Wyatt's arms cradled her gently, but his face was pale with fear. You stopped breathing, he had said softly, like a secret he didn't want to speak aloud.

She blinked up at him. The vault ceiling swam above—etched in spirals and mirrored script—but her focus fractured.

Something was wrong.

The world had a weight it didn't before. The air pressed inward. Thin, stretched. And then—

The dragons came crashing into her mind.

Not one. Not two. All of them.

Brontheus's storm-charged presence surged first, followed by Skylith's fire-fueled warning, Tenebrin's shifting shadow, and Sael's steady hum of light. Virellan—the quietest—was sharp-edged and unreadable, like a blade still sheathed. But it was Sylithra who pierced through it all.

Ancient. Immense. Immovable.

She did not speak with sound, not even mind-speech. Sylithra spoke in memory.

You are not hidden now, said a voice like wind scraping across ruins. *Daughter of echo and flame. He sees. He waits.*

Cam whimpered and gripped her wrist. The black mark there was no longer still. It throbbed, a heartbeat all its own, searing hot beneath her skin.

He knows where you are.

The thought wasn't just hers anymore. It echoed, repeated by every dragon, every part of her magic.

The block she had so carefully maintained—keeping their thoughts, emotions, warnings at bay—had shattered. It was like holding a thousand voices in her skull. Their alarm, their protectiveness, their rage—all twisted into a deafening roar inside her bones.

Brontheus's voice crackled through the static like a lightning strike.

Stormsinger. He rises. The air speaks his name.

The roar of voices pressed too loud, too many, breaking through every wall she'd tried to hold. Her veins flared gold for a heartbeat, her body trembling with it.

Cam clutched at her head, eyes wide. "Too loud," she gasped. Her veins flared gold for a single heartbeat, lighting beneath her skin like wildfire veins. "I can't—"

Wyatt's voice reached for her, steady, a tether in the storm. "Cam. You're safe."

She stared past him, eyes hollow, her voice barely more than a whisper. "He sees me now."

Chapter 61: The Prophecy

The winding stairs stretched endlessly upward, each step heavier than the last. The air was heavier now—each footfall echoing with what Cam had said before the silence swallowed her:

"*He knows I'm here.*"

Kaden led, blade drawn, eyes sharp. Wyatt was right behind him, half-carrying Cam, who stumbled more than walked. She hadn't spoken since the vault. Her eyes were unfocused, lips moving in half-formed words, as if she was still somewhere else. Somewhere he couldn't reach.

She'd seen something.

Someone.

And now the Veil wasn't staying shut.

Kaden paused when the stairway split ahead of them—diverging into two new paths. His brow furrowed.

"This wasn't here before," he muttered.

Wyatt shifted Cam's weight carefully. "You sure?"

"Positive." Kaden's gaze flicked to the left, where the air shimmered faintly, a thread of residual magic lingering like smoke. His instincts tugged. The shadow magic in his blood whispered warnings—ancient, forgotten, and deeply uneasy. He moved toward the right passage.

"This way."

But before he could take another step, Val's voice cut in behind him.

"Wait."

He turned, blade still raised.

She stepped forward, breath unsteady and pulled a worn piece of parchment from inside her cloak. Folded tight, edges curled, and ink faded with age. But it hummed faintly under the magic clinging to the air.

"I found it the other night in the library at Haldrin's Keep," she said quickly. "It was hidden behind a ledger shelf. I didn't know if it would matter—but something told me to bring it. Cam agreed."

"I almost left it behind. It felt... wrong, like it was meant to stay hidden. But Cam saw it and said to keep it. I should've spoken up sooner."

Kaden's brows knit. "You're bringing that up *now*?"

Val unfolded the map, holding it out. "Because it matches this split. It shows both corridors. Left should lead us back. Same floor, same rotation. It's marked."

Kaden stepped closer, eyes narrowing. She was right. The layout was eerily accurate. Detailed. Too much so.

"Then why didn't we see this path before?" he muttered. "We've walked this route twice. That corridor wasn't there."

Val pointed to the faint shimmer in the air—like heat waves over stone. "Because it wasn't meant to be seen."

His magic stirred again. A whisper, threading through his mind like a warning—but it wasn't sharp like danger. It was pulling.

He looked toward the left passage again, unsettled. Whatever was down there wasn't part of the ruins' original design. It felt older. Like it had been waiting.

"We don't have time to chase ghosts," he said. "We need to get her out."

"I know." Val's voice softened. "But Corin said—if we found anything of value..."

Kaden exhaled sharply. "That wasn't a suggestion to get ourselves killed."

Wyatt didn't speak, but Cam stirred against him. Barely conscious.

And then—soft as breath—she whispered:

"Left."

The memory struck like a bell.

The sun had barely crested the outer wall. The courtyard buzzed with quiet motion—packs being secured, blades checked, orders passed down in low tones.

Kaden adjusted the strap on his shoulder and turned toward the keep's entrance, where Val stood near the arched doors. She wasn't talking—just showing Cam something. A piece of paper. Thin. Crinkled. Old.

Cam leaned in to look, her expression unreadable.

She nodded once, firmly.

Val tucked the paper into her satchel without a word.

Kaden hadn't thought anything of it at the time.

Cam had seen that map—recognized it. She hadn't questioned Val then, just nodded.

And now, despite everything, she was pointing them toward that same hidden path.

Left.

Kaden looked right—toward the way out. The safer road. The one they could survive.

Then back to the left—where the shimmer in the air was already beginning to fade.

He cursed under his breath. "Damn it."

He stepped back toward the hidden corridor, blade still in hand.

"We go left," he said, voice low. "But fast. And eyes open."

As they crossed the threshold, the shimmer vanished behind them—like a door locking shut.

And Kaden couldn't shake the feeling that this wasn't a detour at all.

It was the real path.

The one meant to find them.

They followed him through the left path, winding through narrow stone corridors until a hatch of carved metal appeared overhead—woven with symbols neither new nor entirely old. Kaden pushed it open.

What lay beyond wasn't on any of Corin's maps.

A chamber bloomed before them—vast, circular, with carved columns of dragon bone and shelves that spiraled like the inside of a seashell. Scrolls, books, and artifacts filled the vault, glittering faintly in the dim light. Magic saturated the air, thick and humming. The smell of dust and lightning hung sharp.

He turned back. "Val, Tessa—check the outer shelves. Look for anything familiar."

Cam didn't respond. She was blinking slowly, swaying in Wyatt's arms, fingers twitching near her temples like she was trying to push something out of her head.

Kaden stepped back to let the others enter, but his eyes stayed on her a moment longer. Whatever she'd seen... it wasn't over.

◈ ☽✦☾ ◈

Val felt it the moment she crossed the threshold.

Not power exactly—something older: Awareness.

This place was alive in a way she didn't trust.

Tessa's fingers grazed a shelf. "These aren't regular archives," she whispered. "Dragon memory. Some of these are hundreds of years old—maybe older."

"Some are humming," Val said. "Look."

Certain scrolls glowed softly, others were cold and dark. She let her hand hover over one that pulsed gently with violet light and felt a jolt deep in her gut. Veilbind magic.

"Tessa." She held it out. "This—this might be part of what we're missing."

Tessa opened it carefully. Her brow furrowed. "Veilbind fragment. Maybe two pieces." She turned to Kaden. "These go to Corin. He'll know what to do."

"Take them," Kaden called back.

Val slipped the fragments into her pack. Something caught her attention to her right—a section of damp stone walls sealed away from the rest of the vault like a forgotten tomb. Dust motes danced in the narrow shafts of light that slipped through cracks above, settling on rows of ancient scrolls, crumbling books, and artifacts long untouched by time.

But beneath them, tucked in a hidden compartment, was a small, sealed packet—its parchment worn but intact. The seal bore the faded emblem of Caerthalen's archivists, a reminder of the secrets locked away here, waiting to be uncovered.

She hesitated only a moment before slipping it into her pack, knowing that some truths were best kept hidden... until the right time.

Then she turned toward the heart of the room.

Wyatt stood steady, close enough to catch Cam if she fell. She hadn't spoken since they'd entered, but her body leaned forward like something unseen was tugging her along.

Her eyes locked on a massive stone slab embedded in the far wall; its surface carved in deep, ancient runes. At first glance, the markings were unreadable.

Then they lit.

◈ ☽ ✦ ☾ ◈

The words burned gold.

Her vision blurred as the letters ignited, not just gold—but alive, crawling through her veins like memory. The runes didn't speak. They became her. Ancient syllables pressing behind her eyes, demanding voice

She wasn't reading them—not exactly. They were becoming her thoughts as she stared, the letters unraveling across her vision, falling into place like a song she'd always known but never learned.

The light seared across her vision. Her knees buckled, breath catching as the runes unraveled in her mind—not like words, but like memory. They weren't written; they were embedded. Buried in her. She wasn't reading them—she was remembering.

"Cam?" Wyatt's voice was far away.

Her throat scraped raw as the words dragged out—shaky, hollow.

.·˙◈˙·.

Three shall rise when the Veil thins:
one by fate,
one by fire,
and one by fracture.
Balance lies not in their power, but in their bond.
From silence, the flame shall stir.
From shadow, a blade shall break.
From light, the watcher will choose.

.·˙◈˙·.

The sound died in her throat. She staggered back a step.

The air seemed to still around her. Even the vault fell silent, the stone vibrating faintly beneath her feet. Her gaze drifted to Kaden, then Wyatt—eyes wide, unsure, terrified.

"It's not just about me," she said quietly.

Wyatt's eyes softened. "What do you mean?"

Her voice shook, but she forced the words out.

"It's not just about me. It's all of us—me, you, Kaden. And..."

She faltered. The air pressed tighter, as if waiting.

Kaden's gaze was fixed on the runes, his jaw tight. His voice dropped, grim and certain:

"The one who failed."

Cam swallowed hard. Her lips trembled as the name slipped free, falling into the vault like ash.

"...Kaelith."

The sound seemed to cling to the stone itself, heavy, wrong, and final. For a heartbeat, no one moved. Even the air pressed in tighter, as if the vault had heard and remembered.

She hesitated then, lowering her hand slightly, eyes scanning the lower carvings. The stone beneath was darker here—etched more faintly, as if the light itself feared to linger.

"One shall awaken who was never meant to sleep.

Born of hollow purpose and endless night,

he will carry what was left behind—"

Valerie stepped forward, voice barely a whisper, "This part... it's incomplete. The ending's missing."

Tessa's fingers brushed over the uneven runes. "Or erased—because the truth was too dangerous."

Kaden's gaze hardened. "Born of hollow purpose... endless night... That's not us."

Cam swallowed hard. "He. The one who was never meant to sleep."

She looked up sharply. "That has to be Kaelith."

The name tasted like ash in her mouth. Her pulse pounded in her ears. Everything in her rebelled against the recognition—yet she knew. It was him. The shape beneath her nightmares. The hollow weight behind every echo. The one who failed but hadn't fallen.

Wyatt's eyes darkened. "The failed first."

Kaden's voice dropped. "A shadow waiting beyond the Veil. Something broken yet still moving."

Cam's hands trembled, though she tried to steady herself. "The prophecy... it's not just about us rising. It's about what never died."

Val's breath caught. "And what waits for us when the gate opens."

Cam stared at the fading runes. The silence pressed into her ribs like a hand around her heart. Somewhere far below—past stone and shadow and time—the hollow heartbeat quickened.

Chapter 62: Cracks in the Circle

Tessa had been the one to find the exit—though she hadn't meant to.

After Cam spoke the prophecy and the runes dimmed, the chamber felt... altered. The air was thick with silence, charged like the moment before a storm. Everyone had scattered slightly, half in shock, half searching for answers that weren't there.

Tessa's head ached from the pressure of the vault's magic, so she wandered, tracing the curving walls with the flat of her palm, needing something familiar to ground her. Her fingers brushed a line of old carvings—nothing unusual at first—but one of the stones felt warm beneath her touch. Not magic-warm. Alive-warm.

She paused. Pressed her hand fully against it.

And the wall shifted.

Stone slid against stone with a low groan, revealing a narrow opening behind what looked like solid wall. Dust and stale air poured out in a rush, and a worn staircase spiraled upward beyond the hidden threshold.

"Tess?" Val had called, stepping over quickly, eyes wide. "What did you do?"

"I didn't—" she started, then swallowed. "It just opened."

Kaden and Wyatt were there a second later, helping Cam steady herself. No one questioned it. Not really. They were too shaken to argue. And the prophecy—the weight of it—was still pressing against their ribs, a soundless echo none of them could shake.

They ascended without speaking.

The ruins lay quiet, but not still.

Shattered stones jutted from the earth like broken ribs, and the wind moved strangely here—curling back on itself, never quite escaping the circle. Tessa stood near one of the older pillars, her fingers grazing a line of ancient script that pulsed faintly under her touch. The magic in the stone was wrong. Off-key. Like a song sung too low.

Behind her, Kaden moved in tight circles, boots crunching gravel and broken glass. His brows were drawn, lips pressed thin. His usual calm had frayed into something sharper.

"We shouldn't linger here," he muttered, more to himself than anyone else.

Tessa turned, watching him scan the perimeter again, eyes narrowed. She could feel it too—something in the air, pressing in. But for Kaden, it was worse. His magic was usually sharp as a blade; senses tuned to every ripple of shadow and shift in air. Now he looked like he was trying to see through smoke.

"The wards are scrambled," he said when she approached. "Twisted... like they've been reversed and layered. I can't see clearly."

"You think it's a trap?" Tessa asked, already knowing the answer.

Kaden didn't nod—but he didn't deny it either. Instead, his eyes flicked past her shoulder, and when she turned to follow his gaze, she saw Alex.

He stood a little apart from the others, near a half-fallen archway. One hand rested on the hilt of his sword, the knuckles white. He wasn't watching the tree line. He wasn't watching anything.

Just staring down. Still.

Tessa stepped toward him, slow and quiet, careful not to spook him. She touched his arm. He flinched.

"Alex," she said gently.

He didn't look at her. Just shifted away, pulling his arm free.

"We need to stay alert," he muttered. "This place isn't safe."

"You think I don't know that?" Her voice softened. "Talk to me."

Still no eye contact.

Tessa studied him closely—his tension wasn't just battlefield nerves. He wouldn't meet her eyes. His hand hadn't left his blade once since they existed the stairs leading to the hidden vault. She reached for his hand anyway, threading her fingers through his.

"Alex. Whatever it is... tell me."

His grip tightened, then loosened. He let go.

"Not now," he said, voice low. "Later."

But later never came, and Tessa felt the weight of it like a crack waiting to split. That cold void where warmth should've been. He wasn't just shaken—he was hiding something. And it clung to him like shadow.

Kaden's voice snapped across the space: "We need to move. Now. The longer we stay, the worse this gets."

Cam was still seated on a low ledge, pale, her fingers tracing the lines of a fractured glyph. Wyatt stood near her, silent and tense, but steady.

No one argued with Kaden—but no one moved either, not yet. Like they were waiting for something... anything... to make the decision for them.

Tessa glanced up.

The sky above the ruins churned with thick clouds, too fast, too low. The wind was whispering again.

And somewhere in her chest, a sharp coil of instinct twisted tight.

Something was coming.

They stood just out of sight from the others, the ruins humming faintly behind them, the air thick with the aftertaste of vision and veiled memory.

Cam stared at the ground, hands clenched at her sides. Gold glinting in her veins from her being pulled into the veil.

"I... I saw him," she said finally. "Not in a memory. Not in a dream. He pulled me through. Spoke to me."

Wyatt didn't interrupt. He just waited—quiet, open, steady like he always was.

"Called me mirror. Sister. Said I was what he failed to become. That my soul remembered him. He said I was what he could not be. That we were meant to be one voice."

A pause. Then quieter: "But I turned his echo into a flame."

She lifted her gaze, eyes unfocused.

"There was a carving in the stone. The second part of the prophecy. About someone who was never meant to wake."

Her breath hitched. "It wasn't warning about us. It was about him."

Wyatt's brow furrowed slightly, but he didn't speak.

Cam inhaled sharply. Then, for the first time, she said it aloud:

"I'm afraid of what part of him might already live in me."

The words fell into the air like a confession.

A heartbeat passed.

Wyatt reached for her hand—not to silence the fear, but to hold it.

"Whatever you carry," he said softly, "it doesn't own you."

Her fingers trembled, but she didn't pull away.

"Even if part of him lives in you..." Wyatt's voice didn't waver. "It's still you choosing what to do with it."

They moved through the broken arch of the ruins, the sky above slipping from violet to blue-black. Stars barely blinked through the growing haze, as if the heavens were already retreating. Cam kept close to Wyatt and Kaden, boots crunching over gravel and fallen leaves, the forest edge pressing in from the cracked stone path ahead. Moonlight glinted off shattered pillars, half-buried in moss, their carved runes worn smooth by time.

Everything felt still.

Not peaceful—still, like the world was holding its breath.

A pressure built behind her ears.

Something's wrong.

She paused mid-step, breath catching. "Do you hear that?"

Wyatt turned toward her, brows drawn. "I don't hear anything."

That was the problem.

No birds. No insects. No breeze.

Just the distant rumble of something unnatural. Faint, low, growing. Like metal grinding beneath stone.

Run.

The voice slipped like wind through her thoughts. A whisper—but not her own.

Run... girl with the mark. You must run.

Her pulse skipped. Her hand fell instinctively to her side blade. "Kaden—"

"I know." He stepped in front of her, muscles tense, eyes flicking to the cliffs above. "Something's off—"

The first arrow struck stone. The second hissed past Kaden's shoulder. By the third, fire split the tree line, and the ruins exploded into chaos.

"DOWN!" Kaden shouted.

The air shattered. Arrows rained in glowing volleys from the cliffs, stun-spells crackling as dragonfire spiraled down to scorch the treetops. Stone burst apart in front of her—she dropped flat, ears ringing.

A roar answered from above.

Sael.

His wings beat like thunder as he dove, vast and pale, shielding them from the next volley. Flame broke across his hide harmlessly—he turned, spun, and drew fire away.

Hold on, Sael's voice surged through the dragonlink—sharp and resolute. *There are too many. I'll buy you time. Move.*

"Knighthood," Wyatt growled, dragging her behind a scorched boulder as another blast lit the underbrush. "They brought the damn Knighthood—"

"Not just them," Kaden hissed, reappearing behind a cliff ledge in a shimmer of magic. He reached for them both—but a ward flared nearby, snapping bright and violent. "The cliffs are warded! I can't reach!"

Another voice pierced her mind—bright, female, familiar:

"Cam! They don't know who you are—stay in the dark!"

Tessa. Desperate. Urgent.

Cam's heart clenched. Where were they?

They had been right behind her—not even twenty paces back when they'd entered the ruins. She remembered Val's voice, calm and clipped: "Stay sharp. We don't know what else Caerthalen buried down here." Tessa's hand had briefly touched her shoulder in reassurance.

Now—nothing.

Cam's eyes darted through the smoke. There—a flash of violet lightning, Tessa's silhouette sparking against the haze. A shout followed, Val's voice, clipped and steady. Relief surged—

—and then the ground convulsed. A blast tore through the slope, fire blooming upward, hurling rubble into the air.

"Val!" Cam screamed, throat raw.

No answer.

Shapes moved in the smoke, but she couldn't tell if they were friend or foe. Alex went down in silence, swallowed by shadow and flame. Her pulse spiked, panic clawing through her veins.

Kaelith's whisper crawled back into her thoughts, cold as ash: We were meant to be one voice.

But this was silence. Names vanishing. Screams cut short.

The fire below did not speak—it devoured.

Then—*Thwack.*

Kaden jerked, stumbling. A sharp, startled cry escaped him.

"Ah—damn it!" he cursed, grabbing at his upper arm. His fingers met a glowing shard buried deep in his bicep. "It's a damned null-warded arrow," he spat, breath ragged.

"Cam, go!"

Brontheus's voice tore through the link—rough, breathless. *Tessa says to go!*

"No—" Cam breathed, torn between instinct and dread.

Then Val's voice joined it. Calmer. Grounding.

"Go, Cam. Don't let them find you. Just stay free."

The words settled like a weight in her chest. Cam's hands trembled. The smoke stung her eyes, but she couldn't look away.

Brontheus's form swept past, diving with talons outstretched to knock an enemy dragon off course. Tenebrin followed, twisting like shadow, flame curling in his wake. Magic burst above the canopy—green, black, and gold colliding in a violent storm.

Cam reached for Kaden, grabbing his good arm and yanking him upright. "Come on—we're not leaving them—!"

Wyatt shouted Sael's name. The dragon dove again, clearing a path with one final sear of fire.

Cam hesitated; eyes locked on the flames below—on where Tessa and Val had just been. She couldn't see them anymore. Only fire, smoke, and the roar of dragons.

"Cam—" Wyatt's voice broke through, urgent. He grabbed her hand and pulled her toward Sael. "We have to go!"

She stumbled after him, heart tearing. Her legs moved, but her soul stayed behind.

He boosted her onto Sael's back, then climbed up behind her, holding her steady as their dragon crouched low, ready to launch.

Tenebrin landed a breath later, dark wings shielding them. Kaden limped into view and pulled himself up with one arm—just in time.

Then both dragons leapt skyward, leaving the blaze behind.

Below them, fire bled through the trees.

And then—nothing. No more lightning. No more shouting.

Tessa and Val vanished beneath the smoke and ruin.

Cam held tight to Sael's spine, her knuckles white, throat raw from unshed words.

And she understood, too late, that the voice that had first warned her—*run*—hadn't come from any of them.

Not Val. Not Kaden or Wyatt. Not Tessa.

It had come from the dragons.

The ones bound by the Knighthood.

The ones who still remembered the world before the Veilborn.

Chapter 63: Ashes of Guilt

Dragonfire devoured the sky, spilling through the canopy like molten breath. Trees snapped and collapsed in thunderous groans. Smoke stung his eyes, thick and clinging, and the air shimmered with heat. Somewhere overhead, Tenebrin's wings cut the haze in sharp, precise circles.

Kaden ducked, dragging Cam and Wyatt behind a half-fallen tree. The bark was scorched black, still steaming.

"We have to move!" he called, voice raw. His magic flared in his palm—then sputtered. The wards were thicker here, coiling around him like unseen chains. He clenched his fist. Not now. Not now—

Anchor to me, Tenebrin's voice echoed through the link, strained but steady. *You're slipping.*

He reached for his teleportation, grabbing Cam's wrist. A single spark flickered—just enough to blink them a few paces away before a blast of dragonfire scorched the ground behind.

Then he saw them.

Tessa—wounded—half-kneeling, lightning sparking wildly from her arm. Valerie—his Valerie—had thrown herself across her, shielding her as best she could. Blood ran down Val's side. Her blade was gone.

Time stopped.

"No—"

He surged forward, reaching again for the flicker of teleportation—come on come on—

Pain tore through his upper arm. Not fresh, constant. His hand flew to the arrow already buried just below his shoulder, its shaft glowing faintly with runes. The magic in his veins buckled, dimming to nothing.

"Damn it!" he hissed, breath ragged. "Null-warded arrow."

His chest heaved. Tenebrin swept low, roaring as a Knighthood dragon dove toward them from above. Heat lashed the air. Everything was chaos.

He looked back—Tessa still hadn't moved. Val was bleeding, barely upright.

I have to get to them—

But the dragonlink flared like a heartbeat in his mind. Valerie's voice reached him, steady despite the fear underneath:

"Kaden, rescue us. We'll stay alive. Just stay free—go."

His throat tightened.

Through the smoke and falling ash, Tenebrin dropped lower, wings slicing the haze like blades. A moment later, Sael appeared beside him, white and spectral in the burning dark.

"Move!" someone yelled—Wyatt, maybe. He wasn't sure.

Cam was still frozen, eyes darting to where the girls lay beyond the fire. But Wyatt grabbed her hand and pulled her onto Sael's back. She didn't resist—just moved, stunned and silent.

Kaden bit down the pain, pushed through it, and ran. Cam and Wyatt reached Sael just before he reached Tenebrin. They didn't hesitate—none of them did.

Kaden scrambled onto Tenebrin's back, gripping the ridges of scale with his uninjured hand. His bad arm was burning, useless, but he clung with everything he had.

Then they were airborne—wings cutting the firelight, smoke curling in their wake.

They flew away from the burning forest.

Away from their friends.

He turned in time to see Cam glance back, wide-eyed, torn. Brontheus roared—not in pain, but in a raw, heart-wrenching sound that made Kaden's stomach twist. He knew that sound.

Tessa had told him to go.

And Sael, already lifting off with Wyatt and Cam, echoed the call—a warning. A farewell.

They were leaving them behind.

Kaden didn't fight it. Couldn't. He was barely standing.

Brontheus swept low in silence, wings wide, shielding their retreat with defiant grace.

Kaden swallowed the scream in his chest, forcing his legs and good arm to cling to Tenebrin's back. His magic—silenced. But his mind clung to that last whisper from Val:

'Just stay free.'

◈ ☽✦☾ ◈

He felt Cam's fingers slip from his the moment Sael tilted skyward.

Not entirely—just enough.

She was still in front of him, her back pressed against his chest, shoulders rigid. Her breath came fast and quiet.

The bond between them, once burning gold and full, flickered like a candle in a storm.

Something's wrong.

Wyatt's eyes scanned the chaos below as Sael rose through a smoke-choked current, heat rippling along his skin. Flames devoured the treetops. A dragon shrieked behind them—one of theirs.

Not Brontheus. No. That was—

"Sael, dive—!"

But the white dragon had already curved sideways, veering hard to avoid a blast of fire meant to clip their wings. Kaden vanished in the smoke to the right, Tenebrin soaring past like a shadow through fog.

They were too spread out.

Wyatt swore under his breath and reached for Kaden through the link. Nothing. Static. A low, iron hum of wards dulling everything.

He tried Cam instead—but her thoughts were dim. Not absent but clouded.

She was holding something back.

"Cam—what is it—" he twisted, but she only shook her head, eyes wide, glowing faintly. She wasn't crying—but her face said she wanted to.

Below, he saw them.

Tessa. Valerie. Still on the ground.

Wyatt's stomach dropped. Blood. Smoke. The glow of a warded arrow pinning Kaden's magic shut—

And yet they were flying away.

He was flying away.

His whole body screamed to turn around.

To leap off Sael's back.

To burn it all down and stay.

He could almost hear his own voice—the version of him that used to believe fate had a plan. That they were all chosen for a reason. But that voice was quiet now.

Drowned in fire and silence.

"They trusted us."

His hands trembled where they gripped the saddle.

He thought of Corin. Of the prophecy. Of the twins born on the solstice.

He thought of how long he had waited to find Cam—only to fail the people who made her real.

"Sael," he whispered, throat raw, "tell me we're not too late."

The dragon's voice was quieter than usual—distant, as if echoing through glass.

We live. For now. You must live, too.

And though it was not cruel, it hurt.

He turned enough to glance back once. The forest burned beneath them—red and gold, like the end of something sacred.

Brontheus swept through the smoke alone, roaring into the flames.

Tessa and Val had stayed behind.

Because they knew.

Because they chose.

Wyatt shut his eyes and finally let the guilt crash into him.

They were going to survive. But not all of them would walk away whole.

Wyatt didn't look down. He couldn't. But the words clung to his chest like ash, unspoken but shared.

We left them. This is on us.

Then Brontheus's roar tore across the burning sky, raw and unbroken.

Tessa froze at the sound. To her, it wasn't just a roar. It was heartbreak given wings.

Ash drifted like snow through the air—slow, deceptive. The trees burned around her in wild orange arcs, dragonfire and chaos clashing through the forest. Brontheus's roar rang overhead, but distant now—torn and grieving.

Tessa stumbled through the smoke, coughing. Her mind reached for Brontheus's—empty. Panic clawed her throat.

"Alex!"

Through the smoke, she caught him for just a heartbeat—his silhouette sharp against the firelight, blade raised, eyes locking with hers. Relief surged—until, instead of coming toward her, he pivoted. Turned. And disappeared into the thickening clouds of haze and smoke.

Tessa's body ached. Her side was bleeding; her magic bound by the cursed suppression rune that still clung to her skin. She could feel it like a weight pressing her down, suffocating her magic at the source. No storm answered her call. No crackle of sound. She was grounded—cut off.

She gritted her teeth. "Damn it. Not now."

Val was beside her, crouched low, breath heavy, hands still clenched like she could punch her way out of this. Her sword was gone, her coat singed at the edge, but her eyes—her eyes still burned with purpose.

"You okay?" Val asked, voice tight but steady.

Tessa huffed. "Peachy. Just bleeding a little and completely magicless."

Val smirked, but it didn't reach her eyes. "I've got your back."

"You always do." Tessa swallowed hard, heat and smoke stinging her throat. "This was a trap."

Val's jaw clenched. "We hold until they get out. Kaden, Cam, Wyatt—they'll come back."

Tessa hesitated, eyes flicking around. "Where the hell is Alex?"

Val's brows furrowed. "I thought he was right behind us."

"He was. Just—" Tessa scanned the tree line, her chest tightening. "He was supposed to stay close. Then everything exploded, and I lost sight of him."

"He's here," Val said, but there was doubt in her voice. "He has to."

Tessa exhaled, eyes turning skyward. She couldn't feel Brontheus anymore—not like before. The bond was still there, but faint, fading behind distance and pain. The roar earlier—it hadn't come from injury. It had come from heartbreak. The absence of Brontheus's mind was louder than any scream.

"He left because I told him to," Tessa murmured.

Val glanced at her. "That's why they'll come back."

A bitter laugh escaped Tessa's lips. "You're disgustingly hopeful sometimes, you know that?"

"You're still standing," Val said, gripping her shoulder briefly. "That's enough for me."

They both looked up then—through smoke and flame and the flicker of sky beyond the trees. Somewhere, just beyond their reach, their friends were escaping. Brontheus. Sael. Tenebrin.

"Kaden's going to lose his mind," Valerie muttered.

"Let him. We'll keep ours," Tessa blinked hard, focusing on Val. "When they come for us—stay close."

"I will."

Then boots pounded through the burning brush. Voices. Magic swirling through the trees—foreign, cold, wrong.

Val's hand found hers for a second—strong, certain.

And Tessa braced herself, not to die, but to endure.

She wasn't done. Not even close.

◈ ☽✦☾ ◈

Valerie tasted blood.

Heat curled around her ribs as she blinked through smoke and pain and the iron press of magic gone wrong.

The ground trembled beneath her boots. Trees wailed as they burned—splintering, collapsing. Screams folded into dragon-roars, into the clash of steel and spells. The air was thick with ash and something worse: the stench of broken magic.

Tessa stood beside her—barely. Pale, wavering, lightning sparking weakly across one arm. Her fingers twitched toward a blade that wasn't there.

Val wanted to steady her. Wanted to fight. But her limbs ached, and her magic—gods, her magic was gone, swallowed by the same suppression spell that blanketed the forest like a curse.

Still, she stood.

Because Tessa did.

And they weren't finished. Not yet.

Somewhere behind them, Alex had been shouting. Val remembered that.

But his voice had vanished—cut off too soon. Not like someone overtaken, but... pulled away.

He hadn't come back for them.

And Alex wasn't the type to vanish without a fight.

Where the hell had he gone?

She'd seen his silhouette once—briefly—between the trees, blade raised, eyes locked on hers through the smoke.

Then he turned. And disappeared into the fire.

Maybe he was flanking. Maybe he was chasing someone.

Or maybe he ran.

A dragon shrieked—Brontheus, sounding like heartbreak given wings. But he was flying away. Forced to. Tessa had told him to.

Val swallowed, the taste of iron sharp on her tongue.

Boots thundered closer. Hands grabbed her roughly, gauntlets cold as iron as they hauled her up. Her knees nearly buckled, but she stayed upright through grit alone.

Cuffs snapped shut around her wrists—glowing faint blue, forged with runes meant to suppress, to bind. Spell-wrought, like shackles made from betrayal.

Through the chaos, no one noticed her fingers—mud-streaked and trembling—slipping beneath her shirt.

Two scrolls.

Veilbind fragments. Ancient. Dangerous. The kind of truth people burned entire bloodlines to erase.

Just thin enough. Just fast enough.

Her hand closed around them. Pressed them flat against her skin, beneath the waistband of her trousers, and let her shirt fall over them again. She didn't dare breathe too deep. Didn't dare move too fast.

A voice barked near her ear. "Mark them for transfer. The one with the red hair, too."

Cowards.

She let them shove her forward.

A wagon loomed at the edge of the clearing—dark wood etched with shifting runes. The door creaked open, its threshold glowing with a faint red that burned against her skin as she was pushed inside.

She didn't resist. Not yet.

They wanted prisoners. Let them think they'd won.

Let them think she was broken.

But Val's mind was sharper than ever, and rage—quiet, coiled, patient—warmed her from within.

She would remember every face. Every voice. Every sigil etched into the armor of the ones who thought they could cage her.

If the others made it out—

They'd come back. And when they did?

Val would make sure the world remembered why they should fear what they tried to bury.

Smoke billowed upward in black coils, choking the last glimpse of the battlefield below. Sael's wings beat against the rising heat as they soared higher—away from the burning trees, the broken ground, and the ones left behind.

Cam clutched the ridge of Sael's neck, her body pressed close to Wyatt's behind her. His arms were tight around her waist, unmoving. Silent. She could feel the tension bleeding through him like a second skin. He hadn't said a word since they'd taken off.

She risked a glance down.

The clearing was distant now, a bleeding smear of flame and shadow. Brontheus's anguished roar still echoed in her chest—not of pain, but loss. Tessa had told him to go.

Tenebrin flew beside them, sleek and swift, with Kaden astride him. Blood soaked his sleeve from the suppression arrow, but his eyes never left the ground. His jaw clenched. His magic—silent.

Cam leaned forward, as if proximity to the chaos could reverse what had just happened. As if her heart could anchor them long enough to turn back.

Her body tilted, weight dragging forward. The wind caught her cloak like hands pulling her down. For one terrifying heartbeat, she leaned too far—grief and guilt coaxing her toward the fire below. She nearly let herself fall.

"Cam, don't—please!"

Kaden's voice cracked through the wind, sharp and raw from Tenebrin's back beside them.

Their dragons flew close enough that she could see the desperation in his face, could feel the restraint trembling through their bond.

Cam's breath hitched, torn between gravity and guilt.

Down below, she saw the soldiers in black cloaks. She saw the glint of the runed wagon. She saw chains.

And she saw Val's face—only for a heartbeat—lifted toward the sky as she was pulled away.

Cam's voice was a whisper, drowned by the wind but heard in her own soul. "They were after me. And now they have the wrong ones."

No one answered. The sky swallowed her words.

Wyatt's grip on the saddle never loosened, but his head stayed bowed, face hidden behind dark curls that the wind could not shake.

And Cam stared downward until the smoke was just a shadow on the horizon.

Then—barely audible, aching like a wound—she whispered the truth.

"This is my fault."

Chapter 64: The Cost of Holding

They flew in silence for hours.

Even with the wind in her face and Sael's breath steady beneath her, Cam could still feel it: the gold hadn't dimmed. It shimmered faintly beneath her skin—veins at her throat and wrists threaded with molten light, a leftover burn from the Veil. Not overwhelming, not yet. Just a low pulse, like an ember refusing to go out.

The wind felt wrong—carrying soot instead of sky, ash instead of promise.

Dawn should have been cresting in the east, spilling soft gold over the ridges of the Valthorne Peaks. But when Cam glanced southwest, light flickered just over the tree line.

Not sunrise.

Her breath caught. She sat straighter in the saddle, fingers tightening against the ridges of Sael's neck.

That glow—too low, too violent. The clouds above were dark, yet the horizon pulsed with a sick light. Black and red, not gold and blue. And in the wrong direction.

Not morning.

Fire.

She heard Kaden curse under his breath.

Brontheus, Tenebrin, and Sael descended sharply, wings tucked tight. Only three riders had returned—where once six had taken flight. Tessa, Val, and Alex were still missing—captured. The weight of it pressed into Cam's ribs like armor that no longer fit.

Her limbs still ached from the Veil, her veins shimmered faintly with molten gold beneath her skin, but there was no time to rest.

Haldrin's Keep was burning.

They landed hard on scorched grass. Sael bellowed before Cam even dismounted, his body curling protectively behind her. Tenebrin whipped back into the sky, slicing toward a cluster of aerial Veilborn with a scream of shadow. Brontheus unleashed a fork of lightning so bright it split a dozen shadow-creatures mid-air.

Cam dropped to the ground and ran forward.

The world was in chaos.

The outer wards were down—shattered stones littered the outer field, magic broken and leaking like spilled blood. Dark flames licked at the once-shining runes along the Keep's western wall, black fire that twisted and hissed against the stone. And on the field ahead—

Bodies.

Too many.

Some were soldiers. Some mages. Some... civilians.

Cam nearly stumbled. Her pulse hammered in her ears. Not from fear—she didn't feel that anymore. Not the way she used to.

But grief was heavy, and it clung to her ankles like chains. She stepped over a fallen woman with sigils burned into her palms, eyes wide and glassy. No breath. No time.

Movement to the left.

Veilborn.

They lunged—too fast, too close.

Cam's hands ignited instinctively. A surge of heat burst from her palms, searing through the closest one with violet gold fire. Kaden swept beside her in a flash of wind, slicing through the second creature with twin blades. Wyatt struck from behind—magic blazing white-blue.

Another wave came.

Larger. Sharper. Flying.

Cam didn't hesitate.

They fought back-to-back—Cam burning, Kaden teleporting and cutting through shadows, Wyatt anchoring them both with radiant shields and firelight. But for every creature they struck down, another came crawling from the forest. They weren't going to hold like this forever.

Cam turned sharply toward the shattered wards, eyes glowing like tempered metal.

Then she saw it.

The survivors. Hidden inside the Keep, barely visible through the smoke, scrambling to repair the circle. Mages were carving new runes into stone, soldiers bleeding to buy them seconds.

That's what the Veilborn were after—distraction, not destruction. They were trying to keep the wards *down*.

Cam inhaled deeply. Gold swirled under her skin again.

She tapped into the dragon-link.

"Wyatt. Kaden. Listen." Her voice echoed in their minds through Sael and Tenebrin's open link. *"I know what they're doing. They're keeping the pressure here, so the wards can't be reset. But if I can punch a hole—just for a few minutes—the mages inside can finish the circle. I don't need to hold forever. I just need to break their focus."*

Kaden's thoughts brushed hers, sharp and steady. "You've got a plan."

She nodded aloud. "Yeah. But I'm not asking you to follow."

Wyatt stepped beside her, eyes already blazing. "You don't need to."

Kaden grinned faintly. "Let's light these bustards up."

Cam turned toward the breach.

The glowing in her veins flared brighter.

And together—without hesitation—they charged.

They tore through the inner yard, boots pounding against stone and dirt. The chaos of battle closed in around them—mages sprawled where they had fallen, groaning or gone still; broken wards flickering across shattered walls; civilians clutching one another in doorways, eyes wide with terror. Smoke stung Cam's lungs as she pushed forward, the metallic tang of blood clinging to the air.

They skidded to a halt just outside the broken ward line, the ground scorched and trembling beneath their boots. The forest floor erupted in dust and embers around them. The shattered ward lines crackled weakly behind them, magic unraveling like torn thread. Beyond the breach, Veilborn charged through the smoke, their bodies slick with shadow, their shrieks fractured and inhuman.

Cam didn't think—she felt.

Magic welled inside her, rising like a tide too vast to hold back. Her skin glowing with golden threads of light beneath the surface. The light intensified, threads brightening until they looked carved into her skin. It wasn't strength—it was a fracture line, her body straining against magic that threatened to split her open.

She stepped forward, hands outstretched and unleashed a burst of elemental force that slammed into the first wave. The light wasn't controlled; it wasn't precise—it was desperate and full of grief.

Wyatt moved with her, a solid presence just off her left. He didn't need words. His aura glowed a faint, soft white-gold as he raised a shimmering barrier that caught the next blow meant for Cam's side. The shield vibrated with strain. Beneath the torn edges of his sleeve, thin gold veins had begun to etch across his skin, crawling up from his wrist like cracks in porcelain.

"Kaden—right flank!" Wyatt called out, voice tight.

"I see it!" Kaden rasped, his tone raw. He spun into the shadows, forcing the spell through his body. Wind lashed out in a violent arc, scattering the Veilborn—but it was jagged, uneven, like something was choking it at the root.

Cam saw the strain hit him instantly. His shoulders jerked with the release, his arm trembling violently as though the magic itself rebelled against him. Sweat slicked his temples, and blood had spread fresh across his tunic where the wound festered. Even from here, she caught the faint shimmer trailing beneath his skin—gold threaded through shadow, colliding with the dark runes still seared into his arm.

The suppression spell was still burning in him. Every cast looked like it cost more than it gave. His breathing faltered, his stance unsteady—but still, he forced himself forward. As stubborn as he was, Kaden couldn't hide the toll.

"Kaden, fall back. You're bleeding," she said between spells, her voice hoarse.

"I know, but we need more time," he hissed, driving a blast of air into a charging creature. "They're rebuilding the wards—I can hear them behind us."

Cam reached for the dragon-link. *"Wyatt. Kaden's too close to the edge."*

"Cam. So are you. We all are."

She didn't argue.

Another wave of Veilborn surged. Cam closed her eyes and reached deeper—not to control, but to release. The golden light burst outward from her chest, searing the earth and air in a wide arc, enough to stagger the front line.

Cam's chest clenched. She saw it—the golden cracks racing up Wyatt's throat, veins flaring like molten lines. The same burn that already shimmered beneath her own skin. She knew that pain. Knew how it seared through bone and blood, how it threatened to split you apart from the inside. Seeing it on him was worse than feeling it herself. If he pushed any harder... she didn't know if either of them would survive it.

"Cam, your—"

"I know."

Kaden gasped and dropped to one knee. He tried to rise, but his shadow magic flickered out like a dying flame. Golden light webbed faintly along his ribs and arms, fighting to break through the sweat and blood. "I'm—burned out. What's left... it's killing me to use it—"

Wyatt moved without hesitation, shoulder slamming into Kaden's as he shielded him from a lunging creature. The barrier held, barely, before shattering with a thunderous crack.

"Cam, I can't cover both of you—" Wyatt's voice cracked, part fear, part fatigue. He turned toward her, eyes wide. "You have to stop. You have to—before you burn."

Cam's breath came fast, her limbs heavy. The glow beneath her skin blazed brighter than ever. "Just a little longer," she whispered. "Just until they seal the ward."

From somewhere behind them, a voice rose above the chaos—harsh, desperate, hopeful.

"Get the wards up now!"

It was the signal. The rebels were ready.

Cam looked at Wyatt. His shield magic was flickering at the edges, his body swaying, but he was still on his feet. His expression was raw—equal parts pain and love and the unbearable sight of his twin crumpled in the dirt.

Kaden looked up at them both, barely conscious. "Don't die for me," he managed, voice weak but defiant.

"We're not," Cam said softly. "We're surviving with you."

Then she let go.

Something answered.

Light surged—not from Cam alone, but from all three of them. Wyatt's white-gold, Kaden's shadow-laced wind, Cam's violet flame—threads of power that shouldn't have touched wove together. For a breath, it wasn't three elements, but one—brilliant, volatile, alive. It seared through them with as much pain as strength, veins glowing, breath breaking. Not harmony. Not control. But threaded—raw and impossible—and it held.

It wasn't perfect. It wasn't pure.

But it was true. Elemental. Desperate.

Their combined energy roared like a storm breaking through dawn.

And it was enough.

The Veilborn reeled and fell back, clawing at the shadows. Just enough time, just enough breath, for the final runes to flare bright. The outer ward shimmered into place like a translucent dome, sealing them off from the next surge.

Cam fell to her knees. The glow sputtered like a candle in a storm—then flared too bright before collapsing into nothing. Darkness swept in, not gentle but absolute, as her body gave way.

Wyatt collapsed beside her, his golden veins flaring one last time before fading to dull embers. His eyes rolled back as he slumped forward, unconscious.

Kaden was already down, his body unmoving but breathing, shallow and strained. The light beneath his skin flickered once—then went still.

Cam reached for them both with trembling fingers. Her vision blurred. But she continued to push forward, her light blazing now. She felt her arms burning as she pushed to stay conscious.

Her fingers curled toward Wyatt's sleeve—just short. Heat shimmered in her lungs. The world swam.

Then—*a sound.* Not from the battlefield. Deeper. Older. A cry that wasn't a roar but a calling—low and ancient. Wind shifted, laced with power not her own. She smelled it before she saw it: starlight, smoke, and snow.

The sky split open.

Skylith and Ben dove like flame. Sylithra descended, slow and steady, her wings eclipsing the ash.

I've got you now, Little Flame, Sylithra's voice whispered in Cam's mind.

And Cam let go. Then darkness.

Smoke clung to the rafters like ghosts.

Each step echoed too loud against cracked stone, the silence of the Keep pressing in like a held breath.

Corin walked with purpose, though his knees ached and his senses burned with too much magic in the air. The battle outside raged quieter now—held at bay, for the moment—but this place had already fallen.

Ash curled beneath his boots; blood marked the walls like sigils.

He passed fallen rebels and mages alike, their faces frozen in fear. Some had died clutching their chests, not from blades—but from something else.

He moved deeper. Toward the sanctum. Toward the source.

The air shifted.

Colder. Thinner.

He felt it in his teeth first—a pressure like static, low and buzzing. Then, deeper still, a wrongness in the weave of magic.

And there it was.

One wall, untouched by fire or spell, etched with a sigil that pulsed dark silver beneath the blackened stone.

The mark wasn't carved recently—it had been revealed.

It wasn't just a mark. It was a message.

A gate.

A promise.

A signature.

Veilborn magic, but not like what they fought in the forest.

This was older. Intentional. Patient.

Corin's breath caught. His foresight flickered—no clear image, just the sharp taste of dread, the sense of doors unlocking where none had existed before.

Cam. Wyatt. Kaden.

They were out there, burning themselves to hold the line. And still—he could feel it. This wasn't the battle.

It was the *invitation.*

His voice, when it came, was barely more than a whisper.

"He's already inside."

And something in the Keep listened.

Chapter 65: By Chance or Fate

The courtyard was too quiet for a place that had just survived a war.

Ash still hung in the air, thick and metallic, clinging to armor and skin and burning in the back of Ben's throat. Survivors moved like ghosts—those who could walk helping those who couldn't. Blood stained the cobblestones. The infirmary was already full. Still, more arrived.

He hadn't left Cam, Wyatt, and Kaden until the healers forced him. All three had collapsed after the last pulse of magic faded—like a dying star. He'd carried them himself, one by one, their bodies limp with exhaustion, skin hot with magical burn.

Something happened at the ruins. He knew it. He'd felt it even before the final wave hit—the shift in the air, the snap of pressure, the roar of something ancient stirring. But what exactly they faced... they hadn't said. They hadn't been awake long enough to try.

He stood just outside the infirmary doors now, armor open at the throat, gloves in hand. The weight of command pressed down like chainmail soaked in water.

Footsteps approached. Controlled. Familiar.

"You stayed with them."

Ben didn't turn. "Of course I did."

Corin came to stand beside him, gaze fixed on the people moving in the ruins below. His tone was quieter than usual. He wasn't here to lecture.

"You felt it too," Ben said after a moment.

Corin's jaw tightened. "Yes."

Ben exhaled slowly. "It wasn't just an attack."

"No," Corin agreed. "It was a test. A trap. A warning. Take your pick."

A pause settled between them. The kind that carried too much weight not to break.

"You think someone let them in?" Ben asked.

"I know someone did," Corin said quietly. "But they didn't expect the others."

"Cam, Wyatt, and Kaden—they weren't meant to be there," Corin added, voice edged with something close to awe. "Their arrival wasn't part of the betrayal."

Ben turned, startled. "Then their arrival—?"

"A stroke of luck," Corin murmured, almost reverent. "Or fate. Either way, it bought us just enough time. If they hadn't come when they did, the last of the wards would've fallen. And then..." He didn't finish the sentence.

Ben swallowed hard. "So, someone opened the gates—but even betrayal didn't account for them."

Corin nodded, gaze distant. "It wasn't a rescue—it was a shift."

Another long beat passed. Ben stared down at his hands. Still faintly shaking. Not from fear—but from the quiet rage of helplessness. Of seeing your people fall, knowing the blade came from behind.

"Do you know who?" he asked finally.

Corin's response was calm, too calm.

"I have... suspicions. But I won't say them yet."

Ben clenched his fists. "And what? Wait until they try to kill us again?"

"No. We wait until they reveal their endgame," Corin said, voice steel under silk. "And then we cut the root."

A call rang out from the rampart above. Supplies arriving. Another injured group came in from the eastern watchtower.

Ben nodded once, then looked to the infirmary doors.

"If they don't wake up—"

"They will," Corin interrupted, steady but firm. "They're not finished yet."

Ben didn't answer. He wasn't sure he believed that anymore. Not because he doubted them—but because this war was no longer about strength.

It was about trust. And someone had already broken it.

Chapter 66: A Dream of Her

In the dream, she was burning.

Not from fire, not exactly.

But from something brighter. Something ancient.

Cam stood in the middle of the broken forest with what was left of their light cupped in her hands—glowing gold, fractured like starlight held together by will alone. Her breath came fast, uneven. Her veins shimmered beneath her skin. She was past the edge. Far past it.

And still, she pushed.

Wyatt tried to reach her, tried to call her name, but his voice never made it through the trees.

The wind swirled with ash. Shadows curled like fingers around her feet.

Then the light shattered—

And Cam was gone.

But he didn't wake. Not yet.

Instead, the world around him shifted.

The forest faded. The air cooled.

Now he was standing beneath a sky without a moon, the stars so bright they looked close enough to touch. The world was soft here, silver-edged and silent. The kind of silence that wasn't empty—but waiting.

He looked down. Cam was walking beside him.

Whole. Unburnt. Calm.

She smiled at him like she'd always been here. Like this was the only place she could be.

She reached for his hand and laced her fingers with his.

"Happy birthday," she said. Her voice was warm. Soft. Real.

Wyatt froze. The words sank into him like a blade and a balm at once. His birthday. Their birthday. He hadn't thought she'd even known, not after everything—certainly not here, not like this.

"But it's not—" he started.

She shook her head gently, still smiling. "I didn't want to miss it."

The stars above them pulsed—once, gently—and then the ground beneath his feet broke open into light.

Wyatt jolted awake.

His lungs filled with air so sharply he coughed. The stone ceiling above him blurred for a second before settling into focus. His body ached everywhere, but—

He turned his head fast—

Cam.

She lay in the cot beside his, unmoving but peaceful, her face slack with sleep. Her hand twitched lightly, a faint gold shimmer still clinging to her fingertips. Beside her, Ben was seated like a statue, his sword across his lap, head tilted forward—dozing but vigilant.

Relief hit so hard it knocked the breath from Wyatt's chest again.

She's safe. She's here.

A soft rustle broke the quiet.

Wyatt's lungs seized on air, sharp and raw, as if he'd been underwater. The stone ceiling above him blurred, then steadied into focus. Every part of him ached—heavy, hollow—but voices pulled him closer to waking.

"It wasn't enough," Kaden muttered, low and tight.

"You did what you could," Corin answered, calm but weighted.

Wyatt blinked hard, the sound of them dragging him the rest of the way into himself. He turned his head, throat dry, catching sight of Kaden first—upright in the next cot, shoulders rigid, his hands clenched like he was holding something back. Corin sat beside him, steady as ever, though the lines around his eyes looked deeper than Wyatt remembered.

Wyatt swallowed, voice rough. "Kaden... Uncle...?"

Both of them turned toward him, their words halting, as though they hadn't expected him to wake yet.

Wyatt blinked at the sound of their voices, the fragments of the dream still clinging to him. "Are you alright?"

Chapter 67: The Turning Point

Pain brought him back first.

Not the searing kind, but the dull, all-over ache that meant his body had been pushed to its edge and left there too long. Kaden opened his eyes slowly, blinking against the dim light of the outpost infirmary. His head throbbed. His arms felt like stone.

But he was alive.

Bare stone walls. Lanterns burning low. The scent of poultices and dragon ash. Familiar.

His eyes adjusted just in time to see Corin sitting at the edge of his cot, a book closed in his lap.

"I knew you'd be the first to wake," Corin said, voice low.

Kaden sat up too quickly, winced, and bit back a curse.

Corin didn't flinch. "Easy."

Kaden looked past him, scanning. "The others?"

"Wyatt's still out. Cam too. Ben hasn't moved from her side."

Kaden nodded, throat tight.

Corin waited. "Tell me what happened."

Kaden rubbed his temples. "Too much. And not enough answers."

Corin waited.

Kaden inhaled slowly. "We reached the ruins. The chamber beneath it wasn't abandoned—it was rigged. Not with traps, but something worse. There was... a presence. Veilborn or something close to it. Shadows crawled everywhere."

Corin's jaw tightened.

"They split us up," Kaden continued. "Val, Tessa, Alex—they were taken. I don't know how, but one second, they were with us and the next—"

He stopped, forcing the words down.

Oh gods. Valerie.

Her name clanged through him like a dropped sword.

"They're alive," he added quietly, "but they've been moved. Caerthalen."

"Are you certain?" Corin asked, brows drawing tight.

"No one saw exactly where they were taken," Kaden said. "But I'm sure it was Caerthalen. Val, Tessa, and Alex were put in a runed wagon baring the Capitals crest along with the Knighthood."

He still saw her face—streaked with ash and defiance—as they dragged her toward the runed wagon. The way her eyes had found his through the smoke, steady even as chains closed around her wrists. Her voice lingered too, sharp in his chest, commanding him to go when every part of him wanted to stay. His arm ached with the memory of her grip, a phantom weight that burned hotter than the nulling spell in his veins.

"There was something else," Kaden said, voice low. "In the vault beneath the ruins—there's a prophecy. We only saw part of it, but it wasn't just about Cam."

He hesitated. "Wyatt and I... we're in it too."

Corin's head lifted sharply.

"You're sure?"

"Positive. There's a second part to it. The message was clear—we're tied to whatever's coming next."

For a moment, Corin said nothing.

Then Corin exhaled, slow and long, as if it carried something heavier than breath. "Then we don't have much time."

Kaden nodded stiffly. His hands clenched in his lap.

He hated this feeling. Helplessness. The idea that Valerie might be suffering and he couldn't stop it. Couldn't reach her. Couldn't—

"You did what you could," Corin said.

"It wasn't enough," Kaden muttered.

Before Corin could respond, Kaden caught the rasp of breath and turned. Wyatt was awake, blinking against the weight of exhaustion that still clung to him. His gaze darted once, unfocused, before settling on Cam. Of course. Always Cam first. Kaden understood—more than anyone—but when Wyatt's eyes finally lifted to him, the tension in Kaden's chest eased just a fraction. Then his brother looked to Corin.

"Kaden... Uncle," Wyatt said, voice rough with sleep. "Are you alright?"

Corin offered a tired smile. "I'm managing. We were just discussing what happened."

Wyatt nodded slowly, the tension clear in his jaw. "How much do you know?"

Kaden exchanged a glance with Corin before answering. "The vault, the prophecy... Val, Tessa, and Alex were captured. We think they're being held in Caerthalen."

Wyatt's jaw locked. "Then we go after them."

"Not yet," Corin said, tone quiet but firm. "We don't move until we understand what we're walking into. This wasn't random. The timing was exact. Whoever ambushed you at the ruins knew what they were doing."

"You think someone in the rebellion—?" Wyatt began.

"I think someone *somewhere* has been watching us very, very closely," Corin said, voice hardening. "And they've started making moves."

Kaden exchanged a look with Wyatt.

He didn't want to say what he was thinking.

But that conversation wasn't for now.

Corin stood slowly, adjusting the folds of his long coat. "From now on, we proceed with caution. No more trust without proof. No more moves without foresight."

His voice wasn't angry. It was ice.

He looked at both his nephews. His last family.

"You two are at the center of this now," Corin said. "Just like Cam."

He glanced toward Cam, still sleeping in the cot, then back to Kaden and Wyatt.

"No more pretending otherwise."

And with that, he turned and left them in the silence he carried like a shadow.

Wyatt stared at the door after Corin left.

"No pressure," he said, voice flat.

Kaden managed a dry smile. "None at all."

Kaden clenched his fists. Whatever was coming, he wouldn't wait in the dark again. Not while Valerie, Tessa, and Alex were still out there. This time, he'd meet it head-on.

Chapter 68: The Tether Snaps

The mark burned.

Not like fire. Not like a wound.

It pulsed beneath her skin—deep, insistent. Like it had a heartbeat of its own.

It dragged her upward from unconsciousness.

The infirmary air was still. Too still.

She opened her eyes slowly, vision blurry with light and memory. The scent of smoke clung to the stone. Something sweet hung under it—healing herbs, numbing salves, blood.

She shifted slightly.

A figure stirred beside her. "Cam?"

Ben.

He leaned forward; exhaustion etched into the lines of his face. His sword was leaning against the cot, a bruise blooming at his temple. His shirt was rumpled, eyes bloodshot, as if sleep had only ever hovered.

She blinked at him. "Dad...?"

"You're back," he said, his voice rough with relief. "Thank the gods."

She tried to sit. The pain in her limbs answered sharply.

"Careful." He moved to steady her. "You've been out for three days."

Cam's breath hitched. Three.

"What happened?" she whispered.

Ben exhaled slowly. "You made it back just after the first of the Veilborn attack. You, Wyatt, and Kaden—barely conscious. The Keep was on fire. The wards were gone. You held the line." His eyes darkened. "Then you collapsed. All three of you."

Images surged as her memory came back.

The ruins.

Tessa screaming.

Alex's blade flashing before being swallowed by flame.

Val's final glance—fierce, unflinching—as she stepped between Cam and death. Her final words to her were to save herself.

And then they were gone.

"We were ambushed," she said, hoarsely. "At the ruins. We couldn't save them. Val, Tessa, and Alex... they were taken."

Ben nodded grimly. "I know. Wyatt and Kaden told me."

Cam shook her head, her voice cracking.

"They stayed—fought so we could run. And I still left them. I should've gone back."

"If you had we wouldn't be here," Ben said, almost sharply. "The second you reached the Keep and saw it burning, you could've collapsed. Given up. But you didn't. You held off the Veilborn long enough for the others to restore the wards."

"No," she whispered. "Not me. Not alone. Wyatt and Kaden—Wyatt wouldn't leave me behind. Neither would Kaden."

Ben's expression softened. "I know. I saw you all. I flew in on Skylith just as the wards flickered back to life. You three were a ruin. I carried you in myself."

Cam swallowed hard.

There was a long silence, broken only by the quiet hiss of candle flame.

Ben exhaled his shoulders heavy as he sat forward in his chair. His voice, when it came, was low and thick with feeling.

"You know... I've never been prouder of you."

Cam's eyes lifted to meet his, uncertain. The quiet between them pulsed with something unspoken.

"But gods, Cam," he said, a hand dragging down his face, "you scared the hell out of me."

"I didn't mean to," she murmured. "I just... I kept going. I had to. I thought if I could just hold them off—"

"You didn't just hold them off—you bought time. Time that saved lives."

Ben leaned closer, his voice sharp but steady. "Don't downplay that."

He rested his elbows on his knees, the exhaustion clear in every line of him. "But that doesn't mean you should've done it alone."

"I wasn't alone," she whispered. "Not really."

"No," he agreed. "But you carried the weight like you were. You always do."

His voice softened. "You're reckless. Just like your mother. Brave to a fault. And just as damn impossible to stop once you've made up your mind."

That drew a faint smile from her, fleeting and broken around the edges.

"I saw you," he said. "You held on longer than anyone should've had to. Kaden and Wyatt were already unconscious."

Kaden had been lying face-up, eyes closed, chest barely rising. Blood streaked his side, but he was breathing. Wyatt had fallen just out of reach—curled on his side, unconscious, one hand outstretched toward her.

She remembered how badly she'd wanted to move—to reach him—but her limbs had refused.

"And you..." Ben exhaled, shaking his head. "You just kept moving. Like your body didn't know it was done."

She stared down at her hands. The tremble in them hadn't stopped.

"I don't think any of you even realized how close you were to shattering."

She swallowed hard.

"Cam," Ben said gently, "you don't have to break yourself to save everyone else."

A beat of silence passed between them, thick with grief and pride and fear, and most of all love.

Then the door creaked open.

Corin entered like a shadow through smoke—composed but weathered, a faint stiffness in his movements betraying pain beneath his stillness. His coat was soot-stained. A new cut ran through the edge of his sleeve.

"She's awake," Ben said.

Corin gave a nod and approached. "Cam," he said gently. "How are you feeling?"

She offered a hollow smile. "Like I shouldn't be here."

He studied her face for a beat, then sat in the chair beside her bed. "Tell me everything."

So, she did. From the ruins to the fall. The flight home. The Keep burning. The Veilborn attacking the wards. The rawness of the light she barely understood flooding her skin. The mark on her wrist—a thing not dormant but waiting. Watching.

And something else.

"A vision," she said slowly, hesitating. "No—not a vision. A memory that isn't mine. Or a warning. At the ruins, just before we were ambushed. It felt like... a prophecy. But only part of one. Like something's still missing."

Corin's eyes narrowed. "You believe there's a second half?"

"I know there is," she whispered. "I can feel it."

Then—

The world shattered.

Heatless light swallowed everything.

Cam stood—not in the infirmary—but on a throne of black ash.

The sky above her was torn, gaping. The sun eclipsed in shadow.

Wind screamed. The ground cracked.

And rising behind her—

Kaelith.

Wreathed in shadowlight. Waking.

Her vision ripped apart like shattered glass—Cam jolted back into herself with a cry, lungs burning as if she'd been drowning. The infirmary was there again, too bright, too still. Ben shot to his feet. Corin's chair scraped harshly against the stone.

Cam stared down at her hands, chest heaving. Her skin felt cold and too tight all at once. The mark on her wrist throbbed.

Her voice came barely above a whisper.

"The gate is opening."

Corin didn't flinch. But something behind his eyes snapped.

Not loud. Not visible. But real.

"Then we are already behind."

Chapter 69: The Gathering Before the Storm

The trees beyond the wardline whispered with the sharp breath of winter. Candlelight from the Keep was a distant glimmer through the pines, but out here, the dark pressed close. Snow crunched underfoot as Cam stepped into the small clearing where the others waited.

Six dragons stood in a wide circle, cloaked in moonlight. Sylithra's dark blue scales glistened like oil; Sael was pale and still as ice. Tenebrin lingered in the shadows, wings half-draped around his body like a shroud. Skylith curled protectively around Ben, her orange-red body crackling softly with residual heat.

And two more—Brontheus and Virellan—stood at the edge of the clearing, their heads bowed, bodies tense.

They had no riders beside them.

Cam's chest ached just looking at them. Brontheus's talons scraped the ground every so often, resisting the urge to pace. Virellan's wings were half-unfurled, trembling as her silver eyes scanned the horizon like he expected Val to appear at any moment.

"They feel it," Cam murmured, though the words were more for Sylithra.

Of course they do, Sylithra answered, her voice a low hum, rich with sorrow. *Their bond isn't broken—only stretched thin. It's agony. They dream of their riders every night.*

Cam's throat tightened. "And I still left them."

Sylithra lowered her head, golden eyes steady. *If you hadn't, all of you might have been taken. You endured long enough for the others to rebuild the wards. You made the only choice you could.*

Cam nodded weakly. "It doesn't feel like enough."

Sylithra's thoughts brushed hers again, gentler. That's how you know you still care.

A gust of wind shrieked through the forest, cold as iron. The dragons didn't flinch—but Cam did.

She stepped away from Sylithra and turned toward the others. Wyatt stood beside Sael, silent, his gaze distant. But when she moved, his eyes locked on hers—sharp, steady, grounding. He took a step closer, as though bracing for what she might say.

Kaden's arms were crossed, jaw set, his shadow stretching long behind him. Ben and Corin had fallen quiet, both watching her now.

She should have been thinking about the plan. The rescue. The spy.

But her mind was elsewhere.

The prophecy.

The mark.

The way her blood still felt scorched under her skin.

Silence pressed in. Too heavy.

Cam looked at them—her circle, her family, the dragons who had carried them this far. Her voice trembled but didn't break.

"It's started."

The mountains had held the dark for too long.

And now, it was coming for them.

Epilogue

They shoved her forward, and the iron door slammed shut behind them.

The cell was cold. Not just in temperature, but in its bones—stone built to leech hope from anyone left inside. The air tasted of mildew and rust, of old screams still caught in walls that remembered too much.

Val didn't move right away. The chains around her wrists ached, biting into skin rubbed raw during the journey. Tessa sat slumped against the far wall, blood dried at her temple. Alex lay curled near her, unmoving but breathing. They were alive. That was the only thing that mattered—for now.

Her knees gave out before she could stop them, and the weight of her body met the floor with a hollow thud. She let her head rest against the damp stone behind her, but her eyes stayed open.

There were no stars in the narrow sliver of sky above the cell grate. No moonlight to soften the dark.

The Capital had taken them.

Stripped them of weapons, magic, dragons, dignity.

But not everything.

Val pressed her palm to her chest. The absence of Virellan throbbed like a phantom limb. The bond was strained, distant—but not broken. Not yet. Somewhere out there, her dragon still burned. Still waited.

They had underestimated her. All of them. The ones in robes. The ones in armor. The ones who thought silence meant surrender.

She could feel it in her blood.

This wasn't the end.

The game had changed. And she would change with it.

Even in the dark.

Especially in the dark.

Acknowledgments

To my mom—thank you for encouraging me, even in the moments when I doubted myself. Your belief carried me further than you know.

To my sister—who patiently listened to my endless ramblings and half-formed ideas, even when the threads of this story made no sense outside my head. Your quiet support mattered more than words.

This book is as much yours as it is mine.

Author's Note

When I first began writing Heritage, I thought the story was about prophecy, dragons, and rebellion. And it is. But as the chapters unfolded, I realized it was also about something quieter—something that lingers in every shadow of this world: what we inherit, and what we choose to carry forward.

Cam inherits bloodlines she never asked for, a prophecy she doesn't understand, and a power that both saves and endangers. Wyatt and Kaden inherit the legacy of their family name, the burden of Corin's watchful eye, and the secrets of a broken Capital. Even the dragons carry a kind of heritage—ancient memory, bonds that stretch beyond time, and grief for what was lost.

But this book isn't just about the weight of what's passed down. It's about the choice each character makes with it. Heritage can be a curse. It can be a gift. Most often, it is both.

At its heart, Heritage asks:

Do we accept the story written for us, or do we write a new one?

For Cam, Wyatt, Kaden, and all the rest, this journey is only the beginning.

— Alysabeth Vale

About the Author

Alysabeth Vale is a storyteller who believes in the magic of beginnings and the power of breaking free. When she's not lost in worlds of dragons, rebellion, and elemental magic, she's chasing inspiration in the quiet corners of life. Heritage is her debut novel, and she can't wait to share more tales where fate and choice collide.

Alysabeth writes with the hope of giving readers both escape and belonging—stories that remind us we are never as powerless as we think. She draws on her love for folklore, epic fantasy, and the timeless pull of myth to craft journeys filled with courage, connection, and the kind of magic that lingers long after the final page.

When not writing, you can usually find her with a notebook full of scribbled ideas, a stack of fantasy books close at hand, or outside searching for new horizons to spark her imagination. She believes every story begins with a spark of wonder, and hers are written with the intent that they'll find the readers who need them most.

Next in the Series: Inheritance

The Veil is thinning. The Capital is watching. And not everyone will make it home. As Cam, Wyatt, and Kaden struggle with the cost of their power, shadows gather in Caerthalen—where their friends are being held, and where the next piece of the prophecy waits. Bonds will be tested. Secrets unearthed. Choices made that can't be undone.

And in the dark beneath the Capital, something ancient begins to stir.

Excerpt of Inheritance

The cold had teeth down in the dark cell.

Tessa pressed her back to the wall, knees drawn close, one trembling hand clutching her ribs. The wound still wept beneath the filthy bandage—hot, angry, pulsing like it had a will of its own. The stone behind her felt like ice, but she stayed there. If she moved too much, she might not stop.

She didn't know how long they'd been trapped. A week? Longer? Time bent strangely in the dark. But she remembered when they took Alex—three days ago.

Three days of silence from the cell across the hall. Three days of not knowing if he was alive.

She breathed shallowly, each inhale scraping. The air tasted of rot and iron and damp stone. Every heartbeat throbbed in her wound.

But she held on.

"Cam. Wyatt. Kaden."

She whispered their names in her mind like a spell, like if she repeated them often enough, they'd hear her—through the walls, through the world.

They would come. She knew it in her bones—deeper than fear, deeper than pain.

When the guards sloshed water into her cell, she dipped her sleeve into it and pressed the wet fabric to her side. Fire clawed up her spine, but she bit back the cry. The fever had already taken root.

Her mind drifted. Flickers of lightning cracked behind her eyes. Brontheus's roar rolled faintly through her skull—storm and defiance. She remembered wind in her hair, Cam's wild grin, laughter that hurt her stomach.

Then it was gone.

Darkness stretched wider. Her limbs felt too heavy.

Still, she clung to one word. A whispered tether.

Hurry.

And then, the dark took her.

Cam woke with a violent gasp, as if dragged from drowning.

Her fingers clutched the blankets, sweat-soaked and tangled. Her chest rose and fell in shallow bursts. Moonlight spilled across the stone floor, and the room felt too quiet—eerily still after the echo of Valerie's voice.

Not a dream.

She sat up, hand pressed to her heart.

"I saw her," she whispered to the dark. "She was there."

The details clung like thorns: the way the trees bled into fog, Val's unblinking eyes, Tessa fevered and broken, Alex—gone. Chains. A trial.

They were running out of time.

Cam threw off the blankets, swaying as a chill slapped her damp skin. She dressed fast—boots, tunic, and cloak. No armor. No questions. Only movement.

The Keep was hushed at night, its torches flickering against old stone. She passed guards, but none stopped her. Something in her stride—or maybe the fire in her eyes—warned them off.

She slammed open the door to Kaden and Wyatt's quarters.

Kaden jolted upright, reaching for a blade. Wyatt was already half-risen, shirtless, one hand on his sword.

Cam didn't wait. "Val reached me," she said, voice low and sharp. "Not a dream. She mind-walked. She found me."

Wyatt was already out of bed, crossing to her. For a split second, Cam's gaze snagged on him—on the sharp lines of muscle, the lamplight brushing across his chest. Heat stirred unbidden, and she shoved it down as if it were dangerous. She couldn't afford distraction.

"What did she say?" he asked.

"Ah… Tessa's alive but fevered. Scared. Alex—they took him days ago. She hasn't seen him since."

Kaden's eyes were cold, awake. "Caerthalen?"

"Below it," Cam whispered. "Guarded. She said there's going to be a trial. A test. To see if one of them is the chosen one."

The words landed like a blade dropped in silence.

Kaden rose slowly, unreadable. "Then they've started again. The experiments."

Wyatt's jaw clenched. He had seen the Capital's cruelty. But what held him wasn't dread—it was Cam. The fire in her eyes. The steadiness in her voice, even as it cracked. She looked like a storm barely contained. And gods, it made his pulse stumble.

"We leave now," he said. The words came iron-sharp, but beneath them was an ache to take the weight off her shoulders.

She nodded. "I'll wake Corin. Tell Ben. We move before dawn."

Cam turned, but Wyatt caught her shoulder, his hand warm, grounding. She froze, just for a heartbeat. Her hand brushed his forearm in return—anchor to anchor. Then she slipped into the corridor, cloak a shadow in the torchlight.

Wyatt stood in the silence she left behind, her presence still humming in his chest. That unspoken pull tugged again—quiet, relentless. But he shoved it down. There would be time for nothing else. Not until their friends were safe.

Tonight, rest was over.

Don't miss out!

Visit the website below and you can sign up to receive emails whenever Alysabeth Vale publishes a new book. There's no charge and no obligation.

https://books2read.com/r/B-A-DKVFF-VGIAJ

BOOKS 2 READ

Connecting independent readers to independent writers.

www.ingramcontent.com/pod-product-compliance
Lightning Source LLC
LaVergne TN
LVHW100501110826
845146LV00002B/471
9798994528464